Destiny Reborn

PF Karlin

PF KARLIN PUBLISHING
SUGAR LAND, TEXAS

ISBN: 978-0-9890247-6-1

Destiny Reborn

By Karen Pugh…a.k.a. PF Karlin
Linda Fagala…a.k.a. PF Karllin

Published by:
PF Karlin Publishing
Sugar Land, Texas

This is a work of fiction. Characters, places, and events portrayed in this book are either a product of the authors' imagination or used fictitiously, with the exception of certain towns and locations which were used to provide the reader with a sense of locale of the storyline. Any similarity to actual places, events, or persons, living or dead, is coincidental and not intended by the authors.

ISBN: 978-0-9890247-6-1

Printed and Published in the United States

ACKNOWLEDGEMENTS

We owe so much to our families, friends, and fans for helping us muddle through to the completion of our second romance novel. We intended to end the love story of Belinda and Robert with this book. However, the encouragement we received has spurred us to write a third book, <u>Fulfilling Destiny</u>, in a series we now call the <u>Kismet Collection</u>. Many thanks to all of our readers, whose encouraging comments and reviews have been invaluable.

Destiny Reborn

CHAPTER 1

~ Belinda ~

NINE MONTHS AGO, when I fought for my life against the fogginess, the darkness won.

This was different. Now I sensed myself rising instead of sinking. I moved my fingers over the textured fabric at my side, which felt nothing like the stiff, scratchy hospital bedding. My head rested on something soft. A goose-down pillow? Hospitals don't have goose-down pillows.

I exhaled. I am not in the hospital.

"Belinda... Belinda. Can you hear me?" Abby's voice grew louder. "Wake up."

A warm sensation encompassed my right hand, followed by a pat. Her touch encouraged me to fight off the heaviness and focus. Lifting my eyelids to slits, I found I lay on a king-size poster bed in a low-lit room.

"She's waking up." A big smile spread across Abby's face as she bounced on the edge of the mattress.

"You scared the hell out of us?" Garrett, Abby's husband, stood behind her.

"What happened? How did I get here?" I scanned my surroundings full of traditional mahogany furniture with an ocean blue and gold color scheme. The room reminded me of the furnishings in the Pennington's home in my dream. My pulse sped up. No. No. There's no way this room looked like the one in my dreams. My breathing increased.

"The New Year's Eve party was the last thing I remember." I continued to scan the room. What the heck was going on?

"That's right. We're in the Pendleton's bedroom." Abby's stare intensified. Concern washed over her face.

"I came with you and Garrett." I grabbed her hand. "Abby, I saw Ro... "

My gaze froze on a figure at the foot of the bed, dressed in a black tuxedo. I trailed my eyes up the tall, lean body to his lips. Lips that reminded me of toe-curling kisses I'd experienced with him, or someone who looked like him, while I lay in a coma. I continued up to his glacier-blue eyes. His styled, dark brown hair made me want to jump out of bed and rake my fingers through the perfect strands. A breath caught in my throat and my pulse pounded.

My Robert?

"You fainted." Abby squeezed my hand.

I waved for her to come closer. "Do you know who he is?" I nodded toward the guy at the foot of the bed.

Abby hovered near my ear. "Yes. Robert Pen-dle-ton." She pulled back. Her eyes grew as big as silver dollars. "Close, right?"

"Pendleton? Pennington?" I bit my lip. The man at the end of the bed looked like the Robert I fell in love with and married while I dreamt in a coma.

"No, no. Have you ever met him before tonight?" My voice came out strained.

She stiffened. "Tonight was the first time."

My brows furrowed as I glanced at Robert and then back at Abby. "Robert Pendleton...and you've never met him before tonight?"

"Tonight is the first time. I swear." She raised a hand. "Let me introduce you to him." Abby flipped a wrist in his direction. "Belinda, this is Robert Pendleton."

As I forced a smile, an army of jumping beans hopped around in the pit of my stomach.

She tilted her head toward me. "Robert, this is my best friend Belinda, Belinda Davies."

He smiled, nodded, and maintained his straight posture. Robert didn't show any sign that he had seen or met me before.

I propped myself up on my elbows to scrutinize him better.

He pushed the jacket back, then stuck his thumbs in his pants pockets.

I studied him before I spoke. "Out there, you said my name. Do you know me?" My name had floated like silk from his lips. When he placed his hand on my shoulder, a wave of exhilaration made every cell in my body jump into hyper-drive from his touch.

Robert scanned the other occupants in the room, starting with Garrett, and then Abby and back to me. His gaze slipped down to just below my wreath necklace. With a slight shake of his head, he refocused on my face. "My mother told me your name."

I peeped down at myself and saw my position had accentuated the upper swells of my breasts. That's one way to keep his attention. After nudging Abby to move back, I sat up on the edge of the bed.

The man in front of me didn't know me. After all, I'd made him up in my head, but would he be willing to talk?

Abby leaned in closer and whispered, "Is that him?"

I shrugged. "I don't know. I just met him, too."

She rolled her eyes. "You know what I mean. Does he even look like him?"

I paused and then nodded.

Abby let out a gasp. "Oh, my God!" She flung her hand to her throat and pulled back.

After a soft rap, the bedroom door opened, and the hosts of the party entered the room.

"Oh good. You're awake." Sandra Pendleton, the woman I recognized as Robert's mother, beamed. "You had us worried. Are you feeling all right?"

"Yes, ma'am. I'm fine. Sorry, I hope I didn't cause a scene." A shudder rocked me as I imagined myself sprawled on the floor with everyone gawking.

"Oh, no. Robert caught you and carried you in here before anyone even noticed."

Little did she know her son was the reason I fainted.

I tilted my head at him. "Thank you."

"My pleasure." One corner of Robert's mouth slid up.

"Honey, we're glad you're all right. Let us know if we can do anything." Mrs. Pendleton reached for her husband's arm.

I nodded. "Thank you."

Robert turned to follow his parents.

"Robert, can I talk to you?" I rubbed my hands over the gold brocade comforter.

With his back to me, he stopped. He turned his head to the side and nodded.

"Abby, I need to talk to him. Could you two give us a few minutes alone?"

Abby swooped down close to my ear. "You told me the two of you acted like bunnies in your dream. Can I trust you with him?" She pulled back.

I scoffed. Did she think I was going to jump his bones right here and now? I grabbed her shoulder and pulled her close. "Abby Barnett, I only want to talk to him."

Abby looked over her shoulder at Robert and gave him the once-over. Nodding her head, she stood. "Sure." She winked before she latched onto Garrett's arm, led him out into the hall, and closed the door.

~ *Robert* ~

An irrational urge to run took over. I fought with every ounce of self-control not to go to the blue-eyed beauty sitting on the bed.

Aw, hell. When she propped herself on her elbows, her breasts... I had to look away before another part of my body made a bigger ass of me. Damn. Her long, golden-brown hair did the same when it glistened in the light, taunting me to entangle my fingers in every strand.

The presence of others in the room required a sense of decorum. Now, I questioned if I could continue the control.

The sensation I'd had when I touched her filled me with desire. My heart sped up to the point I thought it'd jump out of my chest. I couldn't explain what happened, but I sensed a familiar, unexpected connection. It made me want to be close to her, to get to know her, to love her.

One thing was obvious. I wanted to reach out and stroke her beautiful, angelic face. I wanted to feel her full lips on mine—to taste her. Aw shit... I wanted to experience every part of her.

Those thoughts scared the crap out of me. I crossed my arms over my chest and tucked my hands as they clenched into tight fists, fingernails digging into my palms. Small beads of sweat formed on my brow. Could I be alone with her?

Leave! Leave the room now! Just go for the door and run! But my feet didn't move toward the escape route. Instead, I walked over to the window and stared out, confused. What the hell was I doing?

My cell vibrated in my jacket pocket, but I ignored it. I'll call her back later.

Oh God! I couldn't. No, I shouldn't have these thoughts, these feelings. For God's sake, I just got engaged to Sharyn a couple of hours ago.

What was wrong with me? If Belinda gave me any encouragement, I might not stop.

I needed to stay away. She meant trouble for me.

~ *Belinda* ~

A faint light crept in through the window to silhouette Robert's profile. A sense of longing ignited but switched into a stabbing pain in my heart. He reminded me in so many ways of the Robert from my dream. The man I loved.

He ran one hand back through his hair. The other he planted on his hip. The tuxedo hugged his form, making his broad shoulders more than I could resist.

I rose to stand behind him.

He didn't move and seemed oblivious to my proximity.

I couldn't refrain from touching him any longer. My breath quickened as I raised my hands and hovered them over his shoulders. I slid them down his tuxedo-clad back, feeling the firmness of his muscles as he tensed under my touch.

He lowered his arm, and, to my surprise, stood there, allowing my exploration.

Air stopped rushing through my lungs as my pulse sprinted. I slid my arms around his chest, hugged and then pressed my cheek against his back.

The faint sound of air rushed from his lungs.

His masculine scent of musk with a hint of spice flooded my nostrils. I sighed. He wore the same cologne as my Robert.

I spread my fingers and inched my hands over a firm chest covered by stiff shirt fabric. My arms tightened to experience the essence of this living version.

~ *Robert* ~

A sigh escaped me, knowing I'd lose the battle to stay away. I twisted around to face her.

Belinda released her hold and reached up around my neck. Unable to stop myself, I wrapped my arms around her waist. Our eyes never faltered until she closed hers. Tilting her head back, she exposed her neck in submission.

My mind was a haze of overwhelming desire. God, I wanted her. I bent down and placed one kiss on the soft, warm curve of her neck. A hot sensation surged through me, just like when I'd touched her shoulder. But underneath my desire, something else touched the deepest recesses of my soul.

Something I remembered, something familiar, something I knew.

The combination of my attraction and the strange sensations compounded my longing. I tightened my grip and pulled her closer as I feathered kisses up her neck. My blood boiled with every touch of my mouth against her sensual flesh.

A soft moan escaped her with my first kiss. Her body tensed and arched while I skimmed my lips up her neck. My overpowering hunger for her engulfed me.

~ *Belinda* ~

In my dream, Robert's touch excited me. But now, the undeniable reality made it more powerful. The strange new feeling ignited my soul.

I entwined my fingers in his hair, adhering to him. What I wanted the most—his lips—I found. Our mouths crushed together in a scorching kiss. Oh God, yes! An electrifying tremble surged through me, straight to my core. Oh, how I'd missed him. I never wanted this to stop.

The kiss consumed me, and when my legs collided with the mattress, we toppled over. Robert's weight covered me. He gripped me tighter around the waist and lifted me over to the middle of the bed, our lips never breaking contact. My back arched as he deepened the kiss, our tongues tangling and exploring.

I wove my fingers through his thick hair and pulled him close, not intending to stop him from doing whatever he wanted. The connection with the Robert in my dream had heightened my senses, but the real-version ignited the electrified sensation. My skin prickled. My pulse pounded. My body trembled to the point I wanted to devour every inch of him.

~ *Robert* ~

Blood throbbed through my veins. Our kisses became fast and feverish. Her lips parted, and I plunged my tongue in, exploring, caressing, and twisting around hers.

She locked her fingers in my hair and held me close while I savored her intoxicating taste.

A groan deep in my throat escaped as our tongues danced around one another. I pressed against her willing body, and she reacted, molding herself to mine. My sexual need for her blazed out of control as my body responded to her hip movements. Her moans excited me, pushing me almost to the edge of losing all control.

I went to slip off my jacket, but my phone vibrated. That moment reminded me, I needed to separate myself from her before I had us stripped naked.

My blood boiling and my respirations heavy, I pushed away to support myself on my hands, ending my lapse of poor judgment. With heavy respirations, I peered down at the woman who lay beneath me.

For a second, I studied her. "I… I can't do this." I sprang off the bed, stuffed my hands into my pockets, and paced, trying to control my desire to reach out for her—to touch her—to continue the passion.

To save my sanity, I needed to run from her as fast as I could and put as much distance between us as possible.

"I can't do this." I hurried to the door, but stopped and looked back.

Belinda sat up. She slid over to the edge of the bed and clenched the comforter with balled fists. "Please, don't leave."

The sound of her distress incited a need to comfort her, to protect her. Unable to stop, I walked over and kneeled in front of her. "Angel, I can't now. I have to go."

She gasped and clutched at her throat.

My muscles stiffened as my own words rang in my ears. Why on earth did I just call her 'Angel'?

I stood, rushed back to the door, and stopped. My hand hovered over the doorknob. "I'll get your number from Garrett and call you." I never looked at her before I left the room.

In the hall, with my insides a mess, I raked my fingers through my hair. Did I just experience an overwhelming impulse to make love to a woman whom I just met?

I leaned my forehead against the door and grabbed hold of the knob. Just a twist of my wrist would put me back in the arms of that sensual, willing creature.

But opening the door made me a cheater and a liar. Hell, I'd just asked a wonderful woman to marry me, and she deserved an honest man. I prided myself on my honesty and I loved Sharyn, but now I had questions.

It took willpower not to go back into the room. I drew in air to gain control and then yanked my hand off the knob as if it seared my flesh.

The incident tested my integrity. Why in God's name did I tell her I'd call? That would never happen. No, the safest thing—put distance between us as fast as I could.

Garrett and Abby entered the hall just as I turned to leave.

Abby stopped mid-stride and stiffened. "Is everything all right?"

"You should take her home. She seems tired." I slowed my pace. "It was nice meeting you, Abby. Goodnight." I nodded at Garrett.

Once out of sight, and to avoid the rooms full of guests, I bolted out the patio door near the primary bedroom. I didn't even take the time to tell my parents goodbye.

I slid into the driver's seat and grasped the sides of my head. "What the hell is going on with me? With her?" I needed to get a grip on myself. Sharyn would be furious if she caught the slightest hint of what I'd just done.

Cell in hand, the display screen showed several calls from her. She knew my moods by the subtle changes in my voice. No, if we talked now, she'd know. I needed more time.

Besides, I had another problem. I'd missed our first New Year's kiss as an engaged couple.

I headed back toward Sharyn's parents' house. My knuckles blanched on the steering wheel as I struggled to keep my mind on driving.

What did all this mean? Why now? Why couldn't I have met Belinda a few weeks ago before I asked Sharyn to marry me? Why did fate decide to play this cruel trick?

My feelings for Sharyn were nothing like the passion I'd just experienced with Belinda. We had a comfortable relationship based on respect. Sharyn was there for me, willing and able whenever she was in town.

Yet, what I sensed with Belinda was so different. It seemed deeper. I had connected with her from the first time I touched the soft skin of her shoulder, and now, just thinking of her sent sexual waves through my body.

My arousal swelled. No way could I walk into my future in-laws' house in my present state. So I turned off the beltway to drive the feeder road. The stop-and-go from the red lights gave me time to get a grip. Thinking about work calmed my physical problem.

About thirty minutes later, I pulled into the circular drive, ready to greet my fiancée. Sharyn waved from the front window. A knot twisted my stomach.

I sucked in a lungful of air and made my first New Year's resolution—to forget about Belinda and what I did. I wasn't willing to hurt Sharyn. My loyalty needed to be with her since she'd stood by my side during the lowest point of my life.

As I closed the front door, she rushed over, threw her arms around my neck, and planted a sweet kiss on my lips. I pulled her tight, but it bore no resemblance to the exhilarating emotions I experienced with Belinda. *Keep her out of your head.*

"That's your New Year's Eve kiss you missed. What took you so long?" She protruded her lower lips and lowered her lashes.

"Sorry, Honey. After talking with my client, I started talking to other guests and lost track of the time." She accepted my half-truth.

I forced a smile and changed the subject. "Let's get back to celebrating." In my book, I was a cheater. I'd ended the year engaged to one woman and started the new year in a lustful embrace with another. Now, I had to live with that and prayed Sharyn never discovered the truth.

"Our engagement?" Sharyn's face lit up.

I gave her a squeeze and a peck on the cheek. "And that too."

I offered Sharyn my arm.

She latched onto it and rested her head against me, nuzzling into my jacket. She pulled away. Her brow furrowed. "Is that perfume I smell?" Her nose wrinkled as she sniffed my jacket again. "That's Angel Scent?"

My heart skipped a beat. I just spouted the first thing that came to mind and hoped it satisfied her curiosity. "Oh, Mom said she'd like to have some. So, I bought it for her."

Sharyn lifted a brow. She tightened her grip around my arm. The light I saw on her face a few moments earlier vanished as she led me into the party.

~ *Belinda* ~

Unable to control my tears, I tried to listen to the muffled voices in the hallway. Then they went silent.

Seconds later, the door opened. I stared through moist eyes at Abby and Garrett. She rushed over and sat next to me on the bed.

Garrett shifted from foot to foot near the door. "I'll just go say goodbye to the hosts and get our things so we can leave."

Abby scanned my disheveled hair and dress. "What just happened?"

I answered between sniffles, still dazed from my flurry of emotions and Robert's unexpected response. "I don't want to talk about it."

◁▷

Garrett and Abby kept flashing glances at each other on the drive home. I could tell they weren't sure what to say or even if they should say anything, but I appreciated they didn't pry.

Instead, I stared out the window and replayed the kiss. My eyelids drifted shut as I let the thrill grow inside. I had experienced a passionate embrace with a real person who looked and felt even better than the Robert I'd loved.

The car came to a stop in front of my home. Garrett jumped out and opened the back passenger door.

Before I climbed out, I reached over and placed my hand on Abby's shoulder. "I'll call you tomorrow. We can talk then."

She covered mine with hers. "Belinda, he didn't hurt you, did he?"

"No, no. We'll talk tomorrow."

Garrett held the door open. I gave him a quick kiss on the cheek. "Thank you." He'd done all he could to help in this damn strange situation.

He glanced at the ground. "I'll wait until you get inside."

With every step closer to the front door, I dreaded having to face mom. Maybe she went to bed early, but I expected the worst. She'd demand the details, and the light from the family room was not a good omen.

One turn of the key locked the door. I took off my shoes. With them dangling from my hand, I tiptoed across the dark foyer to the stairway. I glanced into the lit room. Mom slept on the couch. My shoulders slumped and the tension in my neck eased as I continued my escape. The only territory left between Mom's "twenty questions" and peace, the stairs.

I took one stair at a time until a loud squeak freed itself from one tread. I froze, hoping.

"Belinda, is that you?"

Crap!

"Yes, Mom. I didn't want to wake you." I swallowed hard.

She sat on the edge of the couch and yawn. "How'd the night go?"

I didn't have the energy to divulge every detail. "Mom, not tonight. I'm exhausted. Can we talk over breakfast?" I held my breath and waited.

"Oooka... Good night, Honey."

I let out a pent-up breath. "Good night."

I ran up the stairs, safe but tired. In no time, I hopped into bed and slid between the sheets. "Brrr." The cold fabric sent a shiver through me. I prayed sleep came fast.

But that didn't happen.

My skin prickled, and my mind raced from the memory of embracing a live version of Robert Pennington.

CHAPTER 2

~ Belinda ~

THE AROMAS OF eggs, bacon, and coffee consumed the air, beckoning me to the kitchen. I buried my face in the pillow to block the remarkable scents, but my growling belly wouldn't permit any peace. On instinct, my feet reached the floor. I raised my nose to sniff. And there it was, the tantalizing smell of pancakes added to the mix. Mom knew how to entice me out of bed. A strategy she used to pump me for details since I was five and it worked every time.

My nose sucked in the air. "Blast my mother!" I wanted to lie in bed and relive the events of last night. Thank goodness everyone had encouraged me to go. If I hadn't, Robert would still be a dream.

A low, rolling rumble deep in my stomach seemed to go on forever as the kitchen aromas continued to penetrate the room.

"Blast my mother! Blast her!" I tried to lie back down and shield my face with a pillow, but my feet had a different idea. No longer able to resist, I went to the bathroom for a quick pit stop, then scurried downstairs to face my inquisitor.

I worshipped my mother, but her uncanny ability to spout off rapid-fire questions sometimes annoyed me. Before I could answer the first, she'd ask five more. As I grew older, I turned her probing into a game. She'd ask, and I'd hold back on the facts. That drove her nuts, and I cherished the satisfaction that gave me. When she caught on to my deviousness, we'd laugh and start the process all over at the next inquisition. I often wondered why she fell into my trap each time. Maybe she enjoyed our matches as much as me.

Mom stood at the stove about to flip a pancake. She glanced my way. "Good morning, Honey. Did you sleep well?"

I shrugged and grimaced, walking over to pour myself a cup of coffee. "Would you like one?"

She smiled and nodded.

I carried the cups to the table and slipped into a chair, braced for the onslaught of questions.

Mom placed two plates of bacon, eggs, and stacks of pancakes on the table. Then she made herself comfortable across from me.

My mouth watered from the smells wafting around the kitchen. I hoped to get a few bites down before I had to recount the eventful night.

"Where's Dad?" I drizzled syrup over my buttered pancakes.

"He went across the street to help Jack with his car. But I think it's just an excuse for them to drink beer and watch football until nine or ten tonight." She stopped slathering her pancakes with butter and shook the knife. "Those two don't have a clue what they're doing with cars."

We both laughed.

"I agree. It's male bonding over football." I cut the stack into pieces and took a bite.

The delicious culinary mixture passed over my lips. I swirled the soft, syrupy delight around in my mouth and savored each slow chew, then swallowed. This is heaven.

Another stab filled the fork. About to indulge my taste buds, I hesitated and waited for the first question. Nothing happened. What was she up to? Had she decided not to play? The pancakes went into my mouth and slid down my throat. I studied the woman who gave me life, and planned to time my attack by stopping her cold with the bomb I was about to drop.

I'd keep quiet longer, down several more bites of my wonderful breakfast, and sip coffee to wait and see how long before the first "rapid-fire" question began.

I didn't have to wait long.

"So, did you have fun last night?" Mom shifted in her seat and stuck a forkful of pancakes into her mouth.

I answered with a simple, "Yes," and continued eating.

"Were there lots of people there?"

"Yes." Wait for it!

"Was there lots of interesting food?"

"Yes." Wait for it!

"Did Abby look nice?"

"Yeah." Wait for it!

"How did her dress look? Did she wear her hair up? Did Garrett have on a tux? How big was the house? Meet anyone interesting?"

Bingo! Rapid-fire. I smiled and sat back in my chair. "Slow down, Mom. I can only answer one question at a time." I stared at her and giggled, attempting to control my need to laugh.

She snickered.

Within seconds, we burst into laughter.

Mom sat back in her chair. A huge smile spread across her face. "If you'd give me the information like any polite human being engaging in a sensible conversation, I wouldn't have to ask so many questions!"

I widened my eyes and shook my head. As requested, I'd engage in a sensible conversation and give her the information she desired, information that would shock her to the core.

While the tale unfolded, she'd connect the dots between the realities.

I propped my elbows on the table, leaned in closer, and began my story while Mom listened and ate.

"You know, I wasn't thrilled to go to this party, but I'm glad I did. The house, well, it was a huge Tuscan-style home on several acres. And the foyer. It was amazing. It was about twenty-five feet tall with this enormous chandelier." I waited to see if she offered any signs of recognition.

She glanced at me and gave an encouraging nod while she ate.

I placed more bait in the trap with facts that described the Pennington dream house that only she and Abby knew.

"The most unusual aspect of the foyer was the horseshoe-shaped stairway flanking the walls. Two Bombay chests with huge, hand-blown, cobalt-blue vases perched on top stood on either side." I made a slight sweeping motion to add drama to the mental scene I painted.

Mom stopped sipping her coffee and peered over her cup at the description of the vases. Steam rose around her nose.

I leaned closer and continued. "You can imagine after seeing how opulent the house was, I was eager to be introduced to the owners."

I stopped and took a bite of my cooling pancakes. Then I chewed as slow as I could, watching her to time my next tidbit of information at the precise moment.

She lifted her fork, about to take another bite, when I blurted out, "Turns out, their names were Robert and Sandra Pendleton."

As predicted, Mom stopped cold. Her steel-blue eyes squinted. Her mouth was agape as her dropped fork clanged against her plate.

A sliver of a smile formed on my face. Satisfaction warmed me, knowing I achieved my aim. I just took another bite of food and reveled in her reaction. Soon, we'd laugh, and I'd pray the nightmare ended. For a short time, laughter might deaden the pain, but I knew better. Robert had no memory of our life in my coma, and I'd never forget I met a living version of my husband at a New Year's Eve party.

After a few seconds, Mom spoke, "Did you say Robert and Sandra Pen-dle-ton? Not Pennington?"

"Yep. Different last name. But similar."

She swallowed hard. "Almost like in your dream?"

I nodded. "Oh yeah, and you'll never guess who else showed up. Robert, their son!"

Her eyes grew even wider as her hand flew up to her mouth.

For the first time in my life, I rendered her speechless. I hadn't expected the long silence. "Mom, are you okay?"

Her face crumpled. She clutched my hand. "You have been through a lot since the accident, and waking up from the coma. I don't want to see you hurt anymore."

I understood her concern.

The accidents.

CHAPTER 3

~ Belinda ~

AFTER A QUICK kitchen clean-up, I dashed to my room to log into my laptop.

Right after my discharge, I had spent endless hours trying to find anything about Robert Pennington, but all my attempts led to dead ends, and I gave up.

Armed with his correct name and Roman numeral, I plopped on the bed, sitting cross-legged, and stared at the glow on the screen. I closed my eyes, inhaled, and let out a slow exhale. Fingers posed, I typed in "Robert P-E-N-D-L-E-T-O-N the IV of Sugar Land, Texas.

My heart raced as a profile opened with his picture. I kissed my forefinger and then pressed it to his cheek. I continued to scroll through picture after picture of Robert and his family, which included a complete history. Then a picture of him looking straight into the camera popped up and stopped me cold.

Haunting blue eyes bore into my soul. My girlie parts ignited as butterflies made multiple laps around my heart. The connection of our love I experienced in my dream flooded in. A connection I experienced for a few fleeting minutes at a New Year's Eve party the night before. A connection I might never have again.

I kissed a finger, then covered his cheek.

"My love."

I filled my lungs and read the attached article about his college years. The next picture showed him surrounded by cheerleaders. In an instant, my blood pressure rose a few notches.

"Great! Still a player." I snapped the computer shut. "I need a nap."

I woke up about three p.m. and realized I didn't even dream of Robert, or at least I didn't remember it. The void made me uneasy, and that worried me. I felt something had been ripped away from my heart.

In less than twenty-four hours, a live version of Robert walked into my life and had taken over. It made sense that I'd fantasize about him while asleep.

But I didn't.

After I woke up from the coma, I had vivid dreams that felt real. The excitement from my toe-curling kiss should've been all I needed to put me back in Robert's arms, even if only in a dream. That didn't happen this time. Why?

Since Robert's appearance, far too much has happened. I needed to talk to someone who wasn't my mother. A dose of Abby would do the trick, besides I'd promised my friend a call. She'd want all the gory details of what happened behind the closed door of the Pendletons' primary bedroom. And everything I discovered while searching the internet.

"We needed a 'girls' night in," something we started when we were roommates in college. Strangely enough, we kept it up in my dream and throughout my recent recovery. She spent every night with me after I returned to the land of the living. We were close before, but the late nights brought us closer.

She earned a special place in my heart for her selflessness and the added title of sister.

She answered in her usual cheerful voice. "Hi there. It's about time."

"Hey, you up for a sleepover?"

She chuckled. "Yes. I am dying over here. I have to take care of a few things, then I'll be right over."

"What, Garrett can't go a day without ravishing you?"

"Belinda Davies, get your mind out of the gutter!" A hearty laugh rebounded over the phone. "I will be over in about an hour. What I have to do won't take too long."

I almost commented on Garrett's stamina when Abby chimed in, "Don't even go there. I will see you in a few." The phone went dead.

Garrett had become accustomed to our sleepovers, and I appreciated his patience. I figured he was as eager about the details as much as Abby and if being without his wife for a night was what it took, so be it.

I was fond of Mr. Barnett. He was strong, smart, and handsome. Abby started dating him in college, and I had to admit my Green-Eyed-Monster reared her ugly head on multiple occasions back then. I saw how Garrett treated Abby and wished Matt, my deadbeat boyfriend, had shown me that same attention.

Through my sessions with Dr. Rosen, I figured out that I'd based Dream Robert's responses on Abby and Garrett's relationship. On some level, I knew the relationship with Matt had fallen short. In my "Dream Reality," I had filled the hollow space with a similar version of Garrett and named him Robert.

Dream Robert was much better than Garrett, and from what I experienced last night, the Real Robert surpassed the imaginary.

I hopped off my bed and strolled downstairs. "Mom, Abby is coming over. What do we have to munch on?" I passed her sprawled on the couch in the family room, reading her newest romance novel, *Shattered Fate*. Within seconds, she followed me into the kitchen.

Mom did anything to make Abby feel welcome. She referred to her as "a sparkling star" because rooms lit up when she walked in.

"What do you want me to fix?" She opened the pantry door and peered inside.

"I love you, Mom." I flaunted a big smile and then planted a kiss on her cheek. "What kind of wine do we have?"

"I think there's two bottles of Zinfandel on the fridge door."

I sauntered toward the refrigerator and opened it. "There you are, just like Mom said."

"What? You didn't trust me."

"Mom."

The doorbell rang just as we finished the snacks, one hour after the call with Abby. As days went, this one was a seesaw of emotions, but as soon as I opened the door, that would change.

One tug put me face-to-face with Abby and my mouth dropped. There she stood, dressed in hot pink, satin, boxer-cut shorts and matching camisole. The pajama's color paired well with her striking green eyes and shoulder-length, auburn hair. In one hand she toted an overnight bag and in the other, a bottle of wine. Zinfandel, of course.

"I said I'd be here in an hour."

"Have you no shame? Get your butt in here." I grabbed Abby's forearm and tugged her over the threshold.

"What? They cover up the important stuff." Big-eyed as she grinned.

I planted my hands on my hips. "What if you had an accident?"

"Then everyone would've gotten an eyeful, wouldn't they?" Abby laughed as she swanked past, swinging her hips. She dropped her tote bag on the tile floor near the steps. The loud thud bounced off the walls of the foyer.

"Or they'd think you're a hooker. I'm glad my dad's not home."

Abby spun around with her mouth agape. She covered her lips with her fingertips and gave the best Marilyn Monroe pose ever, shoulders hunched, and one leg raised as she balanced on the other. In a voice a few octaves higher, she proclaimed, "Oh! I didn't think of that. If he saw me like this... I'd be so embarrassed." With dramatic flair, she flung her hands out and inspected her sassy outfit. Her puckered lips changed to a giggle.

All the theatrics meant she felt silly. She felt comfortable with the world seeing her in her alluring outfit, but my father was a different story.

"Well, you're safe. He's across the street watching football."

Abby let out a sigh. "Thank heaven." She swung her head around and peeked into the family room. "Where's Dora?"

Mom walked in from the kitchen.

"Hi, Mrs. D. How are you?" A toothy grin spread across her face.

Mom eyed Abby from head to toe and just shook her head. "I'm fine, Sweetie. Happy New Year." She hugged her with the tenderness of a mother and gave her a gentle kiss on the cheek. "Love the outfit."

Over the past few months, the two had become close while they stayed near me during the recovery phase. Mom grew to think of Abby as her second daughter and loved the girl's exuberant personality.

"You two go on and I'll bring the snacks up."

In the bedroom, I dug through the dresser and pulled out a soft blue camisole and matching boxer shorts. "I'll be right back." I slipped into the bathroom and emerged several minutes later, ready to enjoy a 'girls' night in.

Abby dug around in her tote and pulled out her tablet. "I just watched a great chick flick staring that hunk Jonathan Morse. We can stream." She held up a finger. "But first." She flipped on her stomach as her elbows supported her head propped in her palms.

"Well?" She waved a hand. "No. Wait. I need wine first. I'll pour you a glass." She pointed toward the desk. "Your Mom brought all that stuff up here." Abby scrunched her nose. "Is she trying to get us fat?"

"Not you, me."

"Why? You look better than you did before the accident." With two glasses of wine, she joined me on the bed.

"Tell that to my mom."

Abby took a sip. "Later. Now tell me everything."

I explained what had happened behind the bedroom door. I gave her every detail, especially the passionate part with Robert's lips pressed hard against mine and his tongue doing delicious things.

My skin warmed and tingled while I relived the events. Heat flashed in my cheeks with every word and Abby's embarrassing attentiveness.

"Why'd he let you touch him and then kiss you like that? And get you on the bed?" Abby's brows furrowed as she sipped her wine. "But he acted like he didn't know you, or at least didn't admit it?"

"How could he know me? In my head, he's a dream." I downed half of my glass. "Do you think he's hiding something?"

"He called you Angel before scurrying away like a rat. That says something."

I pursed my lips. "I don't think he's a rat. He said he'd get my number from Garrett before he left. I assumed he asked him when I heard them talking in the hall."

Abby lowered her lashes while she sipped her wine. "Belinda, he never asked for your number. He just said you were tired, and we should take you home."

I scrunched my face into a frown and sat up straight. My chest ached as my butterflies made a nosedive. "How could he not want to see me again after what happened?"

Abby piped in, "Although that doesn't mean anything. Robert's the VP of the company and has access to the client accounts." She walked her fingers across my calf. "One of which you are."

The explanation mollified me until a horrible thought entered my mind. "Or maybe he just thinks I'm nuts and wants nothing to do with me."

Deep in the recesses of my mind, the promise of his call gave me hope, which now melted away.

"Don't say that. I'm sure he's a resourceful guy and can find your number without Garrett's help."

It was too late. Self-doubt raised its ugly head, a talent I'd nurtured most of my life. With the help of Dr. Rosen, I'd made great strides in the past few months not to second guess myself.

I'd worked hard to build up my self-esteem. No one, not even a person who looked like Robert, was going to make me throw my accomplishments out the door.

I took a deep breath. "If he calls, fine. If he doesn't, his loss." I'd continue with my life plans. But tucked in the back of my mind, I prayed he'd call.

The light glinted off Abby's tablet. I picked it up and handed it to her. "Let's do this." Maybe seeing someone else's "Happily Ever After" would put an end to my self-imposed pity party.

"Do you need the Wi-Fi password?"

"Nope. Turn on the TV."

I reached for the remote off my nightstand and pointed it at the TV. "Guess what? Jonathan Morse was in my dream. When you met him, you couldn't stay away from him." I settled back on the bed. "Garrett wasn't a happy camper about it because you crushed on Jonathan so bad."

Abby punched me.

"Ouch." I rubbed my upper arm. "Why'd you do that?"

"You never told me about Jonathan Morse. Why dream about him?"

"I don't know. Was I a fan of his before the accident?"

Abby cocked her head and flattened her lips. "Not really. Not like me. You knew who he was because I wouldn't let you forget." She placed her finger on her cheek and tapped. "You know, we were flipping through a magazine plastered full of photos of him at my Hollywood-themed bridal shower."

"And on the way home, I had the accident." Abby opened a can of worms. That gave me an opening. I plunged into the details of my almost sordid affair with the sexy

Jonathan Morse during my "Dream Reality." Abby reveled in the details, as I recanted the story.

"He's certainly eye candy." She placed the back of her wrist on her forehead to fake a swoon.

A giggle escaped. "And a heart stopper." But not as much as my real heart stopper, Robert.

CHAPTER 4

~ Belinda ~

THE ELEVATOR DOORS closed, and I pushed the button for the third floor. Butterflies took a slow turn around my stomach, and I couldn't wait to see how Dr. Rosen would react to the news I'd soon convey.

During our sessions, he'd answer my questions with another question, prompting me to explore my inner self. This time, I'd be the one asking the questions.

I flipped a light switch next to the inner-office door, which lit a dim red light on the opposite side, alerting the fine doctor of his next appointment.

After a few flicks of the magazines on the coffee table in front of the worn leather couch, I sat in an overstuffed wing-backed chair, to wait my turn.

Within a few minutes, the inner door opened. "Hi, Belinda. I hope you're having a good new year so far."

The disheveled Dr. Rosen motioned for me to enter the room. His hair seemed longer than at our last meeting but had its signature-uncombed appearance. As usual, his clothes looked like he had slept in them for days. His jaw sported a five-o'clock-shadow although it was still morning.

As I passed him, I recognized the familiar click when he flipped the switch, turning off the light above the door. We both made ourselves comfortable in our usual seats, facing each other.

He picked up his pad and pen, then rested back in his chair. "Well, where should we start?" His eyes lowered to the paper as he scribbled something.

Instead of mincing my words, I used a more direct approach. "Remember the New Year's Eve party I told you about?"

He nodded, not lifting his head from his pad of paper on his lap.

"Well, I met Robert there." I leaned back in my chair to observe the doctor's reaction.

He raised his eyes to mine but said nothing. Finally, with a tap of the pen on the pad, he asked, "What do you mean you met Robert?"

"I met a real version of Robert at the New Year's Eve party, but his last name is Pendleton." I crossed my arms over my chest. A full breath filled my lungs, knowing I had the upper hand.

Dr. Rosen cocked his head. "Please explain."

Sighing, I rolled my eyes and told him what took place.

He jerked his head back. "His last name is Pendleton. Huh. That could explain why you found nothing about him in your search." He scowled before continuing. "This could complicate your recovery."

"No foolin'."

"So, where do you want to go from here?"

There it was, the question to answer a question. I scanned the room and reviewed all the scenarios. The one I prayed for had Robert calling me. We'd hit it off and then ride off into the sunset to start our new life together, living happily ever after.

In the other one, Robert didn't call because he figured I was crazy. My skin prickled at the thought. Yet my practical, logical side knew I had to live with those two possibilities.

I straightened in my chair and addressed the doctor. "I'll need a Plan A and a Plan B. In Plan A, if he calls, I'll make room for Robert. In Plan B, I'll go on with my life… without him."

As the words passed my lips, my stomach tightened. That sent a shot of pain just below my ribs. I took a few breaths after bending my head. Going on without Robert wouldn't be the ending I hoped for, but it might be the likelier outcome, and I'd have to learn to live with it.

The doctor and I explored my feelings and the consequences of my recent experience for the next forty-five minutes. He glanced at the door and then at his watch.

I turned to see the glow of the red light. His next patient had arrived and my session ended.

"We can increase your sessions again if you need to." Dr. Rosen walked me to the door.

One session solved nothing, despite the fact I felt stronger than I'd ever been in my life, both physically and emotionally. "We'll see how things go. Thank you." I walked out of the office.

I had a lot to think about on my drive home. I knew I couldn't put my plans on hold just because a person who resembled Robert had appeared.

What choice did I have? If by a quirk of fate, he and I found a life together, I'd alter my plans. For now, I'd shop for a house, find a job, and start dating.

That last one scared me the most.

CHAPTER 5

~ Belinda ~

SINCE OUR ENCOUNTER at the New Year's Eve party, I hadn't seen or heard anything from Robert. That pissed me off after the way he acted. Although I didn't like the reality, I dove into Plan B.

The first week of February, I put a contract down on the perfect patio home. Located close to the stables where I boarded my horse, Beau, and minutes from my parents. With everything my parents went through during my six-month slumber, I needed to stay close.

To complete the purchase, I needed a good understanding of my finances. Garrett managed my funds invested with nothing other than the Pendleton Financial group.

Compliments of the real accident and the trucking firm who acknowledged their responsibility for my demise, they established a trust fund. The rather substantial amount would've paid for my care for years. Instead, lucky me, I woke up six months later with loads of money to spare.

So, when Garrett interviewed for the job last November, I told him he could bring me along as a client. That gave him a leg-up over the other applicants and landed him the position.

I didn't know his new job would throw me in the arms of a real version of Robert.

"I'm not sure. Can't we talk about this at your place?"

He understood my apprehension and tried to reassure me. "Look. The odds of you running into him are next to nil."

"How about you come over to my parents? I'll make dinner for you and Abby."

"Belinda, that won't work, not that dinner wouldn't be nice, but the information I need is on the office computers."

"So bring a laptop to dinner."

"You don't understand. I can't. The information can't leave the office." Silence filled a gap. "Belinda, I could lose my job."

That was the sole reason I agreed to the meeting. "What time?"

I left an hour early to head for the Pendleton Financial group's office located blocks from the Galleria shopping mall to make my 1:30 p.m. appointment.

From the second I backed out of my parent's driveway, I broke out into a fine sweat despite the full blast from the A/C. Driving in Sugar Land was a piece of cake, but once I merged onto I-69 my heart raced and I prayed I'd stay clear of any big rigs.

My new Honda CR-V rode higher and diminished the threatening nature of the semi-trucks. But my gut still twisted every time I drove alongside one of those monsters.

The scenario changed as a semi approached from the rear. The sight of all the shiny chrome in the rearview mirror caused my chest to tighten to the point I couldn't breathe.

In both accidents, the thing that was lodged in my memory was the picture of chrome grills barreling down on me.

Dr. Rosen labeled my panic attacks as Posttraumatic Stress Disorder, better known as PTSD. He assured me the fear of large, shiny grills would diminish as I desensitized myself to highway driving. Even with his insistence, I avoided expressways and rush hour traffic, which didn't help with my desensitization.

Today, I had no choice. I-69 to 610 was the fastest and easiest way for me to meet Garrett.

If I won my emotional chrome battle, as a reward, I planned to shop at the Galleria. The huge mall housed every store imaginable in three buildings, all connected by walkways. I'd spend a few hours in my favorite shops and, if I timed everything right, leave before I'd get stuck in rush hour traffic on the way home.

The elevator doors opened at 12:45.

The office space, bright and very contemporary in design, looked rather impressive. I approached the reception desk and introduced myself.

"Oh, yes. Mr. Barnett told me to escort you to conference room B. If you would, please come this way." The receptionist rose and motioned for me to follow.

Glass-paneled partitions formed offices and allowed sunlight to fill the area. Teak-covered columns served as supports for the glass. To warm the space, soft shades of blue and green graced the solid walls.

The place was empty as we walked past the glass rooms filled with sleek furniture. The quietness gave the space a serene feeling.

By the appearance of the office, Garrett had done well for himself and the décor screamed "prosperity."

We stopped in front of a door labeled "B." "Here it is." The woman opened the door. "Everyone will be back from lunch soon." She extended her hand and bade me to walk inside. "May I get you some coffee or tea?"

I shook my head and smiled.

The receptionist pointed to the credenza. "There's fresh water next to the phone. If you change your mind and need anything, just dial extension two." She smiled. "I'll let Mr. Barnett know you're here as soon as he returns." She closed the door and left.

This space looked different. It lacked the fishbowl effect the glass gave the offices. Other than two doors and windows on the opposite side of the hall door, this room was private.

A dark oak table with six chairs sat in the center of the room. At one end lay a keyboard. Mounted on the wall opposite the credenza was a gigantic television screen.

My racked nerves from the drive settled in this less intimidating surrounding. The second door led into an adjacent room. I peeked inside, only to discover another conference room, but much bigger.

Unlike the smaller room, this one consisted mostly of all glass. Floor-to-ceiling windows along the outer wall gave it a full view of Loop 610 and beyond to Memorial Park. The opposite wall, also glass, allowed anyone from the hall to look in. A large oval table and chairs that could seat up to twenty sat in the center. At the far end, stretched along the wall, sat a counter with a coffeemaker and an espresso machine.

Okay, now what? I'd given myself the nickel tour of my temporary confines and glanced at my watch. Only three minutes had passed. Hoping to locate a magazine, I gave the smaller room a quick glance.

Nothing.

I peered into the larger room and eyed one at the far end of the long table. A sigh escaped as I took a step into the room. At the far end, laughter filled the room from a group of men who entered.

They hadn't noticed me, so I stepped back through the doorway and out of sight. I decided not to bother closing the door. With nothing else to do, I walked to the large windows to watch the activity on the streets below.

~ *Robert* ~

A few of my business associates and I gathered around the coffee bar to help ourselves to an after-lunch expresso. The extra kick of caffeine helped us finish out our day. We were all about the same age wearing tailored suits with ties in perfect order against our starched coordinated shirts.

Conversations drifted from one subject to another as we seated ourselves around the table.

Saji started talking about his upcoming weekend date. "This woman is something else. She's the most gorgeous female I've ever met."

Harrumphs circled the group.

Saji threw his hands out with palms up. "What?" He scanned the group. "George, you can't tell me you've never met a girl that didn't stop you in your tracks." He pointed a finger. "I was at your wedding, remember?"

I sat back and watched the testosterone ladened group try to one-up each other. That's until Saji pointed a finger at me. "What about you, Robert? Tell us about the most beautiful girl you ever met."

"Me? Let me think. There's so many." I'd play along, pushing back into the leather-covered chair and interlocking my fingers behind my neck. I took a moment to relish in her memory and allowed a wisp of a smile to form across my face.

"It was in college. I was cutting across the commons when I noticed her approaching." Pausing, I tilted my head back to stare at the ceiling. I wanted nothing to distract me from her. "She was wearing a pair of the best-fitting jeans I ever saw."

The vision in my mind made me smile again and my heart seemed to stop for a split second. "She had the sweetest smile and long, golden-brown hair that glistened in the sunlight."

The room fell silent. "I was watching her, and when she came within ten feet, that's when her big, blue eyes met mine. That was it for me... I was hers and I didn't even know who she was." I scanned the dumbfounded expressions on my colleagues' faces.

Saji leaned forward and rested his arms on the table. "Did you ever meet her?"

With a nod, I blocked out the others for a few seconds. I didn't move but knew my momentary drift down memory lane already gave them too much information. Instead, I plotted a way out of my minor dilemma as I slid a devilish grin across my mouth.

I slapped my palms on the table and straightened in the chair. "Yeah. I married her."

The group darted glances at each other.

Luckily, my quick wit afforded me the ability to convince people of my sincerity. It made me successful at what I did for a living. Being part salesman and part confidant, I had a way of putting people at ease, and they trusted me. I snapped back in a joking manner, "You fools! I've never been married. Go ask my father."

Deep, hearty laughs erupted. The group went on to other subjects of interest.

None of them noticed I remained more reserved, still lost in the recall of my golden-brown-haired beauty who stayed burned into my memory.

Through the glass wall that bordered the hall, I eyed Garrett. He repeatedly took several steps and then paused, tapping the edge of a manila folder against his palm. He stopped and scanned inside the glass enclosure. When our eyes met, I saw his brow furrow.

Garrett's chest rose with a deep breath when he walked in. He headed straight for me, only giving the rest of the group a nod as they left.

The room emptied and grew quiet. I remained seated, sipping my drink. The last member of the group departed as Garrett reached me.

"I'm having a problem with this account. Do you think you could help?" He flashed the folder in front of me.

"I'll see."

He opened the folder and spread its contents on the table. We discussed the possibilities.

I could tell Garrett didn't fully understand the complexities of the fund, and I offered my help. "Is your client coming in today?"

"She's here now." He tilted his head. "In the small conference room."

I cocked my wrist to check my watch. "Would you like me to discuss this with her? I could do it now."

He hesitated for a moment, tapping the papers with his index finger. "I think that might be a good idea, but I'll have to check with her first to see if she'd feel comfortable talking with you."

Comfortable with me? That piqued my curiosity. I raised one brow but shook off the feeling and returned to work mode. "Of course. Go find out."

"Thanks. I don't think I can give her the best advice about this fund. My client needs a good understanding of her financial status."

Garrett took a few steps toward the small conference room and stopped. His reluctance confused me.

I learned to be patient. I'd watch and wait, reading the body language of people. If I gave them enough time and asked a few leading questions, almost everyone would open up and volunteer information.

"Ah… Robert, I think it's only fair I tell you who my client is." He shifted from foot to foot. "It's Belinda Davies."

My jaw tightened. I rubbed the back of my neck, glancing at the closed door, and aimed a finger at it. "She's in there now?" Had she heard my detailed description to my colleagues? Think. Was the door opened or closed?

Garrett nodded. "Look, if there's someone else…"

"No." I was confident I could manage a professional stance by keeping a physical distance between us. "Go see if she'd mind."

Garrett nodded and walked away.

Air stuck in my lungs. The encounter with Belinda at the New Year's Eve party had never left me. I couldn't get the woman out of my head. Despite my resolution, she was affecting my relationship with Sharyn.

My throat thickened. Did I just put myself in her path? I tugged at my collar, swallowed the thick saliva, and then straightened my tie. If I kept my distance and didn't touch her, I'd be fine… I hoped.

~ Belinda ~

The voices from the big conference room grated on my nerves. I pressed my lips together and huffed as I tapped my fingernails on the windowsill. Now, privacy seemed like a good idea.

I gave the sill a pound with a clenched fist, then walked toward the door. About halfway there, Robert's deep, silky voice floated into my ears. Garrett had sworn there wasn't a chance I'd run into him. My lower lip took a beating the second I grabbed it between my teeth.

He spoke again. His words made my heart leap.

I backed against the wall next to the door and leaned in closer to the opening. His voice became sweet music the more I listened. That is until his words rang clear. Is he describing his girlfriend? Whoever she was, she stole his heart. The peacefulness I experienced from his voice shifted and dampened my mood.

Enough. I closed the door and walked back to peer out the window, putting an end to his voice's effect on me.

The traffic on 610, loaded with eighteen-wheelers, moved at a snail's pace. I leaned against the sill. I'd be driving home in that mess.

A muffled knock made me jump. Garrett entered and closed the door behind him, then leaned against it. The corners of his mouth drifted up. "Hi. Sorry, you had to wait."

I'd never been so glad to see someone. "It's okay. Can we get started?" The sooner we'd finished, the sooner I'd get away from any chance of running into Robert. I had doubts about the traffic.

He explained he'd need the help of a colleague with the different components of the fund. The minute he told me Robert Pendleton would do the honors, my stomach dipped.

"Belinda, I don't want to put you in an uncomfortable position. If you don't want to see him, I'll make other arrangements."

I listened to what he said. I took a deep breath. "No, I'm fine. I'll listen to Mr. Pendleton."

It didn't seem right calling him Mr. Pendleton.

Garrett left and closed the door behind him. I paced in front of the window, wringing my hands so hard I thought I'd reach the bone. This would be my first encounter with Robert since the party. The memory of his touch made my heart flutter like the wings of a hummingbird.

On the windowsill, I planted my palms, lowered my eyelids, and swallowed hard. The pale blue of his eyes still wrapped around my mind and didn't want to let go until the door opened.

Wide-eyed, I turned to face them. My gaze rested on Robert's face. My pulse jumped into overdrive and this encounter felt... foreign. Not prepared to see him.

In my "Dream Reality," Robert always dressed well and so did this version. He sported a tailored gray suit, white shirt, and dark blue tie. The jacket hugged his broad shoulders and tapered at the waist. He looked gorgeous, and that made my pulse pound.

It didn't feel right having to act as if I didn't know him, but I had no choice. With every nerve-ending tingling at his closeness, I stiffened and walked toward him.

A golf ball-sized lump formed and caused me to clear my throat. "Mr. Pendleton, it's nice to see you again." I extended my hand.

He didn't step forward to take it. He just stood there.

~ *Robert* ~

Just a hand on her shoulder at the New Year's Eve party had almost caused me to lose control. I couldn't touch her. Not even her hand. So, I ignored the gesture.

She hiked an eyebrow at me.

"It's nice to see you again. Please, sit." I pointed toward a chair at one end of the table. On the other side, I took a seat across from her that established enough distance between us. Garrett sat at the head of the table and started typing on the keyboard.

"Garrett tells me you need a detailed explanation of this fund." I opened the folder and selected the needed papers.

"If you'll look at the television, I'll begin." I maintained my professional persona. Garrett managed the tech duties while I reviewed everything she needed to know about her financial position.

I'd occasionally glanced at her during the presentation. Avoiding eye contact to minimize the captivating effect of her phenomenal blue eyes. As I finished, I asked, "Do you have any questions?"

Belinda's eyes rested on mine.

Everything stopped. My breathing. My heart. Time.

Those eyes grabbed my soul and looked deep into my inner being. Air gushed into my lungs and caused me to look away. That broke the spell. I leaned forward and shuffled through the papers spread out on the table to prevent direct eye contact. "Here. This one summarizes everything I just went over."

While Belinda scanned the paper, I studied her for the first time. She looked more beautiful than I remembered—a natural beauty. Her long hair framed her face. It seemed her eyelashes almost extended to the center of her cheeks. Her flawless skin enticed me to reach out and stroke it.

The impulse intensified when her lashes fluttered up.

I had to fight the desire to touch her.

To my relief, I got a reprieve when Garrett interrupted. "Robert, how much time do you have? I have another piece of her portfolio. I think you'd be able to explain better than I could. Do you mind?"

I snapped my head in his direction. "That's fine." I held out my hand, expecting him to give me the information right then, but he excused himself from the room.

My mouth filled with cotton. With the click of the door, I found myself alone with her. I stared at the frosted glass inset to give myself a few seconds to think and hoped she wouldn't bring up anything that occurred on New Year's Eve. I didn't quite understand what had happened and didn't want to explain. Besides, this wasn't the time or place.

To avoid any further visual contact, I got up and ambled toward the pitcher of water and glasses arranged on the credenza behind her. "Would you like some water?" I kept my voice cool and controlled.

~ Belinda ~

The sight of Garrett's back brought my world to a halt. He had just left me alone with Robert. Suddenly, I couldn't swallow. Water might be a good idea. "Yes. Please."

I bowed my head to allow myself to get a grip. It didn't help. Breathing became more difficult. In my head, I screamed, "Garrett, come back! I can't be alone with him!"

A flurry of emotions erupted. The questions I wanted answered more than the fear of his closeness—why he responded the way he did at the party and why he hadn't called—needed to be asked.

I sat there and stared at the stupid summary page to give myself something to do.

But when he walked behind me and stood at the credenza, the heat from his body radiated off him like an electrical current. Musk with a hint of spice hovered in the air. My back stiffened, and I prayed. Garrett, please come back.

What seemed like hours passed before I got up the nerve to turn around. Our gazes collided, and we attempted to talk at the same time. He politely said, "Ladies first."

I smiled and turned away. The sight of his handsome face fried my senses, rendering me speechless. His penetrating eyes just made me want to leap into his arms and kiss his luscious lips.

Instead, I nibbled at the side of my lower lip. Determined to ask the questions gnawing at me, I planted my palms on the table and squared my shoulders. I had no choice but to look at him again. With a serious expression, I peered straight into his captivating eyes.

Parting my lips, I got out one syllable. "Ah."

The sound of the door opening caused Robert to turn. In that brief second, Garrett's untimely entrance deprived my opportunity.

Robert placed the glass of water in front of me, then approached Garrett and took the folder, and opened it. "You know, I just remembered I need to get to an appointment. Sam can help with your questions on this one as well as I can. I'll send him in."

He glanced my way and made a half-assed gesture at politeness as he double-timed it for the door. "It was nice seeing you again."

"Same here. Thank you for all your help," I called out to his retreating back. My voice resonated with a bit of sarcasm mixed with disappointment as my chance for answers dashed down the hall.

"You're welcome," he shouted back from over his shoulder. I tilted my head, amazed he even heard me.

∞

The meeting with Sam and Garrett ended with me satisfied. I'd have enough money to live very well. If I went back to teaching, even part-time, I'd have plenty to provide for a very comfortable retirement.

For now, I'd pay cash for the patio home. I'd also pay off my parents' mortgage. I knew they'd try to talk me out of it, but I wouldn't take "no" for an answer.

I left confident about my financial affairs, but I couldn't say the same about my emotional state. Seeing Robert had been harder than I imagined. I didn't understand why he wouldn't talk to me, or maybe he saw me as nuts. For whatever reason, he made it clear he wanted little to do with me.

Garrett walked me to the elevator. "Are you okay?"

"Yes. Why?"

"Just making sure. You know, after seeing Robert."

"I won't lie. It wasn't easy."

"I'm sorry."

I kissed him on the cheek and hugged him. "Don't be. I just found out I'm richer than I thought." We laughed. "Tell Abby I'll call soon."

A familiar ping preceded the opening of the steel doors. Garrett left when I entered the elevator.

As I turned around, I saw Robert standing next to his desk, watching me through the glass wall of his office. For the past few hours, my emotions had been on a roller coaster ride. Seeing him again became more than I could handle. Tears welled up as I gazed into the depth of his soft, glacier-blue eyes. For a second, I swore I saw him take a step in my direction, but he stopped just as the elevator doors closed.

Alone, I rested my head against the back wall. Never again did I want to experience being close to him and not be able to be with him. I swept away the tears before the doors opened on the garage level.

Along the wall, closest to the elevator, I noticed a red BMW Roadster in a reserved parking space. It was the same make and model Robert drove in my "Dream Reality." I stood next to the car to see the plaque secured to the wall. My muscles stiffened, paralyzed by what I read. **Robert Pendleton, IV.**

CHAPTER 6

~ Belinda ~

WELLED TEARS FLOWED. All afternoon I kept them at bay. Alone in my car, the floodgates opened. As hard as I tried, my mind wouldn't let Robert go. Too many questions about the New Year's Eve party needed answers.

I leaned my head against the headrest and focused on the red roadster. A sniffle escaped. The muscles in my neck tightened, so I rolled my head to relieve the tension. I took a deep breath and let my head tilt until the red roadster, a symbol of all my frustrations, came back into view.

"I'm acting like a fool." I gave the steering wheel a pop. Then I studied the situation as all the sessions with Dr. Rosen jumped from one to the next. Those sessions and what I had learned gave me emotional strength. The only sensible conclusion was not to run from Robert.

I decided. From this day forward, I would no longer be a passive player. I wiped my cheeks. I wanted to know what happened on New Year's Eve and why he hadn't called. Something didn't seem right.

My mission, discover his motives. I opened the glove box and pushed its contents around, fumbling for something suitable to write on. Two fast-food napkins would do the job. I blew my nose in the first one. Then I picked up a pen from the console and wrote a note on the other.

Robert,

Thank you for your help this afternoon. You took a difficult topic and made it easy to understand. I sincerely hope that if I have any further questions, you'd be willing to answer them. 555-632-9743.

Belinda

A snicker escaped as I reread the note. Nothing like the direct approach. Then I opened the door, hopped out, and strolled over to the car.

At the front fender, I scrutinized the windshield wiper. I hesitated and grabbed my lower lip between my teeth. Tsking, I rolled my eyes. I lifted the wiper blade and tucked the note under it. "What did I have to lose?"

Robert was attracted to me. Hell, his actions on New Year's Eve and the tension I just experienced proved it. Now the ball was in his court. I had to see if he would volley it back.

As I walked past the car, I slid my fingers along the side and fondly remembered my first ride in the blue roadster Robert owned in my dream.

With my memories tucked aside, I had clothes shopping to do. I straightened my back, lifted my head, and took confident steps toward my car, feeling just a smidge prouder of myself.

The meeting ran longer than I expected and that cut into my power shopping. To avoid the sea of highway vehicles, I'd stay longer and leave when traffic died down. My new plan, enjoy the rest of my afternoon by trying on new clothes that looked more presentable than jogging shorts and tees.

The mall was only three blocks away. Fighting the traffic and finding parking took forty-five minutes of my life I'd never get back.

The second I entered the Galleria, the sheer size overwhelmed me. I'd forgotten how much space the mall engulfed.

The place hummed for a Thursday, full of business types bustling past to reach their destinations.

In the first store, I browsed and tried on clothes. It had been a long time since I'd enjoyed myself this much. When I woke up, buying new clothes made no sense. As I gained weight with the help of physical therapy, jogging, and riding Beau, my muscle tone increased to the point I looked more like my old self.

The plan to power shop diminished as I walked from one store to the next and I lost track of time.

During a brisk walk between stores, I glanced at my watch. It was 5:30 p.m. and I'd be in the middle of bumper-to-bumper traffic. Time to change plans.

I'd continue to shop, grab a bite to eat, and then drive back later to Sugar Land when the traffic died down. But first I needed to call my mother. My social life was non-existent, and I knew she'd be thrilled I was doing something other than sitting around the house.

The sides of my bag annoyed me as they collapsed on themselves. I dug around in the depths for the phone while I walked along. With my nose buried in the recesses of the purse's black hole, I hit what felt like a brick wall. The impact jolted the bag out of my hands, which deposited the contents around my feet.

"Crap." My mouth dropped open as I watched a tampon gracefully roll over and stop at the toe of a man's shoe. Could this day get any more embarrassing?

I immediately kneeled to grab my things.

Heat rushed up the sides of my neck to my cheeks. Horrified, I snatched the feminine hygiene product up, praying the man didn't notice.

My gaze crept up the crease of a gray, tailored pant leg to a dark blue tie that ended with the glacier-blue eyes of Robert studying me.

Yep, the day just got worse.

My face flushed hotter. My heart pounded. My fingers fumbled over the mess until I had to look down to see what I was doing.

Robert stooped down and helped shovel the contents back into their home. Neither of us spoke while we worked shoulder to shoulder, our hands inches apart.

This was my chance. I didn't know when I'd be close to him again. To touch him and watch for a reaction.

I placed my hand across his and left it there. As passion stirred within me, I took a deep breath through my mouth. I glanced at him and found him breathing faster. His eyes intensified in a soft way that made my skin heat. His scent swirled around me. I became light-headed.

Robert slipped his hand away, breaking our bond. He reached into the scattered objects. "I dropped my phone." He picked it up. "You got this?"

I nodded.

"Need help getting up?" He didn't extend his hand.

"No. I'll manage." I shoved the remaining items into my purse.

Robert talked to another man while moving a few feet away.

When I stood, I wobbled. I was about to go over when a hand grabbed me.

"I gotcha." The man offered a warm, welcoming smile as his other hand settled on the small of my back. "Hey, you're the girl from the Pendleton party. Belinda. Right?"

"Yeah." I grabbed onto his arm. "I must have gotten up too fast." Or maybe it was my heart-pounding, vein-splitting reaction to Robert's touch.

I inhaled a few times. "Thank you. I'm all right."

I remembered all 6'4" of Colin very well. This attractive, sandy-headed man had paid exclusive attention to me at the party until I made my disappearance in Robert's arms.

"You sure?"

Robert joined us. So there I stood between the two of them. With one man saving me and the other tearing my insides apart piece by piece.

Robert attempted to talk, but Colin jumped right in. "Remember me? I'm Colin Brockman. We shared a few dances." He let me go. "What happened to you? You just vanished. One minute you were there, the next POOF!" He made a bursting motion with his fingers.

I gazed into his bright blue eyes and smiled. "I didn't feel well, so I left early. Sorry, I didn't get to say goodbye."

Out of the corner of my eye, I noticed Robert stiffen.

"We're on our way downstairs to get something to eat. We're meeting his girlfriend. If you don't have any plans, why don't you join us?"

Girlfriend?

Colin glanced at Robert. "You don't mind. Do you?"

A muscle flexed in his cheek. "No."

How could I resist the invitation? I couldn't believe my luck. Not only would I be able to be close to Robert, but I'd also have the chance to see his response to his... girlfriend.

"I would love to join you. I'll just need to let my parents know I'll be late. They still worry about me. You know how parents can be." I wagged my phone as I walked a few feet away for privacy. I hit the number two on the phone. What I heard next rendered me speechless.

"Hello, Robert."

I didn't know what to say and hesitated, then blurted out, "Oh! I'm sorry. This must be the wrong number."

"Who is this?! How did you get Robert's phone?" The voice resonated.

I read the display. It said Sharyn. I put the phone back to my ear. "Could you hold on a minute?"

No reply.

I walked over to Robert, who now stood in front of a store window. "Excuse me. I think we switched phones." I held the phone out to him. "You might want to take this."

Here was another opportunity to test his response. I wrapped my fingers around his wrist, and to my surprise, he tensed and twisted, attempting to pull away.

With eyes slit, I tilted my head and studied his face.

His chin lifted and his eyes widened into a fixed glare as his breathing quickened. My grip tightened with every twist. I knew he could get loose if he wanted, but his effort seemed feeble.

His eyes gradually softened, and he relaxed, melting me with his warm gaze. For a split second, time stopped and no one else existed. My neurons fired as an electrified sensation zipped up my spine.

What the hell was I doing? For heaven sake, we were in the middle of a mall. I slapped the phone into his palm and let go. But the brief episode confirmed his attraction to me. And me to him.

~ *Robert* ~

I turned away as soon as she released me. Jeez? Her first touch left me dazed, and I had trouble recovering. This time, the heat that shot through me intensified. I had to walk away. I needed distance.

The phone display blazed Sharyn's name. I must have picked up and put Belinda's phone in my pocket. I was texting Sharyn when Miss Grabby slammed into my chest and dumped everything from her purse at our feet.

When the white, cylindrical object stopped at the tip of my shoe, that was funny. Sad for her, but funny for me, until she looked up at me, and my heart skipped a beat.

Oh hell. The only thing I could do was help her pick up the crap. Everything would've been fine, but oh no, she had to grab my wrist. I couldn't think of anything else besides jumping her bones after that.

My chest rose with a deep breath as I swiped my fingers through my hair. Now, I had to deal with Sharyn. I placed the phone to my ear and scrunched it with my shoulder to hold it in place. "Hello, Sharyn? Hang on a minute."

I pulled Belinda's phone out and peered at it, raising an eyebrow. It looked identical to mine, down to the protective cover. I pinched the damn thing between my fingers as I walked over and flicked it at her. I flattened my lips into a thin line and furrowed my brow. When she didn't take it I narrowed my eyes and fixed them on hers, giving the phone one more hard flick to make my point.

She finally opened her hand, palm up under the phone. I dropped it in and gave her one last glare.

I walked far enough away to make sure they couldn't hear me. "Hey, Honey. Where are you?"

"Robert, who was that?" Sharyn sounded annoyed.

"She's one of my clients and our phones got switched. They're exactly alike." To avoid too much explanation, I gave her just enough information. "She was at the office. Colin and I bumped into her at the mall." I left out the literally bumping part.

"I'm in the parking lot. I'll meet you in front of the pub. Love you."

"I love you too. See you in a few." Thank heaven she believed me.

~ Belinda ~

I started my fact finding mission with Colin. "How long has he been dating Sharyn?"

"Let's see. He told me they reconnected last Fourth of July at the Pendletons' pool party."

"Reconnected?" Fourth of July pool party? The dream coincidences were adding up. No. More like piling up.

"Yeah. They'd run into each other occasionally. She came with her parents to the party last year, and they seemed to hit it off, but they didn't really start seriously seeing each other until late July."

While listening to Colin, I sized up Robert. In August, I was in a coma. In my "Dream Reality," Robert was in summer school and spending time away from me with Erin Pendelson. I thought it strange the two names were so similar, Erin in the "Dream Reality" and Sharyn in my "New Reality." Then there were the Beamers. And he called me Angel, a nick-name my Dream Robert gave me.

I watched Robert stare at his phone and noticed a slight shift in his posture as he approached Colin and me.

"Sharyn will meet us at the pub."

He showed no detectable emotion and he never even lifted his head. He just studied his phone in an indifferent manner.

"Let's go." He slipped the phone into his pocket, turned, and started walking. Colin and I picked up our pace to catch him.

As I walked between the two men, Colin continued with congenial small talk while Robert added nothing. A few times, I brushed against his arm and my senses went berserk. My thoughts centered on a man who knew nothing about me. Tonight, my goal, to discover all I could, despite the news of a girlfriend.

Robert pointed toward a woman leaning against the rail of the ice rink. "There she is."

The second he was within her reach, she threw her arms around his neck and gave him a tender kiss on the lips. He had to bend down because of their height difference of at least seven inches.

He spoke to her, and her short, layered, blonde hair bounced as she threw her head back and laughed.

Although I found Sharyn attractive, I didn't quite see her and Robert as a match. They didn't seem to fit.

She moved her left hand to his shoulder. The massive diamond sitting on her ring finger almost blinded me. Well, shit. Robert's engaged!?

Hand in hand, he turned to introduce her. "Belinda, this is my fiancée, Sharyn Mendelson. Sharyn, this is Belinda Davies, the client I told you about."

Erin Pendelson? Sharyn Mendelson? That coincidence pile just got higher.

I hesitated, trying to keep myself under control. I stared at the massive diamond she sported. Monster, my old jealousy friend, chimed in with a jerk of her tail. It wasn't until I noticed the questioning expression on Sharyn's face that I responded to the introduction.

"Hi." I tried to be casual and polite under the circumstances. "Beautiful ring."

"He proposed on New Year's Eve before he ran off to meet some clients." Sharyn flashed her hand in my face. She glanced at Robert and smiled.

He kept his head down, but slid a sideways glance at her. "He wanted us to be engaged so we could start the year off together."

She nestled close and rested against his chest. "He's so romantic."

Robert lifted his head. His eyes appeared soft and pleading. He glued them on mine and shook his head ever so slightly. I understood his request and met his expectations by not mentioning our bed-rattling meeting.

With a quick snort and a raised eyebrow, I gave him a fleeting glance.

What kind of man becomes engaged, then makes out with another woman a few hours apart? A player!

The engagement, however, explained why he hadn't called and why he seemed so nervous after our episode.

"May I see it?"

Sharyn proudly posed her hand so I could inspect the rock.

I stepped in closer. "It's gorgeous. Did you help pick it out?"

"No. It was a total surprise." Her face glowed until she cocked her head and her expression changed. "What perfume are you wearing?"

I wanted to scream, but needed to be polite. "Angel Scent."

I glanced up at Sharyn to see a frown contort her face.

She nodded. "I see. It seems to suit you."

My butterflies pummeled the walls of my insides from her tone and the news of the engagement. I returned to pretending to study the stunning ring to give myself a few moments to recoup. "It's really beautiful."

I straightened my posture and lifted my chin, now pissed because Robert resembled an ass.

As I walked past him, I took hold of Colin's arm and responded loud enough for the group to hear, "You have good taste." Timing my next step, I bumped Robert's shoulder with mine and whispered, "Romeo."

CHAPTER 7

~ Belinda ~

AT A QUITE table in the rear corner of the restaurant, everyone settled into their seats. I hadn't had time to call my parents since the phone mix-up. On impulse, I hatched a plan.

"Excuse me. I'll be right back." I grabbed my purse and flung it over my shoulder. Full of confidence, I turned and sashayed away, putting my modeling-class strut to good use. If my plan worked, my exaggerated hip movements would make the view enjoyable for those who wished to watch, and I prayed Robert was one of them.

Most of the time, I avoided drawing attention to myself, but not tonight. I wanted the whole damn place to notice me, especially Robert. A few male patrons turned their heads in my direction, so I amped up the swing.

Was I angry? You bet I was. On New Year's Eve, I received the most exciting, sensual kiss I'll ever experience from a real man I had loved in a fake life. Tonight, my butterflies went from doing laps to dropping on the floor, where Robert stomped on them with the engagement announcement.

Is this vindictive? Yes, it is, but this was my only chance. Maybe he'd never be mine, but I wanted him to get a taste of what he was missing.

~ Robert ~

"Oh. My. God!" came out of Colin.

Colin's face lit up and his mouth dropped open. I tracked his eyes and saw Belinda, with her sexy rear, walking through the restaurant.

I couldn't look away. I enjoyed the effort she put into every step and how her hips moved with the grace of a dancer. The tight jeans cradled her butt, accentuating the upside-down heart shape. My teeth clenched as my jaw tightened.

The fantasy that formed in my imagination about caressing her ass never had a chance. Sharyn punched my arm and knocked the thought right out of my head.

"Ouch!"

She scowled. On instinct, I threw my arm around her shoulders and tugged her close.

"I love you." A gentle kiss found its way to her mouth. A nice kiss, but a lacking kiss. Since the kisses I'd shared with Belinda, I had trouble showing Sharyn the affection she deserved.

Belinda's luscious mouth had gotten in my head and refused to leave. She radiated sensuality, and underneath, I sensed a connection I'd never experienced with Sharyn. The whole time I stayed lip-locked with my fiancée, I savored the image of Belinda, as any cheater might.

A stiff drink was in order after Belinda's head-turning walk, and I figured the panting Colin needed one too. I placed an order for two scotch-on-the-rocks and a repeat of wine for the ladies. Sharyn continued to dominate the conversation with tales about recent business trips.

Colin showed a half-assed interest in her dissertation in between the sideways glances toward Belinda's hip-action departure. He was waiting for a repeat performance. He acted like he was in heat, which annoyed me, but I couldn't blame him.

To keep the peace with Sharyn, I focused my attention on her while I kept Colin in my peripheral vision, making it easy to watch his reactions. The smile spreading across his face indicated Belinda's return.

My attraction to Belinda made being around her and my fiancée pure hell. Sharyn was no dummy. I didn't need to give her a reason to suspect she wasn't the only woman for me, as I opted to watch Colin enjoy the view.

Over his shoulder, I noticed several tables of men turning their heads in the same direction and smiling. I followed their gaze and realized Colin wasn't the only one ogling Belinda. She had the whole damn restaurant watching her.

I hated those drooling men and fantasized about punching each one to wipe the smirks off their faces. At that moment, my blood boiled.

A big smile spread across Belinda's face when Colin jumped up to pull out her chair.

"Mission accomplished." Her gaze fixed on me as she sat.

The muscles around my eyes tensed. Was this jealousy? No. I had no right. I needed to get a grip and calm down.

Remember your resolution, screamed in my head. Hell, why did she bother me so much? I tossed back the rest of my drink and waved to the waiter to bring me a refill.

During dinner and after the last scotch, I relaxed. Our conversation jumped from subject to subject. That helped distract my mind from those swinging hips seared into my memory. Our relentless teasing of Colin also provided much comic relief.

He wasn't from Texas and had moved here from Los Angeles. He'd experience his first summer in his new state in a few months. We all joked and warned him about the heat, humidity, and hurricanes.

"Do you get advanced warnings about hurricanes?"

We all laughed.

"You'll get sick of hearing about the damn things. That's all everyone will talk about if there's a chance it's heading for us." I raised my glass.

Colin repeated the gesture. "That will be a good time to visit my Mom."

Comments flew around the table to call him a wimp and that he'd never become a true Texas because he had no grit.

~ *Belinda* ~

I found it extremely difficult to sit across from Robert with Sharyn hanging on his arm. But the look he gave me after my little walk spoke volumes. As the evening progressed, we both seemed to relax. Maybe the wine and the scotch helped. I was having a good time, and Colin took every opportunity to flirt with me. It felt good to have a male's attention.

At one point, Robert and I reached for the saltshaker at the same time, and his fingers wrapped around mine. My eyes floated shut as the all-too-familiar sensual quiver ran up my spine. His index finger gently stroked the top of my hand until he slipped it away and turned back to Sharyn.

The whole incident went unnoticed by anyone else. What seemed to me like minutes took place in seconds.

Those few seconds confirmed his attraction, but the news of his engagement placed a different slant on the situation. I'd never allow myself to be "The Other Woman" at any cost.

"Belinda, how do you know Robert and Colin?"

Sharyn's question turned all eyes on me, and I took a few seconds to adjust from my dream down memory lane. "I invested through their group."

Everyone stopped talking when Colin blurted out, "I first met her at the Pendletons' New Year's Eve party!"

I gave a glance toward Robert. He'd lowered his head and I couldn't read his reaction.

However, Sharyn's face showed her interest piqued. I needed to backpedal. "A friend's husband invited me, who is my broker at the firm. I didn't even make it to midnight because I was under the weather and left early." The answer stretched the truth.

"Oh, I see." She paused and studied me.

"What do you do for a living?"

Thank God she changed the subject. How do I answer that? I'm a lucky bum who's wealthy as crap and doesn't need to work. "Well. Ah. Right now, nothing."

"Nothing?" Sharyn's voice rose an octave and so did her nose.

"I'm recovering from a car accident, but my degree is in art education."

Sharyn zoned in on the accident. "An accident? What happened?"

"I was on my way home from a wedding shower last April when a semi smashed into my car at the intersection of Highway Six and I-69."

Robert's head swung around toward me, his brow furrowed. "When was your accident?"

"The first Sunday in April. Why?"

His head tilted. "Was it about seven o'clock at night?"

I nodded.

"A silver SUV?"

I nodded again.

"Wow!" He sat up straight as an arrow and shook his head. "I was sitting next to you at the light, waiting to turn left onto Highway Six. I was texting. When the light turned green, I noticed the SUV moving in my peripheral vision." He raked his fingers through his hair. His face drained of color. "I looked up from putting my phone down and saw this semi fly through the intersection and slam into your car." He gulped down a swig of scotch. "If I had pulled out first..." His voice cracked. "I would've been hit instead of you."

Sharyn gasped. Colin froze. Robert gave me a penetrating gaze, and for a second, we connected.

"I jumped out to see if I could do anything. All I saw was blood and hair, and realized, if the woman in the car was alive, I had no business moving her. So I called 911." He swallowed hard. "The truck driver crawled out of his rig, but the woman... you. They had to use the 'Jaws-of-Life' to cut you out."

He took in a deep breath. "After I talked to the police, I sat in my car for about an hour. I couldn't do anything until they cleared the highway. I had a front-row seat. From how the EMTs were handling you, I knew you were alive."

I sucked in air, not realizing I had been holding my breath, captivated by his story of my near demise.

When he finished, he gave me a strange look. "Are you okay?"

My thoughts ran rampant. What if the truck hit him? What if he'd died? Oh, God. I wouldn't be sitting... we wouldn't be sitting here tonight. I never would have met him.

I covered my heart, my eyes blinking rapidly, and took a breath. "Yeah... it's just... this is the first time anyone has ever put into words what happened that night. I read the police reports, but it's different hearing it, especially from someone who witnessed it."

"When I saw them loading the stretcher into the ambulance, I said, 'God, help her.'"

"Thanks. I guess He heard you."

Robert nodded, and half smiled. He lowered his head and fiddled with his drink, rubbing a finger up and down its side.

He appeared distressed, and my heart ached for him. I wanted to grab his hand to tell him everything was all right now that I found him. Of course, I didn't dare, with Sharyn sitting next to him.

A hush fell over the group. Robert's graphic description put a major dent in the lite-hearted mood. I didn't need pity. So I readjusted myself and leaned forward on the table.

"Well, anyway, because of the collision, I spent six months in a coma. I woke up near the end of September."

Robert didn't lift his head, but his finger stopped rubbing the side of the glass the second I mentioned the coma. Another hint of a coincidence. Or was I reading too much into all his reactions and comments?

To lighten the mood, I gave the air a wave and glanced at Sharyn. "And today I found out I'm rich. So, no job in my immediate future."

Sharyn scrunched her nose. "Excuse me for asking, but what do you mean you found out you're rich?"

"After the accident, the trucking firm set up a trust fund for me that would take care of my medical expenses for years. No one expected me to wake up from the coma six months later."

"You were in a coma for six months. You don't even look like you had any injuries. Especially by the way you walk." Sharyn's eyes turned to slits, and her mouth rose at the corners just a smidge. "Do you remember anything from the time in the coma?"

I held my sight on her for an instant, to collect my thoughts and to make sure I didn't divulge the life I had lived with Robert in the "Dream Reality." No one needed to know anything about that aspect of my life, except maybe Robert.

"I remember some, maybe more like dreams."

I glanced at Robert. He just sat there with his head down, not moving. "They expected me to die, but my doctor said my dreams kept me fighting for my life."

Robert peered up with those intense, glacier-blue eyes.

"What dreams?" Sharyn cut her fish and took a bite.

"Things associated with the sounds I heard around me and the movements I felt."

"I see." She picked up her glass and smirked before she took a swig of wine. "You look pretty healthy."

"The doctors explained my recovered was because I was young and in pretty good shape before the accident. I also have my horse to thank. The physical labor of cleaning up after him and riding was a wonderful exercise to regain muscle tone and coordination."

She scoffed. "Robert is an excellent rider. He could've made the Olympic equestrian team when he was in college."

I tilted my head toward him. "You ride?" Finding out this bit of information caused my spirits to lift. Dream Robert knew nothing about horses.

Robert opened his mouth, but Sharyn butted in. "He loves his horse so much he still lives in his parents' guesthouse." She stroked his arm.

He turned toward her. "I'm sure Belinda can understand that. She probably feels the same way about Beau."

I sat up more erect. How does he know the name of my horse? I had never mentioned it, and I didn't remember that coming up in a conversation.

"Robert, how do you know the name of my horse?"

He stiffened but answered without hesitation. "Garrett mentioned it at work."

I studied him for a few seconds. His answer sounded reasonable, but that coincidence pile inched up a bit more. "Sharyn, do you ride?"

"OH, NO! I hate the filthy animals."

I gave a polite nod as if I understood her distaste.

"Well, Belinda, I'm glad you made it." Colin leaned in toward Sharyn, lifting his drink. "And I *do* appreciate her walk." He sneered the whole time in Sharyn's direction before he turned back to me.

"If you hadn't made it, I would've missed out on getting to know you."

I chuckled. "How could you have missed me? You never would've known I existed."

From across the table, I thought I heard Robert mumble, "But I would've."

A hint of a smile grew across my mouth, and I threw that comment on the coincidence pile.

Sharyn left the table and headed for the restroom. Colin hopped up seconds later to do the same, leaving me alone with Robert. Now was the chance to ask why he kissed me at the party. But would there be enough time for a discussion before the others returned? I waited.

The waiter placed my dessert order in front of me, a piece of chocolate cake.

"Thank you."

I'd never mention his indiscretions in front of Sharyn, but I wanted to see Romeo squirm. So I opted for payback to ease my frustration at how he treated me at the party and since. The least he could've done was call to tell me about his engagement. That bit of information would've saved me days of agony.

Not taking my eyes off the sweet delight, I raked my index finger through the thick, creamy chocolate icing. Then I slipped my tongue out and slowly ran it over my loaded finger, licking a little off. "Mmmm." I briefly closed my eyes and shimmied my shoulders.

To enhance my delight, I plunged my finger into my mouth, puckering my lips around it, and rotated it back and forth to suck it clean. I dragged it out and examined it. A trace of chocolate remained. So I flicked my tongue over the few bits. Savoring the delicious taste, I closed my eyes again and sucked in a deep breath as I ran my tongue around my lips, cleaning off every speck of icing. With a seductive glance, mouth parted, I looked up through my lashes and arched an eyebrow.

The expression on Robert's face spoke volumes as he seemed to force air into his lungs and shifted—uncomfortable—from side to side.

Satisfied. Another mission accomplished.

I turned my attention back to the cake, picked up a fork, took a bite, and acted like I'd done nothing out of the ordinary.

~ *Robert* ~

Belinda's unexpected display caught me off guard. That tongue. That mouth. I froze and my stomach knotted while I watched her erotic exhibition, unable to look away. A lower part of me reacted.

Reaching for each side of my chair seat, I gripped it as tight as I could to control myself—to keep from leaping over the table and making a spectacle of myself. I wanted nothing more at the moment than to capture her tongue, her mouth, and do... STOP! Remember your resolution. I couldn't believe she had the nerve to do that.

With a ghost of a grin, I narrowed my eyes at her and said, "You're bad."

She batted her lashes. "Uh-huh."

Sharyn and Colin returned at the same time. The second Sharyn sat, she bitched about the waiter just leaving her dessert, now a soupy pie à la mode, on the table and hailed him down to voice her displeasure.

"No. I don't want a replacement. Just clear this stuff away." She waved her hand over the table and huffed.

The waiter started clearing the dishes. Sharyn sat cross-armed and pouted. She elbowed me after the waiter left. "Don't leave him a tip."

I sighed. "Okay. Honey, where did you park?"

"In the lot just outside the restaurant. Why?"

"Just trying to get the parking order down so we...", I pointed my finger between Colin and myself, "can make sure the two of you...", I pointed to Belinda and her, "get to your cars safely."

I asked Belinda where she was parked. "I'm at the other end of the mall in the covered parking lot." Colin had parked in the middle, and I, to my surprise, had parked in the same lot as Belinda.

A discussion of how everyone would leave took a few minutes. First, the group would walk Sharyn to her car. Colin, Belinda, and I would proceed through to the center of the mall, where we'd part with Colin. Then I'd escort Belinda to the farthest parking lot.

Knowing I'd be alone with her tied my stomach in knots, and I prayed Sharyn didn't notice.

I escorted Sharyn to her Mini Cooper. Normally, I would've been going home with her. However, she was leaving early in the morning to catch a flight to Europe. She decided it wouldn't make sense for both of us to go without sleep. I was glad because, after being around Belinda all evening and my active imagination, I wouldn't have been able to be intimate with Sharyn.

"I'll call you when I get home."

"Okay." She smiled and stroked my cheek. "I love you, and I'll miss you." She reached up and kissed me.

"I love you too." I opened the door. "Drive safely." She slid in. I pushed the door shut, stepped back, and waited.

~ *Sharyn* ~

I threw the gearshift into reverse, and the car rolled backward. I turned my gaze toward the mall door and straight into Belinda's watchful stare. Bitch!

I clutched the steering wheel tighter, blanching my knuckles. I had to be careful not to appear angry. Ever since Robert returned from his parents on New Year's Eve, he'd been distracted and less attentive. After popping the car into drive, I drove past Robert and threw him a kiss, then smiled to disguise the tense muscles my suspicion created.

The perfume scent I'd detected on his jacket when he came back from his parents' party made me think there could be another woman. Maybe Belinda? Colin confirmed she'd attended.

All evening, I fought my impulse to punch the bitch.

Angel Scent. Robert's jacket reeked of the stuff. Whomever he rubbed up against at the party had to be close, very close, and on top of him kind of close.

His tightened jaw and tensed shoulder muscles told me something was up. I'm not blind. I saw how he looked at her.

I took a corner a pinch too fast. The car swerved. If I wasn't careful, I'd be the next one in a coma and Ms. Angel Scent would have him all to herself.

Like hell.

I prayed my fear was unfounded, but if he strayed, I'd never know until after the fact because I traveled so much for my job. Still, when I was home, we spent every free minute together. But since the party, he'd been making excuses and hadn't touched me sexually.

"Angel Scent!"

The more I dwelled on the possibility, the more it ate at me.

~ Belinda ~

Just inside the door, Colin and I waited. I had a full view of Robert and Sharyn's interaction in the parking lot. Monster blinked a few times at the affection they showed to each other. That should be me, not her.

When Sharyn stared at me before driving off, ice water surged through my veins. I understood she meant trouble for me and I need to stay clear.

"Belinda."

"Yes." I turned toward Colin.

"I'd like to see you again. I planned to ask for your number at the party but waited too long, and we know how that played out."

I glanced back and saw Robert walking in our direction. Air lingered in my lungs before I forced it out and decided there would never be a Plan A.

He wouldn't be part of my life because I could never be "the other woman." Despite Sharyn's death-ray stares, I had no reason to hurt her, nor did I have a reason to torment myself. Some things are better just left alone, and my New Year's tryst with Robert was one of them.

Colin was an added benefit. If Robert and I were meant to be apart in my "New Reality," then I'd enjoy the company and affections of another man. Colin could provide that as part of Plan B.

"Give me your phone." I tapped in my number and gave it back without saying a word. With this small action, Plan B went into motion.

Robert walked in. "You two ready to go?"

We walked with me in between the two men, one who might be my future and the other tearing my insides apart.

At our next destination, Colin said his goodbyes to Robert and told him he'd see him at work in the morning.

He turned to me and gave me a gentle kiss on the cheek. "I'll be in touch." I smiled and gave a nod as he walked away.

Robert seemed tense as he stood with his hands in his pockets and tightened jaw muscles, looking at the ground.

"Should we continue?"

As his head rose, the glare he gave me sent a shiver up my spine. Was he angry about Colin?

"Let's go."

"Is everything all right?"

Air rushed out of his lungs and slowly back in. "I'm just tired. Let's get you to your car."

Alone, neither Robert nor I said anything while we walked—our pace slowed as if we didn't want this time together to end.

He broke the silence. "Where do you keep your horse?"

My butterfly flurry settled, and I was glad he picked a good silence breaker. "The stables right next to your subdivision."

"The ones that share the trails by our house?"

"The very ones."

"I'm on those trails all the time. How come I've never seen you riding?"

"I don't know. I'm out there every day." I offered a more feasible explanation. "I ride in the morning, most likely when you're at work."

Silence filled the gap until he spoke up. "Um, thank you for your note."

A slight giggle escaped. "It was still on the windshield? I didn't know how else to say thank you. So I just left it." I tucked my lip between my teeth and stopped walking. "I'm sorry about the phone number. I didn't know you were engaged." I studied the floor. "I don't expect a call."

I lifted my head. He stood there and said nothing at first. He smiled and his gaze thrilled my soul. A smidge of hope rose.

"I understand." He took a step. "Shall we continue walking?"

The parking garage door came into view, meaning our time together would end. I wished with all my heart that I could hold his hand as we walked. I had to remind myself this wasn't the Robert of my "Dream Reality" and this one was spoken for.

We reached the glass door that divided the mall from the parking lot. Just outside, I saw a red BMW Roadster as he held the door open.

I walked straight toward his car, putting a bit of a sashay in my strut. Just like the first time, I saw Robert's car in my "Dream Reality." I slid my fingers over the surface, starting with the back fender, moving across the door, and then the front fender before turning on my heels to face him. "Nice red car."

My heart almost jumped at the sight.

Robert stood about five feet away from the rear of the car with his thumbs hooked in his pockets and his head tilted down with his eyes fixed on me. He shook his head and the signature smile I grew to love in my dream flashed on this Robert. I melted at the sight. "I once knew someone who owned one of these, but in a different color."

"I prefer red over blue."

Suddenly, his mood changed. He became more serious. I watched the softness fade. He straightened his posture as he lifted his head. "Where's your car?"

I studied him. Another toss on the coincidence heap? My gut told me something wasn't right.

"It's on the next aisle."

Robert headed straight for a Honda CR-V despite several cars of different makes parked in the same row. I stopped. My mouth open. How'd he know what car... Another coincidence? Abby was right. This guy was hiding something.

His pace put him almost next to my car.

What the hell? How did he know?

He turned. "Are you coming?"

"Yeah. You walk too fast." Next to the driver-side door, I hit the fob unlock button. The car chirped.

Robert hovered in close to reach around me and opened the door and didn't move back. His short, hot breaths caressed my cheek. Inches from his mouth, I gazed at him. Our eyes met and locked. Then he shifted to my mouth. My lips tingled at the thought of closing the distance and feeling those lips pressed against mine. Did he want to kiss as much as I wanted him? My girlie parts clenched, and my butterflies buzzed.

His head jerked, and he took a step back, ending the moment.

I exhaled. "Thank you for tonight. You don't know how much this meant to me." I went to climb in, then stopped. "Robert. Did you tip the waiter?"

He snorted. "Of course I did, and it covered the tongue-lashing."

I wanted to ask. To find out what happened between us at the party. To tell him we were meant to be together. I wanted to say it out loud, to hear him tell me he knew I was right. It took all my might to keep my mouth shut as I slipped into the seat and he closed the door. He waited for me to start the car before he walked away.

I gave him one last look. But the question lingered. What was he hiding?

I gripped the steering wheel so hard my fingers tingled. Droplets streamed down my cheeks. Through my tears, I yelled, "He's engaged!"

About to reach the highway, I needed something to distract me. Although traffic had thinned, I was upset and about to enter emotional turmoil territory. Music. That might do—soothing music. I reached over and punched the "on" button. The words of "*Forever in My Mind*," Dream Robert's, and my song floated from the speakers.

"You have to be kidding me." I pushed the radio's off button.

More tears trailed down as the song reminded me of a lost love. Glorious memories of being in his arms, dancing and singing the words to him, and the great times we had spent together in the dream.

"He's engaged." I smacked the steering wheel.

Merging onto 610, I forced myself to calm down. I wiped at the tears and gave a quick flash in the rearview mirror. I did the same to the driver's side mirror to watch for oncoming traffic. My grip on the steering wheel tightened as I cursed the car riding my tail. "For heaven sake, just pass me!"

I'd driven about five miles with the same car following close behind. It appeared small.

In the dark, the reflections of the headlights glared. I couldn't see the color or recognize the make, though the shape seemed familiar. I darted my eyes from the rearview mirror to the side mirror, catching a brief flash of color.

Red. Robert? The car stayed with me to the turnoff to my subdivision. After I made the corner, I glanced in the rearview mirror and saw a red BMW roadster drive past.

~ Robert ~

I slammed the car door. Being around Belinda was more difficult than I had expected. My emotions hit a new high. I wasn't used to being out of control. Ever. I was engaged and had to remember that.

When I opened the mall door at the parking lot, I'd had a hard time restraining myself as her scent lofted into my nose. I had inhaled a deep breath, taking in what little of her I could, then slowed my pace to put a little distance between us.

The space hadn't helped.

When I looked up, her gorgeous sashaying hips were making their way to my car. Watching her fingers slide over the fender had made me wish I could just grab her and taste her delicious mouth again.

Her playful mannerisms took me back to another time. That's until I opened my big mouth. What difference did my color preference make, and why didn't I step aside after I opened her door? Being that close and not showing her any sign of affection wrenched my insides. Shit, I'd come so close to closing the distance, making me a repeat-cheater.

I needed to stay away from her.

The yellow traffic light refocused my attention on her car. I raced through the intersection just before it turned red. In hot pursued of the CR-V I had to be behind it before we reached the next light. If I didn't make the turn, I'd lose sight of her.

Driving like a maniac, I swerved into the next lane and sped up, passing the two cars that separated me from my target. Thankfully, the lead car slowed to make a right turn, which gave me the space to switch lanes and fall in behind the Honda.

I let out a deep breath, relieved I was right where I wanted to be. Her safe arrival home was important to me, and following her seemed like the only way I could watch out for her without stepping over my boundary line. I wanted nothing to happen to her.

I knew I couldn't take that.

CHAPTER 8

~ Belinda ~

BY THE LAST week of February, Plan B was in full swing.

We set the closing of my house for the first week of March. I had mixed feelings about moving out of my parents' home because I loved living there. During my recovery phase, Mom and I had grown closer. Now my relationship with her was on an adult level. She still hovered when needed, but had become more supportive of my need to experience life on my terms. I knew I'd miss having her available 24/7, but the time came to spread my wings in my "New Reality."

In Plan B, Robert was out and Colin stepped in. He called me a week after we had dinner at the pub.

At first, I put him off and gave him the excuse I was busy getting everything together for the closing. Though true to some extent, in reality, my palms sweated and my muscles tensed every time I talked to him. I hadn't had an actual date since Matt dumped me almost a year and a half ago. For now, Colin and I communicate through phone calls and texts. Staying away from him only worked for so long, so I took the plunge. The next time he invited me to go out, I'd accept.

Around four o'clock on Friday evening, I was sitting in my room, lost in the pages of my current romance novel, when my cell let out a beep, notifying me of a text.

Colin: Busy???
I typed in my reply: Reading.
Colin: In your neighborhood. At a meeting.

I took a deep breath before replying. This is it. It's now or never.

Me: Where are you?
Colin: Town square. Feel like dinner?
I studied the phone for a few seconds and then typed in my response: OK!

His answer didn't come as quickly as I expected. I wondered why it took him so long to respond. Finally….

Colin:	Pick you up in 60. ☺
Me:	How should I dress?
Colin:	Comfortably. Nothing fancy. Jeans OK.
Me:	I'll be ready
Colin:	☺☺☺☺☺☺☺Is my excitement showing?!
Me:	Yes! I have a date to get ready for. Bye!

~ *Colin* ~

I just stared at my phone with my mouth open. I couldn't believe it. She just accepted a dinner invitation. I made a fist-pumping gesture followed by a muffled, "Yes!"

My client, Ben Taylor, walked back into the conference room to wind up the meeting as a sense of panic came over me. I knew little about Sugar Land and the restaurants in the area. I wanted to make a good impression. Fortunately, my client lived here.

"Hey, Ben. If a guy wanted to impress a… let's say, a very attractive lady he's been trying to go out with, where would he take her for a casual but nice dinner in this area?"

I, usually as steady as a rock, fought the jitters in my stomach. How funny that a single female could bring a man to a state of such insecurity.

A broad smile came across Ben's face. "Well," he said. "I'd start with some wine at the wine bar across the street. Then have dinner at Sugar End. It's a casual, quiet place for pleasant conversation. I'd finish the night with ice cream or yogurt, eating it around the fountain in the square. If you're lucky, there might be a band playing on the City Hall steps. If not, it's still a fun place for people-watching."

A smile spread across my face, and my jumping stomach settled a bit. "Thanks, Ben. That sounds perfect."

"Well, I guess we're finished here unless you have questions." I gathered up the folders and held them while waiting for Ben's response.

He shook his head and stood. "Yeah, we're done."

I placed the folders in my briefcase, then stood up and extended my hand to him. "Well, as usual, it was nice seeing you again."

We shook hands. I loosened my grip to release him when he tightened his grasp and took hold of my upper arm. "You enjoy yourself tonight and good luck. I have a feeling this young lady is special."

A corner of my mouth turned up. "She is."

I sprinted to my obsidian-black metallic Mercedes Roadster, my pride, and joy. As VP of the planned Canadian branch, I had the money to spend, and the car impressed.

I opened the trunk and attempted to make myself more casual by removing my suit jacket. Then I placed it in the trunk. The tie came next. I peered down at the jacket. The nights in February were chilly, and if the groundhog's prediction turned out to be right, spring wouldn't be here for six more weeks. Out came the jacket. I closed the trunk and walked around to the driver's side as I unbuttoned the first two buttons of my shirt, then slipped the jacket on.

In the car, I flipped down the visor and gave my hair a quick mussing. Satisfied, I retrieved the breath mints from the console and then popped a few into my mouth. I gave myself another once-over in the mirror, pushed it shut, and looked at the car clock.

I had killed fifteen minutes.

"Now what?" I placed my elbow on the door and rubbed my chin. Waiting would drive me nuts. Patience wasn't my thing in situations like this. So I hit the start button and listened to the sound of the engine. It amplified off the concrete walls of the parking garage, setting my heart on fire almost as much as Belinda.

I attempted to drive below the speed limit to her house, but the sheer power of the car made it impossible. Then an idea came to me—I'd stop for flowers.

~ *Belinda* ~

What should I wear? I flipped through the clothes in my closet and finally pulled an outfit together. A good pair of jeans, a white, long-sleeved, collared blouse, and a fitted blue blazer that ended just above my hips landed on the bed. A pair of black, three-inch pumps finished the ensemble.

Since the accident, I hadn't dated. My plans changed, but life still had to go on. Feathers filled my throat, and I prayed I wouldn't make a fool of myself. The dating scene had changed so much since my college years.

In front of the full-length mirror, I made half-turns to be sure everything was in place before I walked downstairs. Telling my parents about the date before dressing would've caused too much stress. I didn't need Mom bustling around trying to help when my nerves were on high alert. Walking out the front door after my date announcement made for a better plan.

I gave myself one last once-over. "Well, it's now or never."

I headed downstairs. "How do I look?" I twirled around.

Mom raised her head from the magazine. "Are you going out?" Dad dropped his newspaper to his lap. They glanced at each other and then just stared at me. Mom blinked a few times but said nothing else. Their lack of a response made me uncomfortable.

"Yes. I accepted a date with Colin. Remember? The guy I met at the Pendletons' party? He called and we're going out to dinner."

Dad didn't move, but Mom's expression softened. "Honey, we're so glad." She glanced at Dad. "Oh. Well, that's more pizza for us."

"I know. It's time." The room fell silent for a few uncomfortable seconds, and memories of Robert drifted in until the chime of the doorbell broke the stillness. I shrugged. "Well, I guess this is it."

At the open door stood a handsome, tall man. Without saying a word, he presented me with a bouquet of assorted fresh-cut flowers he had hidden behind his back.

Tiny wings lifted my heart.

"Thank you. They're lovely." I placed the bouquet to my nose and took a deep breath. The scent should have encouraged thoughts of this sweet man's gesture, but it didn't. Instead, Robert and the roses he gave me in my dream popped in.

I caught myself. If I allowed thoughts of Robert to invade my time with Colin, this poor man would never have a chance. Nor would I. So, I kicked Robert out and vowed to give Colin the break he deserved.

"Let me put these in some water." I opened the door wider. "Come in."

I headed down the hall toward the kitchen.

Mom timed her entrance perfectly. "How lovely. Let me take care of those for you." She took the flowers and gave me a curt smile, then looked at Colin.

I rolled my eyes. "Let me introduce you."

Mom didn't even answer. She just turned and walked toward him.

"I guess that's a yes."

With her hand extended, she headed straight for my date. "Hi. I'm Belinda's mother, Dora." She took hold of his offered hand.

His smile spread from cheek to cheek. "Nice to meet you. I'm Colin Brockman."

Mom opened her mouth. I knew if she got one question out, we'd never see the inside of any restaurant.

"Mom. Thanks for seeing to the flowers. We need to go." I wrapped my arm around Colin's and escorted him to the safety of the front stoop.

At his car, he opened the passenger door. I stopped for a moment to admire the convertible. "Nice!"

"She sure is." A smile spread across his face as he gave me a once-over.

In the driver's seat, he seemed to puff out his chest while he backed out of the drive, making the hum of the engine more exaggerated as he shifted gears.

I chuckled to myself. Men and their toys.

~ *Colin* ~

I took all the credit for Ben's suggestion of this well-thought-out date with this beautiful creature I'd been longing for since the first time I met her.

After the evening's events, we strolled down the street toward my car. I let her walk ahead so I could get another glimpse of her perfect ass. With a pause at a store window, I pretended to be interested in the display, which gave her a few seconds' lead without putting too much distance between us. Then I glanced in her direction to enjoy the sight.

When Belinda turned around and flipped her hair over her shoulder, flashing a huge smile, my breath hitched. My ruse ended.

"Okay, bud!" She pointed a finger at me, wagging it back and forth.

I thought my heart would drop at the sight and felt truly grateful she said yes to the date. Once I caught up, I almost put an arm around her but stopped.

Then I figured what the heck and followed through. To my amazement, she not only let me, she snuggled closer. So I tightened my grip and pulled her to my side.

♡♡

The porch light lit the path to the front door. She placed her key in the lock, twisted it, and then turned toward me. Even in heels, she only came up to my shoulders.

"I had a nice time. Thank you for inviting me."

"I enjoyed myself too. Thank you for saying yes this time." I swallowed hard. Would a kiss be a delicate touch or the premature end to what I deemed as a perfect night? If she didn't mind my arm around her, I figured I'd go for it if the opportunity presented itself.

"I'm sorry. I'm just out of practice and was pretty nervous about dating again. The accident messed up my life." She bowed her head.

I inched closer and raised her head with one finger placed under her chin. I bent over to place a kiss on her full lips. She rose on her tiptoes to maintain contact.

The kiss was so sweet. Not too long and no tongue. It stirred me to the core. As we separated, I gazed down at her with a faint smile on my face.

To my surprise, she placed her arms around my neck as I lowered mine to her waist. Our lips locked again. I pressed her to me and lifted her slightly. I brushed my tongue across her warm lips. The action caused a pleasant reaction, and she parted hers.

I noticed a rush of heightened arousal and could've extended the kiss, but knew not to prolong it past its prime. I didn't want to negate the wonderful night by expecting too much at the end.

So, I steadied her on her feet and released her, much to my regret. Belinda's eyes remained closed. I took in the softness of her features.

~ *Belinda* ~

The kiss, to my amazement, was more enjoyable than I expected. His lips were soft, and he handled me like I was a fragile porcelain doll. I lowered my arms from his neck and opened my eyes. He gazed at me with a sweet smile on his face.

"Is this the first time you've kissed since the accident?"

The warm sensation of blood rushed to my cheeks. I looked at the ground. Robert and his kiss. I dare not say a word about that, and I didn't want to lie. As I looked up, I concentrated on Colin's face and stroked his cheek. "It's the first time in a long time someone has shown me some consideration."

He lifted a brow. "When did you break up with the Ex?"

"Almost a year and a half ago." I added, "Remember, almost a year of that was taken up by the accident."

He placed his arms around my waist again and tugged me close. "Well, I have plenty more gentle kisses if you're interested." He skirted my nose with his. "And you're not that out of practice." He reached down and gave me a short, playful kiss. "I think I'd better go. Thank you again for an enjoyable evening. I'll call you later."

I nodded as I pulled back, opened the door, and stepped into the house. "Good night, Colin."

With a bump of my butt, I closed the door and just stood there for a second and reviewed the night, feeling pleased with myself. I had successfully gone on my first date and hadn't blown it. It was rather pleasant. The only thing that would've made it perfect would've been having the date with Robert.

"Belinda, come here. I want to talk to you." I giggled, shaking my head as I walked into the family room to meet my inquisitor. My mother.

CHAPTER 9

~ Belinda ~

I PICKED UP the pen and signed on every line tagged by a pink sticky arrow. The title company agent smiled and dangled a set of keys. "Congratulations! You're the proud owner of your own home."

"Thank you." As I wrapped my fingers around the keys, a slight flicker filled my chest. I'm moving on.

Plan B moved along, but in my heart, I still wished Plan A had won out.

Colin and I had gone on several dates during the last few weeks. Ever the gentleman, he never pushed me for more than I was willing to give. I appreciated having him in my life, but he wasn't Robert. I had to remind myself, my Robert didn't exist.

The points of the key's teeth pressed into my palm as I went to try them out on my front door.

A short drive from the mortgage company placed me in my very own driveway.

One twist of the key unlocked the door. A slight flutter arose in my heart while I pushed it open about a foot. Heat blasted me before I ever took one step over the threshold. I walked in as the owner, even with no AC and I didn't mind.

The flutter turned into a swarm of whirling butterflies. I'm a homeowner.

Walking into this house marked a new beginning. "Did I do the right thing?" I let out a gush of air. Time to become an adult.

With one more push, the door opened wide. I stepped into the foyer. The odor of fresh paint overpowered my nose and, mixed with the heat, made me gag.

Ugh, I'm going to vomit. Taking a shallow breath, and another, the sensation passed.

I scanned the small area and then backed away from the wall, studying it. This is the spot for a table with two lamps and a mirror.

I moved on to the great room. Here I could appreciate the new paint color, a pale gray with bright white woodwork. "But how will I furnish you?"

A bead of sweat ran down my temple, reminding me to move along. A little of my past lack of self-confidence raised its ugly head. I scolded myself. "You're supposed to be enjoying this. Not tormenting yourself."

I walked to the primary bedroom. Another bead of sweat trickled down and tickled my skin. I wiped the drop away and left.

I picked up my pace toward the front door but stopped in the great room to give the place one last look. "Mom and I will turn you into a home."

My parents had told me I could stay with them as long as I wished. This gave me the luxury of taking my time to move when my new home was livable.

Over the next few weeks, my mother and I made multiple shopping trips. We purchased all the smaller basics. However, I questioned every decision about the style, color, and shape of the sizeable pieces of furniture.

"Honey, just stick to different shades of grays and whites. It'll be easy to add color with the accessories later."

I knew Mom was right. I just didn't want everything to be gray on gray. After all, I had an art degree. So putting a room together with scale and color shouldn't be too difficult, but this was in 3D.

The Belinda from my "Old Reality" would have agonized over her situation to the point of hiding. Not so with the new version. I took my indecision by the horns and tackled the dilemma straight on.

I wanted to do it right. So, I pored over multiple websites and videos, studying the terms and the ins-and-outs of design. To my amazement, the subject didn't appear as foreign as I thought, and my fears of failure diminished as I learned.

Two weeks had passed since I took possession of my house. Today, I'd spend more than a few seconds running in and out.

I programmed the AC to a comfortable 76 degrees, and left, heading for an office supply store.

A refreshing stream of cool air greeted me on my return. Today, I could take my time studying my new environment.

I armed myself with a thirty-foot tape measure, a pad of paper, and a pencil and placed the tools needed for the task on the granite countertop of the kitchen island. Then I measured every room in the house.

Two hours later, I completed the first phase of the project.

When I returned to my parent's home, I walked straight to the kitchen table and spread out the supplies. My mother stood at the stove, busy cooking dinner. "Hi, Mom."

She walked up behind me and looked over my shoulder. "What's all this?"

"I'm reproducing my floor plan. This way I can start buying furniture and know it'll fit."

"I don't understand."

"I just measured all the rooms, and I'm going to transfer the measurements to this graph paper. Then when I see a piece of furniture I like, I'll measure it and make a paper version to make sure it fits."

"Good idea. I'll leave you to your work. We'll eat dinner in the dining room so we won't disturb your project."

I only stopped to eat. The digital display on the microwave read eleven o'clock when I put the last measurement on paper. My eyes hurt from the strain of counting the tiny squares on graph paper. In the family room, I heard the monologue of one of the late late-night shows and hoped my mother hadn't dozed off.

"Mom."

"Yeah."

"Can you come here? I'm finished."

She walked in and stood next to me, reviewing my masterpiece.

"Well, what do you think?" I waved a hand over the project.

"I think this will help you get your place furnished." She crossed her arms over her chest. "You know, Belinda, if you bought a bed and two stools for the kitchen island, you could move in. Living there might make it easier to figure out what you want." She placed her hand on my shoulder. "Not that we're rushing you to move out."

I said nothing. I just nodded.

The next day, Mom and I piled into my CR-V and drove north to Gallery Furniture. Given my dislike for freeway driving, I wanted a place where I could pick out everything I needed, a kind of one-stop retail outlet. It would fit the bill.

On one of my internet searches of the store's inventory, I found a contemporary, mahogany, four-poster bed and dresser. We walked straight to the bedroom section and found them.

"Here." I handed the tip of the tape to my mother and we measured the pieces. We repeated the process until I had everything on my list.

Armed with the SKU numbers, we headed for the front of the store when I stopped. "Mom, how'd you think this might look in the living room?"

She stood beside me and studied the painting. "It looks similar to the one you did in college. Why don't you use your pictures?"

"Mine?"

"Yes, yours. I saved them. They're stored in the guest room's closet. Look 'em over before you buy anything. I think I'd rather see your originals on the walls."

Art teachers were required to take a variety of art classes in college, but did that translate into my being able to paint? How creative was I? Did I have any talent?

After waking from the coma, I had no desire to pick up a brush and place it on canvas. It seemed I had difficulty with anything creative. What disturbed me the most, I didn't remember any of my paintings. I gave the forest scene one last look and then turned to follow Mom.

The next stop was the main desk to ask questions about ordering over the phone and delivery. Once I knew everything would fit, I'd call in the order to save myself from another tormenting drive on the freeway.

Jim McIngvale, the owner of the store, seemed more than willing to help me. He answered all my questions and made the arrangements to deliver my purchases once I confirmed them.

"I can have everything delivered and set up this evening if you'd like." Same-day delivery was a unique feature of Mr. McIngvale's business, and he had built a furniture empire around it.

At first, I almost jumped at the chance to spend my first night in my place. But a hint of sadness on my mother's face made me decide that the next day would do fine. "No, I'll wait until tomorrow after I make sure everything fits."

As the delivery truck pulled away, I stood in my bedroom, admiring my new bed and matching dresser. The makeshift floor plan idea had worked, and the bed didn't overpower the room.

I imagined the finished product once the curtains softened the space. I drifted my fingers over the foot of the mattress, now covered in soft Egyptian cotton sheets. Then I moved my hand up the cool, firm mahogany bedpost and stroked it up and down. My mind wandered to where it shouldn't go.

I gripped the post and spun around, then flopped backward and landed in the middle of the bed. With my eyes closed, I clenched the sheet as I visualized Robert over me. My breathing quickened and my back arched, remembering the heat of Robert's flesh against mine. I only allowed myself to enjoy a brief visit to this smoldering memory before I came to my senses.

I stared up at the ceiling. What occurred in my dream would never happen with the Real Robert, and I needed to stop dwelling on the fact we'd never be together. My lungs filled, and I rocked to clear my head. Move on with your life.

With the furniture delivered, we purchased everything I needed to make the place functional. The upcoming weekend was the time to move in.

Colin sat on the floor with pieces of wood scattered around him, attempting to assemble the two bedside tables. In front of him lay the tiny tool that came packaged with the instructions and an open bag of hardware. He held the instruction sheet in one hand while the other repeatedly swiped through his sandy hair.

I giggled at the flurry of sounds coming out of his mouth. "Uh. Gosh! What the heck? WWWhat the…?"

I'd just finished unpacking the last box of clothes. "Those instructions getting to you?"

Without looking up, he thrust the sheet of paper at me. "Here, you try."

I took the instructions and gave them a quick scan. Studying the mess on the floor, I furrowed my brow. "Hmmm. I'll be right back. Some wine is in order." The paper floated to the floor when I released it.

About ten minutes later, I returned with a small but well-stocked toolbox, a cookie sheet with two wine glasses, and an open bottle of wine. An empty cupcake tin lie on the cookie sheet.

Colin scrunched his nose. "Are you going to bake something?"

"This should help." First, I poured us each a glass of wine and motioned for him to join me in a silent toast and then we drank. "Watch and learn."

I picked up the opened hardware bag and separated everything into the cupcake tin. Next, we organized the wooden pieces into neat piles.

Looking over my organized, disassembled side table, I extended my hand toward

Colin. "Instructions please."

He shoved the rumpled paper into my palm. We followed the directions one step at a time and assembled the first table.

Two hours passed before the second table found its new home next to the bed. A crystal ball lamp sat atop each table. A soft glow of light emanated through the white shades.

I walked over and turned off the overhead light. The mood of the room changed. It softened.

Colin joined me at the foot of the bed to admire our handiwork. When finished, it would be a tranquil, comfortable room, and my sanctuary from the outside world.

I smiled. "Thank you for your help."

"Umm, you're the one who got it organized."

~ Colin ~

Would she ever invite me into her bed? I studied the king mattress. Would I even fit?

We'd been on several dates, and I had been more than willing to help her with anything she needed. Our relationship was comfortable, but with intimacy, she held back.

We'd kiss, and that sent me through the roof, but she wouldn't go any further. When our kissing got hot and heavy, notching up the relationship was all I thought about. Belinda was a sweet, gorgeous, sexy, intelligent woman, and I was a healthy male filled with raging hormones.

I asked a question that would either get me kicked out or open up an invitation. "Do you think the bed is long enough for me?" I kept my eyes straight ahead and waited for her response.

Without saying a word, she turned and walked out of the room.

I lowered my chin to my chest.

I was going to be kicked out. "Belinda! I meant nothing by that." I followed her down the hall into the kitchen. "Belinda, please?"

She picked up another breathing bottle of wine and two clean wine glasses. "Okay, sit. We need to talk." I did as commanded. She poured the wine and joined me at the island. Her chest rose with a deep breath and she began. "Colin, I like you—"

I finished the statement with, "But I'm not—"

Belinda placed her finger over my mouth, stopping me from speaking. "Let me finish."

I nodded, and she removed it. "I liked you from the first time we met at the Pendletons' party. You're everything I could ask for if I was going to get involved with someone."

~ Belinda ~

My face flashed warm. I lowered my head, hoping he wouldn't notice, and paused for a few moments. "The accident, well, I'm just not ready."

I gazed into his bright eyes and wished I could tell him the complete truth, which included Robert. That'd hurt too much for me and him. For now, the partial story had to do.

I did the best I could to explain what rattled around in my brain. "There's a lot I remember. I still have gaps. My friends and family have helped me fill in lots of the empty spaces because they experienced those times with me. Yet there are still areas of my life I can't remember. Bits and pieces are just gone."

I cupped Colin's hand. He covered mind. His eyes were full of understanding.

I continued, "Like experiences with people I don't see anymore. For example, there are parts of my relationship with Matt I may never get back. I spent three years with him and remember very little of what we did when we were together."

"Since the accident, I've experienced episodes. I'll be in a restaurant or a store that triggers a memory. Everything revolves around me, and I'm just standing in the middle of this blur. Then, as the spinning slows down, details come into focus and fall into place like a puzzle. When it stops, I have a piece of my memory back. It's very confusing, and it takes a few minutes to recover from it. This has been happening more frequently lately."

I squeezed his hand. "My psychologist doesn't think it wise for me to be involved with anyone while I'm still having these episodes, and I agree with him."

~ Colin ~

My heart tightened from the sad, lost look on Belinda's face, and made me appreciate how much she'd been through. Her soft eyes, glazed with tears, twisted my gut.

I reached over and wrapped my arms around her. Warmth radiated from her and she felt so good. I wished I could expect more, but knew that was impossible. I tried to put myself in her place and said nothing.

I pulled away and released her, placing my hands on hers to encourage her to continue. "What can I do?"

"Be my friend. I promise you'll be the first to know if I can take our relationship further." She hesitated. "I'll also understand if you need to move on."

Her sad look killed me inside, melting me until I became putty. I had no alternative but to give her what she asked. So, I would hang in there and pray she would decide to take our relationship to the next level. And hopefully beyond the dreaded friend status. "Okay. Friends it is."

I pulled her close. She rested her head against my chest, and I kissed her hair. We stayed locked in the embrace until I scanned around the empty living and dining room. "What are you planning on doing with these rooms?"

Belinda swiveled the stool seat around to survey the space. "I have no idea."

"Why don't you ask Mrs. Pendleton for some ideas? She's an interior designer. Tell her I told you to call." I gave her a gentle squeeze. "Remember Robert? That's his mom, and she treats me like her second son. I'm sure she'd be glad to help you out."

~ *Belinda* ~

MY heart jumped. He was trying to help in such an innocent way. I couldn't call Mrs. Pendleton... or could I?

Robert would never be a part of my life. Anyway, why should I live my life around anything that involves him? He decided his path. Now I had to make mine and do what's best for me. If asking his mother for help was good for me, then I'd ask her. So I nodded. "You know, that just might be a good idea."

CHAPTER 10

~ Belinda ~

THE CELL PHONE on the kitchen counter taunted me. Making the phone call had drama written all over it.

I hadn't discussed Colin's suggestion concerning Mrs. Pendleton with anyone, especially my mother, and figured I'd call first. Then fill Mom in on my plan to consult the interior designer mother of Robert. Which I knew wouldn't be a hit.

My chest rose and fell as I took in sevrak deep breaths. I picked up the phone and punched in the numbers to the Crescent Oaks Interior Design Company.

"Hello. Sandra Pendleton. May I help you?"

Air froze in my throat. I wasn't expecting her to answer.

"Um. Uh. Yes. Hello. I don't know if you remember me. I'm Belinda Davies, the girl who fainted at your New Year's Eve party." Did I need to remind myself or anyone else of that embarrassing incident? I tapped my fist on the counter.

"Oh, yes. How are you?"

"Very well, thank you." My words faltered. My mouth went dry and my stomach flip-flopped as I squeezed the phone tighter. I was talking to the mother of Robert Pendleton, the man of my dreams.

"Are you still there?"

"Ah. Yes. Yes. I'm calling… well, I need some help. I just bought a home and have no furniture for the great room." A quick smack on my forehead reminded me I sounded like an idiot.

A chuckle came through the phone. "Oh, I fully understand. Is this your first place?"

"Yes. Colin Brockman suggested I call you. He said you might help me out."

"You know Colin? He's such a sweet man."

"He's a friend." I added, "A dear friend."

"Well, I'll have to see it. Are you free today?"

My mind did a balancing act. Can this be happening this fast? "I'm free all day. Just give me a time."

We hashed out the details. As I disconnected the call, butterflies stirred in the recesses of my stomach. Mrs. Sandra Pendleton, Robert Pendleton's mother, would arrive at my home at one o'clock.

As the clock on the kitchen wall neared one, my frayed nerves made me want to pass out. I paced the room, wringing my hands. The excited butterflies in my stomach reached tornado status and wouldn't calm down.

I opened the refrigerator door and wrapped my fingers around the neck of a bottle of wine. About to pull it off the shelf, I hesitated. I didn't want alcohol on my breath to ruin a good impression.

Several laps around the island eased the tension until the chime from the doorbell interrupted. The clock read 12:55. I bit my lower lip to ward off another wave of queasiness. To steady myself, I rested my hip against the countertop and told myself to breathe. A gush of air filled my lungs.

I can do this.

Another chime from the doorbell shattered the air. I jumped. I drew in another deep breath and then headed for the door.

Memories of my "Dream Reality" mother-in-law raced through my head. Would the woman on the other side of the door be similar? I had a bond with Sandra in my dream. Would the bond enter this reality?

About to turn the knob, a strange sensation rushed over me. A sense my life would change the second I opened the door. I studied my hand wrapped around the knob. All I had to do was turn and pull the door open to start the new adventure. My hand closed tighter, but I couldn't turn. I'm being silly and took a second before I placed a broad smile across my face as I opened the door.

There stood Sandra, dressed in a pair of black slacks, a simple white tee, and layers of gold chains around her neck. She appeared comfortable, yet professional. "Good afternoon, Ms. Davies." She extended her hand.

A warm calm washed over me when our hands connected. I stood there bewildered, staring at her with her styled pageboy and perfect makeup. But I didn't release the handshake and was very aware my adventure had started.

~ Sandra ~

I tightened my grip. A familiar wave of emotion stirred deep inside me. I realized this young woman possessed a gentle and kind soul. I prided myself on the recognition of "pure souls." People who weren't vindictive or had an agenda. They were honest, good people who wanted to do the right thing, and Miss Davies fit that description.

I smiled and placed my other hand over hers. "Shall we see your home?" Without giving her a chance to respond, I walked into the great room. "This is a very nice floor plan. I love how open it is. Miss Davies, what would you like my help with?"

The simple question opened the floodgates to Belinda's ideas or lack of them. She showed me what she'd accomplished in the bedroom. Back in the kitchen, with a bit of encouragement, she displayed the graph paper floor plan.

"Mrs. Pendleton, I'm not sure where to go from here. I want to make the right decisions on the scale of furniture for these two rooms." She pointed to the empty living and dining rooms.

"Call me Sandra. Mrs. Pendleton sounds so formal. Do you mind if I call you Belinda?"

She shook her head. "That's fine."

"Well, Belinda, from what I see, you have a good start. The bedroom furniture fits the size and dimensions of the space." I walked into the adjoining living room. "You did the measuring of all the rooms. I can transfer them into my computer program. If you'd like, we can plug in the numbers now." I pointed to the front door. "My computer is in my car."

~ *Belinda* ~

A hint of a curled smile formed, and the tension I harbored minutes before dissolved. "I'd love that. Would you like some wine?"

"I'd love some."

We sat at the kitchen island talking and sipping wine while she entered the measurements into the program. During the conversation, I told her about my accident and the coma, minus the details of my dream life with her son. The subject of Robert did, however, come up several times after I described my impromptu dinner at the Galleria with Robert, Sharyn, and Colin.

Her lips pursed, and then she didn't hold back on her displeasure with Sharyn. "She isn't what I'd call daughter-in-law material, and I don't appreciate that they're engaged. I tolerate her as she does me. Oh, she's nice enough, but..." She trailed off her statement before she looked up from the computer. She stared at me with a serious expression. "He needs someone like you."

My mouth dropped open, not sure how to respond. So, I didn't.

Her mood sobered. "He needs someone who is kind and who'd love him for who he is. For the past year, he seems so lost. He tells us he's fine, but his father and I have noticed a change."

For a few seconds, she said nothing. "I don't know why I brought that. It's not like me to be so open with my personal life to someone I've just met. I'm sorry." Like a light bulb, Sandra lit up and a huge smile spread across her face. She patted my forearm and scrunched her nose. "Shall we get back to work?"

I saw the concern for Robert, but that subject had ended, at least for now. With a smile, I lifted my wineglass to her. She returned the gesture as we toasted and took a sip. I felt a connection to this elegant, soft- spoken woman and knew I liked her.

At six o'clock, we finished arranging multiple configurations of the rooms. Thanks to the three-dimensional planning program. Now, the subject of her fees became the priority. I liked Sandra a lot and wanted her help, but I knew it wouldn't come cheap.

My lower lip took the brunt of my anxiety. "I appreciate you working me in today. I know you can help me. What are your rates?"

"Well, I charge one hundred and fifty dollars an hour."

I quickly did the math and realized I just racked up a bill of seven hundred and fifty dollars. I wasn't sure how to respond and figured the deer-in-the-headlights expression gave me away as I held my breath.

~ *Sandra* ~

I studied Belinda and realized she wasn't breathing. I placed a hand over the shocked girl's before continuing. "Today is free. This was a consultation. I admit it was a little longer than I usually spend, but I was enjoying myself so." I chuckled as I noticed her release a sigh and relax.

"So, where to go from here? There are two ways. I can do everything for you. I'll do the shopping, make sure all the deliveries come on time, organize any needed contractors, and then I'll put the rooms together for you. You sit back and enjoy your new home. That's the expensive route. The more affordable path is using me as just a consultant. This means you do all the legwork, and I'll help you with sensible but tasteful decisions."

I sat back and watched the girl's tense shoulder muscles relax. Her breathing slowed to a normal rate.

"I'll take the second one."

I liked Belinda and knew I'd be more than a consultant to this young lady. I knew we would become friends.

∞

I drove home trying to figure out what I could put together for dinner. My husband, Rob, usually arrived first. Then our son followed about an hour and a half later.

Rob was pretty laid back about my cooking times. Although I tried to have supper ready every night, he understood my career interfered with meals occasionally. Most times I tried to warn him, but today I forgot all about calling because I'd enjoyed my visit with Belinda.

I walked through the back door and saw my husband in the kitchen. He stood at the sink with an apron on, washing lettuce.

"Hi, Doll." He winked. "I figured I'd get a start on salads. I hope that's in the plan."

As CEO of his financial firm, he never ceased to amaze me with his down-to-earth approach to a kitchen. It also reminded me why I found him so attractive. Despite his years, he had maintained a superb physique and looked distinguished with his salt-and-pepper hair. The apron only added to his sex appeal.

"There's no plan, so salads are a good start." I wrapped my arms around him and rested my cheek against his back. "Is Robert home?"

"Yeah. He's out there doing whatever he does." The concern came through in his tone.

To an observer, Robert functioned very well. But in the confines of his dwelling, the scenario changed. About a year ago, he isolated himself. He completed a normal workday, but once at home, he retreated to his bed.

"At least he's awake more."

We knew the signs of depression and attempted to seek help. Nothing we suggested seemed to sway him. So, we did the only thing we could do within our power, be there for him.

Rob stopped washing the lettuce. "I sure would like to know what's going on in his head."

"I'm glad he came out of hibernation and started living again." My shoulders drooped. My chin trembled. "But he's not the same."

Rob turned and wrapped his muscular arms around me. "I know. I wish he'd talk to us."

Tears welled. "A piece of him died, and I don't know what we can do to help him." I looked up at my husband. "You know Sharyn isn't right for him."

"I know." He rubbed his hands up and down my back. "They haven't set a date yet. So there's still a chance he'll come to his senses."

He always knew what to say. "But what if he doesn't? We'll be stuck with her, and she'll make him miserable."

With a gentle swipe, he ran a thumb across my cheek to brush away a tear. "We can't do anything now. Let's finish dinner. Agreed?"

I nodded. "Will Robert be joining us?"

Rob bent down to kiss me, and I stretched up on my tiptoes to reach. He stopped, his lips hovering centimeters from mine. I laced my fingers through his hair on the back of his head and pulled him close until his lips covered mine. An electrifying thrill sizzled through me. My grip tightened, and he did the same until he pulled back. "You know I love you."

"I love you too." I stared into his hazel eyes. "Kiss me again."

"No."

The firmness in his voice made my insides sizzle.

"We won't stop if I do and our son will starve."

I huffed and pushed him away. "I hate it when you're right."

"He told me to call him when you came home."

I reached for the house phone and called handset #2. "Hi, Sweetie. I just walked in. Dad started salads and…" I opened the freezer door and rummaged around for something fast. "How does salad, Dijon chicken, and mashed potatoes sound?"

"That sounds fine. I'm hungry."

"Good. Start walking over. You can set the table." I put the phone down and turned toward Rob. "He sounds good today." A soft smile grew on my face.

"Sharyn must be out of town again. He always sounds better when she's not around."

"Rob, I want to enjoy our dinner." I gave my husband a gentle punch to the arm as the back door opened.

"Robert." My heart lifted at the sight of my only child. "You have a good day?" I wrapped my fingers around his upper arms and kissed him on his cheek.

"Yeah, not bad."

"Good. Tell me about it while we're eating. Dinner won't take long to prepare." I winked at him. "Please set the table." I returned to the stove to cook.

All the dinnerware sat on the table arranged with a man's touch. I shook my head as I placed the food on the counter for everyone to serve themselves. "Thank you, Robert, for helping."

We wasted no time filling our plates and then sat around the table, ready to enjoy our time together. Rob recounted his busy day and then Robert took his turn. The course of the conversation shifted when Rob started a discussion about current news events. It sparked opposite opinions from both men. I knew he loved these heated discussions with his son. In the past year, they were few, so Rob took every opportunity to keep things interesting.

Ten minutes into the political posturing of the two most important men in my life, I'd reached my tolerance level and interjected an explanation of my day.

"Anyone interested in what I did today?" I glared at my dinner mates."

"Sure, Mom. Please."

Rob chewed a mouthful and just nodded.

"I had a meeting with Belinda Davies. She called and asked if I could help her with her new home." I turned toward my husband. "Honey, you remember, she's the very attractive girl who fainted at the New Year's Eve party."

"Oh yes. How's she doing?"

"Fine. I spent the entire afternoon with her. The meeting is why dinner is so late tonight."

I focused all my attention on Rob and didn't even notice Robert's reaction. When I did glance over, he looked like he'd seen a ghost. He appeared pale and just stared at his plate.

My stomach jumped. "Robert, are you okay?"

He panned from me to his father. "I'm fine and was just thinking about something. I'm sorry. What were you saying about Ms. Davies?" His voice sounded cold and curt.

My gaze drifted to my husband. He sat still. His brows pinched together as he focused all his attention back on our son.

An unsettling feeling came over me as I turned back to watch Robert. "You sure you're okay?" This time I put more force behind my words. His expression made me uneasy.

"Yeah, why wouldn't I be? Go on with your story." He lifted his fork and continued to eat.

I studied him but knew it would be futile to press him. So I continued my description of a very delightful afternoon. "I like this woman. She's bright, funny, and a very warm person. I'm excited about working with her."

Robert shifted in his seat.

~ Belinda ~

I drove to my parents' house the minute Sandra left to tell Mom about my plans to move forward with using Sandra's decorating help.

"Mom, I don't see how working with her will be a problem. I think it will be fun. She is Robert's mother."

I knew my mother didn't see it that way and her expression told me so. "You know how I feel about this version of Robert interfering? I don't want to see you get hurt."

"He's not interfering. I'm just working with his mother. What are the chances I'd run into him?" I grabbed a throw pillow and hugged it to my chest. "She'll be acting as my consultant. I won't even see her that much."

With pursed lips, Mom sat back in her chair. Her chin dropped to her chest as she folded her arms across her. She glared up.

"Mom. Please. I need the help."

Dora softened. "I don't like it, but you're not a child and you can make your own decisions."

I reached and placed a hand on my mother's arm. "Come to breakfast with us and you'll see."

∞

"Hi, Mom." I wasted no time with the introductions between the two women. Mom sat across from Sandra. "We waited for you and went over some ideas. After you order, I'll show you."

I handed a menu to my mother. After a few minutes, she placed it on the table. "Are you ready?" She nodded. I waved to the waitress, signaling we were ready to order. Mom and Sandra placed their orders first. I finished with, "I'll have coffee and a blueberry bagel with cream cheese."

Sandra's face lit up. What she said next floored me. "So does my son, Robert. He'd eat them every day if he could."

The Robert from my "Dream Reality" loved blueberry bagels with cream cheese. In the dream, we ate this combination of doughy perfection as often as we could. This was another coincidence I added to my pile.

The breakfast meeting went better than I hoped. Mom and Sandra hit it off and before I could say or do anything, the two were in a deep discussion about furniture.

Several hours passed. Mom warmed to Sandra and her ideas for my home as the three of us enjoyed each other's company.

Sandra glanced at her watch. "Oh, my! I've lost track of time again. I have to leave. I have another appointment." She gathered up her belongings and spread them over the table. "Dora, it was very nice to meet you, and I look forward to seeing you again." Sandra excused herself and left.

I frowned at my mother. "I told you she was nice."

"Okay. Okay. I'll admit I like her." She downed her coffee. "Let's get the check and visit Mattress Mack about living room furniture. Then, while I make dinner, you can look over your paintings."

∞

We raced upstairs to the guest room and swung open the closet door. My hand flew up to my mouth. "Mom, these are all mine?" I stepped into the walk-in closet that contained all sizes and shapes of canvases leaning up against the walls.

"You painted all of them." Mom stood just outside. "Let's get them into the room."

We pulled out the canvases and propped them against anything that would hold the artwork upright.

"Sweetie, I'm going to go downstairs to start dinner. You stay here." The door closed with a soft thud.

I stood, surrounded by paintings, glancing from one picture to the next.

The room spun, slowly at first, and then faster and faster as memory after memory piled on top of each other. Just when I thought my brain would explode, the spinning stopped. I fell to my knees and grabbed the sides of my head as I squeezed my eyes shut. My head throbbed. My breathing sped up.

After a few minutes, the pain lessened, and my breathing slowed. I opened my eyes and stood.

I picked up one canvas at a time and studied the pictures. Each one held its memory, some pleasant and some not. I arranged the paintings in order, from the first one I completed in college to the last one just before the accident.

Once organized, I sat on the floor and savored the memories.

Mom suggested I take home the paintings I wanted. She also encouraged me to take all my art supplies. The back bedroom would make the perfect studio since sunlight filtered in most of the day.

I hauled the paintings to the back bedroom and stacked them upright against the wall. I selected a forest scene and held it out in front of me and studied it. Not half bad and just as good as the stuff I'd thought about buying. Hmm. Maybe I have an artist hiding in me.

I carried the painting into the living room and propped it against the feature wall and then paced in front of it. The colors complemented the room, but the painting seemed incomplete. I left it leaning against the wall to take another look in the light of day.

About to flip the light switch off, I took one more glance. "Yep. Needs something." With one flick of my finger, the room plunged into darkness.

The next morning, I padded into the kitchen. My hair flopped everywhere as I brushed it off my face. This was my favorite time of the day. It was quiet, and the world seemed at peace with itself as it awoke under the morning sun.

The first planned item on today's agenda was a quick stop to tend to Beau's needs. Afterward, I'd come home to change before meeting Mom for lunch.

The K-cup popped when I closed the lid to brew my coffee. My favorite beverage trickled out, and the aroma filled the room. I took a deep whiff. The scent tantalized my nose as I tapped my fingers, waiting. After I added the sugar and creamer, I took a sip. "Ahhh." That first jolt of caffeine coursing through my veins was my only real vice, and I thoroughly enjoyed it.

Armed with the mug of coffee, I walked back toward the bedroom and stopped to study the painting. I raised the cup. Before my lips touched the rim, an idea hit. I grabbed the painting and hurried down the hall to the back bedroom, leaving my morning caffeine fix on the island. There in the morning's light, I unpacked the supplies, set up the easel, and started painting.

I took several steps backward, rubbing my chin while I studied the finished piece. The melodic tune of the cell phone from the pocket of my boxer shorts sliced my concentration. Without checking the caller ID, I answered, "Hello."

"Sweetie, are you okay?"

I heard the concern in my mother's voice. "Yeah. I'm fine. Why?"

"I've been waiting for you for almost thirty minutes."

"What time is it?"

"One o'clock. We were supposed to meet for lunch."

I opened my mouth to answer but stopped when I realized I hadn't even taken off my pajamas. I ran my tongue around the inside of my mouth—or brushed my teeth. A strand of hair took that precise moment to fall in front of my nose. A quick burst of air out the side of my mouth blew it back into place. "I'm sorry. I started painting and lost all track of time."

I paused for my mother's response. Nothing.

"Mom. This is all your fault."

"Mine?"

"Yeah. You're the one who told me to paint again."

A small chuckle came over the phone. "Well, are you satisfied with your work?"

The corners of my mouth crept upward. "Yes, I am."

CHAPTER 11

~ Belinda ~

THE BRIGHT SUN dappled through the trees on this magnificent Saturday morning. I planned to turn my attention to Beau. I had pushed the animal aside with the decorating of my home. Today, I'd lavish him with attention—washing, brushing, riding, and feeding him well.

First on the agenda, a ride.

Over the past weeks, my limited presence at the stables also reduced any chance of running into Robert on the trails.

Now in April, and despite working with his mother, I hadn't seen him since the accidental encounter at the Galleria in January. What I had learned about him came from conversations with Sandra, whose favorite subject was her son. Seeing Robert didn't cross my mind as I set off on the trails.

Beau's steady gait relaxed me. The rhythmic motion of the horse caused my mind to wander and placed me in a semi-meditative state. I closed my eyes and inhaled the scent of cut grass. Birds chirped from the tree-lined trail. This was the closest I'd be to heaven.

A swat from Beau's tail across my shoulder interrupted my bliss. "Beau, remind me to trim that tail of yours."

Up ahead, a rider approached on a chocolate brown thoroughbred. As he rode closer, my heart stopped, and I couldn't breathe. Heaven just turned into Hell. It was Robert.

There was no place to go except back, and what would that prove? I've changed. My therapy sessions reinforced the concept, and this was a prime time to test out that theory. So I straightened my back, tightened up on the reins, and headed straight into harm's way.

"Belinda?" He approached, then stopped his horse alongside.

A lump rose and stuck in my throat, making my voice quaver. "Hi. I'm surprised to see you out here."

"I just got back into town. I haven't ridden for a while and this morning…" He panned the sky. "It was too good to waste."

I studied his face. His smile brought back all the wonderful memories of my life with Dream Robert.

My eyes closed as I plunged myself into a full-blown fantasy. I pictured myself jumping from Beau into the arms of my love and planting a long, fervent kiss on his tempting lips. Tasting them, as my tongue explored every inch of his mouth. I imagined a burst of heat zinging through my veins. A shiver ran up my spine as the embrace led to our love making before we rode off into the morning sun, forever in love. A gentle sigh escaped as I became aroused.

~ Robert ~

Nervous pangs in my gut exploded when I recognized Belinda. She turned my insides upside down. For my sanity's sake, I had to control my emotions before I got any closer. I reminded myself that she didn't differ from anyone else, and I'd treat this situation the same as a casual business meeting.

I scanned the sky and trees and sucked in a deep, slow breath of fresh air. The air escaped as slowly as I had inhaled, allowing my shoulders to drop. I went into my professional persona. I squared my shoulders and pasted my signature smile across my face as I rode alongside to greet her. What else could I do? Take off in the other direction.

Then she faded away as she closed her eyes and seemed oblivious to my presence. Her mouth parted and her breathing became irregular. Flowing waves of hair caressed her face from a gentle breeze. At that moment, she was the prettiest woman I had ever laid eyes on. I watched her as she relaxed, lost in a world of her own.

The feeling I'd had when we kissed took me to a place I'd never been. I immersed myself in her, almost as if I knew what she was feeling. Her blood seemed to move through mine, and for a few minutes, I'd felt closer to her than any other human being. I knew I wanted to be back there with her again.

The caw of a crow overhead caused me to look up. I sighed. My shoulders slumped. This was all a dream. Belinda and I would never be together. I had integrity and would follow through with my promise to marry Sharyn.

Without disturbing her, I took in her beauty and softness for a few more seconds than asked, "Belinda, are you all right?"

~ Belinda ~

My eyes popped open, and I realized how crazy I must have appeared. As I squirmed against the leather of the saddle, the movement increased my sexual arousal from my walk through fantasy land. Why is this happening now? Heat rushed up my neck to my face. I dropped my chin to my chest, allowing my hair to fall and shield my hot cheeks.

I needed my wits about me, and all I was doing was making a fool of myself. "I'm fine."

Through my strands of hair, I peeked at him. A smile grew across his face. He seemed comfortable and more like the gorgeous, loving Robert from my "Dream Reality." His expression put me at ease as I changed the conversation to the thoroughbred. "Your horse is beautiful. What's his name?"

"Scout."

I saw him beam while he stroked the horse's neck. The animal responded to his touch. I giggled. The name didn't seem to fit. "You named that magnificent animal Scout?" By this time, my cheeks had cooled. So I brushed back my hair.

"His full name is Crossed Arrows Apache Indian Scout."

"Oh! I see. Hello Scout." I looked the animal over. "Do you prefer an English saddle?"

"That's what I learned, and it seems to fit Scout better than a Western. I see you ride Western."

"Yeah. I've never ridden with an English saddle. Is it hard?"

"I don't think so." His face lit up. "Would you like me to show you sometime?"

Did he just give me the opportunity to be close to him? I didn't even hesitate. "Yes, I'd like that. When?" When the words came out of my mouth, I realized it was too late.

~ *Robert* ~

I'd put little thought into offering to help her ride using an English saddle. I just said it before I could corral the impulse.

"I have to go out of town again in two weeks for work. This week I have to play catch up. How about I call you when I get back?" Feeling more confident, I felt it easier to put distance between us to correct my lack of judgment.

I knew she saw Colin regularly because she was all he could talk about. Belinda this and Belinda that. All I wanted to do was punch him in the mouth to get him to shut up. Then another part of me wanted to hear everything my friend had to say about this beautiful woman, but I had my loyalties and would not breach those, either. So, I made it clear I was aware Colin was a part of her life.

"Maybe Colin could join us." I cocked my head and waited for her reaction.

~ *Belinda* ~

I snapped my gaze at him, his motives obvious. "That might be nice, and what about Sharyn?" My words spilled out curt.

"She might join the three of us afterward. Remember, she isn't fond of horses. Well, I'd better be going. It was nice seeing you again."

The tightened reins made Scout lift his head. As we shook I noticed a subtle shift in his demeanor. His smile disappeared Robert's weight shifted. Scout moved forward, putting distance between us, then broke into a canter.

I didn't leave immediately. I just turned and watched Scout's tail swish, ending the chance encounter. Robert rode off and never once looked back. No one I had ever known caused me to experience such an array of emotions, especially not someone who was so aloof.

I watched him move further away and huffed. "Yep. Another phone call I'll never get." With a gentle kick to Beau's sides, I rode in the opposite direction.

The rest of the day I spent as planned. After the ride, I let Beau out to pasture while I mucked the stall and lined it with fresh straw. A bath and a good brushing came next. To dry his coat, I turned him loose to run in the late afternoon sun. It glistened off him as he bucked and galloped through the tall grass.

The sight warmed my heart because I loved the horse. That is until he lay down and rolled on his back and flailed his legs above him. He destroyed all my hard work.

"Beau!" I pulled a few of his favorite tasty morsels from my pocket and stretched out my palm. "Hey, Beau, carrots?" The dusty animal ambled straight toward me. While he munched, I attached the lead. "Look at you. You're a mess."

We headed for the stable, where I gave him a quick brush down. "You can bet I'll never let you run loose after a bath again."

Beau's repetitive routine had taken over my daydreams. Robert crept in all day. I knew I'd have to work hard to push him out of my mind. I knew my love for the Dream Robert edged in on the Real Robert—who could be just as charming, sometimes. Those occasional glimpses of charm gave me a small amount of hope to cling to. Although, in my heart, I knew it would never lead to anything.

With the click of the latch, I secured my beloved horse in his box stall. "See ya tomorrow, fella." I gave him a good rubbing behind the ear, then left to get ready for my date with Colin.

∞

The doorbell rang, and I dashed to answer. There stood Colin, my date for the evening, whom I hadn't seen for the past week. As he stepped in, he wrapped his arms around me and planted a big kiss on my mouth. I responded, and we remained locked in our embrace as the kiss grew more intense.

"Boy, if I didn't know better, I'd say someone missed me." Colin smiled with his bright eyes. He pulled me closer and placed a soft kiss on the top of my head.

I tightened my hug around him as I snuggled against his chest. I missed him. He wasn't Robert, but he cared about me and for that, I loved him. "How was the trip?"

He leaned over and sniffed my hair. "Mmmm. You smell so good....The trip was fine. I'll tell you all about it, but now I just want you in my arms."

I chuckled. He picked me up and swung me around as he found my lips.

Still, in our lip-lock embrace, Colin carried me into the kitchen. He put me down and gave me a quick, tight squeeze. The corners of his mouth curled up into a big smile when he saw the breathing bottle of wine on the counter. "Great! Wine!" He approached the cabernet and poured two glasses. "This traveling back and forth is getting to me. I'm here this week, then gone again the next."

After the first of the year, the Pendleton Financial Group started planning its Canadian branch. With Colin as vice president.

While the northern location was in the initial stages, he remained stateside, based out of the Houston office. He informed me his traveling would increase, but he warned at some point he'd be moving.

I had been spending more time with Colin. When he wasn't traveling, he'd been there to help with anything I needed. During the weeks he was around, we spent at least three evenings together. We'd go to a movie and dinner or I'd cook for a night in.

Despite our time together, I still hadn't let our physical relationship progress any further than snuggling on the couch with heavy making out.

I was very aware Colin wanted more, and a few times, I came very close to inviting him into my bedroom. But my gut stopped me from committing. Still, I knew I'd have to decide soon or risk losing him.

When Colin moved, I'd have the haunting knowledge I lost a great guy, and maybe a potential marriage proposal, because of my indecision.

I never committed to Matt, either. Now, I found myself in a similar situation. The one difference, Colin informs me of what the future may hold for him. Matt never afforded me that courtesy. He just left.

My relationship with Colin was the principal topic of my sessions with Dr. Rosen. He seemed pleased with my progress and my ability to form a relationship with a man whose name wasn't Robert. However, no matter how hard I tried to move on with Colin, Robert, or my memory of him crept in.

"You'll make the right decision when the time is right. You've been able to make so many positive choices in the past few months. If Colin is who you decide to be with, your decision will come." Dr. Rosen always encouraged me.

For now, I'd just continue on the present course. Colin was a good friend with whom I enjoyed spending time. I just wasn't in love with him.

Dinner and a movie were on the schedule. I enjoyed my evening with Colin, as usual. When he escorted me back home, I invited him in. He sat on the couch as I filled wine glasses and then joined him. The conversation dropped off as he sat with his arm around my neck, fiddling with a strand of my hair. I leaned my head back against his arm and sipped the wine. The wine and physical labor of caring for Beau earlier in the day relaxed me.

"This place has come together. It's real comfortable," he said, lifting his glass. "Hat's off to the decorator."

We clinked glasses and took a sip. I took pride in what I had accomplished in such a short time. "And to my helper," I added, acknowledging his contribution to manual labor. Raising my glass to him, the rims touched, followed by a drink.

The living and dining rooms were comfortable. Elegant touches were done on a woman's conservative budget. With Sandra and Mom's help, both rooms had a cohesive feeling of luxury.

"There's going to be a cocktail party in two weeks to celebrate the official opening of the Canadian branch. Ah'd be honored, Ms. Belinda, if you'd accompany me as mah date."

I laughed at Colin's attempt at a faux-southern accent. "It would be mah pleasure, sir," I said, batting my eyelashes.

~ Colin ~

My desire for her grew to more than I could take. I placed my wineglass on the coffee table and then did the same with Belinda's. Placing my fingers under her chin, I kissed her full lips. Her arms wrapped around my neck. As I leaned back, she draped herself across my lap and we continued the fast kisses.

It didn't take long for our passion to escalate. I felt a growing need for her as I roamed my hands over her back and then slipped them under her top. I relished the feel of the warm, soft flesh under my fingertips. Moving north, I released the latch of her bra. Her breasts relaxed from their restraint against my chest. This excited me as my need for her grew, pressing against her hip. I reached around and cupped her more than ample, firm breast. My breathing became more irregular—our kisses were now deep. She stopped me momentarily while she repositioned herself and straddled me.

Her sultry stare gave me no sign she had any plan to stop me. Our breathing became heavy. My heart pounded. I moved my hands across the skin of her firm back toward her neck and pulled her close. Now I could feel her heart hammering in her chest.

She seemed willing to continue, so I took a big chance. I picked her up, cradled her in my arms, and walked toward the hall that led to the bedroom.

At the threshold, Belinda stiffened and screamed, "Colin, put me down!"

I stopped cold, closed my eyes, took a deep breath, and set her on her feet. I stood there studying her. She cast her gaze to the ground and wouldn't even look at me.

I sighed. "I think I should go." Belinda said nothing but kept her head down. I hugged her and kissed her on the forehead. "I'll call you." My heart ached as I turned and walked out.

Outside, I quickened my pace to the car, wondering how much longer she'd continue with the roadblocks. How long I'd be willing to put up with them? I was a patient man, but my patience was wearing thin. I slammed the car door and drove off squealing the tires, hoping the power of my car would help relieve my sexual frustration. When I got home, a cool shower took care of the rest.

~ *Belinda* ~

Tonight's date was hard for me. Robert, on Scout, came along in my mind, taking my attention away from Colin. I fought to keep focused.

I had decided tonight, I'd invited Colin to spend the night. I allowed myself to feel the sexual excitement he had ignited within me. In the heated last moments of the evening when he picked me up, Robert's name almost slipped past my lips. I caught myself before I reached the point of no return. At that moment, I felt I was deceiving Colin and knew I had to stop.

CHAPTER 12

~ Belinda ~

MOM HAD BOUGHT a cream-colored, strapless, silk dress with a matching Bolero jacket she planned to use as my funeral garb if I died. I didn't.

Ironically, the dress was identical to the one I'd worn when I married Robert while in my coma. I hung it on the back of the closet door as I ran my fingertips down the front.

A faint moment of melancholy washed over me. Dream Robert held a place in my heart, but I was moving on with my life.

Tonight, I'd put the dress on and attend a party. A black clutch, three-inch black heels, and a simple strand of pearls with matching earrings rounded out the outfit.

In front of a full-length mirror, I studied myself. I twisted and turned to see every aspect of my image. In full view, I smooth the skirt and then adjusted the jacket.

My hand covered the pearls. A flutter settled under my ribcage. Who was I trying to impress, Colin or Robert?

After our last date, I was sure I'd never hear from Colin. But as promised, he called to firm up tonight's details.

The ride to the Wilson Hotel was pleasant. Colin was his usual attentive self and acted as if nothing had happened the weekend before.

In the grand foyer of the hotel, Mr. and Mrs. Pendleton stood in front of the door to the main ballroom, greeting their guests.

Sandra saw me and approached with outstretched arms. "I'm so pleased you could come. How did everything fit in the niches?"

"I made those changes you suggested. Everything balanced nicely."

"Remember my husband, Robert Pendleton?" Sandra reached for his arm. "It's Belinda."

He turned his attention from Colin and extended a hand. "It's nice to see you again. I take it you're doing well."while he studied our clenched hands.

"It's nice to see you again, Sir." Just then, a sensation stirred. Very much like the feelings I'd experienced when Sandra and I first shook hands. The similarity was uncanny.

A faint smile returned just before he looked up and released my hand. "Please enjoy yourself. I'm glad you could join us."

"Thank you. So am I."

Colin and I entered the low-lit ballroom to the sound of a familiar perky voice. Abby rose from her chair and waved. "Belinda, over here. We saved seats for you." We walked toward the table about halfway down the side of the dance floor to join my best friend and her husband.

The smile I wore deteriorated when Garrett stood, exposing Robert, seated beside him. I expected to see him here. After all, his father was the CEO and Robert was a VP. I just didn't think I'd have to sit at the same table.

All The feelings I had for Dream Robert didn't transfer to the Real Robert. The initial excitement diminished with every encounter with this one because he acted like an ass.

For now, I'd be pleasant. I took a seat across from him and gave him a nod of recognition. He smiled and nodded back.

Abby leaned into me. "Does it bother you being this close to him?"

I glared.

"That bad, huh?"

I turned my chair toward her. "You have no idea."

Her brows lifted and, with a slow upward motion of the corners of her mouth, a full-blown smile appeared. She swung her chair around and scooted closer. Abby's detail antenna had risen. She and I were deep in conversation while the party sped into full swing. Music blared as the laughter from the party goers filled the room.

Colin stood and looked toward the door. "Belinda, a client just walked in. I'll make this as quickly as possible."

I guess the peck on my cheek was his signal I approved. He walked away without an answer. Garrett joined him. The two went into work mode. I didn't mind. Abby and I had far too much to talk about.

Robert, on the other hand, didn't leave. Why?

~ *Robert* ~

I had the luxury of hanging back tonight. Sure, I'd have some schmoozing with clients, but not as much as Colin. The party focused on potential Canadian investors. For once, I wasn't in the spotlight.

"Ladies?" Abby and Belinda swung their heads toward me. "Do you need a refill?" I swirled the ice in my glass.

On cue, they both said, "No thank you." Then they went back to their conversation, putting me in my place.

I left and rested my forearms on the bar as I studied my glass, trying to figure out how I got in this fix. Being around Belinda sent my insides into chaos, even from across the table. About to take a drink, a hand rested on my shoulder.

"Robert, I have a big favor to ask."

I turned toward Colin.

"I can't give Belinda much attention tonight. I'm pretty busy. Do you think you can help out and dance with her a few times?" His fingers tightened.

I never changed my facial expression. How could Colin be asking me that?

I didn't know why, but I agreed which shot my evening to hell.

"Thanks, dude. I owe you. I'll go ask her to dance this one, then you can take over." Colin walked over to the table and extended his hand. They headed to the dance floor.

I waved at the bartender. Scotch, straight up on the rocks, fit the bill. Downing it in a few gulps, I signaled the bartender for a refill. With the rotation of my hand, the ice cubes clinked against the glass. I knew she hadn't seen me sitting at the table. Her wide eyes told me so.

The second I saw her walk in, time slowed. She appeared to float with each step. The light reflected off every lock of hair and cast a glow that framed her features. Her hips moved seductively from side to side. The dress she wore caused my heart to race and my breath to cease. When she sat across from me, I stared at her in that dress.

The cool glass touched my lower lip. The vision of Belinda in that dress lingered. I tilted my head back, downed the scotch, then slammed the glass on the bar, getting the bartender's attention. The bartender motioned for a refill. I nodded. With my glass filled, I walked back to the empty table. I'd need to nurse this last drink to get home unscathed.

~ *Belinda* ~

My heart stopped, and I almost forgot to breathe when I heard his soft, masculine voice. Memories flooded my mind, causing my eyes to moisten. I shut them and let my hair cover the side of my face. I took a breath to get a grip. With all the skills I had learned over the past few months, I tossed my hair back and smled. "I'd love to."

He took me by the arm, and I thought I'd die. His simple touch sent a rush of toe-curling sensations through me, but I controlled myself as he led me to the dance floor. I expected him to keep me at arm's length during the slow dance. The opposite happened. Robert placed his arm around my waist and pulled me close. Our eyes connected and what happened next sent blood pounding through me. He reached up to the side of my head and gently pulled it against his chest. With a tightened grip around my waist, he pressed me closer. We floated as one around the dance floor to the tune of my favorite song, "Forever in My Mind."

With my cheek pressed against his chest, my eyes drifted close as I listened to each beat of his heart. I drifted to the Robert I loved and how this one gave me small glimmers of that love. I cherished every minute of being held in his arms.

When the music stopped, neither of us moved. Afraid to look up, I listened to every rhythmic rub-dub, rub-dub beat of his heart. Robert didn't let go. He stroked my hair and placed a tender kiss on the top of my head, which caused me to nuzzle into his chest. The band played another slow song, and we resumed our graceful association with the dance floor.

~ Sandra ~

The sight of my son and Belinda dancing thrilled me. I reached over and patted my husband's arm to get his attention. I pointed in the couple's direction.

Rob glanced at me. He followed my finger to watch Belinda and his son move across the dance floor.

"What do you think of that?" I studied my loving spouse.

"I haven't seen him that peaceful in months."

"Those two belong together, and you know it. Sharyn is all wrong for him." I never hesitated to let Rob know my thoughts about my attended daughter-in-law.

"Sandra, you can't interfere."

"I won't. We're going to just give them a slight push."

"You keep me out of this."

I turned toward my husband. "You know you have to be a part of this. You know that deep in your bones. You felt it when you shook her hand. I know you did." My finger poked his chest. "I saw your expression. You know she's the one for him."

Rob studied my face. "We'll talk about it later."

~ Belinda ~

"May I cut in?" Robert and I separated from our tender embrace when Colin appeared. Robert nodded, returning to the table.

Colin took me in his arms. "Well, have you been enjoying yourself?"

The stir of butterflies reminded me I enjoyed the closeness to Robert. I wondered how much Colin saw of our intimate dance. "I'm having a nice time."

"Good. I've been so preoccupied with my clients." He stroked my cheek. "I'm sorry. I'm not paying much attention to you."

"That's okay. I understand." I tried not to think about Colin's speedy departure last weekend. This man didn't have a spiteful bone in his body and had always been consistent and sincere. I pushed the thought away.

I settled my head against Colin's chest. His steady heartbeat threw me back in the memory of Robert's arms. Robert sent every fiber of my being into turmoil. His tender touch caused my senses to react, compounding my confusion. Despite all my attempts to distance myself from him, my body went nuts whenever he was close. His touch connected me to him just like with my Dream Robert, but with more intensity. That connection also kept my feelings for Colin at bay and that wasn't fair to Colin.

At the end of the dance, Colin escorted me back to the table, and this set the pattern for the night. Abby and I'd visit, and Robert and I'd have a few very close, almost too intimate dances. Dances I didn't want to end. Colin made the occasional appearance, and the cycle started all over. To complicate the strangeness of the night, Colin's focus on his clients caused him not to notice Robert's affection which I didn't discourage.

Near midnight, Abby yawned and poked Garrett. "We need to leave."

She stood and gave me a peck on my cheek. "We'll talk this week." She looked over at Colin. "I hate to leave you here by yourself."

"I'll be fine. The worst case scenario is I get an Uber."

"We could drive you home."

The idea appealed to me, but I didn't want to rock the boat with Colin. "No. I'll give him about thirty minutes, then tell him I need to leave." I patted her hand. "I'll be okay."

"You sure?"

"Yes."

I watched Garrett and Abby walk toward the door. She turned to wave. I waved back, and then I was alone. I propped my chin on my palm. At the far end of the room, I watched Rob, Colin, and Robert talk. From their facial expressions, they were in an intense discussion. As the conversation wrapped up, Colin and Robert approached the table. Now more intrigued, I waited to hear what else this strange evening offered.

My date seated himself beside me, and this time, Robert sat next to him. Colin scooted his chair back to include Robert in the conversation.

"I'm going to have to stay for a meeting with a client, who has to fly back to Toronto in the morning. Mr. Pendleton is staying. Robert agreed to drive you and his mother home, if that's all right with you."

I bit my lower lip and stared at Robert. My gaze wandered back to Colin. I knew how important advancing his career was to him. I placed my hand on his. "That'll be fine." If I get through the ride home. Maybe an Uber might be a better idea.

He smiled back and kissed my cheek. "Thank you. I have to go, but I'll call. Robert said he can leave whenever you and his mother are ready." He walked away and left me alone at the table with Robert.

It felt awkward. I reached for my wineglass and hoped my jittery nerves didn't make my hand shake. I shifted in my seat when a warm hand rested on my shoulder. Sandra's smiling face gave me the diversion I needed.

"I'll be ready to go home soon. It's getting late and most of the guests have left, leaving me only a few more obligatory "goodbyes" and "thank yous." Sandra winked. "Why don't you two dance while I finish up?" She panned between us before she left.

Robert looked at me and extended his hand. My butterflies bombarded my diaphragm as he led me to the dance floor.

The lights dimmed for the last dance of the night. My heart raced as he, not saying a word, peered into my eyes and pulled me close. With one arm around my waist, he clasped my hand in his between us. I placed my other one around his neck, and he leaned into it. He breathed deeper. His muscles relaxed as he held me close.

We moved across the dance floor as if suspended in air. I found myself transported to a time when I knew the deepest love I'd ever experienced, and I didn't want it to end.

The music faded away, but we continued to dance. In the background, the M.C. thanked everyone for attending. The lights brightened and broke the trance. I blinked and my heart sank, returning me to reality.

He smiled and then scanned the room, but didn't release me. "My mother is waiting at the door. Looks like she's ready to leave." He looked down at me. I stared back. A faint smile swept across his face. "Are you ready to go?"

"Mm-hmm." Nothing else came out. He escorted me to the table to retrieve my bag. I was glad Abby and Garrett left earlier, sparing me from having to explain myself. I was already having enough difficulty trying to make sense of the evening.

Sandra stood at the exit. Her smile grew wider as we came closer.

From her finger dangled a key-ring. "Robert, here's the keys to your dad's car."

At the car she claimed the back, leaving me to sit up front. The traffic was light, so the ride home only took about twenty minutes. However, that was the longest twenty minutes of my life. Robert's scent filled the air and I swore so did his body heat. Sandra sitting in the back was the only reason I didn't reach over and grab him.

When the car stopped in front of my house, Sandra spoke up. "Robert, be a gentleman and walk her to the door."

~ Robert ~

Mom's words grated at me. What the hell did she think I would do? Just dump her out? I had every intention of making sure she was safe before I sped off into the night. I turned toward her. She wore a familiar broad smile on her face. Her expression brought on a sudden twinge of concern. I realized my mother was up to something, but I had no idea what.

I exited the car and walked over to open Belinda's door. Mom said goodbye while I waited. With the pleasantries completed, I escorted Belinda to the small porch.

~ Sandra ~

I opened the back car door and stepped out. For a second, I gave a discrete glance in the couple's direction as they faded into the dark recesses. I was pleased. I knew they belonged together and, in time, the mess known as Sharyn would work herself out of my son's life. With my confidence renewed, I opened the front passenger door and slipped in. Taking care not to slam it and risk disturbing the couple if they were in an embrace. My smile broadened. Getting them together might be easier than I expected.

~ Robert ~

Belinda dropped her house keys while she attempted to unlock the door. I bent down and picked them up. The metal red rose attached to the key chain jolted a memory. I studied it for a moment before sliding the key into the lock. I opened the door a crack, then turned and blocked her path. There was something I'd wanted to do all night. Something I shouldn't do.

All evening, I was a bundle of nerves. She was the woman I belonged to. The one I should plan a life with. I knew this in my soul, but I had committed Sharyn. However, Belinda's closeness made it too hard to keep my resolution.

Despite my promise to myself, I placed my hands on either side of her head, tilted her head back, and stared at her rosy, enticing lips.

Slowly, I moved closer to them.

I hesitated before my lips pressed against hers. She didn't move. I gave her a soft kiss. Still, she gave no sign I should stop. I slanted my head and covered her mouth, deepening the kiss as I maneuvered her back into a darker region of the porch. Away from the possible peering eyes of my mother, who I should've dropped off first.

~ Belinda ~

The coolness of the brick against my back momentarily shocked me. I placed my arms around Robert's back and lost myself in the softness of his lips.

He kissed me with more fervor as both our respirations deepened. His hands went to my lower back, tugging me close. Our intimate parts pressed together. A thrill rushed through me. I slipped my arms around his neck and entwined my fingers in his hair. I pulled him as close, never wanting the feeling to go away. His hands roamed my back.

I rolled my head to the side as he brushed kisses down my neck. He ran a hand up the bare skin of my thigh. Gasping, I pulled him closer, the heat of his body penetrating the sheer fabric of the dress.

Unlike our first encounter, I got a strong sensation Robert didn't intend to stop his advances. His hands roamed my body, heightening my longing. He touched me with the familiarity of a love I once knew.

A hushed, pleading whisper escaped my lips before I could think about the ramifications of the words. "Robert, don't do this. Then leave." In that instant, the passion diffused.

He straightened. Sadness washed over his face. His breathing sped up. He contorted his mouth and reached for my hands, releasing them from around his neck, and exhaled. "You'd better go in."

I sneered and clenched my fists. "No! You tell me what's going on. You're not doing this to me again. And what about Sharyn?" With each mounting second of frustration, I dug my fingernails deeper into my palms.

He stepped back. His breathing was fast and his facial expression was confused. "I don't know... I mean... I don't know... I can't." He let out a breath. "Please go in."

I didn't want to make a scene with Sandra sitting at the curb. I glared at him while he just stood there, offering me nothing to explain his actions. Did he think I was a toy he could play with when the mood struck him? The first kiss was a mistake. The second put me to close to the role of the other woman.

"Why?" With open palms, I hit him squarely on the shoulders. The force caused him to stumble back.

"Please go in."

In a huff, I pushed past him and ran into the house, slamming the door behind me and locking it.

With my back pressed against the door, I heard the car drive away. Tears streamed down my cheeks as I slumped to the floor.

"Why is he doing this to me?"

An ache attacked my chest. Didn't he know how much this hurt?

~ Robert ~

Remember your resolution, remember your resolution kept repeating over and over in my mind. I questioned myself and my motives. Feeling guilty as hell, I slipped into the driver's seat without glancing at my mother. To my relief, we didn't talk on the way home. I pulled the sedan into the garage. Mom waited until I came around to help her out. My parents raised me to be a gentleman, but now I felt like a cheater.

"Are you all right?" She took hold of my arm.

"I'm fine. I'm just exhausted. I'll probably sleep in tomorrow, so I'll see you in the afternoon. How about we take the horses out in the evening?"

"You have a date. I'll see if your father wants to come along." She crossed in front of me and walked toward the door.

I reached for her arm and kissed her on the cheek. "Mom, I love you."

She smiled and patted my arm. "I know. I'll see you tomorrow. Sleep well."

I waited for her to lock the door before I left for the guesthouse. Normally, I would've taken my time, but tonight I sprinted across the lawn to the front door. As I ran, I loosened my tie and pulled off my jacket. Once inside, I rushed straight for the bedroom.

In there, my thoughts of Belinda sped up. I had shoved her into the recesses of my mind during the drive home. Now she came flooding back.

The little voice in my head screamed, *remember your resolution.*

I thought I had prepared myself and could handle seeing Belinda Davies tonight. But when she came floating across the floor in *that* dress... I could feel my resolve melting.

Holding her, smelling her, and feeling her warm body pressed against mine proved more than I could resist. I relived the taste of her luscious lips as I remembered the feelings that stirred deep inside me. That strange connection I experienced with her drove my mind and body to uncontrollable heights. She was my narcotic, and I knew I must go cold turkey.

I needed to stay away and there couldn't be any type of physical contact. With one touch, I turned into a moth so attracted to her flame that I can't help but fly into it, making me vulnerable.

Remember your resolution. What did I think I was doing, anyway? For God's sake, she was Colin's girlfriend, and I was engaged. It wasn't as if we were free agents and able to do whatever. Two other people were involved in this little foursome, even though they were in the dark.

My boxers were the last piece of clothing to hit the floor. I looked down at myself and sighed over the distress a little one percent of my body could cause. Rolling my eyes, I snatched a towel off the chair before hitting the shower.

The tepid water rolled over my head and down my body. I braced myself against the cool tile and let the water work its magic. About forty-five minutes later, I emerged from the bathroom wrapped in a towel around my waist.

I picked up my clothes and started putting them away. As I hung the jacket in the closet, I couldn't believe what wafted up my nose. Angel Scent, Belinda's perfume. "Damn, damn her." I couldn't win.

I slammed the closet door, ripped off the towel, crawled into bed, and pulled the sheet up to my chest.

The only problem, I wasn't alone. Belinda crawled in with me. My mind ran rampant with images of her.

Her eyes—those gorgeous baby blues mesmerized me when she looked at me.

Her mouth—that luscious taste that made me want more.

A shudder rocked through me.

That dress…

Her body—all those soft curves pressed against me in all the right places.

A slight movement of the sheet drew my attention.

A teepee rose in my nether regions.

"Oh, God. Get her out of my head," I groaned as I threw my arm over my face.

Remember your resolution.

Remember your resolution.

Remember your resolution.

CHAPTER 13

~ Belinda ~

DR. ROSEN STROKED his five o'clock stubble. "We have to analyze why you are continually putting yourself in these predicaments."

"What do you mean, my need? Was I supposed to walk home? I had no choice!" My voice raised in an angry tone along with my blood pressure. This guy knew how to push my buttons.

He stopped stroking his beard and gave me his "Do you want me to believe that?" look.

"Okay. I could've called for an Uber, but in my defense, I stopped the kiss." I huffed as I crossed my arms and sat back in my chair. "But I didn't want to." I looked down at the floor, twisting my mouth. I had a love-hate relationship with a man I had no right to want.

As time went on, we explored how I could protect myself against the emotional upheaval called Robert. I came to recognize the differences between the two. The real one wasn't as confident as my dream man. In short, the Real Robert had character flaws that made him different.

As far as he was concerned, I wasn't even sure I liked him. Yes, there was that irresistible, sensual connection we experienced. Not to mention the sexual tension a chainsaw couldn't cut through.

But he was engaged to Sharyn, which was a blessing in disguise. His involvement with her kept him away, and that allowed me the time I needed to heal psychologically.

My biggest lapses of memory pertained to my relationship with Matt. Those details came from what others told me, but no one witnessed our times alone. That left missing pieces.

At one point, I'd considered calling him, but I really didn't want to talk to him after the way he had treated me.

Dr. Rosen encouraged me to make a few trips back to my college in East Texas. Being on the school grounds, in places Matt and I had frequented, helped me discover several of the missing links. The downside, I remembered how he left and how it made me feel—used and abandoned. No one would do that to me again.

Armed with the few memories of Matt made me thankful he left. The idea of being married with children, having no career, and a loveless marriage haunted me. So, I figured the only sensible thing to do was cover the wound with a king-sized band aide, tuck it away and leave Matt in California.

Dr. Rosen had other plans. "No. No. No. Belinda, you need to look at your feelings about Matt and how he made you feel."

"Why? I can't change the past."

"Maybe not. But you can change your future."

So he helped me rip those memories wide open. I realized I had chosen the wrong guy because of my lack of self-confidence.

An added benefit of going back to the campus was saying goodbye to my beloved dream husband. With every visit, a piece of him turned into a pleasant memory I'd always cherish. The grieving process followed a healthy path. Although he never existed, my emotions told me he did. As a result, I went through the grieving steps as if I'd lost a real person. Letting go opened up my life's potential.

Eight months had passed since I woke up. It was now May. Spring was in full swing and with every passing day, the sorrow I felt from the loss of my love in my "Dream Reality" weakened. I grieved and grew stronger as my memory healed. The spinning, which I had experienced in the beginning, occurred less often, replaced by flashes of pictures. Sometimes a whole scenario popped into my head. Once the incident finished, a piece of my life unfolded without the disorienting dizziness.

"I'm glad to hear the memory issues are calming down. This means you can move on. Start making new plans for the future." Dr. Rosen reminded me in every session. Then he'd always ask, "How's the relationship with Colin?"

"Okay. I guess." I'd give my pat answer because I really didn't know.

Colin, he was a whole different dilemma. I loved being around him. Although his job took him to Toronto, we talked daily. Over the weekends, we spent every second together. I knew time was running out. He'd put off the relocation as long as possible, but more and more, the demand of his job was up north. Soon, Colin would pack up and leave.

Going with him was my next and most pressing dilemma.

Whenever we talked, he'd hint about me moving with him. A few times, he mentioned marriage. Either prospect caused me to breakout in a cold sweat.

So, why did Colin and a future with him scare me so? I guess this was more food for future sessions as I tried to figure out what was stopping me.

As Colin's job kept him busy, and I completed the decorating of my house, I had more time. I also saw less of Sandra as her client base picked up.

Undecided about my future with Colin, I moved into the next phase of my plan, job hunting. It was the perfect time to pursue a teaching position.

After my enlightened session with the good doctor, I called Abby for help and to get her thoughts, since I'd wanted to work in her school district.

"I think it's a great idea. But do you want to work full time?"

"I'm not sure. I could sub. Then I could work as much as I wanted."

"That doesn't pay much."

"I know. That's not an issue. Remember the settlement?"

"So why work at all?"

Good question. "I need something productive to do. See what you can find out. I think I'd like working with you."

Abby never missed an opportunity to do some digging. "Do you think he'll ask you to go with him when he moves?"

"I don't know….he's hinted around. I'm not sure I'd consider moving to Canada. Maybe I'll visit and see how things go." I collapsed back onto my mattress. "Oh Abby, every time he's dropped a hint, I change the subject. But I know I'll miss him."

For a moment, Abby remained silent. "What about Robert?"

I laughed under my breath. "Which one?"

"You know which one."

I let out an enormous sigh. "He's engaged, and other than those marvelous kisses we experienced—"

"Stop! Back it up. Kisses? He kissed you again? When?"

"Yeah. Colin couldn't take me home after the party, so Robert did. When he walked me to my door, he planted one on me and then the jerk just left without an explanation. He's screwing with my head."

"Wow. I think he likes you, but can't act on it."

"Well, he sure has a funny way of showing it. As I was saying, most of the time he doesn't seem interested in me. He's acting like a man who's getting married."

"Or having second thoughts because he's hiding something," Abby blurted through my cell.

I rolled my eyes at the phone. "Or just a player."

"Hmmm? I don't think so."

"Why?"

"Just gettin' a feeling something ain't right."

"Well maybe, but I can't do anything about that now."

I changed the subject and we talked for another half hour before we ended the call.

~ *Sandra* ~

I placed a cup of hot coffee on the table in front of my husband, then took a seat and puffed out my lower lip.

Rob looked at me from over his cup while he sipped. "Okay, bumper lip, you have my attention."

My lips curled into a smile. "Well, you know my business is growing. So I think it's time I hired someone to help me."

"And this involves me how? You run your business as you see fit." He took another sip of coffee.

"I want to hire Belinda Davies. Robert told me she has a horse named Beau. I want you to move him to our stables," I revealed, with batting lashes and teeth flashing.

Rob, now in mid-swallow, almost choked. He sputtered out, "What!?"

I offered my distressed spouse no comfort. I knew he'd survive, but now I held his undivided attention.

"You know Robert and Belinda belong together. You felt it." I placed a hand on his forearm. "You saw how they acted at the party, and if it wasn't for the tentacles Sharyn has wrapped around him, I'd be calling Belinda my daughter-in-law."

Rob raised an eyebrow at me, his wife of thirty-five years. "I can't believe what I'm about to say, and I hope I don't live to regret this." He gave his index finger a slight wave in the air. "So I'm supposed to just horse-nap the animal and move him to our stable in the depths of the night?" He furrowed his brow. "You know they still consider horse stealing a crime in Texas."

"P-p-please. No, silly." I swatted his upper arm. "Let me see if I can get her to work with me. In a week Robert leaves for European. He'll be gone three weeks. Just enough time for us to put my plan to work."

I took a sip.

"If she agrees to help me, we'll invite her to stay for dinner and to take a late ride with us. Then you can suggest she bed down her horse in the empty stall... because of the late hour and all. After a few times of doing that..."

"Will you please take a breath and come up for air?"

Robs brows knitted after I gave him another swat. "Let me finish."

"Okay. Finish."

"Then you insist she stable the horse here for convenience and safety's sake. After all, you wouldn't want your future daughter-in-law riding around in the woods after dark."

Rob gave me a sharp glance.

"Then when Robert gets back, she'll be practically living with us at least three days a week."

Hovering over his now cooling coffee, Rob shook his head. "All right, but what if your plan backfires?"

"I'll worry about that later." I stood and sashayed toward the sink, exaggerating my hip swing. Looking over my shoulder, I said, "Today, I need to hire me some help."

Around eleven o'clock, I called Belinda.

"Hello."

"Belinda, it's Sandra. Are you free for a late lunch?"

"Yes. What time were you thinking?"

"How about I pick you up about one?"

"I'll be looking forward to it. Sandra, may I ask why you want to see me?"

"I just miss your beautiful smile and need a dose of Belinda."

"Oh." She chuckled. "I'll be ready."

∽

I didn't see Belinda as a client any longer, especially after I saw my son's reaction to this delightful young lady. She seemed so different from my intended daughter-in-law.

When Robert first started dating Sharyn, they seemed well matched. Her family was well-off, she had received an excellent education, and she had selected a good career path. At first, the two showered affection on each other like most couples in a new relationship. After the New Year's Eve party, things changed.

Before that, Sharyn came over to visit. Back then, I gave her a chance. Even that changed. She stopped visiting altogether. With her absence, Robert also left, spending more time at his fiancée's apartment. The only time I saw my son was when she left town.

I also noticed a shift in his mood. When he was around Sharyn, he was quiet, almost reclusive. However, she traveled a great deal, which meant he stayed home. At those times, I could enjoy my son as the child I loved.

My greatest fear was that she'd prevent him from seeing me after they were married. I imagined we'd just get the leftovers after he made the biggest mistake of his life. I had to prevent the marriage to save him.

If my plan worked, I'd welcome Belinda into the family.

~ *Belinda* ~

My imagination ran wild while I paced and bit my lower lip. "What could Sandra possibly want to talk about?"

The doorbell chimed precisely at one o'clock.

"Hi, Sandra. Nice to see you again. Come in." I opened the door wider to allow my visitor to enter.

She walked into the open concept rooms and peered around. "You've made more changes. They look great." She smiled from ear to ear.

"Thanks. I still have done nothing with the extra two bedrooms. Sometimes I think buying a three-bedroom house made little sense."

Sandra raised her finger and shook it. "Always think resale. Having those bedrooms will help this house sell better than a one or two-bedroom. Be prepared for when you may decide to sell." She smiled and extended an arm. "Shall we go? I'm hungry."

⚭

Once we placed our orders, Sandra explained the reason for her invitation. I listened with intensity to the proposal. The idea intrigued me. This would put me on an alternative career path, but there were a few obstacles I'd have to consider.

"Are you sure I can do something like this?"

She smiled. "Look what you've done in the past few months. You taught yourself the program I used to design rooms. You've grasped the concepts of what makes a room work… I have faith in you, and you have the background, being an art major and all."

I thought for a second, skimming through all the reasons to take her offer.

Then I reviewed the reasons not to. The only one on the list, Robert. For me, I couldn't let him stand in the way. His engagement and absence showed he didn't want to be a part of my life.

Dr. Rosen and Abby's voices screamed at me. "Go for it!"

In that split second, I looked at Sandra and gave her a nod.

~ Sandra ~

A smile shot across my face. I was so pleased with myself. I leaned back in my chair. Like magic, the first step of my plan fell into place to make Belinda my daughter-in-law.

CHAPTER 14

~ *Belinda* ~

A WEEK LATER, on Monday morning, I parked my CR-V in front of the Tuscan-style house on Crescent Oak Circle, home of the office of Crescent Oak Interior Design Company. Sandra opened the door, inviting me into the kitchen to talk and have a cup of coffee.

My resident butterflies fluttered their tiny wings. The deeper I strolled through the rooms that I hadn't seen since the New Year's Eve party, the more those wings flapped.

Robert might be around any corner, although that likelihood was slim since he worked 9 to 5. Still, the butterflies picked up more speed and took flight. Was I making a mistake?

"How do you take your coffee?" Sandra walked over to the kitchen counter.

"With cream and sugar."

She pointed toward the table. "Go have a seat and I'll bring everything over there."

I walked to the large oval table nestled at the end of the room in front of an immense bay window. From that vantage point, the barn was visible, and I could see the horses' heads bobbing in and out of their stalls. "How many horses do you own?"

Sandra placed the tray on the table. "Three. We each have one, but there are six stalls. We use one as a tack room, one for feed, and one is empty." She motioned for me to sit. "We'll go out later to meet them if you'd like. I'll need to turn them out." She handed me a cup of piping hot coffee, then motioned to the tray. "Help yourself."

"Thank you." A smile spread across my face and those damn butterflies settled. "I like barns. I like the smell of fresh hay and horses." I scooped sugar and creamer into my cup and stirred. "You know, I have a horse." I lifted the cup to my lips. "I keep him at the stables on the other side of the woods. His name is Beau."

"Really?" When you come back on Wednesday, why don't you plan to stay for dinner? Then afterward, we can go for a ride. Rob can run you over in the car to get Beau."

"Will Robert be joining us?" I attempted a sip of the hot liquid. A sting on my lips told me to wait. So I basked in the aroma and inhaled.

"No. He's in Canada for three weeks. He'll be working for the first two, then he and Sharyn are going on vacation for a week. Your partners will just be Rob and I."

Relief swept over me. I let out a slight sigh. Robert wouldn't be an issue, and I could concentrate on learning my new job. "That sounds like a plan. I'll bring some riding clothes with me."

"Bring a swimsuit, as well. I like to take a dip afterward and sit in the hot tub. It's very relaxing. We can have some wine and talk."

~ Sandra ~

I had just set the stage for part two of my plan. Now I had to make sure Rob did his bit. If he did, the scheme would come together without a hitch.

The last step in my plot was for Robert to allow his attraction to Belinda to take hold. Then, after they formalized their relationship, Rob and I'd explain. By that time, the happy couple would understand the reason for our meddling and they'd forgive us.

While we sipped coffee, I explained the reasons I needed to hire someone to help with the design business, as well as the expected responsibilities.

"I won't expect you to do anything you don't feel comfortable doing, and if I give you too much to do, you need to tell me to back off." I extended my hand to my future daughter-in-law. "Agreed?"

She clasped my hand. "Agreed."

~ Belinda ~

I grinned. I liked Sandra and felt at ease around her. She made things simple, and I related to her more as a friend than as my new boss. The two of us laid out who would do what and how to cover all the aspects of the job.

"I have a few errands to run this morning. Would you feel comfortable answering the phone while I'm gone?" She leaned back in her chair. "Just tell everyone I'm out with a client and take their number."

"Sure. I think I can manage that. Just show me to the phone."

"I can do better than that. I'll show you the office and your desk." Sandra motioned for me to follow her. She led me up the stairs in the kitchen to an ample-sized room at the back of the house.

It was nicely decorated and had hardwood bookshelves lining two sides. The bookshelves were heavy with samples of fabrics, window coverings, flooring and other items for interior design.

At the far end of the office, large windows overlooked the barn, pasture, and the pool. An overstuffed sofa sat in the middle of the room, facing the windows, dividing it in two. Positioned behind the couch sat a French Country style farm table that served as Sandra's workstation.

She led me to a desk facing one window. "I hope this will be all right."

Then she gave me a brief tour of the office that ended at the farm table.

"I have to go, but while I'm gone, explore, get the lay of the land." She reached for her purse. "If you want anything from the kitchen, help yourself. I'll be back before lunch." She headed to the door. If it's all right with you, I'll pick up some sandwiches. We can eat lunch by the pool."

"That sounds great."

She smiled and closed the door behind her.

I glanced around the room, trying to figure out where I should start. My desk. I sat in the ergonomically correct rolling chair and tested the positions until I found the best one. Then I probed into the drawers and located everything I could need to perform my job efficiently. In front of me sat a brand new state-of-the-art laptop. It appeared she'd spared no expense making sure her assistant was comfortable.

Over the smooth top of my new workspace, I rubbed my fingertips. Then I placed my elbow on the shiny surface and rested my head in my palm.

I skimmed the lush scene outside the window and drifted my gaze to beyond the pool area. There the guesthouse, Robert's residence, came into full view. Those damn butterflies did more than flutter. They caused my stomach to knot. I'd have no choice but to watch him come and go while I sat there working.

"No. No. No. This will not do," I said out loud. I scanned the room for another location. After my analysis, I decided the arrangement met a very specific need and moving the desk wouldn't be an option.

I rested my head on my palm and tapped my fingers. A muffled drumming beat filled my ears. A snort puffed out of my nose and the butterflies stuck in my throat.

"Can't fix this. I'll have to make sure I leave before he gets home." I threw my hands in the air. There I go again, talking to myself. A nasty habit I'd started when I was nervous or alone and had been doing it more lately. Come to think of it, I'd started answering my own questions.

Dr. Rosen had assured me on more than one occasion, "It's okay to talk to yourself. It's okay to answer your own questions. However, when a third party steps in, that's cause for concern."

I stopped to listen. No third party. I'm safe.

I pushed my chair away from the desk and swiveled around to face the room. "What else can I poke around in since I can't move you?" Jeez, I needed to stop talking to myself. I'm glad the desk didn't answer me.

A group of framed pictures hung on one wall.

I walked over to check them out. My breath hitched. They were pages from a magazine article showcasing the Pendletons' house.

The first picture featured the front of the house with a BMW roadster parked in the circular drive, with Robert leaning against the car door. The next one exhibited the foyer with the Bombay chests, cobalt blue vases, and the horseshoe shaped staircase. Another was of the dining room. In the picture of the family room, Sandra and Robert Pendleton sat on the leather couch near the massive fireplace. Robert posed behind them with his arms crossed on the back of the couch. I ran my fingers over the smooth glass that covered his face. "Robert."

Sandra's right hand was draped over Rob's knee. On her ring finger, she wore a three-stone diamond ring, an exact duplicate of the one Robert gave me when we became engaged in my "Dream Reality." I slid my fingertips down the glass. "My ring."

"When were these taken?" I found the date at the bottom of each page. It was one month before I fell into a coma.

"I must have looked through this magazine before the accident."

"I just plugged your family and your house in." Butterflies swirled in my chest. Each photo represented a part of the house I used in my dream. In a split second, another piece of my memory puzzle fell into place.

The only thing I couldn't figure out was how I knew what drawer the wine bottle opener was in on New Year's Eve.

The last picture was of Rob standing in the kitchen with his back to the camera. He had his left hand on the neck of a wine bottle resting on the counter, and his right one hovered over a drawer at his side, holding a bottle opener. The very one I had retrieved it from at the party.

I let out a sigh. "Dr. Rosen will have a field day with this." Oops, there I go talking to myself again. Maybe I need a brain scan.

Butterflies dropped and hit the bottom of my stomach. I should've been happy. These pictures filled gaps but were also a forehead-smacking reminder. My Robert never existed.

Tears clung to my lashes. A sniffle escaped.

The droned shrill of the phone called me to work. I swiped my eyes and pursed my lips and then released a long sigh.

I spent the next hour answering the few calls that came in.

The design program filled the screen of the laptop as Sandra walked in. "How did it go?"

"I think I did okay. There were a few calls. Nothing earth shattering."

Sandra chuckled. "I'm glad. Lunch is downstairs. I'll get to the calls after we eat."

We ate lunch for a relaxing hour under the covered patio that overlooked the sparkling, clear water of the pool and waterfall.

The gentle trickle of the water cascading down the rocks relaxed me. I could become accustomed to this quickly and wondered how long the honeymoon phase would last.

∞

Wednesday morning, I found myself excited to get ready for work. The job not only gave me something to do, but I liked the direction of my alternative career path.

Sandra had filled me in on the ins and outs of the design profession and what it would take to become a certified designer. It appeared I was well on my way because of my chosen academic field. So, with experience and a few more courses, I could apply for the title of Interior Designer through the State of Texas.

The day proceeded with me, making myself useful as her new assistant. She did a great job of mentoring me and juggling her present clients. Her ability to multi-task and keep her cool at the same time amazed me. On Friday, I would accompany my boss on a new build project of a 7,000 square-foot home. She wanted me to see how the design process worked from the ground up.

At four o'clock sharp, Sandra walked over to the phone and sent the calls to voicemail. "Did you bring your riding clothes and swimsuit?"

"Yes, ma'am."

"Okay. Go change and meet me downstairs. You can earn your keep by helping me with dinner. Rob will be home in about thirty minutes. One perk of being the boss is he gets to leave before rush hour when he's not in a meeting."

I met Sandra in the kitchen and pitched in. About to set the plates on the table, I stopped. Rob moseyed in with his glasses perched down toward the tip of his nose, shuffling through a handful of envelopes and didn't seem to notice me. He put the mail down on the counter and wrapped his arms around the waist of his wife, who stood at the kitchen island. He nuzzled into her neck and kissed her ever so gently. She seemed to soften as she leaned into her husband in response to his loving gesture, engrossed in their moment.

I tried to keep my head down, but the compulsion to watch the CEO of a major corporation in such an intimate embrace with his wife proved too strong. I saw something very familiar. She responded to him the same way I had to Robert.

Rob became more intimate as his left hand moved north on his wife's torso, clearly targeting her breast.

Just before he made contact, she cleared her throat. "Honey, we have company. Belinda is joining us for dinner. Remember?"

His hand stopped moving. With his nose buried in her neck, he looked up from under his brow at me standing by the kitchen table. I gave him a quick restrained wave. It seemed uncanny how the pair acted like Dream Robert and I.

He let out a brief snort and gave his wife one last kiss. "Later."

She smiled. "I hope so."

He released her and acknowledged me. "It's nice to see you again. I'm glad you could join us." He started backing out of the room. "I'm going to go change." His voice became fainter halfway across the family room. "I'll be back to help."

Sandra gave me an impish smile. "We may be older, but we're not dead."

The statement broke the tension, and I let out a small giggle.

"Laugh. It was funny."

I finished setting the table while she went back to cooking.

Rob didn't take long to return dressed in jeans and a t-shirt. For someone in his fifties, he had a nice physique that matched his slight ruggedness. He looked as if he would be just as comfortable running a ranch as he was running his company.

"Well, what's left to do, or did I time it right and get lucky?"

She glanced at him. "You always try to get out of helping me."

"And most of the time, I'm successful."

She gave him a sharp smack from the corner of her towel.

He jumped. "Hey. Watch that."

They both gave each other a playful smile before he grabbed her and planted a kiss on her lips. "Now what can I do?"

"Make the salad."

With the ease of a chef, he went into action, collecting everything he needed.

"I can help cut up vegetables." I sat on one stool at the island.

Rob completed his gathering and set up shop alongside his wife. He handed me a knife, a cutting board, and a cucumber. He then turned to get something else.

Sandra had her back to her husband and never lifted her head. "Here, Rob." She held out a cutting knife to him. He turned around, took it without saying a word, and returned to the counter to finish his task.

I tilted my head. It appeared she had read his mind.

~ Sandra ~

I timed dinner to take longer than usual. As planned, Rob drove Belinda to the stables to saddle up Beau. He and I would come with our horses to meet her.

He returned to the barn to find me waiting atop Mouse, my horse. I had saddled his horse, Billy, and held the reins. "Remember what you're doing tonight." I jutted the reins toward him. "I did my part with a late dinner."

"How could I forget?" He sighed and took the reins from me and walked Billy outside. Then he checked his cinch before mounting the animal.

We met up with Belinda and took a relaxing ride that lasted until after dusk. The ride ended back at our barn.

I dismounted and held Mouse's reins, waiting to make sure Rob remembered his part of the plan. He dismounted and led Billy toward the barn. I cleared my throat and caught his attention. Then I tilted my head toward Belinda as I turned to lead my horse into the barn. The exchange I heard, met with my approval.

~ Belinda ~

I stayed mounted and wasn't looking forward to riding the dark trail back to the stable. We should've started earlier, but I enjoyed the time spent with my hosts. "I'll ride Beau back. Rob, would you mind picking me up so I can come get my car?"

"Belinda, Sandra tells me the two of you were planning on sitting in the hot tub. Since it's so late, why don't you leave Beau here for the night? We have an empty stall."

I thought about the proposition for a few minutes. It made sense, so I agreed.

With the horses bedded down, the hot tub came next on the agenda with a relaxing glass of wine to round off the night. The three of us sat and enjoyed each other's company. I learned more about my new boss and her husband. In return, they were learning about me. I felt a bond with them and knew I liked them. They were not stuffy as I imagined people in their position might be. Both of them were down-to-earth kind of folks who made me feel welcome and wanted.

At ten o'clock, I sat in my car for the ride home. All I could think about was the hours of discussion the evening would spur on with Dr. Rosen, Abby, and my mother.

~ Sandra ~

Rob and I were in a tender embrace in bed. I rested my head on his chest. He stroked my hair.

"Are you happy now?" He gave me a soft kiss on my forehead.

I looked up at him with a hint of a smile. "You did well. Now all you have to do is convince her to move Beau here permanently. Then phase two will be complete."

He huffed, but knew my prying was the right thing to do. Sharyn was wrong for our son.

CHAPTER 15

~ Belinda ~

EARLY THE NEXT morning, I called Sandra to plan to pick up Beau. It wasn't one of my scheduled workdays, but I didn't want Beau to overextend his stay.

"Oh, Belinda, I hope you don't mind. I'm going to be gone all day, so I fed Beau and turned him out with the other horses. He seems to get along with them just fine."

"Thank you, but I don't want to take advantage of your generosity."

Sandra let out a small laugh. "We don't mind at all. In fact, since we're planning to ride again tomorrow night, why not just leave him where he is? It might be easier."

"That'll work for me. You can deduct anything he eats from my pay."

"Oh. Don't you worry about that. If you want, you can come over earlier and help me feed the horses before work."

"I'd be glad to. I would've done the same thing at the stables, anyway." Her plan made more sense than moving Beau back and forth.

"Good. I'll have some coffee on. See you tomorrow morning. Say around seven."

"I'll see you then, and thank you, Sandra."

"You're welcome, Darling."

At seven a.m, I arrived at the Pendleton estate. Dressed in jeans, a white t-shirt and boots, I carried my work clothes up to the office. Today's schedule was full. We'd tend to the horses, clean up and then be ready to go on my first off-site visit. She'd decide with the owner and I'd take notes. Back at the office, I'd write up the report, and she'd complete the layout. On the following Monday afternoon, we'd review the presentation with the owner.

My heart took flight, mixed with a healthy dose of nerves. I wanted to make a good impression and hoped I wouldn't mess up.

The day went as planned and we worked well together. I completed my end of the presentation by four o'clock. Sandra was sitting at her computer working on the design program. I scanned over the report, filled my lungs, and approached her.

"I have the report finished. Do you want to go over it? I'd like to know what I did wrong."

She stopped working and frowned at me. "What you did *wrong*? Darling, we don't do wrong here. We do 'room-for-improvement.'" She grinned, making air quotes. "Give it to me and make yourself comfortable." She pointed to the overstuffed chair by her desk.

Sandra read, making slight facial gestures with each flip of a page, until a broad smile came across her face. She passed it back to me. "You're a fast learner. The report is perfect."

She glanced at the clock and proclaimed with one finger on the voicemail button, "Quittin' time. I'm going to change. See you downstairs."

I bounced down the back stairs into the kitchen to find Rob and her in a passionate kiss. Neither of them heard or noticed me until I cleared my throat.

They turned their heads in my direction. His lips pursed and he let out a sigh. "I'm going to change. See ya in a minute."

"I'm sorry. I keep interrupting you two." The corner of my lip suffered when I bit down.

"You didn't intrude. In fact, you might need to get used to it if you're going to hang around this household. Rob and I are still madly in love and can't seem to get enough of each other."

I envied their passion. They reminded me of my Dream Robert and myself.

With a full week of employment completed at the Crescent Oaks Interior Design Company, I'd learned a lot from my new boss. I also became more familiar with the couple I knew as my in-laws in a memory.

In my dream, I had limited contact with the Penningtons. What I knew about them came from a chance encounter with the magazine article. Now I learned what they were really like. I found it fascinating that the two people from the article, who lived a life I could only dream about, had invited me into their lives.

The evening ended with a relaxing soak in the hot tub. Rob strutted out of the house with three glasses of wine. My heart jumped at the sight of his silhouette. In the dimness of the pool lights, his shape resembled Robert. He sat on the edge of the tub and handed each of us a glass. "Belinda, Sandra tells me your first week went well."

I wasn't sure where this conversation would lead. "I think it did?" I glanced at Sandra, who gave me a nod, confirming my statement.

"So, it looks like you'll be coming back next week?" He lifted his glass.

Now I was confused. "What are you asking me? I'd like to come back next week, if that's okay."

Rob's mouth opened, and a blank look swept across his face. "No, no. That's not what I meant. Look, I'll just come out and ask. Since you'll be spending at least three days a week here…Sandra and I thought it would be easier if you moved Beau to our barn. There I said it." He gave a nod, pleased with himself.

His uncomfortable manner was unexpected from this otherwise confident businessman. I hesitated, but gave his proposal two seconds. Beau enjoyed his new friends, and that was good enough for me. "It makes sense, but there'd have to be some ground rules."

He looked at his wife and then turned back to me. "Go on."

"I'll rent the stall, pay for his food, and help with all the horses' care."

Rob smiled. "Young lady, you have a deal."

~ Sandra ~

I sank back against the lounge seat of the hot tub. The water rose to my neck as I rested my head back to see the night sky. Watching the lights from a distant plane pass overhead, I felt confident phase three of my plan would only be a few weeks away. By the time Robert returned, Belinda would practically be family.

~ Sharyn ~

Robert and I sat in the President's Lounge at the Toronto Airport during a three-hour layover on our way back to Houston. I amused myself by paging through bridal magazines, and he watched the planes on the tarmac.

In the center of one magazine, a gorgeous dress by a top designer held me spellbound. It was breathtaking, but out of my price range.

"Robert." He didn't move. I again repeated in a higher voice, "Robert." Again, no sign he even heard me.

The paper of the magazine crumpled in my hands as I turned them into fists.

This wasn't the first time he seemed preoccupied. Something was bothering him. I noticed a shift in his mood about a week after our engagement. The first time, whatever distracted him only lasted a few days. In February, another brief episode had occurred.

I had hoped being together in a five-star hotel on Lake Louise would spark our romance. It didn't, and he never touched me even when I pranced around naked. All my attempts to arouse him failed with his multiple excuses.

But when Robert sat quietly, he seemed more distant, and that scared me the most. I thought about asking him what was going on, but didn't want to nag. Does Ms. Angel Scent have anything to do with his new distant behavior and lack of need for sex?

I touched his arm. "Robert."

He turned toward me as I lifted the picture of the exquisite dress.

~ Belinda ~

Over the past three weeks, I thought of Sandra and Rob as extended family. Their warm and comfortable manner made it easy for me to forget they were Robert's parents. My workdays centered on my office duties. After the phone switched to voicemail, it was all about the care of the horses and socializing with the Pendletons.

On Friday, about three o'clock in the afternoon, we cut the workday short. I changed out of my work clothes and left for the barn. Sandra and Rob would fix dinner by themselves while I worked on grooming the horses.

Armed with my cell phone, I inserted the ear buds and started listening to some of my favorite songs. After I tethered Beau to a post, my brush strokes increased with the fast beats of the music along with my hip action. When the melody of my favorite slow song played, I raised my arms and imagined myself dancing with Robert, twirling and floating around the barn as I sang.

~ *Robert* ~

The driveway came into view, along with a familiar Honda CR-V parked in the circle drive as I drove past to the guesthouse. My stomach dipped. Surely it's not hers. Why would Belinda's car be here?

After tossing my luggage into my abode, I walked across to the main house and found Mom in the kitchen, cooking. "Sure smells good. I'm starving." I took in a deep breath of the mouthwatering scent and could feel the saliva building in my mouth. "Pot roast?"

She shot me a glance over her shoulder and smiled. "Thanks. You're right, and it'll be ready in about half an hour. I'm finishing the gravy and potatoes. Glad you're back. How was your trip?"

She lifted her cheek, and I planted a kiss.

Her smile widened.

"Good to be home. I think the business trip was successful. We have some new clients. The vacation was okay." He snatched a tomato out of the salad and popped it in his mouth. "By the way, who does the car in the driveway belong to?"

Mom pointed toward the kitchen window at the stables. "Belinda."

I almost choked on the tomato. *Well shit.* "What's she doing here?"

"Grooming her horse."

At the kitchen table, I supported myself on my knuckles to peer out the window. "What's Beau doing here?"

"Living here. Belinda now works for me part-time. She's a really sweet young lady." Mom stopped and looked at me as I glared at her.

"She's working for you and has Beau in our barn?" I waved my hands. "What happened while I was gone?"

"Nothing. I needed help. She needed a job, and it only made sense she start keeping her horse here."

I walked over to the kitchen counter. "How did all this happen?"

Mom blinked her eyes. "Well, a few weeks ago, Colin told her to call me. She needed help with her new place and she impressed me." She gave a quick shrug of her shoulders. "So, I asked her to be my assistant."

With a jerk of my head, I turned back to the window.

"So, why is the horse here?"

She sighed. "We went on a few rides together, and your father thought it best if she boarded Beau here. For safety reasons."

I glared at my mother. Her face bore no expression.

"I see what's going on here." I planted my palms on the counter. "How did you get Dad to go along?"

"Oh. Robert, don't be silly." She wiped her hands on a dishtowel. "Now be a dear and go ask Belinda to come in and clean up."

I could feel myself flush as my heart rate sped up from my low boiling rage.

"Why!?"

"Because she's staying for dinner, and I need her to set the table." She paused. "In fact, the two of you can set it together. Now go on."

My mouth dropped open as stared, but I'd fight this battle another day. I was tired and hungry. All I wanted was to eat and go to sleep.

I turned on my heels and marched out the back door to meet the love of my life I'd lost in a dream.

~ *Sandra* ~

I walked over to the island to watch my son tromp across the lawn. His hands clenched, just like when he was about to have a tantrum as a child. "Some things never change."

Phase three of my plan was now in motion. I just had to wait and pray his attraction to Belinda was stronger than his loyalty to Sharyn.

I changed my position, taking a better vantage point behind the kitchen table to see into the barn without being noticed.

~ *Robert* ~

Blood pounded in my ears. I needed to distance myself from this woman, and my mother plotted to bring us together. How could she do this to me?

I approached the barn, not sure what I'd do when I reached Belinda. She had stuck in my head and hide there like a little mouse waiting to be given the chance to scurry around. For the past three weeks, she was all I thought about, and she was messing up my relationship with Sharyn. I barely touched my fiancée on what was supposed to be a romantic getaway. I almost ran out of excuses.

The way Belinda felt, the softness of her skin, how she moved, how she laughed. She had unloaded her bags and moved right into my mind, refusing to leave. My biggest fear was breaking down and giving in to my impulses, because around her, I seemed to have very little control.

And now this. From the way my mother acted, she'd adopted a daughter, and that only meant one thing. I'd be near Belinda a lot.

When I reached the barn, I was determined to keep my resolution no matter what. There'd be no physical contact of any sort. I'd just pass on my mother's message. At the doorway, I stopped, paralyzed by the sight of Belinda.

As I watched her, she appeared to float as though she danced with an invisible partner—her arms positioned as if around a man's neck. Earbuds in place, she sang, "Dear love, my only sweet true love." With her eyes closed. Her voice filled my ears like the voice of an angel.

I fell against the doorjamb. My balled fists relaxed and the tension in my shoulders vanished as I gazed at her for a few minutes, enchanted.

With deliberate steps, I walked over to her and stepped into her arms, placing my hands on her hips. And there went my resolution. It flew out the door.

Her eyes shot open, and she froze with her hands suspended in front of her shoulders. Inches away, I could smell her perfume mixed with the distinctive scent of horse. I inhaled and raised my palms to hers until our fingers laced. That familiar sensation took over. I concentrated on her face. In slow motion, I guided her arms around my neck. I removed one of her earbuds and inserted it into my ear.

"Don't stop." I tugged her to my chest. She tightened her grip as I glided her around the dirt floor.

~ Sandra ~

Rob walked into the kitchen in his usual manner, flipping through the mail. I stood behind the table. My arms crossed over my chest, still viewing my son and hopefully future daughter-in-law through the window. "Honey, come look at this." I pointed toward the barn.

He stopped shuffling through the envelopes. "What?"

"Look in the stable. See them dancing. See how they're looking at each other? She's his soul mate." I wrapped my arm around his waist and snuggled into his side. "They found each other."

"I know you're right. Now let's see if those two can take it to the next step. Sandra, your part is done. Now it's up to them."

I nestled into my husband's arm and let out a sigh. "Okay, but is it all right if I give them a little nudge now and then? You know, just to keep them on track."

He gave me a squeeze. "You're so bad. That's why I love you. Just don't push too much."

"I promise." We turned back toward the window to watch what else might unfold.

~ Belinda ~

I waited for Robert to release his hold when the song ended. He didn't, so I gave him a shove.

He stumbled backward a few steps. "I guess I shouldn't have done that."

My miffed level rose. What made him think he could just walk in and out of my emotions? "You bet you shouldn't have done that!" I snapped back at him. Yanking the earbud out of his ear, I turned away to finish brushing Beau.

"Mom sent me out here to ask you to come in. I understand you're joining us for dinner."

I stopped grooming the horse and glared at him. "Tell her I'll be right there."

Not saying another word, he turned to leave.

Scout stuck his head out of his stall just as Robert walked past. I watched him smile as he stroked the horse's nose and then rubbed behind his ear. I could hardly believe what I heard. A soft cooing sound came from him the closer he moved toward the horse. Scout's ear was level with Robert's mouth as he continued to make the sound. He stood next to the animal for several seconds and then looked over his shoulder at me and walked out.

My heart melted watching his response to his horse. That was the sweetest thing I had ever seen. I threw my arms over Beau's back and rested against him.

"That SOB. How could he be so obnoxious one minute and so adorable the next?" Beau swung his head back and nibbled at me. I inhaled, then untied Beau to lead him into his stall.

∞

I scoped out the occupants in the kitchen as I opened the door. Sandra stood at the island working, and Robert sat on a stool across from her. He turned toward me. I looked away.

"Sandra, I'll be right down. I'm going to go clean up."

I strolled past him, giving him a sideways glance, and headed up the stairs.

"Don't take too long. I need you and Robert to set the table."

I had made it halfway up the stairs when I heard Sandra's request. "Shit!"

Minutes later, and with the horse smell tamed, I bounced down the stairs. I walked straight toward him. As I strutted past, I elbowed him squarely in the ribs. Maybe a bit of pain would convey the message I was upset. I turned toward Sandra and could see him watching me through squinted eyes. I ignored him. "Sandra, what table should I set?"

"I think the one under the patio cover, dear. Robert will help you."

I took a tray from the center lower cabinet and placed all the needed dinnerware on it. Hands full, I marched toward him and shoved the tray against his chest. "I'll get the door." With a flip of my hair I walked away. By the open door I stood with my arms crossed. The soft pat of my shoe tapped non-stop. "Well. Are you coming?"

~ *Robert* ~

A sweet muffled voice came from my mother as I grabbed the tray.

"Robert, play nice."

I sighed and raised an eyebrow, trying to figure out just what in the heck had I gotten myself into. All I knew was my mother was up to something. I gave her a scowl before turning toward the other woman I found myself pitted against.

Alone on the patio, no one spoke. I placed the tray on the cart across from the table while Belinda arranged the placemats. I picked up the plates and attempted to help as instructed, but approached with caution.

She wrapped her fingers around the edges and tried to take them. "I'll do this. I don't need your help."

My grip tightened around the plates. "No. We'll do this together."

We stood there in a non-verbal tug of war. She gritted her teeth as her grip tightened. I responded the same. After all, I was stronger and would win this battle. The sound of plate grinding against plate caused us to loosen up.

Her eyes rolled, and she let out a loud sigh. "Whatever." She released her hold as a low-pitched tone of the top plate cracking sliced through the air.

I gasped. "Oh shit! This is Mom's good stuff."

Belinda flapped her hands in front of her. "What can we do?" She took the broken plate. "Can you sneak in and get another one? I'll hide this and try to buy a new one tomorrow."

I nodded and started for the door just as Mom opened it for Dad, who carried another tray with the food. I swung around to shield her from their sight. I heard her lift the nearest patio chair cushion and shove the pieces under. She spun around and stood next to me.

There I stood, a man near thirty, acting like a kid who just got caught with his hand in the cookie jar.

~ Sandra ~

Something didn't feel right when I looked at my children. Robert stared back, just as Belinda clutched her wrist behind her and looked at her feet. If I didn't know better, the pair acted like two little kids who just got caught doing something naughty. I knew what his expression meant. It was his "I'm sorry. I didn't mean to do it" face. I hadn't seen that face in years and my heart warmed.

I looked at the stack of plates now sitting on the table. I counted three. "Where's the fourth plate?"

The pair shot repeated glances at each other. Belinda pursed her lips. Several seconds passed before Robert spoke up. "Ah, there's been a slight accident."

I crossed my arms, watching the interactions between the two.

They faced each other. "Go on. Show her."

Belinda reached under the cushion and pulled out the two halves of the plate.

I panned from Robert to Belinda as I scrunched my nose and shook my head. "I just bought those. I guess I'll go buy a few more before the sale runs out. I only paid a buck apiece for them."

Belinda elbowed Robert. "I thought these were her good stuff."

"I'm a guy. What do I know about dishes?"

I watch them stare at each other like two gunfighters about to have a shootout. He broke first and formed a crooked smile.

She gave him a wary stare and pushed out her lower lip, then let out a huff. A smile broke out across her face.

He pulled out her chair and gestured for her to sit. She made herself comfortable.

"Sandra. You know it's all his fault." Belinda pointed her thumb in Robert's direction.

"No, it wasn't!" His scoff exaggerated. "Mom, don't believe her." He took his seat beside her. "She's trouble."

~ Belinda ~

I snapped my head back to Robert. With an impish grin, I nodded. "Yes, it was. It's always the guy's fault. Don't you know that? So just apologize."

A muffled giggle from Sandra and a throaty chuckle from Rob distracted me, but I didn't take my glare off him. "Well. Go on. Apologize."

He exhaled and snickered out, "I'm sorry."

I shielded my mouth and leaned into Sandra as if I needed to tell her something in confidence. Of course, I didn't lower my voice. "It really wasn't entirely his fault, but we'll let him take the blame."

I heard a snorty laugh come from Robert. He just took a swig of his drink and found my antics comical enough to half choke.

Rob's perturbed expression spoke volumes as he busied himself mopping the droplets that flew from Robert's mouth onto the table. Sandra and I busted out in gut wrenching laughter. The two men followed, and the tension broke.

With food passed around the table, we fell into a comfortable conversation.

Robert and I ended the evening in the hot tub, drinking wine alone, because the older Pendletons decided they needed their rest.

CHAPTER 16

~ Belinda ~

FOR THE NEXT week, Sharyn made an appearance and, like magic, Robert disappeared.

I found myself amid helping Sandra plan the Pendletons' annual Fourth of July Party, along with my duties as assistant.

The phone started ringing the minute I entered the front door. I poured a cup of coffee and headed straight for the office. Sandra was already hard at work poring over some plans, ignoring the invasive ringing. I rushed to answer it.

"Good morning. Crescent Oaks Interior Design…"

Over her glasses rims, she peeked and mouthed, "Thank you."

I nodded. "Yes, how can I help you?"

We'd follow this work pattern for the next couple of weeks. Sandra worked nonstop wearing two hats: interior designer and event planner. I'd be her second hand.

She had hired someone to manage the preparations, but because of her need for perfection, my boss micro-managed until the scheduled date. The day of the party, the event became the responsibility of the party planner so she could enjoy her family, friends and guests.

About mid-morning, the phone calls died down. Sandra leaned back in her chair, stretched her arms and rotated her head with her eyes closed.

"Do you think you could give me more of your time for the next few weeks? I'm going to be pretty busy until after the party."

"How much time would you need?"

"I'll take every day, but if you can't, I'll take whatever you can spare."

"Weekends as well?"

She tightened her lips, causing them to form a thin line, and nodded. "But only if you can."

I studied her. I loved my job. She and Rob had been so generous, and I felt this was a way to give something back, to show I appreciated them. "I have some appointments and a week from this Saturday, we both need to be off."

Her head raised and tilted toward me.

"I'm planning a small housewarming dinner, and I expect you and Rob to attend."

She grinned. "Put the party and your appointments on my calendar. You can plan on us." No sooner had she finished the phone rang again.

The rest of the week was hectic. As promised, I increased my hours and achieved full-time-plus status.

On Friday, I had a date. Colin's plane landed at two in the afternoon. I had to admit, my butterflies did the opposite. They took flight.

At five o'clock sharp, I stood. "I'm leaving." I shut down the computer and picked up my bag. "Sandra. Why don't you stop and go enjoy the night with Rob? I'm sure he misses you."

"I'm sure he does, too." She studied the phone. "I miss him."

I walked over and stood behind her, placing my hands on her shoulders. "So stop working and go pay attention to your husband. We can pick up this in the morning."

Sandra took off her glasses and rubbed her eyes. Then she transferred the call to voicemail. "Great idea. I'm done for the night." With a smack of her hands on the desk, she stood. "What are you and Colin planning for the evening?"

"I have no clue. I'll leave that to him."

"Well, have fun," she encouraged as I left the room.

~ Sandra ~

My protégée vanished into the hall. I loved Colin like a son, but their relationship would fade away. I had to be patient.

Belinda didn't talk about him like most young women in love. She had a fondness for him, but I knew she wasn't in love with him. So when Colin made his move to Canada, she'd stay behind.

I went downstairs to find Rob sitting on the sofa with his bare feet propped up on the coffee table. I plopped down beside him and snuggled into his chest. He placed his arm around my shoulders and gave me a squeeze. "Finished for the night?"

"Mm-hmm."

"You hungry? I can make you a sandwich or a salad."

"I'd like a sandwich. I'll come with you. You know, watching you slaving in the kitchen always turns me on." I stroked his cheek.

He smiled, and our inner connection surged through me. I filled my lungs. His soft lips brushed my hand. The connection increased.

"Should we keep going?" I hiked a brow.

His lips were soft and warm. "What time should we expect, our son?"

"In about an hour." I took his cheeks in my hands. "Let's keep going." My lips covered his and for the next hour, we immersed ourselves in love.

~ Robert ~

I pulled out of the airport-parking garage after escorting Sharyn to the security check. She left on one of her two-week trips to Europe.

As I entered the Beltway 8, my gut jumped at the thought I'd see Belinda. With my parents' help, I'd been seeing more of her than I'd planned. At every turn, Mom had a reason to push us together, which made my resolution harder to keep.

An irrepressible urge grew the closer I came to the house. As I turned into the driveway, my heart plummeted. Her car wasn't there. Then I remembered, Colin was due back in town.

"That lucky dog."

Mom sat at the counter, mesmerized by my father's culinary technique. He had a knack for the dramatic and had transformed sandwich making into an art form.

"Hi, Sweetie. Did you get Sharyn to the airport all right?"

"Yep. I'll pick her up in two weeks." I approached the counter to observe my father's handiwork. "Is there enough for another one of those?" I picked at the sandwich fixings. "Mom, where's your adopted daughter?" I popped a slice of roast beef into my mouth.

She and Dad chuckled at my statement. "Out with my adopted son, Colin."

My face contorted. "Isn't that incest?"

Dad smirked. "I guess you can call it that."

"Rob." Mom squealed.

~ *Belinda* ~

Saturday morning, Sandra and I pushed to tie up some loose ends on a design project. We planned to take Sunday off. Colin left for Canada on Sunday afternoon and we had a breakfast date. Sandra wanted time to sleep late and be with Rob. Come Monday morning, the party planning became front and center. July fourth inched closer in front of our eyes.

My eyes grew tired from staring at the screen all morning. Closing them, I took a deep breath and rested my head in my palm. I lifted my eyelids and looked out the window.

Robert was standing with a hose, spraying down his beamer. My mouth fell open. He wore a pair of cut-offs, a snug t-shirt and flip-flops. My eyes stayed riveted on him as he moved from one side of the car to the next. Then, with circular motions, he used a soapy sponge to rub down the hood. The water-soaked t-shirt stuck to his chiseled chest like a second skin. My heart made somersaults on top of my desk, and my fantasies went from wild to erotic.

At this time of the year, the temperature easily rose to around ninety degrees by mid-morning. He hadn't worked too long before he threw the sponge in the bucket and stopped to peel off his t-shirt. Then he swiped that wet garment across his brow.

My belly seized when he looked at the window above my desk. A devilish grin spread across his face. Our gazes never faltered, and in slow motion, he rubbed the sweat from his chest with the t-shirt.

His perfect six-pack screamed at me. I wanted to rub my fingers over every inch of those taut muscles. I gasped a bit too loud.

"Are you all right over there?"

I never took my eyes off Robert. "I'm fine. Just taking a moment."

He again walked from side to side and front to back, rinsing the car. He paused and used the hose to douse himself.

My breathing increased, and I squirmed in the seat as the water rippled, causing his skin to glisten in the sun. My lips parted. *Oh. My. God.* Dream Robert never looked that good.

Once finished, he walked toward the pool. My mouth dried as he unbuttoned the shorts. Never breaking stride, he reached for the zipper next.

I stopped breathing.

When he reached the edge of the pool, he stopped. With his thumbs in the waistband, the flip-flops came off first. Just before pulling down the cut-offs, he looked up at me.

Our eyes locked. Taking in air became difficult. The blood in my ears pounded so loud it was all I heard.

He tilted his head and raised one corner of his mouth, giving me a sultry half-smile. He stripped off his cut-offs and exposed a pair of the snuggest excuse of male swimwear I had ever seen. When he straightened up, he looked down at himself, then back at me. A shit-eating grin smeared across his face. He was as excited as me. Before he dove into the water, he winked.

Air again gusted in. I stood from my desk. "I'm going to the restroom."

~ Sandra ~

"Okay." I watched her as she left the room and smiled to myself. She'll be in there for a bit.

Earlier that morning, I had pulled up the blinds knowing Robert always washed his car on Saturday mornings, followed by a quick dip in the pool. I gave her the excuse I was in the mood for more light, and from the way I'd watched Belinda squirm, my son had put on a good show. Whether Robert knew it, he played right into my plan. A plan that was easier to execute than I hoped. I could report to Rob. I did nothing to interfere. Unless, he considered, pulling up the blinds was meddling.

~ Belinda ~

Bright and early on Monday, I pulled into the Pendletons' driveway and glimpsed Beau grazing in the pasture. I stopped the car. His coat glistened in the morning sun and his methodical movements reminded me I had never painted his portrait. At least, if I did, I didn't remember. I decided to snap a few pictures of my darling horse after I parked.

A flash of red headed straight toward me and scared the crap out of me. I hit the gas to swerve back to the right side of the driveway.

Robert didn't slow down. The only acknowledgement of recognition he offered was an adjustment of his sunglasses as he passed.

The roadster slowed at the end of the drive, turned and faded out of view.

"What an arrogant ass." I parked the car in the usual spot. As I reached for my phone, it pinged a text alert. He has my number?

Robert:	You drive like an old woman.
Me:	You ass. You almost hit me.
Robert:	We don't drive on the left in the US. Remember?
Me:	Are you driving and texting?
Robert:	Hands free. You concerned?

I hesitated. I wasn't sure how to answer and then responded:
Yes!

I waited for a few seconds, hoping.

Robert: I'm glad.

I couldn't help myself and texted: Why???

He never answered.

"Robert, what are you trying to do to me?" My moment of wishful thinking dashed. I studied the phone, then let out a gush of air.

I hopped out and walked toward the pasture fence, armed with my phone set to camera mode. Beau lazily grazed until the snap of a twig sent a crisp crack through the air. I froze. He raised his majestic head but stayed put. So I shot away. "Thanks boy."

I made a quick stop at my car to collect my belongings and the dinner I made for tonight.

I walked into the kitchen balancing a pan of lasagna, salad fixings, and garlic bread.

Sandra sat at the kitchen table watching the juggling act. "What's all that?"

"Dinner for tonight."

"Dinner?"

"Yep. I decided I needed to contribute to the food supply around here. So from now on, every Monday I'll provide dinner."

It took a few minutes of rearranging, but I made room and stored my feast in the refrigerator. I poured a cup of coffee, then slipped into a chair across from Sandra and made myself comfortable.

"You don't—"

I held up a hand to stop her. "Yes, I do. This is one of my ground rules. It's right up there with the Beau rules. Okay?"

She nodded and pressed no further.

We faced another grueling workday. We ate lunch at our desks as we caught up with the design end of the business in between the Fourth of July party planning.

The day passed too fast. At five o'clock, Sandra threw her hands up. "Stop working. We're going to go eat your wonderful dinner and then relax by the pool with drinks."

The invitation to quit was all I needed to shut down the computer. I was more than ready.

I placed the lasagna into the oven to warm. Sandra volunteered to make the salads while I took a brief break to go visit my horse.

Armed with Beau's usual treat, I walked into the barn. "Hey, Beau, carrots?" I held out the morsels as the horse poked his head from his stall to retrieve them. "Thanks for standing still this morning."

I was stroking his nose when I felt the grip of arms around my waist and a simultaneous whisper in my ear. "Did you enjoy the view Saturday morning?"

The intruder nuzzled my hair. He was gentle, and I softened, molding myself to the strong, warm chest pressing against my back. It felt good, and I almost gave in. His phone interrupted our moment, reminding me he was engaged, and I was dating his best friend, but I still enjoyed the closeness.

I whirled around and poked a finger in his chest. "What do you want? And what do you think you're doing?" My face ran hot and my muscles tensed as I clenched my fists.

He poked at his phone, sending a text, most likely to Sharyn. "Just a sec."

I huffed and wanted to slap the stupid thing out of his hands.

"Okay." He slipped the phone back into his pocket. "What did you say?"

"Are you kidding me?" I thrust my hands onto my hips. "Do you always come up behind women and wrap your arms around them to ask a question?"

He shrugged his shoulders. "What?" He wasn't at all apologetic.

"Robert, you can be such an ass."

"Yeah. I've heard that occasionally."

"Did you forget about Sharyn?" I squared my shoulders. "And Colin?"

He stuffed his hands in his slacks pockets, then shuffled his foot in the dirt. "Mom sent me out to tell you the lasagna is ready to come out of the oven."

His attitude took me aback. Was he just going to change the subject?

I huffed past, but I couldn't get the picture of his body out of my head. In fact, no matter how I tried, he never left my thoughts. This Robert was more complicated and challenging. Not to mention a real jerk, because he set my insides on fire every time he came near me. How on earth could I maintain distance when just looking at him made me want to be with him?

Robert dropped back and followed behind me across the yard. Now and then, I glanced over my shoulder. His gaze appeared to have settled on my backside and brought a lopsided smile to his face.

I swung around and stopped. His face came within inches of mine. Puffs of his breath stroked my cheek. I fixed on his lips. I wanted them on mine. Then he reached for his phone and broke the spell. I turned to walk into the house but not before blurting out, "Such an ass."

∞

My adopted family, and I were well into the meal when Robert commented, "Mom, this is great lasagna. Is it a new recipe?"

"No, I didn't make it. Belinda did."

With a heaping helping of the Italian cuisine on his fork, he lifted it to me. "My compliments to the chef," and then mumbled, "My Baby Sister can cook, too."

I scrunched up my nose before mouthing, "Baby Sister?"

Robert shoved the lasagna into his mouth and ignored me.

For the next few days, the pace didn't let up. Sandra attended meetings with the party planner and multiple clients. I manned the office. We always mixed in some downtime, which shot my plan to leave before Robert came home.

I most cherished the time spent away from the office with the Pendletons. As soon as Sandra and I left the second floor and entered the kitchen, the mood changed. The Pendleton family worked hard and put the same effort into unwinding.

A pattern soon emerged. After each dinner, they would invite me to take a ride on the trails, sit in the hot tub, swim or watch a movie. All of which, of course, had Robert in attendance. He was off limits sexually because of our involvement with other people, but I found it stimulating and exciting to be so close.

I no longer saw him as the Robert of my dreams. He was very different, and I embraced him for who he was, not who I remembered.

The path of my grieving the loss of my imaginary husband was on track, according to Dr. Rosen. I always harbored just a pinch of hope that this Robert and I would find a life together, even if it meant just being friends. The more I got to know him, the more I knew friendship was all I could expect until his marriage yanked him away.

Saturday arrived and I'd only put in a few hours so I could finish my preparations. Everyone invited planned to attend. The group was small but manageable.

Mom and Dad arrived early to help. After our hello's, my father planted himself in front of the TV with the remote, surfing for any sports-related show. Mom and I agreed this was the best help he could give us—he was out of our way.

Since the increase in my work hours, Mom and I had little time to spend together. We talked every day, which kept her in the loop about the relationship I was forming with the Pendletons, including Robert. She never hesitated to remind me of her concern. Aware she didn't want to see me hurt again, I always reassured her I'd be careful.

We busied ourselves in the kitchen, arranging the appetizers and eating utensils on the island. Barbeque chicken was the main course, Mom's world-class potato salad, baked beans and tossed salad. She surprised me with dessert, a homemade apple pie and ice cream.

"Did everyone respond to your invitation?"

"Yep! Abby, of course, said yes right off the bat, just like you and Dad. Sandra confirmed again just before I left work this morning. I'll be the fifth wheel."

"Is Colin out of town again?"

I ripped open a container of chicken. "Yes, he is." I grabbed the pieces and placed them on a platter. The doorbell rang. Sticky goo covered my hands. "Can you get that for me, Mom?"

"Sure."

Abby and Garrett arrived with Zinfandel, and the energy level increased the second she entered the kitchen. "Wha'cha doin' in here?" She rested her chin on my shoulder.

"Getting the chicken ready for the grill." I leaned my head into hers. "I'm so glad to see you. Where's Garrett?"

"With your father." We giggled.

"Typical man. Sports win out over a hello."

"Hi, Belinda," came from the living room followed by a "Yes!" which was Garrett's reaction to something on TV.

Abby shook her head. "Men. You just gotta love 'em."

Mom opened a bottle and began filling glasses.

The chime of a doorbell alerted us to the last guests just as I finished washing my hands. "I got it."

I turned the corner into the foyer and planted a radiant smile on my face before opening the door. "Sandra, Rob, I'm so glad you could..." Sandra stepped aside to reveal a third person—Robert. I let out a shallow sigh. The sight of him stopped me cold.

He gave the back of his mother's head a wary look. "Mom, was I invited?"

She twisted around and patted his arm. "Not exactly, dear." She turned back and produced a sweet smile. "You don't mind that we brought him, do you? He would've been all alone tonight."

I took a deep breath under my faked smile. I knew they had been leaving us alone together. One night, the pair excused themselves about forty-five minutes into a movie. On another evening, Rob started yawning in the hot tub and got out to go to bed, with Sandra following.

Not that I minded the closeness to him. It forced me to see him as his own person, very different and yet similar to the Robert of my dreams. The biggest difference, this one had given a ring to someone else.

I looked at him. He shrugged and shook his head. I cast an eye over the small group and snickered. "No, I don't mind. There's plenty of food." With a step taken aside, I let the new arrivals in.

His expression flattened, and I saw him inhale, relieved. He entered and paused, muttering, "Sorry."

"Really, it's all right. I'm glad you're here." I closed the door and followed them into the living room.

The dinner party went rather well. The women talked and laughed and, of course, the men gathered around the TV watching one of the basketball playoffs hootin' and hollerin', except for Robert. He made an occasional visit to the men's side of the house, but most of the time he helped, taking on the role as…host.

He grabbed the chicken off the counter. "This ready for the grill?"

Before I could answer, he strode out the door, his steps wide and determined. All I could do was make sure he had what he needed to barbecue. I picked up the tray and followed him out.

"Okay, have you ever done this before?"

Robert opened his mouth, jerked his head back, and tsked. "Yeah! I do a fair job with a grill. Ye woman of little faith." He snapped the tongs inches from my nose.

"I was just checking. I've never seen you cook before."

"Just because I don't cook doesn't mean I can't." His gaze froze on mine.

Was that fear I saw? "Excuse me. Why did you say that?" His statement had a familiar ring. Dream Robert had used those very words.

"What?" He raised his shoulders and concentrated on the grill.

"Why did you use those words?" Another coincidence jumped on my pile.

He inhaled and didn't answer. He shifted his gaze around the patio. His lips tightened. "There just words."

"It's just I once knew someone who told me the same thing."

He swung his head in my direction. His jaw clenched.

This man had something he wasn't telling me.

He gulped in air and went back to brushing barbeque sauce on the grilling chicken. "I guess Mom and Dad have taught me a few things. I can manage in the kitchen if I need to, but I have Mom." He looked over at me and raised his brows several times. "They also didn't raise a fool. Mom likes to spoil me and I let her. It makes her feel good."

I scoffed and then scrutinized this man grilling away in front of me. Earlier in the kitchen, he and I worked side by side. We waltzed around each other in a synchronized rhythm. It seemed so natural having him in my home. It was as if he belonged there, and maybe he did.

Dinner was a great success. Everyone sat around the table socializing and laughing. Robert's chicken was a hit. It was moist and flavorful, smothered in his tangy red concoction, and blended with the rest of the meal. I'd glance at him while the group ate. A few times, our eyes met, sending a wave of jitters through me. I'd look away, hoping no one else at the table noticed.

After dinner, Robert stayed true to form. He assisted with clearing and putting away the food before he returned to the guests, who gathered on the covered patio. He made sure everyone's glass never went dry for the rest of the evening.

Around two a.m., Abby and Garrett left first. "Belinda, thank you. We had a great time. Now don't be a stranger." She latched onto Garrett's arm. As they walked down the sidewalk, she turned and placed her hand to her ear with a phone sign. "Call me."

"And you can do the same."

In the living room, Sandra and my mother said their goodbyes. Sandra scanned the kitchen. "There's still a lot of cleanup to do. It will be three before you're finished, my dear." Just about then, Robert walked past his mother. "Robert, why don't you stay and help Belinda finish up around here?" She didn't give him a chance to answer before she honed in on my mom. Not taking a breath, she placed a hand on my mother's arm.

"Could you drop us home and we'll leave the car for Robert?"

I caught my mom's look of concern. In a soft voice, I assured her, "That'll be fine."

Then she answered Sandra with a nod.

Once everyone left, Robert and I went to work clearing the mess. I finished by wiping off the counter.

~ *Robert* ~

I retrieved my wine glass from the island and wandered into the living room. In the quiet, this was the first time I'd admired Belinda and her mother's handiwork. "You did a good job on this place."

"Thank you. Your mother had her hand in it too."

I placed my drink on the coffee table. "I'll be right back." Down the hall, I was about to turn into the bathroom when I glanced to my left and noticed one of the posts of her bed. She was still in the kitchen, so I stopped at the threshold of the primary bedroom.

I envisioned the white pillows with her hair splayed across them, enticing me to sift my fingers through the long, golden-brown strands. We'd move as one with our mouths and hands, exploring each other's body in rhythmic motion. Then my mind messed with me. The profile of the man sharing her bed wasn't me, but Colin.

That sent a wave of jealousy racing up my spine. How many times had Colin, and she, entwined in the throes of passion in that bed?

I shut my eyes and clenched my teeth. Next, I pictured her straddling him, his roaming hands finding the sensitive regions of her body. Her head thrown back and mouth agape as she embraced the thrill of searching for her heightened pleasure, moaning.

The entire time, I wished I was the one with her.

Now with ragged breathing and the awareness that my arousal was in full effect, I fell against the doorjamb just as my phone gave off a vibration. I yanked it out of my pocket. Sharyn. She must be psychic. I hit decline while I backed away and proceeded to the bathroom.

After my prolonged stay, I returned to the great room. Belinda sat waiting on the couch. "More wine?" She raised the bottle to refill my glass.

"No, I'd better not."

I walked to the painting hanging on the far wall above the credenza and leaned in close. "I noticed this earlier, but didn't have a chance to really get a good look. Nice composition."

I started with the upper left corner and moved around the painted canvas, observing the forest scene with a path that led into the trees. At the lower left corner, I stopped and looked at the head and neck of a horse entering the picture, heading toward the woods. On the neck of the horse lay a dainty female hand. I straightened and studied the upper right-hand section and examined every detail of the entrance where a small silhouette of a man stood.

"Interesting painting." I studied the lower right corner where I saw the signature, Belinda, written in the script. I whipped around toward her. "You painted this?"

"Yeah. I started it before the accident and finished it recently."

More solemn, I turned back and ran a finger over two angel wings used as the dot over the "I" in the name. "Angel wings. Nice touch." Still studying, I read the title, "Remembering...." With my back to her, I remembered another life I'd never have again. I inhaled, then exhaled. "I need to go. It's late."

She walked me to the door and opened it, standing behind it with her shoulder pressed against the edge. "Thank you for all your help tonight." She glanced at the ground and then looked up through her lashes at me. "I...liked it."

I grabbed the edge of the door and peered down at her. Neither of us moved.

With all my heart, I wanted to take her in my arms. I'd worked at becoming an ass. It was all I came up with to keep things friendly, but I was losing. The more time I spent with her, the more I knew Sharyn wasn't the one for me.

I bent forward and kissed her on the forehead. "Good night, Baby Sister" was all I said, before turning to stroll away.

Halfway to the car, I almost turned around and went back. I knew if I did, Belinda would invite me in. Every inch of my being told me she wanted me as much as I wanted her. Then there was that deep feeling that rocked my soul that told me I knew her and she knew me.

The time I'd spent with her compounded my dilemma. I enjoyed being around her and fantasized about her. She dwelled in my thoughts. My only problem was what to do about Colin and Sharyn.

Neither Belinda nor Colin had said anything about her moving to Canada, a positive sign. But I couldn't bring myself to ask about his intentions. I knew my relationship with Sharyn was deteriorating because of my preoccupation with Belinda. Yet I didn't know how to end it with Sharyn without hurting her. She was in the throes of wedding planning, even though we hadn't set a date.

CHAPTER 17

~ Belinda ~

THE IRRITATING RING from the phone woke me up. The little, devious contraption had a mind of its own and shifted every time I fumbled for it.

"Hellloo." I drew the word out, still half asleep.

"Belinda, I'm sorry. I woke you up, but it's almost eleven." Perky Abby's voice chimed in on the other end.

I yawned. "Oh, hi. I didn't get to sleep until after four."

"What time did Robert leave?"

This was a great opportunity to jerk Abby's chain. "Oh, he's still here." I put my hand over my mouth to suppress the laughter.

Dead silence emanated from the other end of the phone—a first for Abby in the history of our relationship. A few seconds later, a quiet voice spoke up. "Should we hang up?"

I couldn't contain myself any longer and let out a soft giggle that grew into a robust, low laugh.

"He's not there, is he?"

I answered through brief spurts of muffled laughter. "No."

"You witch. Okay, what time did he leave?"

I got up and fixed myself a cup of coffee while I filled her in on all the miniscule and titillating details. I made myself comfortable on the couch because I knew this would take more than a few minutes.

"So you're telling me you're falling for this guy?"

"Ah, maybe. I…guess so. He's really nice." I blew on the hot liquid.

"And engaged, may I remind you?" Abby warned.

"Yeah, there's that minor problem." I took a quick sip.

"What about Colin?"

"I think when he moves, our relationship will change." I took a few more swallows.

"What do you mean?"

"We haven't talked about what will happen when he moves." I tucked my feet under me. "I think we'll just stay friends."

"Well, just be careful. I and a few other people don't want to see you hurt."

The conversation lasted for another hour before she hung up, citing grocery shopping and maybe a movie on the Barnett household agenda.

In the kitchen, I put my cup into the sink when the painting that interested Robert caught my attention. I walked over and stood in front of it to study it. My mind drifted to a life that became more and more a distant memory.

Heaviness filled me as I continued to my room and crawled back into bed. All I had were the toe-curling dreams of slumber. And since that was the only time I'd have his arms around me in the throes of passion, I prayed I'd dream.

After the dinner party, Robert hadn't attempted to be physically close to me, and that filled my every pore with disappointment. He made it a point to keep his distance despite his parents' meddling. I kept reminding myself I had no right to expect anything different. I also realized Colin would never graduate beyond friend status.

Anytime I was around Robert, my emotions sent me into a whirl. My attraction to him sent shivers and goosebumps skittering over my whole body. He was off limits, and my only option was to work on our friendship.

Rob and Sandra didn't help. They continued to leave me alone with their son. Most parents try to keep their children at a socially acceptable distance. Not those two, and their interference made my life more difficult.

Despite their continued pushing, Robert amazed me. He was funny and smart, and also kind and gentle. The only major flaw he had, Sharyn, and that was something I had no control over.

For now, I'd enjoy his company and take every moment I could steal from her.

However, was I becoming the other woman?

The week flew by. Sharyn had planned to return on Saturday morning, taking Robert away for however long she remained in town. But knowing he'd be at home during Sharyn's absences made my heart throb and gave me something to look forward to.

Texting became part of our routine. He started when he turned off Highway 6 and would give me a blow-by-blow account of just how far he was from the house, using hands free. When he drove into view, he'd park the car and send the last text. Like magic, he'd emerge from his car outside my desk window and look straight at me, sporting his signature smile. My gut would tighten and my heart jumped out of my chest to do a happy dance.

Thursday night, Monster stirred more and more. She woke up as I dreamt of Sharyn and Robert together. I tossed and turned because my mind wouldn't release me from the visions I replayed in a deep sleep.

Dreams haunted me of him placing a hand on either side of Sharyn's head. Her breaths would intensify with each soft kiss to her lips, neck, belly, and beyond. Visions of Robert on top moving in a steady motion as his breath quickened. Him looking down at her with softened eyes just before....

Night after night, I'd cry, agonized and tormented. "That should be me with him."

Why am I doing this to myself?

On Friday, the day before Sharyn's arrival home, I kept myself in a miserable state. I felt worn down by the conflict between my dreams and the knowledge that her presence would keep him away.

The plan for this evening included a mix of some serious hot tub time and wine. Of course, I fully expected Sandra and Rob to bow out of the activities, leaving me alone with Robert. After tonight, I expected nothing, until Sharyn flew off again on her broom to France. I couldn't wait.

We finished dinner late. Rob yawned, and that meant one thing. The older Pendletons were on their way to the bedroom.

"Mom, you and Dad can go to bed. Belinda and I got this." Robert picked up a few glasses before he turned toward me and rolled his eyes.

He cleared the table while I filled the dishwasher.

~ *Robert* ~

The last plate found the dishwasher. I leaned against the counter and watched Belinda. She was the most graceful and beautiful woman I'd ever met. I enjoyed how she made the simple task of rinsing dishes seem like performing a ballet and could stand there to be with her all night. "I'm going to miss this."

"I will too." She dried her hands, then folded the dishtowel and laid it on the counter. "I'll go change and meet you outside."

I ran to my place as fast as I could, stripped off my clothes and pulled on my trunks. Then I rushed to make it to the hot tub first. I set the mood by dimming the lights and placed lit candles around the hot tub to increase the ambiance.

With my aim complete, I stepped into the bubbling water, positioning myself so I could watch her come out of the house. I liked the way the light played off her skin. It gave her an alluring glow I knew I'd never tire of seeing.

Belinda walked out in a form-fitting, teal, two-piece suit that showcased her assets. Boy, was I glad to be seated in chest high water.

She carried a bottle of wine and two glasses. The dim light caused her to stop and take notice. Our eyes met and locked. She tilted her head and exaggerated her walk, swinging her hips as she sashayed toward me. The closer she came, the broader the smile stretched across my face.

The warm water relaxed me, washing away the tensions of the week...and the bulge in my swim trunks. As we sipped wine, we talked and laughed.

I was going to miss her. But this week, I had to be fair to Sharyn and break it off. But how?

Belinda captivated me. Her eyes sparkled and danced as her hands gracefully gestured. Her cute giggle touched my heart. At one point when she tossed her head back in laughter, exposing her slender neck, it was all I could do to control my urge to envelop her in my arms.

I imagined skimming feathery kisses up the appealing flesh and across her delicate jaw. Her sweet lips beckoned, teasing me to savor every precious second they met mine.

~ Belinda ~

I cocked my head and smiled. "What are you thinking about? You have this…look on your face."

He just made a half grin with his enticing lips. "Oh, nothing. Just enjoying the evening."

While Robert talked, I remembered how much I enjoyed listening to Dream Robert. Cuddled up in his warm, secure arms, I imagined doing the same with this one. Robert's voice and actions made me comfortable, like I'd known him forever.

I focused on his mouth and recalled our passionate kisses. His warm, moist, soft lips pressed hard against mine and how he made me feel all tingly and hot inside. I ran my tongue over my lips, moistening them, and then bit the lower one.

Oh, how I wished I could inch closer, if only to brush against his arm to feel the stir within. But that meant asking for trouble. Instead, I wrapped my fingers over the edge of the hot tub, gripping it tight. I didn't know if I'd be able to restrain my desires. I wanted to feel my desperate mouth against his, tongues tasting, teasing, and to have his muscular arms wrapped around me pressed in his warmth.

Our excited bodies together.

I was going to miss him, even if it was only for a week. I had to straighten things out with Colin. But how?

~ Sharyn ~

Missing Robert was the excuse I told myself about why I came home a day early. But deep down, a nagging feeling hovered that something wasn't right between us. Ever since his parents' New Year's party, he'd been acting different. I knew it wasn't my imagination.

He made excuses all the time for us to not make love. I'd caught him staring off into space. Now, he wasn't taking all my calls. More and more often, most of them were going to voice mail and not returned. His excuse—"I was busy" or "I forgot." Or was Ms. Angel Scent keeping him occupied?

I made my first call on the plane after landing and then in the airport and again when I arrived home, but got the usual. "Leave a message."

I needed to know and surprise him at his place. Besides, if Angel Scent was with him, he'd spend the evening with me, even if it was out of obligation. I was sure I'd take his mind off her after a few glasses of wine and hot tub action. I wouldn't give in to his excuses. Not tonight. To get him in more of a mood, I armed myself in my new sexy bikini and sheer cover-up.

I pulled into the Pendletons' driveway and parked. With one last look in the visor mirror, I primped to make sure my make-up and hair were perfect. As I headed toward Robert's residence, a strange car parked next to his came into view. *Belinda's*?

The hair on the back of my neck stood up. "Shit! Angel Scent is here." Heat ran up my neck. "I knew he was up to something."

His place was dark. Muffled voices followed by laughter caused my skin to heat. I snapped my head in the pool's direction. I clenched my fists, digging nails into my palms. My breathing shortened with every exchange of laughter that filled the air.

At first, my strides were wide, but they slowed as the romantic setting of the pool area came into sight. The flicker of candles seemed to be concentrated around the hot tub. I made sure I stayed in the shadows until I was ready to make my move.

The tall hedge alongside the pool obstructed me from view, but I could hear plenty. The soft cooing laughter and the high-pitched ping of glass set on the stone deck around the tub told me what was going on.

The familiar voice saying Robert's name made my blood boil. "You bitch. He's my fiancé and I'm not letting him go." I paused. Maybe it's time for a little Robert mini-me to enter the picture. He'd do the right thing and marry me.

I splayed my fingers and concentrated on my breathing to force myself to calm down. Dropping my arms to my sides, I shook them to further relax, as a prizefighter might who was preparing to go into the ring. I took one last deep breath, stepped onto the pool deck and then removed my cover-up, dragging it along, hooked on one finger.

Belinda came into view first with her head tossed back in laughter over something Robert just said. I drew in slow, steady breaths and narrowed my eyes. "Bitch." I could only see the back of his head, but his laughter indicated a huge smile. My chest rose and fell with each deep breath as I slinked toward them. "What's going on?"

Robert jerked his head around, the smile visibly slipped away. "Nothing. Just visiting." Yellow feathers almost fell from his mouth.

I kneeled down beside him, my crotch in his full view, covered by one of three tiny, hot pink patches of fabric held together with a few strings.

"Mind if I join you?"

"Ah, no. Not at all. What are you doing back early? I thought you were coming home tomorrow." His voice cracked.

"I missed you."

And I needed to catch you, just like I did.

I shifted my weight to rest on my hip and then laced my fingers in his hair to pull him within inches of my bustline. This simple act would keep any red-blooded male's attention on me, and Robert was all male. I planted my lips and pushed my tongue into his mouth. After a few seconds, I withdrew, pleased that Robert didn't break our contact.

I slid into the hot tub. Before I straddled him, I glared at Angel Scent. Hands off, Bitch. My attention again focused on my fiancé. I wrapped my arms around his neck and covered his lips with mine.

~ *Belinda* ~

Heat surged through every inch of my body. With flared nostrils, Monster stood up on her hind legs. Smoke puffs emerged.

My mouth fell open. I couldn't believe the nerve of Sharyn, barging in unannounced, unexpected and flaunting her body in that sorry excuse for a swimsuit. She might as well have come naked. How dare she ruin my evening with Robert? This was supposed to be our time before she parked her broom back in his life.

I wanted to yank her off him, but I had no right. He was engaged to her and off limits.

In the middle of the kiss, he glanced up at me. He grabbed Sharyn's shoulders and pulled her away. "Wouldn't you be more comfortable sitting beside me?"

She let out a stupid, mean-girl giggle. "No. I'm very comfortable right here." She kissed his cheek and ground her hips.

"It's getting late. I'd better be heading home." I gave them a sliver of a smile and, without thinking, said, "Have a good evening," and climbed out.

I turned back and watched Sharyn reposition herself, giving her hips another rotation, as she emphasized, "Oh, we will." She ran her hands up his neck and plunged her lips to his, not giving him a chance to say good night. What I noticed, he appeared to restrain himself.

She was really working the hip grinding. Nope, it was only a matter of time before he gave in.

The image made me cringe as I hurried toward the house. Sharyn in her skimpy excuse for a bathing suit. Their lips crushed together in passionate kisses. Their hands groping at each other, out-of-control emotions and reactions…. I shook my head. Tears of anger, jealousy, and hurt welled.

"You leaving so soon?"

In the kitchen, Sandra's voice made me jump. "He has company." I sniffled.

"What?" She walked to the window and peered out. "What's she doing here? She wasn't supposed to get back 'til tomorrow."

"She said she missed him." I kept my eyes down to hold back the moisture welling in them. "I'm dripping wet and need to change." Tears flowed as I turned and ran up the stairs.

~ *Sandra* ~

My future daughter-in-law disappeared from view. I didn't know if I should go after her or leave things alone, but one thing I knew for sure, Belinda had feelings for Robert.

I decided my son needed another gentle push. I could see how close he and Belinda had grown in the past few weeks. His attitude changed in her presence. She was the one for him. Not Sharyn.

I stormed into the bedroom.

Rob was lying in bed reading. He looked up over the rim of his glasses. "What's going on?"

"I'm changing." I was on a mission and hurried past in a huff before I entered the closet.

On the way back, I stopped at the foot of the bed, dressed in my bathing suit. "I'll be in the hot tub."

Rob raised a brow. "Aren't our kids in there?"

"No, Sharyn is! Care to join us?"

"Uh. No thanks. I'll just leave the meddling up to you. Well, have fun." He repositioned his glasses and returned to his book.

"Is that all you have to say?"

He didn't look at me. "I'm sure you'll handle it, Dear."

"Unbelievable."

"Fill me in when you get back. I'll be right here."

"I could use your help."

"Nope."

I huffed and left.

The drone of the bubbles and the two entwined bodies engrossed in a kiss helped ensure my silent approach. Neither Robert nor Sharyn noticed. At the edge of the tub, I hesitated and then stepped in. I seated myself until the water covered me up to my shoulders.

I sat, glaring at Sharyn's back. The shadows cast on her face by the flicker of the candlelight didn't soften her features. They accentuated her nose and gave it a hooked, witchy appearance. I stretched out my arms and rested them on the sides of the hot tub.

It was bad enough seeing her wrapped around my son, sucking his face, but when she started doing unlady-like hip movements on his lap...Oh God, strike me blind. That was it—I cleared my throat, loud enough to reach over the sound of the soothing bubbles.

Yep, this witch needs to go.

~ *Robert* ~

The familiar throaty sound shot through my ears. My eyes popped wide at the sight of my mother glaring at me from across the steamy water. Her expression flashed from perturbed to devilish.

Without hesitation, I grabbed Sharyn around the waist and jerked her off my lap. Her legs came out of the water in a circular motion until she landed next to me.

"What did you do that for?" she shouted, before she noticed Mom sitting across from us with an impish grin plastered across her face. "Sandra. When did you get here?"

"Well hello, Sharyn. We didn't expect you back until tomorrow. I'm sure you don't mind if I join you?"

"No, not at all." She scrunched her nose.

I kept my mouth shut. This was one conversation I had no business getting in the middle of.

~ *Belinda* ~

I changed in the dark so I could spy on the hot-tub drama from the window above my desk.

When Sharyn's legs flew out of the water, I covered my mouth to restrain my laughter. Sandra was sure gutsy. I admired that woman.

But Robert's reaction to his mother's presence was priceless and put me in stitches. I laughed so hard I had to support myself against the desk.

"You go, girl."

~ Robert ~

We all sat in silence. Sharyn nudged me. I figured she wanted to leave, but I didn't move. I sat with my arms stretched out, resting on the edge of the hot tub, giving my body time to recover.

Hell, I'm a normal male with normal responses. Sharyn just wasn't the woman I wanted my body responding to.

I rolled my head back and to the side. Out of the corner of my eye, I detected movement by the cars. I adjusted my view and saw Belinda standing by her car. She swiped her cheek with the back of her hand and then disappeared as she slipped into the driver's seat and left.

A pang of regret pierced my sinking heart, because I wished she was still beside me. I nudged Sharyn. "I'm ready to go."

When I tried to stand, my head spun. I grabbed the edge of the tub to brace myself.

"Are you okay?" Mom leaned forward.

"I'll be fine. I just need a sec." I looked at the empty wine bottle Belinda and I finished.

Sharyn had already hopped out. "Are you coming?" she demanded.

The wave passed. I stepped out, grabbed my towel, and wrapped it around my waist.

"Good night, Mom."

My mother flashed a smirk. "Good night, Son." She stuck her nose in the air. "Good bye, Sharyn."

Sharyn didn't respond. She wrapped her hand around mine and pulled me toward the guest house.

The second inside, she threw our towels to the side, and she was all over me. Her hands went everywhere. When she reached for my crotch, I gripped her wrist and shook my head. "Stop."

She wiggled free and rubbed my abs. "Why?" She stuck out her lower lip and gave me a sad look. Then she brushed her breasts against my upper arm.

I felt a twitch in my trunks. I had a tough night ahead of me.

~ Sharyn ~

Once at Robert's place, behind a secured door, I continued my pursuit.

"Sharyn, I'm tired."

Oh, no you don't. I had to work fast to get my way. I hurried to the cabinet that housed the highball glasses and reached on my tiptoes. "Can you help? I can't reach."

He huffed, but came behind me to remove the glasses from the upper shelf.

"Get two down."

While sandwiched between his warm body and the counter, I took advantage of his closeness and gave my ass a few rotations against him. His body responded.

"I think I've had enough alcohol for one night."

"Please. Just have one with me." By this time, I had turned to face him. His warm breath caressed my hair. I pressed into him, moving my hips. "Grab the scotch." I brushed my lips against his skin and then kissed his chest. His body responded as I hoped.

He placed the glasses on the counter, then backed away.

I wrapped my arms around him and snuggled against his chest. "Pour us a glass."

He did as I requested.

"Cheers." We clinked and downed our drinks.

"Let's have another."

His eyes hooded. "Sharyn. I need to go to bed."

"Just one more."

He pursed his lips but poured two more.

He liked scotch and downed his second drink. These mixed with the wine gave me the advantage I needed. He'd be mine tonight.

This time I poured and filled the glasses with extra. "Last one. I promise."

He took the glass and slugged it down.

I rubbed against him and let my hands wander. This time, he didn't protest and became more pliable. I took hold of his hand and walked backward as I led him into the bedroom. I reached behind my back and released the ties on the bikini—first the top fell and next the bottom. With his calves against the bed, I pulled his trunks off. Once they hit the floor, I pushed him. He fell like a tree trunk across the bed.

"Don't fall asleep. I'll be right back." I pointed to the bathroom.

Robert closed his eyes. "Okay."

Please. Don't fall asleep. I have plans for you tonight.

I crawled into bed and snuggled against his warm back. "Robert." No response. I lifted on my elbow to reach his ear and nibbled. "Robert." Again, no response. I shook his shoulder. Nothing.

I'd miscalculated and fed him too much scotch.

"Shit!"

All I could do was go to sleep.

In the middle of the night, a hand groped my breast and then my thigh. I turned onto my back. Robert pulled himself on top of me.

"Robert."

His eyes remained closed. He didn't respond. He was still asleep. The details didn't matter. Tonight was a good night to get pregnant and I encouraged him on.

Our breathing became fast and hard as we kissed each other with feverish zeal. His hands roamed every inch of my body. I wrapped my legs around his waist to encourage him. We began a rhythmic dance that took us to another place. He had never made love so wildly to me like this before.

With his mouth next to my ear, he moaned, "Belinda."

CHAPTER 18

~ Sharyn ~

I SAT AT the table with a cup of steaming coffee, fiddling with the two-carat solitaire engagement ring on my finger. Robert lay fast asleep in the next room, most likely with a good hangover which I hoped made him miserable all day.

Because of what had happened last night, I knew I wasn't crazy. He confirmed that when he called me Belinda just before he climax in his sleep. I took a sip of coffee and contemplated just what I should do about the bothersome other woman. She had infringed on my territory, and I had to stop her.

A shuffle up the hall toward the kitchen told me my cheating fiancé was up. He walked in dressed in jeans and a t-shirt.

"Hi, Sweetie. You're up early." He bent to give me a kiss on the cheek and then went to make himself a cup of coffee. After popping a cup into the coffeemaker, he hit the brew button.

He opened a cabinet door and pulled out a medicine bottle. "Is there any orange juice left? He poked around in the frig.

I smirked, Good. The bastard has a headache. "Why are you dressed?"

He walked over to the window. "I promised Mom I'd feed the horses." He popped the pills and followed them with a swig of OJ right from the bottle.

I watched his gaze follow as a CR-V pulled in and parked in the driveway right in front of the window. I recognized my nemesis' car.

My blood started a slow simmer. I clenched my jaw but was too much of a lady to start a rant.

I rose from my chair and approached my man with the stealth of a cat. In one fluid motion, I clutched the end of my t-shirt, lifting it over my head and tossing it on the floor, exposing my naked form.

I stood behind Robert. He was too busy watching out the window to notice. I never faltered. I moved my hands around his hips and teased his navel, my bare breasts rubbing against his back.

Robert's breath hitched, and his muscles tensed. He grabbed my wrists and pulled me off of him. "I'm going to feed the horses." He released my hands and turned toward me. "Besides." He massaged his temples. "I have a splitting headache."

He started for the door.

"Don't you want your coffee?" I bent down to pick up the t-shirt.

"I'll get some at Mom's."

He never looked at me. I'm naked, for heaven sake.

I watched him sprint across the yard to catch up to Belinda. His mood changed, and he sported a huge smile when he turned at the back door to open it for her.

"This means war, bitch." I saw red until I shifted my mood and smiled. After all, I got what I wanted last night.

~ *Robert* ~

I held the back door open for Belinda. As she passed, the air filled with Angel Scent. Guilt washed over me. The dream I had about Belinda and I making love last night felt so real, and I couldn't get it out of my head. Oh, my splitting head.

"Would you like some coffee?" She walked straight to the coffee brewer.

"Yes." I took a seat at the table and cradled my head.

A cup of coffee came into view. "Thanks."

"Rough night?"

She took a seat across from me as I peeked through splayed fingers. "Too much drink."

"The wine?"

I shook my head. "Scotch. Sharyn wanted a few drinks, so I joined her."

"Do you need some pain pills or orange juice?"

"Took some Tylenol. OJ would be good." I rubbed my face and then tipped my head back to get the last bit of OJ just as Sharyn walked in. Great. I didn't want to deal with her until the pills kicked in.

She sported a broad smile. "I thought you had to feed the horses." She slammed the door.

Pain shot through my head. "I'm just getting ready to do that." The glass clunked against the table. I glanced at Belinda, who gripped her mug and lowered her eyes.

Sharyn placed her elbows on the table and rested her chin on her hands. Her icy glare meant one thing. She was pissed about something, but what?
I didn't know.

I ran through what happened after I hit the bed. Nothing. I fell asleep. Nothing happened. Maybe that's why she's pissed, but I was glad.

She slapped her hands on the table. "Well. Don't you have horses to feed?" Her brow arched.

I back glared at her. My head throbbed too much for this drama. Yet, how could I leave Belinda alone with her?

A high pitched, "Good morning," blurted out of my mother's mouth as she entered the kitchen. She stopped in mid stride. "Robert, are you okay?"

Thank God. I was never so grateful to see her. She would keep Belinda out of the lioness' claws. "I'm fine. Just wanted a cup of coffee before feeding the horses."

"Don't be too long. I have lots for you to do today." She lifted her cup to her mouth for a sip.

Before I got up to leave, the tension between Sharyn and Belinda became so thick a knife couldn't cut it. I saw the reality of the situation. Here were two very different women. One I was engaged to. The other was off limits.

I downed the last bit of coffee before placing the cup in the sink. "I'll be in the barn."

The Tylenol kicked in with each stride I made across the yard. My head filled with thoughts of the two women I just left in the kitchen.

Sharyn, well, she cared about me. I liked that but realized something else seemed missing—the closeness I'd seen and felt between my parents throughout the years wasn't there. Although we had a decent relationship, I realized I wasn't in love with her.

My thoughts turned to Belinda. Oh, sweet Belinda. She was such a beautiful, gentle creature who left me breathless with a single touch of her soft skin. And when we kissed…my world turned upside down. In the past few weeks, I had grown closer and more comfortable around her naturally—as though I were home. Our movements around one another reminded me of my parents, which brought a smile to my face. When I was with her, I felt a missing part of me fall into place. She was an intelligent woman with a good sense of humor and someone I wanted more than as a friend.

I knew I was in love with Belinda but didn't know how to end it with Sharyn. Biding my time, I prayed somehow, this week, a situation would arise to make a clean break.

~ *Belinda* ~

I reported to work on Monday. Robert's and Sharyn's cars were gone. I accepted my fate for now and would bide my time. Once she left on her next business trip, I planned to take a gigantic leap and reveal my feelings to Robert. I knew I was taking the risk of becoming "the other woman." If he didn't reciprocate, I'd need hours of therapy with Dr. Rosen, along with putting my job in jeopardy. But I'd take the chance because I knew I loved him.

The workweek began with a roar as workmen, housekeepers, landscapers, chefs and tent builders swarmed the estate. To an outsider, it would've appeared as pure chaos, but right in the middle and at the helm stood Sandra. She was the conductor of her own symphony with every point of her finger. She amazed me, and I admired the grace with which she managed every detail.

My prime responsibility became manning the phone and fielding the calls. When something came in that needed Sandra's immediate attention, I would place the call on hold and text her cell. She would then text back a response or take the call. The system worked and allowed the uninterrupted party orchestration to continue.

I watched Robert arrive home around four o'clock. I fully expected Sharyn to follow. That never happened. At five p.m., I switched the office line to "Do Not Disturb" and went to the kitchen. The caterers had prepared plates of food before they left. Sandra, Rob, and Robert gathered in the kitchen, each taking a meal. Sharyn was nowhere in sight. This puzzled me, but I picked up the last plate and joined the trio at the table.

Sandra wasted no time in laying out everyone's duties after work for the rest of the week. "I'm going to have Sharyn running around this week after work, picking up the things we'll need for the party. In fact, that's exactly what she's doing now, so she won't be joining us for dinner. I suspect she'll be busy shopping until the stores close." She dabbed at her mouth with a napkin.

"You two will clean out the barn." She pointed a finger at Robert and me. "In the past, Robert had the job all by himself." She smiled at him. "So having you help him will be an added plus."

Sandra locked her eyes on mine until they grabbed my soul.

I stared back, mesmerized, and heard, "Enjoy your gift of time with him." A chill ran through me. Her lips never moved. Sandra turned away, and the voice vanished.

Not sure what I just experienced, I answered, "Okay."

"Good, now finish eating. The barn needs lots of attention."

Robert and I walked to the barn in silence. Grateful for the unexpected time, I felt in my heart I should say something, but how do I tell a man I love him without acting like a complete fool? So I kept it to myself and waited for a better time.

At the barn entrance, he explained the task. "We have to clear everything out and hose down the place."

"What do you mean, hose it down?"

"Just that. When I was doing this by myself, I'd start with the tack room. Clear it out, then hose it down. Then I'd oil all the leather and clean all the metal. The next day, I'd put everything back. Then I'd start out here, one stall at a time, until I was done. The outside is the last part."

My mouth dropped open as I scanned the barn. "That's a lot of work for one person."

"It usually took me two weeks after work in the evenings. I was wondering when Mom was going to tell me to get started." He folded his arms across his chest. "I guess she figured with the two of us on it, a week was enough time."

"Well, you seem to have a plan, so where do you want the tack once it's hauled out?" I scrutinized the area, hands on hips.

His face lit up. He bowed at the waist and stretched out his arm to his side. "This way, my lady, please follow me."

I giggled and curtsied back before I followed him.

We worked for an hour without saying a word until we had emptied the room, and all the equine equipment lay strewn over the rest of the barn. He disappeared outside, leaving me waiting in the tack room's doorway. When he returned, he held a water hose ready to discharge a force strong enough to remove a year's worth of grime.

"You better get out of the way. This can get messy." He stepped in front of me and turned the hose on full blast.

I backed away and sat on a hay bale just outside the room. A fine mist filtered out of the doorway. It felt good and, because I had worked up a sweat, it cooled me down.

The over spray soon soaked his t-shirt and made it cling to his hard body. I surveyed every ripple of his back muscles as he worked his way around the room. Although I wouldn't have minded seeing his smooth, taut, muscled chest glistening from the water dripping off, I prayed he wouldn't take off the t-shirt. That would be more than I wanted to handle.

His back was still toward me when he turned the hose on himself. My breath hitched. I fought the impulse to jump him.

I imagined rubbing my hands across his broad shoulders, but I controlled myself by grabbing the wires of the hay bale. When he turned off the water, he rubbed his hands over his face and through his hair, sending excess droplets flying. He looked over at me and flashed an enormous smile. "Ready for phase two?"

I held my breath and nodded.

With saddle soap cans and rags, we worked on every piece of leather we could find.

I buffed the last saddle. During a period of deep thought, before I could stop, "Why are you with her?" escaped my mouth. I froze after hearing the words and lifted my head to watch him.

He ceased polishing the bridle but didn't raise his head. He responded with a hint of uncertainty in his voice. "I love her?" He offered no other explanation as he went back to work.

"Oh." My bad. I'd put us in an awkward position. I changed the subject. "Will you be glad when the party is over?" I could see his body relax.

He concentrated on the bridle. "Yeah, but it's not that bad. This year there's more planning because we'll have more guests. As for the barn cleaning, it would have to be done, anyway."

I didn't get to respond. The witch walked in.

"Robert! There you are. Are you almost finished?" Sharyn headed right for him and then entwined her fingers in his hair and held him so he'd look up at her. She bent down to kiss him, but he dropped the bridle and grabbed her wrists to make her release his hair, then stood.

He looked my way. "We can finish this tomorrow. It's getting late."

"You go on. I want to finish," I answered in a sharp tone, not wanting to keep him from the clutches of the woman he loved. He seemed a tad eager to leave, and I didn't want to stand in his way.

"Will you be all right?"

My stare snagged his. "Of course I will." With more sessions with Doc Rosen, but do you care? You're in love. In a huff, I picked up my rag and a bridle, applying the saddle soap with more zeal than I intended.

A quick glance toward the door revealed Sharyn's glare over her shoulder. Her face sported a smug smile that faded into the darkness as they walked out. I threw my rag across the floor, almost panting from my chest tightening with rage. "That witch!"

The next day, I had time to think in between the phone calls. I slumped over my desk. The smooth eraser tip hit my lip as I flicked a pencil between my fingers.

The way I saw it, I could be mad at Robert, or I could make the most of my time with him. He was engaged but not married, and until he slipped a wedding band on her finger, I still had a chance. As far as I knew, there was no wedding date.

So for the next week, I'd be as pleasant as I could. Until she showed up in the evening to steal him away, leaving me with nothing but my green-eyed monster to keep me company.

~ *Sandra* ~

I completed my job on Friday evening by turning everything over to the party planner. I sat on the patio enjoying the serenity. All the people who had blustered around all week were gone. On Saturday morning, I planned to retreat to the privacy of my bedroom. I'd have my meals delivered while I relaxed, reading until time to get ready to receive my guests.

I heard the French door open and hoped it was Belinda. I hadn't thanked her for all her hard work, but hadn't seen her for the past three hours. I wondered if she'd left without saying goodbye.

"Excuse me, Sandra. Is there anything else I can do before I leave?"

I never opened my eyes while I laid on the lounge chair. "Yes, bring out two glasses of wine and come join me."

I heard the clatter of the glasses as she placed them on the table between the chairs. I let out a sigh. "Sit down and make yourself comfortable. I'm glad this week is over." I held my hand out toward her and she latched on. "Thanks for all your help."

"You're welcome. I'm glad I was useful."

"You two did a great job in the barn. I was out there this morning. I don't know why, but eventually, most of our guests end up taking a walk through there. It never fails." I placed a sliver of a smile across my face as I released my grip. "Where's my glass? I'm in need of an adult beverage."

CHAPTER 19

~ Belinda ~

CLOTHES LAY STREWN all over my bed. I had given little thought to my outfit because I'd been so busy this past week. Nothing I tried on seemed to have the "wow" factor. Although I would attend the party with Colin, it was Robert I really wanted to impress. I stared at my reflection. I was turning into the other woman.

Fine beads of sweat formed on my brow. I looked at the clock and calculated how much time I had left before Colin's arrival. Three hours. I scurried into the kitchen and dragged my purse off the counter along with my keys. The door of my car shut, and I drove to the mall.

I returned satisfied I had found the perfect outfit. One hour remained for me to do everything needed for the date. So I hurried, feeling guilty my efforts weren't for the man who'd be accompanying me.

The doorbell rang as I put the finishing touches on my ponytail. I flung the door open and immediately knew I had accomplished my goal by Colin's expression. The outfit worked its magic. He stood there with a huge smile, giving me the once-over from my head to my toes. "You look fantastic."

"Thank you. I'm glad you like it." Pressed for time, I grabbed my purse off the hall table and walked straight out the door. As I passed by Colin, I gave him a quick kiss. I couldn't chance him wanting more. "We better hurry or we might be late."

~ Robert ~

I patrolled the pool area, greeting the guests as they entered. Sharyn hadn't arrived yet, but when she did, she'd join me at my side. She was still in the guesthouse, dressing and running late, as usual.

I had just finished welcoming one of the new arrivals when I saw Colin walk around and open the door of his car. A beige and black, patent leather clad foot emerged. Then the other appeared on the ground. I held my breath. When Belinda stood, I thought I'd die. She wore a skimpy camisole. The skirt came to mid-thigh, which exaggerated the length of her legs in those heels. With her tanned skin, she looked so damn sexy. She wore her hair up in a ponytail that swayed back and forth, keeping rhythm to the bounce of every step she took.

Still captivated by the sight, I heard someone clear his throat. I glanced to my side and saw one of my clients grinning from ear to ear.

He pulled close and whispered, "I'd be staring myself if my wife wasn't with me, but all I can do is sneak a peek." His head tilted in Belinda's direction. "That one's a looker."

Had I been that obvious? I would have to watch myself. "Yes, she is." The two of us snuck a long peek in Belinda's direction before he introduced his wife.

I needed to stop staring so Colin wouldn't notice anything out of the ordinary. Up to now, I had done nothing other than kiss the girl my friend was dating, but that offense seemed bad enough. I swore after the last time, I would never cross that line again because of my friendship with him.

I had respected that boundary, despite growing closer to Belinda. But because of the way she looked tonight, I was on the verge of losing my fight. I could only study her with fleeting glances, when I really wanted to stare at her and watch her every move.

I jerked from the guy-like slap on my back.

"Hey. How've you been?" Colin scanned the guests at the party. "We've got a lot of catching up to do tonight."

"Yep. I think every US and Canadian client showed up."

"Robert, I need to get to work. We'll catch you later." Colin tugged Belinda along. Before she walked out of earshot, I said, "You look fantastic, Baby Sister."

She glanced over her shoulder and rolled her eyes. "Thanks. Glad you approve." A bright, sexy smile appeared, causing me to stiffen. Her expression changed as her eyes darted over my shoulder.

I turned to see Sharyn, nose to nose, just before her lips planted on mine. She threw her arms around my neck and held on tight, almost smothering me.

I maneuvered us around so I could look over her shoulder at Belinda, whose teeth seemed clenched as her eyes narrowed. With a sudden jerk of her head, she turned away, flicking her ponytail.

~ Belinda ~

Country music floated through the air as the dance floor full of guests swayed to the beat. I played my part as the dutiful friend. Thank heaven, that's how he introduced me. I stood next to him during his conversations with the clients, one right after the other.

An embarrassing rumble erupted in my stomach that vibrated clear through me. Colin looked at me. "That was loud."

I reached for his arm. "I'm hungry. Let's go eat."

"Do you mind going ahead? I'd like to finish talking to this client."

I didn't need to hear anything else. My stomach rumbled again.

I gave him a kiss on the cheek, then turned and left for the buffet under the massive tent.

Rob's grilled and smoked meats, his crowning glory for the evening, were placed on a long buffet table. The way he put it, "Well, it's not a barbecue if you don't barbecue." He had spent the week at the grill or smoker. The savory meat smoke had floated into the house, filling it with the most mouthwatering scents.

The memory of the weeklong, taunting smells led me straight to the buffet line. With every step closer, I heard the growl as the aromas that filled the air became stronger.

All the waiters were dressed as cowboys, with crisp white shirts, jeans, boots, and belt buckles the size of Texas. Black hats sat atop their heads.

The wooden picnic tables displayed red and white checkered tablecloths. Salt, pepper, tabasco sauce and flatware filled empty six-pack beer cartons placed in the middle of each table. On either side, rolls of paper towels stood like little sentries.

As I walked away from the buffet with my plate of Rob's masterful cooking, I saw Robert sitting alone. Sharyn was nowhere in sight. So I headed toward him. "May I join you?"

He jumped to his feet and swung around. "Please do."

I took a seat across from him. "Where's Sharyn?" I picked up a rib and bit down, tearing free a chunk of the savory meat. My mouth filled with a burst of tangy barbecue sauce. "I just died and went to heaven." I took another bite. "This is better than sex."

I stopped chewing and looked at Robert.

He snorted before he laughed. "I'll make sure I tell Dad exactly that."

I waved him off. "You know what I mean. So, where is your other half?" I took another bite.

"She went to the guesthouse." He eyed my plate full of food.

"You hungry? I have plenty. Help yourself." I shoved the plate toward him.

"Don't mind if I do. Thanks." He grabbed a rib and joined me.

I took a fork out of the carton, filled it with potato salad and then offered it to him. He reached for the fork, but I pulled it back, wagging my finger at him. "Open." He did as I instructed, and I placed the tangy concoction in his mouth.

"What are you looking at?" My voice was low and seductive.

"You."

"Aren't you worried your fiancée will come back and catch you with me?"

"Why do you have to be such a downer?"

"Me?! I'm not the one who's engaged here."

"You're dating my best friend."

I shrugged. "There's that too."

"Can we change the subject?"

"I would, but I don't think we'd have time." I jutted my chin toward my nemesis, walking toward us.

He didn't bother to turn around. "Sharyn's on her way over here?"

"Yep." I stared at him just before tearing a chunk of meat off the rib bone.

Sharyn didn't look happy, stiffening and clenching her hands at her side. I suspected she saw me feed Robert. I'd swear her eyes glowed red. Halfway to the table, she stopped for a moment, unclenched her fists and then proceeded to Robert, placing her hands on his shoulders. Her eyes narrowed to slits when she bent down to kiss him on the cheek. "Here you are, *Darling*." She stood, still glaring. "Belinda, how nice to see you."

I wanted to puke but responded with equal insincerity. "Thank you. Same here."

"Darling, don't you think we should go talk to more of the guests?" She never stopped staring at me or seemed to care that Robert was hungry.

He appeared to visibly tense when Sharyn addressed him. Had her antics annoyed him? I half believed I still might have a real chance here.

He stood to leave. With her still eyeing me, I smugly said, "You two enjoy your evening now." Then I winked at her as I chomped down on the last bit of meat left on the bone.

~ Sharyn ~

I monitored Belinda. Just who does she think she is? My tolerance level had reached its peak, and I planned to make it clear. I wanted her to stay away from Robert. After all, she was just an employee.

I spotted her walking across the lawn toward the pool, searching for someone.

"It better not be Robert," I mumbled to myself through clenched teeth.

Timing was critical. I made sure he was busy enough so I could slip away to confront her. He was engaged in a financial discussion with someone. I walked toward her as she stood alongside the pool. I approached and grabbed her forearm, giving it a shake. "You stay away from him. Do you understand?"

~ Belinda ~

I couldn't believe Sharyn had the nerve to touch me threateningly. I could feel my anger boiling almost to capacity. Why I didn't lash out at her, I'd never know. All I did was look down at her hand wrapped around my arm. "Let go."

"Or else, what?"

I narrowed my eyes and kept them fixed on her. "Or else you won't have a fiancé when you blow back in on your broom because he'll be mine."

Sharyn's face contorted in the passing seconds as I felt a palm shove against my chest. A shriek escaped as I fell backward into the pool. The sting of cold water engulfed me. From underwater, I heard a muffled scream from Sharyn. "You bitch!"

I bobbed up to the surface, gasping for air and treading water. I recognized Robert's voice next to me in the pool. "Are you all right?"

"You're all wet."

"Are you all right?"

"Yes, I think so." In an instant, his arms wrap around me, lifting me to the side of the pool. He hopped out, picked me up, and marched toward the house.

I felt a burning sensation on my calf and reached for my leg as Sandra rushed to our side, carrying a towel.

"Oh, you're hurt." She dabbed at the wound, blood streaming down my wet leg.

"Robert, put her down on the lounge chair." A few more pats touched the area. "It doesn't look too bad. I don't think you'll need stitches. Come inside so we can get this bandaged."

~ Robert ~

Sharyn grabbed my arm.

I glared at her. "What the hell were you thinking?"

"Robert. Let me explain."

I jerked my arm away. "Not now."

Colin was nowhere to be found, so I went into the house to check on Belinda.

I entered the back door and saw my mother walking through the great room toward me. "Is she all right?" I could hear the concern in my voice and realized I'd never shown that with Sharyn.

"Sweetie, she'll be fine. It's only a minor cut. I cleaned and dressed it. She'll be out in a minute. She'll just need to dry off." Mom gave me a gentle pat before she left out the back door.

I had started for the primary bedroom when I saw Belinda walk into the great room. Her clothes were still wet, and her camisole clung a bit too much.

In the dark room, we met halfway in front of a fifteen-foot arched window. She was barefooted and holding wet shoes, making her a good bit shorter as she looked up into my eyes.

"Are you okay? Are you cold?"

I grabbed the throw off the chair and wrapped it around her shoulders.

"Thank you. Your mother took good care of me."

The first explosion from the fireworks display startled us. We chuckled and turned to see a red starburst through the top of the window. The room glowed red as the burst dissipated to ash. Another one went off with an explosion of red, white, and blue in the night sky.

~ Belinda ~

Robert stood so close my goosebumps multiplied despite the throw around me. I peered up at him, my heart about to leap out of my chest. My breathing became irregular. If he kissed me, I'd be his for the taking. We stood mesmerized by each other, silhouetted against the backdrop of starbursts on the back lawn.

He bent down, moving closer to my lips. I rose to reach his. His quick puffs of breath warmed my cheek. Millimeters away, I heard a screech.

"*Robert*, I want to go *now*!"

He pulled back. His face appeared emotionless. Without a word, he left me standing there as he walked out with Sharyn.

I ran upstairs to the office window to watch them leave. They didn't talk to each other. When they stopped next to his car, a discussion exploded. After several angry gestures from each of them, he threw his hands in the air as she turned and stomped into the guesthouse. Minutes later, she emerged with a suitcase and shoved it at him. She yanked the car door open and crawled in.

He slammed the trunk. With his fists clenched, he walked to the driver's side and stood. He rested his forearms on the roof and fiddled with his keys. Seconds later, he opened the door, dropped in, and sped off.

I didn't understand the significance of what I had just witnessed, but I knew I had a date to find, and I wanted to leave.

CHAPTER 20

~ *Belinda* ~

SUNDAY MORNING, AS planned, Colin arrived. My heart filled with lead. Did I ever give him a real chance? That nagged at me like a toothache. At times, it settled down but always lingered. The subject of Colin even had entered every session with Dr. Rosen. I also vented to Abby. Nothing helped. Was I making a big mistake by letting him walk out of my life?

Today, he'd come over for a light breakfast. Then we'd go take care of the horses. After that, we'd have the day to do whatever met our fancy.

On Thursday, he'd drive out of my life. I had four days to tell him I wanted more than he could offer. My problem: I didn't know if I could.

I opened the door and Colin presented me with a bouquet of assorted fresh flowers. "Good morning, my fair lady."

"Oh, thank you. They're lovely." I sniffed the bouquet. "Let me put these in water." Thank heaven he never brought roses. Those were Robert's and Robert's gift only.

I set the table for a nice, light meal before he arrived. After I arranged the flowers in a vase, I placed them on the table. He sat on a stool across from me.

The breakfast conversation centered on superficial talk about his new place, his office, and how he liked Canada so far. The entire time, I listened and questioned if I was making a mistake. One word of encouragement from me would send my life on a different path. Yet, I held back. A commitment wouldn't pass my lips despite the hints he dropped.

Colin placed the last dish in the rack. "All done. You ready to go?"

"Just let me get Beau's carrots."

About twenty minutes later, Colin turned into the drive of the estate, and I noticed the red Beamer parked in its usual spot. Why wasn't Robert with Sharyn?

Colin parked the car next to the barn. Beau stuck his head out of the stall. I dug in the plastic bag for his treat and held it under his mouth. "Hey, Beau. Want a carrot?" I stroked his neck and cooed to the animal. I gave Colin the extras and asked him to give the other three horses a carrot.

He flashed me a grin. "You want me to put my hand near their mouths?" He shook the bag of carrots. "You know they have huge teeth that could chomp off my fingers." He rubbed his free hand through his hair.

I snorted and then laughed. "Come on, I'll show you." I gave the first carrot to Scout. "Hold your palm open with your fingers flat and out of the way."

The horse took his treat without a problem. "Now you give some to the other two."

He did as I asked. After Mouse gobbled down her tidbit, he counted his fingers and wiggled them at me, a broad smile plastered across his face. "All there."

Taking care of the animals wouldn't take too long because we had cleaned the stalls for the party. The horses just needed turning out, their deposits picked up, feedbags filled, and fresh water. About an hour and a-half's worth of work, if I estimated it right. "Have any idea what you want to do after we're done here?"

"I'd like to go say goodbye to Sandra." Just about the time the words came out of his mouth, she appeared at the barn entrance.

"Well, good morning, you two." She walked over to him and placed her arm in his, locking at the elbows. "Are you all ready for your move?"

"Everything is arranged. I leave Thursday."

She patted his arm. "I'll miss you. You know that."

He gazed down at her and swung his other arm around her shoulder, pulling her close. "I'll miss you too."

They remained in their embrace for a few moments, with him swaying back and forth.

She gave him one last hug. "Would you two be interested in eating any lunch? We have plenty of last night's leftovers." She turned to me and then to Colin, waiting for an answer.

I rubbed my stomach. "We just ate breakfast."

"Well then, how about a swim in the pool after you're finished here? You can cool off and work up an appetite at the same time."

I glanced at him, feeling him out. He shrugged. "Sounds good to me. I never turn down a swim or invite to eat."

"Then it's settled. We'll see you at the house in a little while."

Sandra turned to walk out when Robert walked in. Her surprise expression told me he was unexpected. She greeted her son with a kiss on the cheek. "Good morning, Sweetie."

"Hi, Mom." He gave her a kiss back.

"These two will have lunch later. Will you be around or are you going over to Sharyn's?"

"I'll join you."

Sandra shot a glance my way. Her face intensified, and like before, she held my attention when I heard, "He's yours."

She turned away, and the trance broke, but she never moved her lips. What the hell?

~ *Robert* ~

After last night, I needed a diversion to get my mind off Sharyn. The drive to her house had been the worst forty-five minutes of my life. She never said a word. When we got into the apartment, all hell broke loose. She had accused me and Belinda of every type of sordid sexual diversions. She called her names I'd be too embarrassed to repeat.

My stomach had knotted during her rant. I felt like flames engulfed my neck and face. I couldn't feel my arms or legs. At work, I handled conflict with confidence. It followed a pattern I could predict. Sharyn's outburst gave a new meaning to the art of fighting and breaking up.

I had said little to defend myself and that seemed to enrage her more. So when she threw the engagement ring at me and told me to pack up, I got out of there as fast as possible, a free man.

"Here, Robert, you can finish cleaning out this stall." Colin pushed his pitchfork toward me. "I'm not into picking up large animal waste."

I grinned. "Give me that thing." I began to finish off what he had struggled to start.

While I worked, I glanced in Belinda's direction, watching her as unobtrusively as possible, making sure Colin didn't notice. Her graceful movement drove me nuts. Every time I stood near her, my insides went into a raging war. I wanted to touch her, hold her, caress her hair, take her full, warm, luscious lower lip in my mouth and nibble, but I couldn't because of Colin.

For now, I was doomed to watch but not touch. I would wait and see what played out between my friends. His move could very well be the downfall of their relationship. Was it wrong of me to pray that happened?

Colin constructed a lounge chair out of several bales of hay. He sat there, legs stretched out, gnawing on a piece of hay, looking as comfortable as if he were watching TV.

I nudged Belinda's arm. "Look at that."

She planted her pitchfork. "What do you think you're doing? Get over here and help."

He removed the straw from his mouth. "Nope. You're doin' fine without me."

Belinda snorted and stomped her foot. "Hold this."

She tried to pass me her pitchfork. "Don't even try. Let's just finish. Okay."

"Lazy," she shouted to Colin.

He just waved her off.

I returned to the barn after dumping out the last wheelbarrow. "You two up for a ride?" I turned to Belinda. "Do you still want to try riding English? You can ride Scout. I'll ride Beau and Colin can ride Billy."

Colin shot to his feet from his prone position. "You want me on one of those things? Dude, I'm from LA. The biggest thing I've ever been near with four legs is a Great Dane."

I thought for a brief second. "Okay, I'll ride Billy and you take Beau. He's a good horse to ride, and easy. He'll do everything for you." I glanced at her and hoped she'd back me up after my suggestion.

"Robert is right. He'd be perfect for you."

Colin looked at us. "I just hope I live through it and don't regret this decision." He glanced over his shoulder in the pool's direction. "Taking a dip is sounding real good about now."

I chuckled. "We'll all go swimming after the ride. Trust me, you'll enjoy it more after you get off the hot trails."

He jerked back. "Belinda, I don't do sweaty. I do cool and comfortable, but for you my lady, I'll make an exception. Lead me to my steed." He made a sweeping gesture with his right arm as he brought it in front of him and bowed.

I shook my head, and she giggled. Colin had a flare for the dramatic, and I liked that about my friend. I saw myself as reserved most of the time, and his pendulum swung on the opposite end. He possessed a clownish side I appreciated. In short, he made me laugh. I'd miss him.

With the horses saddled, I informed my mother of the change in plans. We would swim after the ride, then eat.

I walked over to Belinda, mounted on Scout. "Now, he can be high-strung, so make sure you don't let him get away with anything." I pulled at the stirrup strap. "Keep a tight rein on him. Once he tires, he'll calm down. Usually takes about twenty minutes."

I walked around to check the other stirrup. "I'll keep up with you on Billy, and when Scout slows down, I'll give you more instructions."

My hand settled on her calf and gave it a squeeze. I looked up at her. We fixed gazes. I was in love with what I saw—her perfect features framed by supple strands of golden-brown hair and striking, penetrating blue eyes.

She turned away.

"Are you ready?"

She nodded and stared straight ahead.

I turned my attention to Colin and gave him blow-by-blow instructions on how to mount a horse. "Okay, up you go." Despite his height, he couldn't quite swing his leg over Beau's back. I led the horse to a hay bale.

"Stand on the bale." I pointed to it. He did as instructed. His hips were now level with the horse's back. "Get on." I held the reins, so Beau stayed in position. He placed his foot in the stirrup, hoisted his long leg over and landed in the saddle.

I shook my head.

"What?" Colin made an exaggerated movement, inspecting each side of the horse. "Hey. Where's the brakes on this thing?"

A muffled giggle came from behind me. I shrugged. "Belinda, you're not helping."

"I can't help it. Beau looks small with Colin on him. His legs are so long." She giggled again.

I backhanded his calf. "Pay attention. This is how you stop." I showed him how to hold the reins, but most of all, how to pull back by applying the right pressure. "If the ride gets too bumpy, grab onto this." I took hold of the horn. "It'll help keep you in the saddle. I'll help if you have questions or get yourself in trouble."

I mounted Billy and turned to my companions. "We all set?"

With their nods, I tightened up on the reins and pointed toward the trails.

Scout acted just as I had predicted and, thank heaven, so did Beau. Colin had no trouble keeping up with Scout's pace. About twenty minutes into the ride, Scout settled down into a nice, easy walk. We rode three abreast.

"Hey, this isn't as bad as I thought. In fact, I'm sorta enjoying it." Colin gnawed on the straw sticking out of his mouth.

About fifteen minutes later, I figured Scout was calm enough to give Belinda her first lesson on an English saddle.

"Colin, can you hold Beau back while Belinda and I go ahead? I'd like to let her get a better feel for the saddle."

"Sure. I think I can handle that."

We rode up the trail about fifty feet in a fast walk. I began to post and explain to her what I was doing. On her first try, she moved with the horse. We sped up the pace to a canter.

I suppressed a gasp. I couldn't stop watching her. Strands of hair glowed from the sunlight, bouncing off. She made little purring sounds that transformed into muffled giggles with every upward hesitation of each post. Her cheeks lifted to a broad smile. *God, I love her.*

~ *Colin* ~

I just let Beau amble along and do his thing. I sat back in the saddle, relaxed and watched Belinda's graceful movements.

My hope of her becoming my wife had long faded because I knew I'd never move past friend status. For now, I'd enjoy what little time I had left. I wanted it to be as perfect as possible and prayed she would visit me after the relocation.

I fully intended to follow along at a slower pace, but the stubborn horse had a different idea. Once the distance between him and the other horses widened, he helped himself to the smorgasbord of grasses along the trail. Head bent down, he tore at the grass and wouldn't move. I tried pulling back on the reins. With the shake of his muscular neck, Beau just ignored me. I talked in soft tones to encourage him. Nothing. So I gave in and let the animal eat his fill until one of my fellow riders rescued me.

~ *Robert* ~

I shifted in the saddle to turn around, fearing we were getting too far away from Colin. I saw him just sitting on his mount with his arms crossed over his chest and burst out in laughter.

"What's so funny? Am I doing something wrong?"

"No. You're fine." I pointed my thumb for her to check behind me.

She let out a hearty outburst at the comical scene. "Think we should go back and help him?"

"Seems like the right thing to do."

"Wait here." I turned Billy and went back down the trail.

Colin had his arms crossed over his chest. "Nice of you to come back."

"You're not supposed to let him graze."

Colin frowned. "Tell that to Beau."

"Pull up on the reins."

Beau paid no attention to Colin's attempts and continued to eat.

"See."

I jumped off Billy and approached the stubborn horse. About to grab Beau's bridle, I saw Colin's eyes widened as he looked past me.

Belinda's scream caused the hairs on my neck to stand on end.

I swung around to see Scout rearing up. Her legs and arms flailed in the air just before she hit the ground. I shoved Billy's reins in Colin's hand and ran to her side. My knees hit the ground, and I held her down by her shoulder. "Don't get up." My free hand roamed over her body for any signs of an injury. "Angel, are you okay?"

"Baby...I think I am."

"Lie still. Now lift your right leg." She did as asked. "Any pain?" She shook her head. I instructed her to move her left one and then her arms. "Did you hit your head?"

"No."

"You sure?" My fingers massaged her scalp for signs of injury.

~ Belinda ~

I reached for Robert's wrist. "Baby, I'm okay."

I looked deep into his eyes as he stopped his examination and stared back. "I'm going to get up now. Help me?"

He stood and stretched out his hand. We brushed the dust from my clothes. Concern covered his face. "Angel, are you sure you're okay?"

I took hold of his arm to steady myself. "Baby...I'm fine."

He held me close by the waist, and I wrapped my arms around his neck. "You scared the hell outta me. What happened?" He stroked my hair.

"I couldn't help it. A rabbit ran across the trail. The next thing I knew...I was on the ground."

~ Colin ~

I was glad Robert moved as quickly as he did. I knew I would've been useless. While he tended to Belinda, I dismounted and kept the horses together.

My back was to my friends, but I heard how they talked to each other. I stiffened the more I heard. I turned and approached the pair, still embraced in each other's arms. "Excuse me!"

She gasped when she saw me. They released each other. Robert spun around.

Why were you two wrapped around each other? And why is she calling you 'Baby' and you're calling her 'Angel'?" I frowned at her. "Have you been seeing him when I'm out of town?"

"No! It's nothing like that." She waved her hands in front of her.

I shoved Scout's and Billy's reins into Robert's hand.

"Colin..."

I raised a hand. "I'm out of here." Adrenaline kicked in and with one try, I mounted Beau. I rode off, not quite knowing what I was doing or where I'd go. I just wanted away from them.

~ *Belinda* ~

I turned to Robert. "I have to go after him."

He nodded. "Take Billy."

It didn't take long for me to reach Colin. We rode along for a few seconds, not saying anything. I glanced at him and could see the signs of my betrayal all over his face. Knowing I needed to make him listen, I broke the silence. "Colin, we need to talk."

He shot me a hard stare. "Why? What's there to talk about?"

"I haven't been completely honest with you."

Again, he gave me a hard, icy stare. "That's pretty obvious…isn't it?"

"No, it's not what you think. The barn were I boarded Beau is right over there. Come with me so I can explain." I took hold of his wrist and gave it a tug.

His eyes softened, and he nodded. "Okay."

We secured the horses and walked inside the barn. We straddled a hay bale.

He said nothing. I took a deep breath. "Brace yourself. This is a lot to take in."

I started the story where I met, fell in love with and married Robert in my coma. I explained how we split up because he had difficulty staying away from other girls. Then I explained that our love was so strong we reunited only to be torn apart when I came out of the coma. As I realized it had all been a dream, I feared I'd lost him forever.

He looked puzzled. "You met Robert in your coma?"

"That's only half of it." With an explanation of what took place at the New Year's Eve party, minus the whole kissing and bed incident, I finished and leaned back, studying him.

"After the New Year's Eve party, I didn't think I'd ever see this Robert again, but things kept happening. We kept crossing paths." I fiddled with the straw between my fingers. "The next time I saw him was when I went to talk to Garrett at the office. Then again, later that evening, when we accidentally met at the Galleria." I shrugged. "Not to mention the fact that I work for his mother."

"So, when did you two hook up?"

My mouth dropped open. Appalled by his question, I felt my brow furrow. "We never did. He's engaged, and I was with you. I wouldn't do something like that to you or Sharyn."

"Okay then, what was that I just witnessed between the two of you?"

Staring off at the floor, I couldn't answer the question with a logical response. I looked back at him. "I don't know. In the coma, he called me 'Angel' and I called him 'Baby'."

I wrung my hands and sighed. "I can't explain what happened on the trail. This Robert is different from my Dream Robert." I pointed in the direction where we left him. "And this Robert has no way of knowing I dreamt about him because I've never told him." I wrapped his hand around my fingers. "You're now the eighth person who knows anything about this stuff." Tears started running down my cheeks. "I'm sorry I didn't tell you, but you have to admit, it all sounds rather nuts."

~ Colin ~

Belinda's tears ate at my heart. I couldn't be mad at her. Besides, I believed her, as crazy as it sounded. I reached over, put my arm around her neck, and pulled her to my shoulder, cradling her close. "Well, you're kinda nuts, anyway."

She gave me a punch to the back. A non-verbal response I didn't expect.

"Hey. I'm being supportive here."

I held her for a few seconds. Now I had to be honest. My timing might be off and this could end badly, but I took a leap of faith and went for it. "If I had asked you to marry me, would you have agreed?"

She took a deep breath, which she didn't let out until she pulled away from me.

Her lower lip disappeared between her teeth and then popped out. "A few months ago I would've said yes, or at least given the proposal some thought. Back then, I felt there'd never be anything between Robert and me. I figured I needed and deserved a life."

She stroked my cheek. "You're a good man who cares about me." She reached for my hand and gave it a squeeze. "You know I love you."

My heart jumped knowing the other shoe was about to drop, so I finished her statement. "But you're not in love with me." I lifted her chin. "You're in love with Robert, aren't you?"

My statement forced tears to stream down as she nodded.

Disappointment tugged at me, but I knew there had to be a reason she never committed. Now the truth came out, and if I had to lose her to someone, Robert would've been my first choice. From what I witnessed on the trail, I knew he had the same feelings for her.

She sniffled.

"Okay, that's enough crying," I reached up and brushed the tears from her face. "What are you going to do about Sharyn?"

"I planned to talk to Robert the week after you left. She's leaving then, and I decided it'd be then or never."

I smiled. "Let me know how it works out." I moved my eyebrows rapidly up and down several times.

She gave my upper arm a push and giggled. "I'll never kiss and tell."

"Okay then, I'll just ask him." I jumped to my feet.

An 'O' formed on her mouth as she frowned at me. "You wouldn't dare." She stood.

A raised eyebrow followed as a half-smile crossed my face. "Oh, wouldn't I." I pulled her closer, resting her cheek against my chest. Her warmth engulfed me as she softened in my arms.

"You're not mad at me?"

"How could I be?" I kissed her and stroked her soft hair, most likely for the last time. God, I'd miss being with her.

When we arrived back at the Pendletons', Robert's car was gone. We stabled the horses and went into the house to change. We swam, then joined Rob and Sandra for lunch. Robert never came home the entire time we visited with his parents, and I said my goodbyes.

Monday morning, at the Pendleton Financial Group, I arrived to a surprise breakfast planned in my honor by the secretarial staff. The affair lasted about an hour. My friend Robert never showed up, which disappointed and hurt me.

On the way to my office to pack up, I noticed him sitting at his desk. I knew he saw me. How could he not through all the glass walls?

The last item found its way into the box. I made one last sweep of the room. I'd miss this place. With a sigh, I lifted the packed belongings and headed for his office. I walked in and placed the edge of the box on his desk.

"Hey, Bud. Are we still on for our last round of golf tomorrow afternoon?"

Robert looked up, doing a double take. "You're not mad at me about what happened?"

"Should I be? Is there something going on between the two of you?"

"Absolutely not. We're just friends."

"Well then, what's the problem?"

His face lit up as he stood and shook my hand. "You know, my mom is going to miss you."

"Yeah, I know. She couldn't stop doting over me at lunch on Sunday."

His fingers slid partially into his pockets when he looked down at the floor. "Yeah...I just thought it'd be better if I made myself scarce. Sorry about breakfast, too."

"It's okay. We're cool. Now you owe me a fishing trip. I hear there's some good spots just due north of my new digs. So, golf tomorrow as planned?"

"I'll look forward to it."

I lifted the box. At the door, I looked back. "I'm going to miss this place...and you. You know that."

He nodded. "Golf tomorrow, as planned."

CHAPTER 21

~ *Colin* ~

ROBERT And I met Tuesday afternoon at the country club for our last round of golf before my move to Canada.

A cool breeze sent billowy clouds drifting across the blue sky, which blocked the hot sun.

The game progressed at a normal pace through the first five holes. Robert started in rare form, but on the eighth, he became more distracted, causing his swing to veer slightly to the left.

We drove to the ninth hole when I gave my friend a sympathetic look. "Is there something going on? You don't seem to have your head in the game." I bumped him with my elbow. "Where are you?"

"Oh, sorry." He frowned. "Yeah…Ah…Sharyn…we broke up after the party."

I rarely had a mean thought, but the only thing that came to mind was Sharyn problem solved. Belinda's life just got easier. "Do you want to talk about it?"

He jumped out of the cart and selected his club. "Hold on for a minute while I take my shot." I watched him approach the ball, then peer down the fairway. He stepped back, positioning himself, and set the club before taking a practice swing. I admired his form and ability to follow through. He took a step forward, addressed the ball and clobbered it.

"Colin. Eyes!" We watched it land and roll a few feet beyond the hole. "Yes!" Robert exclaimed, pumping his fist. After placing the nine iron back in his bag, he jumped into the cart, and I drove across the fairway toward the green.

I gave him a quick glance. "Well?"

He pursed his lips before starting. "Hmmm. Our relationship started going south after the first of the year. I just didn't know how to get out of it. Now it's done and I'm grateful."

The cart jerked to a stop. I jumped out and selected the eight iron and then addressed the ball. "Maybe I should let you go on being distracted so I'll have a better chance at winning." I looked up at him and grinned, and then turned my attention to the ball. After taking a solid swing, I followed it, watching it land and roll about a foot from the hole. "Okay, talk. What are friends for?" I plopped into the driver's seat.

He started fiddling with his glove. "Where do I start?"

"I have a few cold ones in the cooler. Let's sink these and go park under a tree for a break." I pointed as I drove toward the green. "I have something I need to talk to you about, and I guess this is as good a time as any."

Picking up the golf balls and replacing the pin, we hopped into the cart and drove toward the tree line. I selected a spot in the shade and turned the cart facing the fairway of the tenth hole, toward the setting sun.

The course had a peaceful ambience for a normally busy afternoon. I reached into the cooler, pulled out a beer, and tossed it to Robert. As I fished for another can, the ice chilled my hand, biting at my fingers. Droplets of sweat streamed down my brow and the back of my neck as I rubbed the can across my heated skin. The sound of the top popping, followed by the hiss, reminded me of how much I enjoyed a cold beer with my good friend and hoped this wouldn't be the last.

Robert asked, "Okay, you had something to say?"

I took a hefty gulp, then wiped my mouth with the back of my hand. "You know, I've really enjoyed dating Belinda, but she just isn't...totally into me. After we left you on the trails, we went to Beau's old digs and talked." I took another swig. "Do you remember at the Galleria, her telling us that while she was in a coma, she had dreams?"

"Yeah. Why?"

"She told me she met a guy after she woke up, but the strange part is, she said she dreamt about this guy while in her coma."

I noticed him tense and furrow his brow as he stared at me. "So? People dream about other people all the time."

"The strangest part about this dream is she didn't just dream about him once. She dreamt of a life with him."

He sat quietly and took a gulp of his beer. "And?"

"Here's the weirdest part. I know the guy she dreamt about."

"Colin, just say what you have to say," he insisted, his tone now irritated.

I raised an eyebrow and half grinned. "She dreamt about you, dude." I poked him in the arm with my elbow.

He did a double take. "Me?"

"Yep. I've noticed how she looks at you and the way the two of you act around each other. She's never looked at me that way." I rubbed my hand over the cold can. "Not only did she dream about you, she told me you had some connection that drew the two of you to one another. She also told me you fell in love and got married."

"We got married?" Robert's mouth twisted while his brow ridged. "I'm sorry. I'll admit I'm attracted to her, but I promise you we haven't been seeing each other. I swear."

"Yep. That's what she told me. Don't worry. I believe the both of you." I took another drink.

"You have to admit, she is beautiful." He lifted his can toward me.

"I'll give you that." I tapped the edge of my can against his.

We stared straight ahead over the golf course and raised our beers, taking a gulp.

He broke the silence. "Look, Colin, I have my loyalties, and I would never interfere with you two. I just want you to know that." He finished his statement with a firm slicing motion of his hand.

I took a more laid-back approach. I knew I wasn't winning the prize, so there was no need for me to sweat it anymore.

"Thanks for the consideration, but I'm leaving and she's not going with me. She won't even consider it. I'll never be more than just a friend to her." I formed a funny grin. "That is, unless something happens to you. Then, maybe…" I flashed my teeth, followed by a muffled chuckle, emphasizing the humor I saw in my comment.

"What do you mean, me?" He raised a brow dubiously at me.

"Dude, she dreamt about you when she didn't even know who you were. That says something. Right?"

He didn't respond.

Silence fell over us until I chimed back up. "So, you're two single people who need to talk." I took another swig of beer. "We're supposed to go out tonight, but I'm going to cancel. You go over there instead."

He hesitated, watching the horizon. "It's your last night. Don't cancel on her. I can talk to her after you leave."

"No, I insist." I gave him a stern look. "It's settled. You're getting your ass over there tonight."

I leaned back in the seat, slouching, and propped my foot on the console of the cart. "So we're good here?"

"We're good."

"I've lost interest in this game." I reached back into the cooler, pulled out another can, and offered it to him. "Let's call it quits and just enjoy these beers. Okay?"

"Fine with me."

~ *Belinda* ~

Tonight, I'd have my last date with Colin. I'd miss him, and he'd always be a friend who'd occupy a little corner of my heart.

I had just finished showering when my cell rang. I threw on a thigh length nylon robe and bunny slippers, then ran for the phone. "Hi, Colin."

A raspy voice came over the phone. "Hey, Belinda. I have some bad news. I have to cancel our date." Cough….Cough. "I feel like crap."

"Oh no. Do you need anything? I can come over."

"No. No. I don't want to expose you to it." Cough. Cough. "I think I just need to rest."

"Oh…okay. So, will I get to see you before you leave?"

He hesitated. "How about breakfast on Thursday before I drive out?"

"You have a date. I hope you get to feeling better soon."

"Thanks. I do too. Bye." Cough….Cough.

"Bye."

I let out a huff, rested the phone on the table, and then tapped the case. Heaviness settled in my chest. I'd been looking forward to the date all day. I'd wished things between us could've worked out differently, but Robert sitting in my head wouldn't let me.

I returned to the bathroom to comb out my wet hair. There'd be no reason to change. For a night of TV and munching, my comfortable robe and bunnies fit the bill.

Armed with a soda and a bag of cookies, I sat on the couch with my legs curled up next to me. My finger punched through channels, searching for an interesting movie to fill the boring night—maybe a romantic comedy? I needed something light to fill the hole in my heart.

~ *Robert* ~

About eight in the evening, I finally got up the courage to go over to Belinda's. I'd run over the scenarios of my plan hundreds of times. Each one ended with me acting the fool.

The grocery store at the entrance of the sub-division screamed at me. Just inside, I'd found a display of flowers, including red roses. I'd always bought her red roses. Why change now? I pulled into the parking lot and purchased a single red rose.

The car engine hummed as I pulled into her driveway. Should I get out or run? If I left, nothing was lost. My heart raced. My palms moistened. The cool metal of the door handle filled my hand when I opened the door. I took a deep breath and stepped out.

In a few steps, I stood at her door. I raised my fist, poised to knock, but stopped just before it made contact. "Is this a good idea?" With my fingertips, I tapped on the door, then lowered my hand. "Colin, why am I listening to you?"

"This is nuts. Just like me." I turned around and walked back to my car. About to open the door, I closed my eyes and the vision of the woman I loved exploded before me. "I have to do this."

Without hesitation, I turned, my steps more determined to reach her door. This time, I knocked and then took a few steps back to lean against the cool brick of the alcove.

"Ouch!" I plunged my bleeding thumb into my mouth. Damn, I should've gotten a thornless rose.

~ *Belinda* ~

The unexpected rap on the door surprised me. Who could that be at this time of night? I hurried over to peer out the peephole. My heart skipped a beat, and I let out a gasp. My back hit the wall and my hand flew over my mouth. I turned back to the peephole and studied the lean, t-shirt-and-jean-clad man sucking his thumb. He looked like a two-year-old standing on the porch. "What the hell? What in the world is he doing here?" Then I noticed the rose. Oh, a rose thorn. My brows knitted together. Why a red rose?

The butterflies in my stomach worked their way to my chest and circled around my thumping heart. I clutched the silky fabric of the robe. There was no time to put on a tee and shorts. He might leave if I changed.

I grasped a bigger chunk of fabric, making the robe tighter. I opened the door just enough so only my head poked out, shielding the rest of me.

"Robert? What are you doing here?" My butterflies swarmed as I studied him, propped against the brick.

He didn't answer, but stared at me for a few seconds before he smiled and said, "I'll explain. Do you mind if I come in?" He held the rose out in front of him and stepped toward me, putting it within reach. "I brought a peace offering."

At first, I hesitated, then reached for it.

"Be careful." He held up his thumb. "It got me."

A laugh escaped as I took the rose and sniffed it. "Thanks." I stepped back and allowed him to enter. He closed the door and leaned back against it, not saying anything. He just gazed at me.

"Why are you here?"

His head lowered, and he sighed. "I came to…" The statement trailed off when he looked down at my feet. "Bunny slippers? Really?" He snickered and glanced back at me.

"They're comfortable."

My favorite compelling smile grew across his mouth, and his glacier-blue eyes became lustful as they tracked down my body and back to my face.

"Nice robe, too. All we need is an oak tree."

The butterflies dropped. My breathing halted. "What did you just say?" The conversation sounded very familiar. It reminded me of the first time Robert kissed me in the dream.

His eyes dropped to my chest. I had let my guard and my grip on the robe down. A bit too much of me became visible. I grabbed and wrapped it tighter as I crossed my arms over my chest to keep it in place.

Slowly, I looked up at him through my lashes. My heart sped up and my breathing became faster. His features changed. They appeared to become full of determination.

He took a step toward me. I took one back. He hesitated, tilting his head. His brow raised as he took a few steps closer. I took a few back.

I didn't understand this game. "I should go change. You can wait in the living room." I made a half-turn.

"No, wait."

"Why?"

He stood there and studied me. "Angel."

"What's going on? Why did you call me that?"

He closed the gap and wrapped his arms around my waist. "Because I always have." His palm cupped my cheek. "I love you and have always loved you."

A zing shot up my spine. I went limp. He lifted me off my feet and found my lips. I melted.

Every inch of me quivered. I wasn't about to protest. Instead, I locked my arms around his neck and encircled his hips with my legs. I knotted my fingers in his thick hair—adhering to his magnificent body. My whole being screamed for him to make love to me. I kissed him right back with all the pent-up need I'd kept controlled for far too long. All I could think about was rocking his world like we did in my dream.

Sliding one hand down from my waist to my ass, he kept me airborne and clinging to him. The hand on my back trailed up, locking into my hair. He plunged his tongue between my parted lips, searching.

His tense muscles excited me, and I threw my head back. Short puffs of warm breath brushed my skin as his lips kissed every inch of my jaw and neck, while he edged us into the living room.

Robert bumped into a chair, causing him to lose his balance and stumble. We clung to each other as we landed on the couch with him on top of me. Longer, harder kisses prevailed after short, sweet ones slid up my neck, across my jawline, then back to my awaiting lips, inducing sighs and moans of arousal.

He paused and, with his lustful, hypnotic eyes, he gazed into mine and breathlessly whispered, "I want you. I want you so bad."

Heart hammering, I sucked in air. He grabbed me up into his arms and carried me toward the bedroom. He hesitated at the door and his expression became serious. "I just came to talk but...I didn't plan for this to happen...I didn't bring—"

I placed a finger over his lips. "Don't worry, we're covered." I winked. "I'm on the pill, and I have condoms in the nightstand drawer."

He nodded and let out a sigh as a half-smile swept across his lips. He wasted no time carrying me to the bed.

He reached behind his neck and yanked his t-shirt forward over his head. I gasped at the sight of his taut muscles. He untied my robe and slid it off. It slipped down around my feet, leaving me standing naked. A wide grin appeared as his passionate gaze scanned down my body. "God, you're beautiful."

I traced the rippled muscles of his abdomen down to his buckle. I gave it a tug, causing him to stumble toward me. He seized my hands, pulling them up about his neck, and lifted me onto my tiptoes. He secured his arms around my waist and squeezed our bodies together. Feeling his warmth, I let out a loud sigh and said, "You feel so good."

In one quick fluid movement, he scooped me up and laid me in bed, then sat on the edge. His soft, sensual lips and warm, gentle hands roamed my entire body, setting my reactions in motion. In a matter of seconds, his clothes were off. He kneeled above me and pointed to the nightstand drawer.

I nodded.

With the speed and grace of a gazelle, he was ready and laid partially over me.

I trembled with sexual desire. As my lips found his, our limbs entangled and pressed heat against heat. I relinquished control, letting my body respond to his. Neither spoke—only our bodies communicated.

He slid on top, settling between my legs. My breathing sped up in anticipation as I waited for the pain. With the first thrust, I tensed and pushed my head against the mattress. I moaned and grabbed a fistful of the sheet.

Robert stopped. I relaxed. He peered down at me. A gentle placement of my hands on his ass, accompanied by the downward pressure, encouraged him to continue. He thrust again.

This time my back arched, molding me to him. I moaned with pleasure. Digging my nails into his flesh, I encouraged him again and again until we rhythmically moved as one. Sparks of light flashed against the back of my eyelids when my eyes drifted shut. Every nerve ending in me came alive. About to reach my peak, I dug my nails deeper into his flesh and cried out, "Robert!"

He stiffened as he made a last thrust, followed by a rocking motion that sent waves of ecstasy through every inch of my body. Then he relaxed. With beads of sweat trickling down his chest, Robert rolled over onto his back. Breathing hard, like me.

I couldn't believe what had just happened.

I wanted to relish him as long as I could, so I rolled onto my side and snuggled against his warmth, curling over him. He wrapped his arms around me and tightened his grip, not explaining he nuzzled my hair. I reveled in his embrace. Talk would come later. Now it was time to sleep.

I awoke in the dark to the excited thrill of Robert's touch as his fingers stroked circles on my stomach. At first, I thought I had dreamt of our lovemaking from a few hours ago.

His tantalizing touch sent a zing charging up my spine that made my back arch. Robert's ragged breaths increased in response to my movement. Seconds later, his lips moved across my cheek. I tilted my head up as I reached over and cupped his cheek to direct his lips to mine. He came alive, rolling over on top of me. In united euphoria, we made mind-blowing, passionate love, again.

ᖳᖰ

A slight back-and-forth motion awakened me. A lazy yawn floated over my lips while I stretched and focused on him. He sat on the edge of the bed. Bent over, his back to me, he rummaged through the pile of clothes we had discarded. Is he trying to sneak out? No discussion had taken place about why he even came over. Not to mention how he ravished me without a word. I loved his advances and had waited too long, so I wasn't about to let him out of my sight without a decent explanation.

"Where do you think you're goin', mister?"

Half leaning off the bed, very naked, he jerked his head toward me and flashed his signature smile. "Good morning, Angel. I have a job to get to."

I scowled as my mouth dropped open. Is he jacking me around again? My back went straight. How dare he come over and make love to me? Then I realized he called me Angel. The whole scenario seemed peculiar, and I needed questions answered.

I turned over and reached for my phone on the bedside table, letting the sheet slide down to expose the upper half of my torso.

He stopped rummaging for his clothes.

I had his full attention. I sat up, pressed a number on my cell and never stopped looking at him. He stared back at me as I put my plan into play and left a message for my employer. "Sandra, this is Belinda." I paused as I moved my eyes down his rippled chest muscles. My gaze continued downward to below his waist as I finished the message. "Something's come up and I won't be in today." I disconnected the call and held out the cell toward him.

His breathing quickened. Smiling from ear to ear, he gathered his jeans from the floor. "I'll use mine." He pulled the cell from the pocket. "Caller ID."

He used speed dial and waited for a response. "Gail, how heavy is my day?...Okay, great!...I need you to reschedule those appointments for later in the week and let my dad know I won't be in today. Tell him I'll talk to him later, but I'm all right." He disconnected the call, turned off the phone, and placed it on the nightstand.

With cat like movements, he crawled over the bed to straddle me. He ran the tip of his tongue over my lips and then pressed his to mine. His tongue slipped into my mouth. I threw my arms around his neck and pulled him to me, carrying on our lovemaking from the night before.

Around ten a.m., I awoke from round three. In sheer bliss, I looked at a sleeping Robert. He was as handsome as I remembered from the dream, and I couldn't believe he was lying beside me. I ran my fingers over his chest to convince myself he was real. The all-too-familiar arousing stir filled me and I was satisfied.

But why was he here? What changed that brought him to my door and why'd call me Angel? I had too many questions, but for now, I was content to take in his essence.

As I traced a finger over his lips, his eyes flickered open. He caught my hand and kissed my palm.

"Good morning again, Angel." He smiled. "I need a shower. You interested?" With a devilish grin, he leaped out of bed and extended his hand. I knew that look. It only meant one thing, and I was game. Forty-five minutes later, we walked out of the bathroom.

Wrapped in a towel, I rummaged through a drawer for something comfortable to put on. A camisole and shorts fit the bill.

Clad in just a towel, Robert emerged from the bathroom. With one hand, he rubbed his head. Water droplets sprayed off. He moseyed over to the side of the bed and stopped, staring at the mattress.

I walked over and stood beside him. There on the sheets was a bloodstain, a remnant of my first sexual encounter.

His brow furrowed. He turned toward me and placed his arms around my waist. "You were a virgin?"

I nodded.

"Are you okay with this?"

I giggled. "It's a little late to ask that. Isn't it?" Concern washed over his face. "Why?"

"You're on birth control pills and have condoms. I'm just a little confused." He stroked my cheek.

A heated wave emanated from his fingers. I brushed my lips against his fingers. "If you keep this up, we'll need another shower."

He dropped his hand back to my waist.

I took a deep breath to let the wave pass.

"You and Colin never…"

I glanced away and lightly bit my lower lip. "I started on the pill the week after the New Year's Eve party." I looked into his eyes. "I never slept with Colin or anyone. I've been waiting for you."

~ Robert ~

My breath caught as I studied her. I tugged her to me and hugged her tight, kissing the top of her head again. My heart wanted to leap out of my chest. All my senses went wild with a simple touch. When we made love, I melded with her. Her heart became mine. Her blood flowed through my veins. Our souls became one.

I was determined never to let her go again.

"I love you."

She looked up at me through her thick lashes. "I have always loved you."

I bent to kiss her succulent lips.

She placed a hand on my chest and pushed. "No. You have some explaining to do."

"Fair enough." I nodded. "I don't know about you, but I'm starving. How about you start breakfast, and I'll take care of the bed? Where's your clean sheets?"

She picked up her clothes and went into the bathroom. A few seconds later, she tossed the sheets on the bed and returned to the bathroom.

A few minutes later, she emerged dressed and with her hair in a ponytail. She whizzed past. "Blueberry bagels, coffee and OJ coming up."

"I love blueberry bagels!"

From down the hall, she replied, "I know."

~ Belinda ~

On the credenza, behind the couch, lay a red rose. It was the farthest thing from my mind after Robert's advances. I picked it up and held it under my nose, then took a deep breath. Why a single red rose? I walked into the kitchen, found a suitable vase and placed the rose in and then set my new possession in the center of the table.

I busied myself with making orange juice and toasting bagels. He entered the kitchen barefooted and clad only in jeans, carrying an armful of sheets. "Where do you want these?"

I scrunched up my nose and pointed with the knife to the door at the end of the kitchen.

Seconds later, he returned. "Dish soap?"

I pointed to the bottle on the sink.

"Good for getting out stains." Then he left for the laundry room.

I heard the lid of the washer drop and water ran just before he emerged again. "How about I make the coffee?"

I nodded. "Please wash your hands first." He let out a laugh as he walked over to the sink. "I'll use the dish soap."

After placing the OJ and freshly made coffee on the table, he sat down to wait for me. I followed and placed his bagel in front of him. It was lightly toasted and spread with the right amount of cream cheese, just like I remembered from my dream.

"It looks perfect." He took a bite and nodded. "It's perfect. I couldn't have done it better if I made it myself." He raised his juice glass. "My compliments to the chef."

After another bite, he grabbed the back of my chair. "Pull your chair in front of me." His jaw tightened. He shifted in his seat to face me and encouraged me to do the same. Taking my hands in his, he said, "Angel, we have a lot to talk about."

CHAPTER 22

~ *Robert* ~

"ROBERT, WHY DO you call me Angel?"

I took a deep breath and exhaled, rubbing my thumbs over the top of her hands. "What I have to say may sound a little crazy, and I can't explain how this happened or why. Just bear with me."

She tightened her lips and nodded.

"A year ago last April, after witnessing your car wreck, I went to bed and had a dream about a woman riding a chestnut horse on a college campus. I was walking with some friends across the commons when the horse reared up in front of me and her eyes met mine. From that moment on, I was hooked and in love."

Her eyes grew to the size of saucers. An audible gasp escaped. She threw her hand up to cover her mouth.

I watched her for a second before I continued the story. "Night after night, I found myself in the same dream. I lived a life with this woman. We even got married. Everything seemed great until July. She left because she saw me kissing my study partner, Erin, in my blue BMW Roadster."

"Robert." Her voice quavered.

"Before you say anything, let me finish." I took hold of her hands before I pressed on.

"I fell madly in love with this woman and did everything I could to be with her. I'd come home right from work every night and jump into bed so I could be in the dream. My parents believed I was depressed. They tried to get me to see a psychiatrist, but I refused.

"By July, the dream had become more important to me than reality. I knew I'd go insane if I didn't do something. That's when I started dating Sharyn. I'd stay awake more and the funny part is the dream reflected my absence."

"In the dream, the woman moved to Atlanta about the same time I started up with Sharyn. My life with my dream girl turned into phone calls and texts, but after weeks of talking, she agreed to meet me for one night in September. We reconnected and decided we'd work at our marriage. After that, I didn't dream about her again, and *you* were gone."

"Then around November, I had one last dream. It picked up the morning after we spent the night together. I found a note telling me she went to run an errand, and she'd be back soon. I went to buy our favorite breakfast..." I waved my hand over the kitchen table. "Bagels and coffee." More serious, my respirations increased. "As I pulled up to the bakery, I saw her pull into the intersection. A semi came out of nowhere and broadsided her. I thought my life would end right there. I ran to her and cradled her in my arms. Blood covered her and me. That was the last time I ever dreamt about you." I swallowed hard.... "I thought you died."

Tears welled, and my chest tightened from the pain and the grief. She reached up and stroked my cheek.

"When Mom called New Year's Eve and said a young lady by the name of Belinda asked about me, my heart froze. She described you and I knew immediately who you were. I rushed home. Mom pointed you out. The minute I spotted you, I knew you were the Belinda of my dreams. What surprised me the most was when I touched you. It was the same experience. I got an arousal of all my senses, but more intense. I felt an immediate connection to you. Up to now, I've been afraid to say anything out of fear. I thought you'd think I was crazy. To tell the truth, I felt crazy and wasn't sure if you were the same sweet, caring person I dreamt about."

I gave her hands a slight squeeze. "Pretty nuts, huh?"

I watched her for signs of acceptance. Her pupils widened and narrowed, her mouth parted, taking in short steady breaths. Her head moved from side to side occasionally.

She reached for my face and cupped my cheek. I grabbed her wrist and placed tiny kisses on her palm. Tears streamed down her cheeks. "Robert, I love you," floated over her lips in the tone of an angel.

My soul took flight. Her words validated I wasn't insane, and she understood. We'd have a lifetime. This I knew for certain.

"I love you too, Angel."

A tear-stained face looked back at me, corners turning up to form a sweet smile.

Leaving the cold bagels and coffee abandoned on the table, we retreated to the bed to continue the conversation. She lay curled up in my arms as we talked.

"Robert, what you just told me about your dreams.... Well, as strange as this sounds...I...I...I dreamt about you in my coma, and it sounds like it was at the same time you were dreaming about me." She repositioned herself so she could see me.

"I know."

"You know?" She rolled onto her side and propped herself on her elbow. "How?"

"Colin and I played golf yesterday, and he told me. That's why I came over. He told me if I didn't straighten this out with you, he'd kick my ass. My plan was to just talk, but when I saw you in that robe and those bunnies...the memory of our first dream kiss...I couldn't control myself."

She bit her lip. "Robert, how could this happen?"

I shook my head. "I don't know. What I know is I found you and I don't want to let you go." I tightened my hold around her. "That's only if you want to stay."

Her eyes moistened, wetting her lashes. "I'm right where I always wanted to be."

A faint sniffle escaped her nose. I chuckled, wiping each eye with my thumb. "No more crying. Agreed?" She nodded and nestled her body against my chest.

"They're happy tears."

"Good. Still no more." I gazed at the ceiling. "You asked me why I call you Angel. There are two reasons. First, the night of the New Year's party when I saw you, I felt I was seeing an angel. In our dream, I thought you died, but there you were—alive and real." I paused and gave her a tug, bringing her closer. "It devastated me after the dreams stopped. I mourned for a person who didn't exist." My insides shook.

"I did the same. I spent hours in therapy after I found out our life was a dream. If I hadn't come out of the coma, I could've stayed with you." She made lazy circles over my abs.

I winced, rubbing my hand up and down her upper arm. "Don't say that. Us. Being here now wouldn't be happening if you hadn't."

"So, what is the second reason?"

"Because I called you Angel in our dream. They sent you to me from heaven." I took hold of her hand and kissed it.

Her eyes soften. "That's so sweet."

"Just like you."

She snuggled close. "Robert. Did you try to change the outcome of our dream?"

"I couldn't. I tried a few times, but nothing happened. It was like I was a character in a movie. I got the experience, but had no control over what happened. I was just along for the ride."

"You mean you really felt everything?"

"Angel, it was as real as you being here with me now." I exhaled. "How did it feel to you?"

"Oh, very real. When I woke up from the coma, I expected to see you in my hospital room. I didn't understand why you weren't there." She rolled over on her stomach and faced me. "But you're here now..." Her fingers touched the skin on my chest and I tensed. "What does it feel like when I touch you?" She continued toying with my skin. My eyelids lowered and my breathing became shallow.

I took a deep breath. "Like my body is about to explode. It's like every nerve ending is on fire, and you are the only thing that will put out the flames. But there's something else. When I'm around you, I don't feel alone. I feel like I'm home." I looked into her eyes. "Does that make sense?"

She nodded. "Perfect sense. When you touch me...a rush of sensations shoot through me.... It's the most sensual feeling you can ever imagine. And when I'm around you, I feel this connection, like my life is now...complete."

Belinda danced her fingers across my stomach and down to the button on my jeans. I swallowed hard, sucking in air as I watched her finger playfully circle the button repeatedly. Until she freed it from the buttonhole. A zipping sound followed, opening the fly.

Her hand slipped down the front of my pants. My body tensed and a groan arose from deep in my throat. Her eyes flared as her lips parted. She hopped onto her knees, grabbed the waistband of my jeans, and tugged. I reached for her camisole and pulled it off, throwing it across the room. Her shorts sailed through the air next. I stripped off my jeans, and she straddled my hips.

Breaths short and fast, she peered down at me. "But this, you, they're so much better than in our dream." Her fingers kneaded my chest. I reached for her and rolled on top, positioning myself to begin our lovemaking.

~ Belinda ~

My eyelids fluttered open to find Robert propped on his elbow, watching me. My heart filled with joy.

Then, like the semis that crashed into me, Sharyn flooded my head. I couldn't return his gaze.

I had turned into the other woman.

"Belinda, what's wrong?"

I pulled the covers up around me, wringing the smooth sheets with my balled fists. "What about Sharyn?"

"Oh." He rolled onto his back, placing his locked fingers behind his neck. "We broke up. After the New Year's Eve party, everything changed." He adjusted the pillow under his head. "She figured out something was going on the night she joined us in the hot tub. Then at the party when she walked in on us in my parent's great room on the Fourth, she snapped." He sighed. "We had a huge fight. She packed everything she had at my place. When we got to her's, she threw a trash bag at me and told me to pack up. Then she tossed me out on my ass."

"I saw you fighting by the car."

He rolled his head toward me. "I stopped making love to her."

"What?"

He positioned himself on his elbow. "I couldn't touch her. I felt like a cheat every time she came close." He slanted his eyes. "Nuts?"

"Maybe." I shrugged. "Then again, Colin was in the same boat."

His lips turned up slowly into a crescent shape. He nodded his head. "Yeah."

I smacked his chest. "Robert."

"Sorry."

"Any regrets about Sharyn?" Air stopped filling my lungs while I waited for the answer.

"Nope. Not a one. I'm glad it's over, and I'm right where I wanna be."

Air passed in and out. I could breathe again. He was a free agent.

"When we were in the hot tub and Sharyn showed up, I wanted to yank her away from—"

He interrupted, "Like you did to Lora?"

I jerked toward him and smiled. "Yeah. Just like Lora. I hated her too."

His hand cupped his cheek. "I can still feel the sting from the slap you gave me the second time you caught me with her."

"You deserved it. Ah, I mean he deserved it."

"I know." His tone lowered, and his fingers stroked my cheek. "I'll never do that to you. I'm not like that Robert."

My lips parted at the sadness on his face. I combed through his hair. "You're not. I figured that out several months ago, and I like this version much better." My cheeks flashed hot. "Besides, hands down, you're a far better lover."

He shook his head and raised the corners of his mouth, lifting his cheeks. "I like this version of you better, too." Robert brushed his fingers over my breast. My breath hitched. "Oh, yeah." He nodded. "Much better."

Giving me the once-over, he slid a smug smile across his face that turned devilish. "Besides. It's not every day a guy gets to take a girl's virginity twice." His brow lifted and his mouth thinned.

Blood rushed to fill my cheeks. "Robert, you bad boy."

He rolled onto his back, laughing. "That's me." As quickly as he started laughing, he stopped and sat up in bed. "I need another shower." With one jump, he stood at the side of the bed. He tilted his head as he bent in closer, scooping me up. "And you're coming with me."

I threw my arms about his neck, feeling myself go airborne. A stir of butterflies danced in my stomach. This was real.

CHAPTER 23

~ Robert ~

AT FOUR O'CLOCK in the afternoon, Belinda and I left for my parent's place. We owed them an explanation for playing hooky.

I pulled into the driveway and parked next to the guesthouse. We strolled arm in arm across the back lawn.

"I think we should go in and see Mom first before we tend to the horses. We need to let her know we'll be eating here tonight."

Belinda's brow knitted. "I haven't eaten all day, thanks to you." She gave me a gentle slap on the chest.

I snorted under my breath. "Well, we have been pretty busy. But I don't recall you protesting, unless I misinterpreted all that moaning…" A sharp poke in the rib cage got her point across. However, the little chuckle from her told me she had seen some humor in it. We headed toward the back door of the house.

"Mom!" I called out. There was no answer. I looked at the clock on the kitchen wall. "She must be in the office." I started upstairs with Belinda in tow. At the door, I stepped aside and motioned for her to go in first. Her slow, faint smile told me she understood.

I positioned myself outside the door so I could see Mom, but she couldn't see me. I knew seeing Belinda and me together completed her plan. After all, my parents weren't very subtle in their attempts to push us together.

"Sandra."

Mom was bent over her desk, supporting herself on her elbows, concentrating on the plans spread out in front of her. It took a second to acknowledge Belinda.

"Hi. What are you doing here?"

"I came to take care of the horses." No sooner had the words come out of Belinda's mouth than I appeared beside her, slipping one arm around her waist.

My mother stood. She covered her heart with her hand.

I gave Belinda a slight tug, pulling her closer. I never broke eye contact with Mom until I bent down and placed a kiss on Belinda's forehead. Looking back at her, I waited for a reaction.

Mom didn't speak, but sported a broad smile of dazzling teeth. I hadn't seen a smile like that on her in years.

She stepped toward us and took one of each of our hands in hers. "This sure took the two of you long enough." She placed a kiss on Belinda's cheek and then mine.

"And this goof wouldn't take a hint, no matter what I did or said." She stretched up to ruffle my hair. "Bend down here. You've gotten too tall."

I rolled my eyes and bent my knees. "Yeah. Well, I'm disappointed in you. You knew I wouldn't do anything as long as I was engaged. Nice try though." I winked at her.

"We wanted to let you know we'll be staying for dinner. But first, we're going to take care of the horses, and then we'll come back and help. Okay?"

"That'll be fine. But don't rush." She turned back toward her work and picked up a page from the plans strewn across the desk. "Dinner won't be until around seven. Your dad had a late meeting."

"Good. That'll give us time to clean up as well. See you later."

"There's a bag of baby carrots in the vegetable bin."

I grabbed Belinda's hand and raced down the stairs, stopping at the refrigerator for the carrots. At the back door, I swung her around, slamming her into my chest. I wrapped my arms around her and kissed her full, warm lips. I loved the contours of her back, her warm soft form pressing against mine. My breath became more ragged as my mind filled with images of how her soft, naked body had felt against my chest. I slid my hands into her hair and it excited me. She responded, kissing me back. I was about to suggest we go to the guesthouse when two palms pressed against my chest.

"Robert, as much as I want to, we'll get nothing done if we keep this up." She gave a push to put an arm's length between us.

I released a huff. "Okay. You're right." I opened the door and let her pass but inhaled as deeply as I could, drawing in her Angel Scent.

~ *Belinda* ~

I agreed to play water boy while Robert cleaned the stalls. I filled the trough outside. He came out of the barn with the last wheelbarrow of horse excrement mixed with wet straw. A distinctive sweet smell that screamed horse and one I was fond of.

I watched his arm muscles tense and relax with every maneuver. The sweat-soaked tee clung to his chest, and his well-developed biceps glistened in the sun. I continued enjoying the view until he vanished around the side of the barn *en route* to the compost pile.

I listened. The squeaking of the front wheel told me he was on his way back. Timing was critical. I broadened my stance and took aim with the hose, and waited for him to come around the barn corner. The squeak grew louder and louder. I waited. The wheel entered my line of vision first. Next came the bucket of the wheelbarrow and, finally, Robert. I let him have it, soaking him with a steady stream of cold, stinging water.

"That's for starving me all day. I ate some carrots just so I could survive."

The wheelbarrow went flying onto its side. He jumped over it and landed on his feet. He stopped. His face sinister. He balled his fists, lowered his head and tucked a shoulder, charging straight for me. I screamed, spinning on my heels, and took off running, weapon in hand. I had a small lead, so I turned back and blasted him again, momentarily slowing him down.

His hands flew up to his face, attempting to protect himself as he dodged from side to side. He reached down and grabbed the hose, giving it a yank. The nozzle flew, landing a few feet from him.

I watched him juggle it until he had a firm grip. The coil of hose by the faucet made me realize I stood in the danger zone. I made a half-turn as the bite of the forceful stream hit my side. I lifted my leg and arms.

"Robert!"

It didn't help. The stream kept coming. He grabbed my forearm, and I flailed my arms.

He dropped the nozzle. We continued to struggle. Laughter mixed with my squeals the whole time.

I twisted and wrenched to get out of his grip. The heel of my boot landed in a puddle of slimy goo, and my leg slipped out from under me. In a fraction of a second, I hit the ground with a thud, lying flat on my back. The muddy water soaked through my t-shirt, chilling my skin. It oozed into my hair and down around the waist of my jeans.

To get up, I turned onto my side, but he jumped on top, straddling and pinning me down at the wrists. His voice turned ominous. "Where do you think you're going?"

"Robert, let me up. I'm all wet."

"And I'm not?!"

We stared at each other. A steady spray of water continued to settle under me, soaking me, but I didn't care. The allure of his face captivated me.

I gave up my fight and lay studying his eyes. They had a glint I'd never seen before, not even in Dream Robert's. He looked damn sexy, and I wanted him.

"Do you remember?"

"How could I forget our water fight the day after our wedding? We were washing your car, and I ended on my back in a puddle of cold water."

A shiver ran through me and my teeth chattered. "And here I am again, on my back, lying in a puddle of water, but this feels colder."

I shivered harder.

Robert's face changed to concern. "You must be freezing." He sprang to his feet and offered a hand. "You need a hot shower to warm up."

"And you'll be right there with me to make sure I get warm?"

He snorted and winked, his voice low and sexy. "Yep."

I clamped onto his forearm, and before I knew it, I bounced to my feet, plastered against him. The expansion of his pupils told me he had one thing on his mind and something I knew I'd enjoy. "You're right. I think *we* need a shower."

A soft breeze rustled through the trees. A shiver raced through me.

"Let me turn off the water and pull in the hose. Start walking back. I'll catch up."

I walked across the back lawn toward the guesthouse and noticed Sandra standing on the patio, waving. "You're a mess."

"Thanks, Sandra."

"Here, take these. I know the tee will fit. The shorts might be a little big, but I think they'll be comfortable and *dry*."

I veered to get the bundle and smiled at her as Robert came up from behind and wrapped his warm arms around my waist. He rested his chin on my shoulder, his hot breath caressing my neck. His breathing was fast and shallow from his quick jaunt.

"We're going to take a shower. When we're done, we'll come in and help with dinner." He clasped onto my hand and moved toward the guesthouse. "She needs to get out of these wet clothes."

I turned back to her and waved. "Thank you."

"You're welcome. You have about an hour and a-half to do whatever."

My mouth dropped open. I jerked my head toward Robert. I caught him in mid-wince.

He lowered his head and shook it. "I can't believe my mother just said that."

~ *Robert* ~

Belinda and I entered the house through the back door. Mom was standing at the stove stirring something in a pot. The table had plates arranged on placemats with glasses and flatware fixed in the artistic way she did everything. The aroma of pork chops filled the air.

"What can we do to help?" I stuck my finger into the bowl of pudding on the counter.

"Get out of there!" she squealed. "You're not three years old anymore. Go watch some TV. I've got this under control. Your dad's not far and should be here soon."

"I love your pork chops." I walked behind her and kissed her cheek to distract her. Timing my next move, I poked my finger back into the creamy confection. "We'll be in there." I pointed my pudding-laden finger toward the family room before popping it into my mouth and sucking it clean.

"Robert!" She swatted at me but missed. "I hope you have clean hands."

I responded with a dismissive "Ha" and clamped onto Belinda's hand.

She waved and shrugged as she passed my mom.

We settled on the couch. She curled up under my arm while I surfed the channels. "News okay?"

"That's fine." She paused. "What day is it?"

"Wednesday. Why?"

"Where's my phone? I have to call Colin. I have a breakfast date planned with him in the morning." She patted at the nonexistent pockets of the shorts. "Oh, I remember. I left it on your nightstand."

I shifted and pulled mine from my back pocket. "Here, use mine."

She settled back against my side and scrolled through the contacts. "Any girls in here I should know about?"

"Nope, just Sharyn, and you already know about her."

~ Belinda ~

I tapped Colin's picture and waited. "Hi, Colin."

"You're on Robert's phone?"

"Yeah." I chuckled under my breath.

"So, does that mean you're together?"

"I guess you can say that."

"In bed?"

"Behave yourself. Besides, it's none of your business."

"Wait, a minute. Who sent him over to your place? Ingrate."

"Okay, we can talk about it over breakfast. By the way, thank you."

"You're welcome."

I glanced at Robert. His mouth twisted and brow knitted.

"Are we still on in the morning?" He asked.

"Yeah, how about we meet at Billie Boys off the Southwest Freeway?"

"Okay, see you then."

"Belinda."

"Yeah."

"Bring that sorry-ass boyfriend of yours along. I'd like to get his take on the two of you." I heard a faint chuckle.

"Colin!" A snort escaped. "I'll ask. See you in the morning."

Robert's mouth appeared less contorted when I turned and handed him the phone. "So it sounds like you'll be going to breakfast with him in the morning."

"Yep, and he told me to bring your sorry-ass with me."

His eyes narrowed at me.

I raised my hands, taking a defensive stance. "His words, not mine. So, do you want to come?"

He raised a brow. "You know I always want to do that."

I caught the double meaning of the words. "Robert Pendleton. That is not what I meant." I glanced into the kitchen, then back at him. "Well, do you want to accompany Colin and me to breakfast?" I dared not use the word "come."

A grin formed, and he pulled me close. "Yes, I'll go with you but afterward be prepared." A sudden jab to the ribs made him wince.

~ Robert ~

Around seven o'clock, the door from the garage opened. With his glasses perched on the bridge of his nose, Dad thumbed through a stack of mail. Belinda and I watched as he walked past the couch. He glanced up, "Hi, Robert. Hi, Belinda."

About to take another step, he stopped and turned toward us seated on the leather sofa. He studied our proximity to each other.

"Hi, Dad." I peered at my father, confident my arm around Belinda caused his sudden interest. He didn't say a word, but his mouth spread into a slow smile. He turned his gaze toward the kitchen.

I repositioned myself to see mother propped against the arch to the kitchen with her arms crossed in front of her. Her head lifted and a wide smile grew across her face.

He moved toward her. In a fluid motion, he raised his hand as hers met his, making a smacking sound as they high-fived each other. He kept walking and disappeared into the hallway that led into the primary bedroom. She returned to the stove.

I settled back on the couch beside Belinda.

"What was all that about?" she asked.

"My mother's way of telling my father all her meddling in our affairs paid off. What I don't understand is how she talked him into helping her."

I watched my parents throughout dinner. They acted as if Belinda and I had always been a couple. The conversation flowed, and the laughter came naturally. The part that puzzled me the most was Dad's participation in Mom's plot.

My mother often meddled in my life, and he objected to her nosiness when I was younger. As I grew older, I could see she only interfered when my decisions could've placed me on the wrong path. I learned to appreciate her parenting technique because when I followed it, things turned out better.

My father stayed on the other end of the spectrum. He guided me, but in a much different way. We had man-to-man talks, as he liked to call them. Through them, I learned things about him. This is why his part in her recent scheme didn't fit his personality. All of my life, he drew a line with her plotting. He tolerated it but stayed clear.

I scrutinized my mother and wondered what was different this time?

"Belinda." Mom crossed her arms in front of her on the table. "You worked so hard helping me with the party. I think you deserve some time off."

I studied her. She's meddling again. I sat back, wondering what she would say next.

"Why don't you take the rest of the week off and come in on Monday?"

I watched her give my father a gentle squeeze on the arm.

Dad had just filled his spoon with some pudding and shoved it into his mouth. He swung his head toward her. "What?"

Mom raised a brow and jutted her chin toward us.

He swallowed and wiped his mouth with a napkin. "Oh." He blurted out, "Robert, why don't you do the same? I'll cover for you and have Gail rearrange your schedule." He sat back and winked at Mom. She reached over and stroked his cheek.

I looked at Belinda, who watched the interaction. Neither of us had responded to my parents' comments, but the decision was final. We had the rest of the week off.

CHAPTER 24

~ Robert ~

I SCANNED THE restaurant and found Colin seated at a window booth.

He stood as we approached and gave Belinda a big bear hug, swinging her from side to side. He leaned down to give her a kiss, but stopped. Flashing me a quick glance, he chuckled as his gaze returned to her. His eyes concentrated on her luscious lips. "I guess those are off limits now."

She huffed, "Not to you." She pulled him close and planted an adequate but respectful kiss on his mouth.

I waited for them to separate before I stepped forward and offered him my hand. Very aware I was the third wheel at this breakfast.

"Hey, Colin."

The handshake he gave me had a hefty quality. He nodded and gestured toward the table for everyone to sit.

"Sit down. I had the waitress bring a pot of coffee." He scooted to the middle of the bench seat. Fiddling with his napkin, he unfolded it, then shot a fleeting glance at us, seated across the table. He wasted no time getting to the point.

"Sooo, what's up in your world?" He made an exaggerated movement by folding his hands in front of him on the table and glanced between us. He waited for a few seconds.

I wouldn't be the first one to open my mouth. Nope, I had more sense than that and suspected I'd be on the couch for at least a week. I waited. Belinda said nothing and just sat there.

"Oh, for heaven sakes. So are you or aren't you? And don't tell me you're just friends." A stern look flashed toward her.

"Are we or are we not what?" she spat, with a hint of irritation.

He moved closer to her. "Are you or are you not a couple?"

Continuing to keep my mouth shut, I wanted to hear how she would answer. I had a good idea, but it still piqued my curiosity.

Her lashes fluttered, and then she bit her lower lip. "We're more than friends and might work on being a... Colin, it's only been one day and I don't know what this is." She pointed wildly between me and herself. "What we are?"

She seemed frustrated by the question. I patted her arm. "It's okay, Angel." I gave him an icy stare. "He's just messing with you and seeing if he can bait me as well. It's what he always does." I made a circular motion with my hand in his direction. "Ignore the evil tall, blonde man sitting across from you."

A grin slid across Colin's face as he pointed a wagging finger at her. "I'll accept your answer because it tells me what I wanted to know. So Miss Davies, by my calculations, you two have been waiting for the go ahead for some time. Well, now you have it." He pushed himself back against the backrest of the booth. "I also know the two of you are my best friends. I just want to see the both of you happy. Do you understand?"

She reached across the table and spread her fingers over his hand. "I understand clearly, and thank you."

He winked.

I spoke up as he filled the coffee cups. "The other day when you told me about Belinda's dream.… I didn't tell you the complete story." I pursed my lips

He stopped pouring and looked up at me. "Okay, you have my attention."

I placed my arm around her. She turned toward me and nodded, telling me to go on.

"I didn't tell you I was dreaming about Belinda when she was in her coma. As far as we can tell, I was actually in her dream."

Colin squinted and his mouth opened as he tilted his head, with signs of confusion written all over his face. "Let me get this straight. Are you telling me you had the same dream?"

"Yeah. At the same time, but it was more than that. I actually experienced the dream. Feelings, smells…just as if I was awake. I walked around in the dream as if it were real."

He stiffened, sitting up straighter. "How does that happen?"

She took a sip of coffee before chiming in.

"We can't explain it but he was there. From what we have been able to figure out, his dreaming started the night I fell into the coma and ended when I woke up. When I saw him at the New Year's Eve party, I thought I was going nuts. I didn't know he recognized me. After all, logically, he'd have no way of knowing who I was." She turned toward me. "But I was so attracted to him and when we kissed in his parents' primary bedroom, I knew he was the man I fell in love with during those six months in the coma."

Holding up his hand, Colin asked, "Whoa! Hold up. You kissed?"

She turned toward him, biting her lower lip. I focused on her mouth and watched her nibble the way she did during every one of our chance encounters. I loved it, and it made me want to bite her tempting lip too. Over the past months, all I did was watch and want. Now I could and would nibble away at will, but later.

"Colin, I left that part out when I told you about my coma. It didn't seem like a good thing to do."

"So tell me now."

~ Belinda ~

I filled him in with the rest of the primary bedroom drama I had omitted when we talked in the barn. Colin listened, mouth open and looking befuddled.

"The night at the Galleria, when I found out Robert was engaged, I had no choice but to make plans to go on with my life. That's why I gave you my number and later agreed to go out with you. Colin. The night we almost ended up in my bedroom—"

"Ah. This might not be the best time to go into that." With knitted brows, he shot Robert a glance.

The waitress appeared at the edge of the table, shifting the attention to her. "Are you ready to order?"

Colin exhaled and scrambled for his menu.

As soon as the waitress left, I wasted no time getting back into my explanation. "Colin."

Mid sip of coffee, he gazed at me under his brows. "You're going to insist on finishing?"

"Yes, I am. It's important to me you understand what was going on between you and me....Why I couldn't make a commitment to you."

"Sweetie, I think I figured it out. You don't owe me anything." He extended a finger in Robert's direction. "This goof over here got in the way and that's okay. We'll just blame everything on him."

"I don't think that's fair," Robert piped up. "First, it was her dream. I had nothing to do with it."

Colin scoffed. "From what she just said, it sounds like you enjoyed it as much as she did."

"I may have enjoyed it but I also thought I was going crazy." He shifted in his seat. "That's something I never want to go through again."

I swung around and cooed, "Robert." I reached for him, and he kissed my palm, exhaling.

"Look guys. I understand. There's no hard feelings here, but I have to admit your story is rather strange. You should talk to someone who can explain this to you."

"I have an appointment with Dr. Rosen this afternoon. Robert's going with me. I can't wait to see his face when he meets Robert, but we're also going to ask him for some help. It's got us stumped."

~Robert ~

I pushed my plate away, poured myself another cup of coffee, then offered my two companions the same. I glanced at Colin. "When do you leave for Canada?"

He propped himself with his back to the window and stretched his long legs out on the booth seat. "As soon as we're finished here. I plan on driving as long as I can today, but I'm taking my time. I've never seen much of the country north of here and figured I'd take some time sightseeing on the way. The St Louis Arch, Chicago skyline,

Starved Rock State Park, etc., etc." He sipped his coffee. "Robert, I expect you to come up to go fishing next summer." He shook a finger at me. "I hear the black flies are rather friendly that time of the year."

I sucked in a short laugh. "Bet they're nothing like the roaches down here."

"I'll give you that one. I don't think a black fly can grab the can of Raid from you and spray you with it." Tapping the tabletop, he swung his legs from his reclining position. "Well, I'd better get going, or I'll only get as far as Dallas today." He looked at us. "You know, I'm going to miss you two."

Belinda and I escorted him to his car.

He turned to face us. "I guess this is it for now."

"You'll be back for meetings. I'll try to talk my dad into giving you a reprieve from the frozen north this winter, so you don't freeze."

"You've got a deal." He engaged in a brisk handshake which turned into a hug. As he pulled away he gave my shoulder a pat. The corners of his mouth turned up. "I might learn how to ski."

With arms spread wide, he approached Belinda. "As for you, young lady..." He engulfed her as he held her close, giving her a firm squeeze. Slightly pulling away, he cocked his head and said in a serious tone, "You know I love you."

She let out a gasp. "I hope like a sister."

His mouth contorted. "No, I think a little more than that." He pulled her close again to kiss the top of her head and then stroked her hair. He stared at me as he raised his eyebrows up and down swiftly.

I peered back at him, but knew it was his way of goading me. We're good friends, and I had nothing to worry about, even if he knew more about her than I cared for him to know.

Belinda retrieved her phone from her purse. "I want to take a selfie of the three of us by your car." We posed, and she snapped the picture. "Let me look at it to make sure it's okay." She showed it to us. Colin was headless, and I lost half of mine.

She's shorter than us, and that made it hard for her to achieve the right angle. Colin took the phone and retook the picture.

"Let me see." Her nose scrunched up. "We're three intelligent people. You'd think we could figure this out." She held the phone so Colin and I could see it. Only the top half of her face showed. "Colin, you're too tall. Robert, you try." She shoved the phone toward me. A slight scurry followed as the three of us jockeyed into position.

"Everyone say cheese." I heard the telltale click and scrutinized the picture. A smile grew across my face. I thought it captured each person's essence. Colin, with his casual self-confident stance. Belinda, perky and beautiful, sporting her faint smile that made me wish I could just kiss those lips. And me...reserved as ever. I held it out for them to see. "Good."

He threw a thumb up.

She, all smiles, replied, "We're good."

Colin slid into his car. He closed the car door, started the engine, and placed it in gear.

"I'll send you the picture. Call us tonight and let us know where you are. If you don't…" She shook her finger at him. "I'll send the cops after you."

"Okay, Mom. Well, you two take care and remember to name the first boy after me." One of his shit-eating grins slithered across his lips just before he broke out into a laugh. I opened my mouth to spit out a rhetorical comment, but he drove off, waving out the window. He turned out of the parking lot onto the frontage road that would lead him to US Highway 59 and north to his new home.

CHAPTER 25

~ Robert ~

"WELL, WE HAVE a few hours before your appointment with the fine doctor. What should we do?" I hoped Belinda would agree to go to her place and crawl in bed, but there'd be a slim-to-none chance of that happening. I realized, at some point, the lustful need would die down as we settled into a more normal routine. My practical side told me to plan on a lifetime of settling with her. Something I had looked forward to for a long time. Now my fantasy came as a living human female.

Not only did this woman excite the hell out of me, I loved everything about her. The way she tilted her head, her breathy giggles, the sparkle in her eyes, her nose, her hair, her lower lip, and the list never ended. I'd have four uninterrupted days of exploration with her and couldn't wait.

"We're close to Memorial Park and it's a beautiful day. Let's go for a walk and talk more about our dream. Compare. Kind of plan what we'll tell Dr. Rosen." She slid into the front seat of the Beamer as I held the door open.

"I like that idea.

"Top up or down?"

She retrieved a scrunchy from her pocket and pulled her hair into a ponytail. "Definitely down."

I warmed just looking at her. God, I loved this woman. I started the car, retracted the roof, and drove toward Memorial Park.

~ Belinda ~

With the flip of the switch in Dr. Rosen's office, I signaled him his next client had arrived. I took a seat next to Robert on the couch and wrapped my arm through his. On our three-hour stroll in the park, we had talked about the dream and made comparisons. We found we could explain a good portion of the events, either as a memory or some blank I filled in. How we both experienced the same dream stumped us.

The door to the inner office opened. Dr. Rosen opened his mouth as if he was about to greet me, but hesitated instead.

I rose. "Hello, Dr. Rosen."

The doctor didn't reply. He just stood in the doorway with a blank stare on his face. I led Robert past him, not saying a word. I pointed to one of the two upholstered chairs that faced a single one across from a wooden coffee table.

Robert wiggled around in the seat and clutched the armrests. He leaned back and glanced around the room and then started bouncing the heel of his right foot. He shot me a faint grin.

I sat and reached for his hand. "Are you okay?"

"Yeah. Yeah. I'm fine." He readjusted himself in his chair.

I smiled and leaned in closer. "It'll be all right. He doesn't bite."

Dr. Rosen took his time joining us. I watched him study us. He rubbed the stubble on his chin until he stopped behind the chair he'd sit in. "Belinda, may I ask what's going on?"

I plastered a big smile across my face. "I'd like you to meet Robert Pendleton."

He stood to shake the doctor's hand. "I'm glad to meet you, sir." He waited until Dr. Rosen moved from behind the chair and took his hand.

"Nice to meet you as well."

Robert sat down. This time, he leaned forward with his arms resting on his legs. He addressed the doctor, "You've been the topic of several of our conversations. Belinda tells me you've been very helpful with her recovery. Thank you for that."

Dr. Rosen found his way to his seat and picked up his pad of paper and a pencil from the coffee table. "Thank you for the compliments. Now Belinda, please tell me what's going on?"

I looked at Robert. "Go ahead," he encouraged.

Swallowing hard, I began. "We thought it'd be a good idea if he came with me to see you. I hope you don't mind." The doctor didn't respond, but motioned with his finger for me to continue. "As you can see, our relationship has changed." I bounced forward in my seat. "We're in love...we love each other." I glanced over at Robert with a half-smile and then turned back toward the doctor.

"When did this happen?" Dr. Rosen supported his chin, resting it in his palm with one of his fingers rubbing over his cheek.

"Tuesday evening." My voice almost mouse-like.

The finger stopped moving. He took a deep breath and leaned forward. "Okay. Before we go any further, you understand I can't discuss anything about you in front of him because of privacy issues."

I panned from the doctor to Robert and back. "I didn't think about that. But we have to talk to you about something. It's important."

"Very well. Robert, would you be willing to participate?"

"Yeah. Sure."

"Belinda, do I have your permission to discuss your case with Robert if needed?"

"Of course."

He went over to his desk, rummaged through the mess, and pulled out some papers, spilling half of one stack on the floor. He placed several forms on two clipboards and then stepped over the pile on his way back to us. "I'll need these papers signed before we can continue." He gave a clipboard to each of us.

I started reading the forms. Robert leafed through his. "I think I have yours."

We switched clipboards.

Once we returned the papers, the doctor resumed his position in his chair. With his elbow on the armrest, his hand supported his head with a finger cupped over his mouth, rubbing his upper lip. "So…you think you're in love? Belinda, what changed since our last meeting?"

The floodgates opened as I recapped the story of Robert's break up, Colin's departure, and how he encouraged Robert to visit me. I told him we had spent the last several nights together.

"You seem to be moving very fast, and that concerns me. Robert, how do you feel about all this?"

"I agree, sir. This might seem fast to an outsider, not that you're an outsider…I mean." He flopped back into the chair. "Look. I've never done this therapy stuff before, and I'm not sure what you expect."

"I expect you to talk to me. Tell me how you feel so we can explore what needs to be understood." Dr. Rosen continued to rub his upper lip.

Robert sat straight up in his chair and glanced at me. "Can I tell him?"

I nodded.

"I know she has told you all about our lives together in *our* dream."

When he emphasized the word *our*, Dr. Rosen raised an eyebrow.

"Ah. I see you noticed when I said *our* dream. You see, when I was asleep, I was with Belinda.

We've talked about it and compared notes. I can remember details and feelings about her just like she can about me. Now I know there are several things she has explained. Things like how she plugged my parents' house into the dream. What we don't understand is how I had the same experience. That's where we need your help."

Dr. Rosen sat back in his chair and tapped his fingers on the armrest. I suspected he was trying to process what Robert had just said. "I don't know. You're telling me you experienced the same dream Belinda had about you?"

"Yes. Right down to smells, tastes, what we had for dinner, and how wonderful she felt."

"And I experienced the same. When Robert came over on Tuesday, we didn't even really talk to each other. He saw me in my robe and bunny slippers, just like in our dream, picked me up, and that was it. I can't explain this, but it's like I've always known him." I turned toward Robert. "Like we belong together."

Dr. Rosen studied us, making me feel awkward. I'd learned to read his non-verbal signals over the past year, but this seemed different. He appeared dumfounded. Several seconds passed in absolute silence.

"Well, what do you think?" I asked.

Dr. Rosen threw his hands up in front of him, barely hanging on to his pencil, and flopped back against the chair. "I don't know. This is a new one on me."

"We were hoping you could help us figure out how this happened," Robert said.

The doctor twisted his mouth several times. He shot his index finger in the air. "I might have something." He jumped out of his seat, walked over to a bookshelf, and started scanning. He came to one title and tapped the spine.

"No." Starting up again, he stepped sideways, moving down the bookshelves spanning one wall of the room. Stopping, he pulled a book from the shelf and thumbed through it.

My heart sputtered. Will he be able to explain what happened?

He snapped the book closed and returned it to the shelf.

"I'm sorry. I thought there might be something in that last book, but no." He thumbed toward the bookshelf. "I'll ask around and do some research to see if any of my colleagues know or have heard about anything like this before." He returned to his seat. "Everyone's brain maintains in their memories everything they have ever done or seen. Some people are excellent at recalling those memories, while others have a harder time. Obviously, in Belinda's deepened sleep, she accessed the memories hidden in her mind."

He looked at Robert. "The mind is complex and full of areas still not understood. I have no way to explain how you ended up experiencing the same dream. What if there isn't an explanation? This might just have to be accepted. How would you two feel about that? Robert, you go first."

"I don't think it would really matter. The way I look at it, that's an extra six months of having her in my life. A bonus."

"But is she the same person as in your dream?"

"Pretty much. There're differences. She's more confident than the Belinda in the dream. This one has no trouble telling me what's on her mind. She stands her ground."

"Belinda, what about you? Is it important you find out how this happened?" the doctor asked.

I smiled at Robert before addressing the question. "No, I don't think it really matters. We talked about Dream Robert in my other sessions, but this Robert is better. In the last few weeks, I've learned he's sensitive and more grounded. He loves his parents. He's an honest man, and he loves his horse." I cooed at him. "Who can't love a man who loves his horse, but he has his faults?"

"Faults?" Robert spat out.

I swung my head in his direction. "Stop it. You're not perfect and neither am I. But we're real and that's what's important."

Dr. Rosen interrupted. "Robert, what happened to your dream when Belinda woke up?"

I watched Robert's face go white. He focused on the doctor. "I thought she died, and that's why it ended."

"And how are you doing? Do you feel you've worked through the grief?"

"I don't know."

I noticed the glare of the red light above the door. Our hour was up.

Dr. Rosen picked up his appointment book from the coffee table. "We'll have to continue this at our next session. Are you all right with that?" We nodded.

"How about I continue to see Belinda on Thursdays as scheduled? On

Wednesdays around four, I'll see the two of you together." He looked up waiting for our answer.

"I can do that," Robert agreed.

"So can I."

"Robert, if you feel you'd like some sessions without her present, I can set some time aside for you. I'll let you decide."

He nodded as he pushed out of the chair. Dr. Rosen and I followed. He extended his hand once again to the doctor. "Thank you. I'm finding this very interesting."

He shook Robert's hand and then gestured toward the back door.

"So, what do you think?" I asked as we walked toward the car.

"Interesting."

"He has helped me a lot, Robert. Give it a chance."

"I will. Who knows, he might tighten a few of my loose screws."

"Ha. Ha. So what do we do with the rest of our time off?"

He rubbed his chin and twisted his mouth. "How about the company beach house in Galveston?"

I grew a smile a mile wide. "Perfect, but I have to call my mom and Abby. They'd never forgive me if I didn't fill them in. Especially Abby."

"You can call them on the drive down."

"That works."

CHAPTER 26

~ Belinda ~

BRIGHT AND EARLY Friday morning, Robert and I hopped into the roadster with the top down and drove south toward Surfside Beach near Freeport, Texas. We would spend the next two nights in the corporate luxury beachfront house, doing whatever.

On the drive down, I called Mom and Abby, to fill them in on the needed details. Of course, Abby needed more.

Mom came first. I presumed her call would be less involved. I filled her in on what transpired, again with an edit, giving just enough information to satisfy her.

"Yes, Mom. That's right. Robert and I are on our way to Galveston."

"That sounds like fun. What are you going to do?"

"I don't know. I guess whatever we want. We're staying in his company's beach house."

"Belinda, are you sure this is a good idea?"

She had nothing to be concerned about. It was Robert. "I'll be fine."

I studied him while he concentrated on his driving, looking all hot and sexy, in his white t-shirt, jeans and designer sunglasses. Flip-flops completed the outfit. His elbow rested on the door as he slouched back in the seat with his hand flopped over the steering wheel, his head bobbing to the music blaring from the radio.

"You call us if you need a ride home or anything?"

I filled my lungs and let out a deep sigh that made enough noise to inform her of my frustration. "Yes, Mom. I'll call if I need anything, but I'm all right."

He turned his head toward me and dropped his sunglasses, so he looked over the rim, one eyebrow raised. "Yeah, tell her you're at the mercy of a serial killer."

I covered the mic. "Robert! Behave yourself and watch the road."

"What did he say?"

"Oh nothing, Mom. Someone just yelled an obscenity out their window. I'll come over on Monday and we can talk more."

Abby. I have a date with her on Monday.

"Mom, I haven't told Abby yet. You know how high maintenance she can be. If I need to change our day to Tuesday, would you mind?"

She snickered. "Tuesday fine. Just let me know."

"Great. I'll call when I get back."

"Sweetie, take care of yourself. I love you."

"Love you too. Bye."

"What was that about? Are you trying to make an enemy out of my mom?"

He threw his head back and let out a laugh. "She loved me in our dream and she'll love me now. No sweat."

"I'm glad you're confident. But, until we know for sure, play nice. Okay." I gave him a stern look, wagging a finger. "Do I have your promise?"

He exhaled and like a little boy he muttered, "Okay."

I loved that innocent look he gave me. If his charisma continued to have the same effect on me, he'd get whatever he wanted. Too bad he's driving 70 mph down Highway 288. Otherwise, I'd reach over and given my sexy hunk a kiss on those marvelous lips.

"Now, Abby, you're next." I shook my phone and pressed her number. Glancing at Robert, I saw him watching me with a smile the size of Texas. "Eyes on the road, please."

He snapped his head forward, like a good boy, still grinning.

"Hi, Abby."

"Hey, whatcha up to, friend?"

"I'm on my way to the Pendleton company beach house."

She said nothing for second. "Is there a company party down there Garrett failed to tell me about?"

"Well, I guess you could say I'm going to a private party for two."

"Didn't Colin already leave for Canada?"

"Yes, he did."

Things went silent until the screech that came through the phone nearly deafened me. I held it about six inches from my ear, waiting for the screaming to stop. She started asking rapid-fire questions, wanting all the details of how, why, and when Robert and I happened. The conversation lasted the rest of the trip to the coast.

He pulled under the carport and turned off the engine.

"Abby, I have to go. We're at the beach house."

"Monday, and I want everything."

"Monday, and I promise."

Apparently, the last hour of information just didn't seem to be enough. At least I'd have more spicy tidbits for my dear friend after my two-night stay in a romantic beach setting. But I would never kiss and tell. I would edit the more intimate details.

~ *Robert* ~

I waited on the deck while Belinda went inside to change into her suit. I stretched out on a lounge chair and closed my eyes. Over the past few nights, I hadn't been getting much sleep, and expected the next two nights wouldn't offer much more. I'd be going to work Monday, dragging. At some point, sheer exhaustion would smack me in the face.

I relaxed, allowing the rhythmic sound of the waves hitting the beach to fill my ears. The caw of a shorebird blurted in now and then—some close, some in the distance. The heat from the warm July morning embraced me as I drifted off.

"Robert. Baby." My eyes fluttered open to an apparition of a woman's image above me with a glowing light encircling her long, flowing hair. The warmth of a hand pressed against my face.

"Robert." The angelic voice called to me. "Are you awake?"

I rubbed my eyes and cleared my throat. Adjusting my position, I sat up. "How long was I sleep? What time is it?"

"About two hours and it's a little after noon. You're not in the shade anymore, and I didn't want you to burn. Are you hungry? I made some lunch."

"Yeah. That sounds good."

She turned to walk back into the house, wearing a sea foam green, two-piece bandeau swimsuit.

"Hey, that suit looks familiar."

She giggled. "I had it before our dream. I guess I just plugged it in and wore it to the dream pool party." Her shoulders briefly lifted. "Come on, let's go eat." She held her hand out for me.

The sun backlit her silhouette. I couldn't make out her distinctive features, but I thought she glowed as the sun formed a halo outlining her. I clasped her hand as I stood and tugged her close. "Thank you."

"For what?"

"For loving me." I wrapped my arms around her and pulled her close. Her warmth against my bare skin filled my heart and enticed a growing need for her.

She smiled at me. "Lunch is going to be much later, isn't it?"

Nodding, I bent down and gave her a soft, light kiss. She drifted her hand up the back of my neck, pressing me closer. She parted her lips, and I took the invitation to caress her willing mouth with my tongue. Her back arched and she let her head fall back. I sent kisses floating down her neck to her breast. With every tiny touch of my mouth on her velvet skin, she drew me in, taking my soul and mingling it with hers until I felt our spirits wrapping around each other as one. Our breaths quickened, and I tightened my grip around her smooth, firm back. I kissed her hard and enjoyed how she responded.

Enthusiastic catcalls and wolf whistles from the beach rang through the air. I glanced up and, with a thumbs-up, acknowledged the men passing by. I was happy to share my beautiful girlfriend with the world, but I had my limits.

I bent close to her ear. "Angel, we need to go inside before I forget we're on the deck." In one swoop, she filled my arms. My stride was long and fast. I wasted no time taking her to the bedroom.

~ Belinda ~

I lay on my beach towel on the soft sand, soaking up the sunrays. I flipped onto my stomach. "Put some sunscreen on my back, please." I loosely held the bottle in

Robert's direction.

"Do you think that's a good idea? We might end up back in the sack again."

"Well, you do it or I'll have to ask some poor schmuck walking by to help. You do want to get back in the bedroom sometime again on this trip? If I have a sunburn, I'll be off-limits."

One side of his mouth raised, and he grabbed the bottle. "Point taken."

I sucked in a deep breath as the cold lotion hit my skin, forming a figure eight on my back. A firm hand pressed and rotated the oily liquid over my shoulders, spine, and lower back. The other one joined in and they moved in harmony, working the lotion into my skin. Then fingers reached under the back strap of my top and release the clasp. More massaging ensued. Two thumbs pressed every vertebra of my spine as they moved up and down. Skillful splayed fingers kneaded the tense muscles, working their way over my back and then toward the flanks. I moaned. The impromptu massage felt wonderful. His hands settled even with my breasts, followed by the sensation of fingers moving closer to cup and caress them. The heaviness of his chest covered my back. He pushed the envelope a little too far for a public beach and it killed me to ask him to stop. "Robert, I think that'll be enough. Please hook the strap."

A puff of air hit my ear as the pressure lifted. When the strap reconnected, I sat up. Maybe some cold water might cool down the situation. "Care for a swim?"

He crinkled his brow and snatched up a towel, placing it over his mid-section. "Give me a minute."

I sputtered out a muffled giggle and covered my mouth.

He glared up, his eyes smoldering. "Belinda, that's not helping."

My chest tightened, trying to suppress the need to laugh. I pursed my lips tight. A giggle erupted out of the sides of my mouth.

His eyes glowed like embers, burning into mine. The more he tried to be serious, the funnier the situation seemed. I couldn't control myself. Out of the sides of my mouth a laugh erupted. I clinched my arms around my stomach. Seconds later, uncontrollable tears streamed down my cheeks.

"Okay. You're asking for it." He tossed the towel aside and lunged toward me.

I squealed and jerked out of his reach. I made a beeline for the water and hit the surf. Raising my knees high, I attempted to put some distance between us.

He was in hot pursuit, with his long legs reaching through the waves.

The whitecaps crashed against me in the waist-high water, slowing my speed. I glanced behind to judge the distance as two arms grabbed me and yank me under. I turned and pushed against strong shoulders and kicked to free myself.

I went limp. Struggling was futile. He pulled us to the surface. Laughter rang in the air. Waves hit us as we bobbed, struggling to stay upright. "You can't get away from me that easily." He pulled me up and kissed me.

~ Robert ~

The full moon rose over the gulf and hung in the sky, illuminating the night. Moonlight reflected on the water, touching the tips of the waves with a hint of silver as they rolled toward the shore. At high tide, the waves rushed in, consuming the beach. The closer to the deck they came, each lap against the shoreline became louder, causing a gentle rhythmic sound.

Belinda and I sat curled in each other's arms on a lounge chair while we sipped wine.

"Angel. The dress you wore to the cocktail party. Did you have it before our dream and just plug it in?"

She rested against my shoulder and swallowed. "No. My mother bought it for me when I was in the hospital."

"Why would she buy you a dress?"

"I found it hanging in her closet when I was getting ready for the New Year's Eve party. I didn't even know she had it until then. She told me she was on the way to the hospital and saw a sale sign in the shop window. She could never pass up a sale, so she stopped in. She saw the dress and thought I'd look great in it."

"Belinda, you were in a coma. I don't understand."

Her voice took a more serious tone. "My parents decided to take me off life support. There was a good chance I would die, so as Mom saw it, there were two possibilities. One, I would wake up and live to wear the dress, or two, she would bury me in it."

I stopped breathing and tightened my arms around her. I had lost her once already and the thought of her being gone for good reignited feelings. Then again, I thought I was nuts for being in love with a dream.

I rested my cheek against hers and ever so lightly swayed back and forth. "Angel, I'm glad you got to wear it. You looked as beautiful in it at the company party as you did on our wedding day. I couldn't stop staring at you when I saw you walk across the room to the table."

"Aaah. That explains why that night was so strange." She snorted. "And I thought I was in some weird universe."

I placed my mouth next to her ear. "When we got married in the dream, it was the happiest day of my life. Even if it wasn't real. Then seeing you in that dress at the party made me feel like I was back in the dream. Colin had no idea what he was doing to me when he asked me to keep you busy. Us being thrown together that way, the dress, your favorite song being played when we got up to dance…it all caught up with me."

"You know, on my porch, if you'd given me any sign you'd stay, I would've done anything for you."

"I know, but I'm glad you told me to take a hike. It stopped me from cheating on Sharyn and lying to my best friend."

She turned to face me. "I'm glad we stopped. I couldn't hurt Colin or Sharyn either, but I hated you because you walked away." She repositioned herself and rested against my chest. "Besides. It gave us time to get to know each other as friends. I think we both realized neither of us wanted to cross the lines we drew, and I'm glad we didn't. Things worked out for the best."

"Except for Sharyn. I hurt her."

"I think we both did, Baby. But would it have been better if you married her?"

I didn't answer for a few seconds. "No, I knew it had to end."

We sat in silence. I wrapped my arms around the woman I loved more than anything as I swayed from side to side under the moon-filled night.

On Sunday night, Belinda and I stayed at her patio home. As I predicted, exhaustion caught up with both of us. We lay wrapped in each other's arms and slept.

CHAPTER 27

~ *Robert* ~

MONDAY MORNING, REALITY started with a quick breakfast of our staple blueberry bagels.

I picked up my coffee cup and bent over to give Belinda a quick peck on the lips. Her soft expression engulfed me, and I placed the cup back on the table. Cupping her face, I engaged her full, soft lips and gave her a tender kiss. She reached for my wrist and kissed me back, exciting me. I loved it when she returned the kiss. A slight quiver in that lower lip of hers churned my insides with desire.

The smallest touch from her sent me soaring. I could never put into words what I felt when she touched me. I had tried to explain it, but my words always failed.

Every fiber of my soul told me to keep going, but I stopped. We had jobs. I pulled back. "Don't work too hard. Meet up at my parents for dinner and a ride?"

"I can't. Abby, remember?"

"Oh, yeah." If we met up at my parents, I'd at least have a chance of ending up in her bed again. "So, I guess I'll stay at my place tonight?"

She stiffened and acted as if she was thinking. One important maneuver my business sense taught me was to keep your mouth shut to give the client time to think. Of course, she wasn't my client, but the same principles applied in love and war. I prayed her next words were what I had on my mind.

"Ah. I might not be home until around ten, but I'd like it if you were here when I arrived." She swallowed and then looked at me from under her mile-long lashes. My heart melted. She had a keyless lock, but I had the combination and now an invitation.

I winked at her, and a smile slid up the corners of my mouth. "I'll keep the bed warm for you." She giggled. One last peck on the nose persuaded her to release her hold. I picked up the cup, and after putting it in the sink, walked out the door.

As I stepped onto the driveway and took hold of the car handle, I hesitated and glanced around. The morning was quiet, the sky big and blue as only the sky in Texas could be. The air smelled fresh, and I took in a good lungful. I couldn't remember the last time I actually felt this alive.

From the first time I experienced the dream with Belinda, it set me on a path to a downward spiral. As much as I craved being with her, the dream caused me to become unbalanced. I spent so much time sleeping, trying to live in our dream that to the outside world I acted depressed.

It took a toll on the family, my work, and my social life. I fought to survive in both worlds, but had no choice in the end. To keep my sanity, I pulled back on my sleep. I started dating Sharyn, which plunged me back into the real world, but that decision caused me to lose the only woman I loved.

I took one more deep breath and pulled the car door open. Yep, today was a great day to be alive. I had the love of my life and she was real.

~ Belinda ~

I punched the code into the pad and opened the front door. I'd had a long workday which led into dinner with Abby. Although I loved her to death, her questions exhausted me. The thoughts of a hot bath and my comfortable bed made me sleepy just thinking about them.

The only lights in the house came from the hood over the stove and the primary bedroom. They gave the place a warm glow and lit the rooms enough for me to have a clear path down the hall. I rounded the corner of the entry and stepped into the kitchen. Placing my purse on the counter along the wall, I noticed a new red rose with a note attached.

"For my beloved Angel."

Hand-drawn hearts surrounded the words. I traced the lines of the tiny symbols of love.

"He's real," slid softly over my lips. I looked down the hall toward the bedroom. Giving the rose a quick sniff, I placed it in the vase with its older brother and then switched off the light over the stove.

Robert looked up from his book and watched me climb into the bed. I curled up and snuggled against him as he wrapped an arm around me and pulled me close.

"Hi, Angel. How's Abby?"

"Exhausting as ever. That girl just has too much energy. It isn't right for someone to be that way at any time of day." I let out a gigantic sigh. "Thank you for the rose."

His arms tightened their hold as I nestled closer. "Anything for my Angel?"

My heavy eyelids drifted close. The bed and his radiating heat were just too inviting. Sleep overcame me.

I felt the bed rock from side to side. My shoes were slipped off. Followed by a thump as they hit the floor. That annoyed my ears. The zipper slid down and the pants slipped over my hips, then freeing my legs. Fingers unbuttoned the blouse and warm lips placed a kiss on my stomach just before I was lifted into a sitting position. My arms were helped out of the blouse. Fingers unlatched the clasp of the bra as my head rested comfortably against a shoulder. Fingers brushed softly over the left breast, but the sensation only lasted a second before my head and arms were guided into soft fabric. Last, I remembered the softness of the pillow under my head as a smooth sheet and comforter floated over me.

The warmth of him wrapping around me made me feel safe. A whispered voice puffed out the words into my ear, "Good night, Angel," as I drifted off into a deep sleep. I would need the rest in order to repeat another workday and night of questions and answers as I ate dinner with my parents on Tuesday.

Four months passed, during which Robert and I were inseparable. In the evenings we'd spend time with the horses. Music blared while we worked around the stable. But each time, the night ended with our finale, a dance around the stable dirt floor.

Afterward, we'd retreat to my patio home. We felt more comfortable there. We were close enough to both sets of parents, yet far enough away from well-meaning but possible parental interference.

Little by little, the guesthouse became void of Robert's belongings as I made room for my true love. I gave him the walk-in closet in the empty third bedroom. The only storage for his folded clothes became the floor of the same room. In the morning, he'd rummage through the stacks of clothes that lined the walls.

Early one Saturday morning, while we lay in bed waking up, the doorbell rang. He sprang out of bed, rushed to put on some clothes, and then vanished from the bedroom, closing the door behind him. I yawned and fell back to sleep.

Voices and bumping sounds from the hallway forced me to wake up. I listened for a few seconds and heard him, but couldn't identify the voice of the second man. I jumped up and scurried around to find something suitable to wear. The grunts and groans seemed louder as I approached the door. "What the hell?" I opened the door to find him and a deliveryman struggling with a six-drawer dresser, trying to make the corner into the third bedroom.

"We have to be careful. I don't want to nick the walls or woodwork. My girlfriend will kill me if we do," he instructed the deliveryman.

Robert had his back to me as I leaned against the doorjamb of the primary bedroom. I crossed my arms and smirked as I watched the two-man maneuvering act. I felt embarrassed I hadn't suggested we buy one, but also a little POed about his sneakiness.

The deliveryman's eyes shot my way, and he stopped assisting with the progression of the dresser.

Robert held the tilted dresser against his shoulder. He seemed to realize he carried the brunt of the beast as he shifted his weight. He peered over the top edge to find the deliveryman now offering little support and his eyes fixed on something.

"My girlfriend is behind me, isn't she?"

The man just nodded.

In a flash, his head spun around, sporting his signature smile of perfect teeth. "Hi, Angel. I'm kinda busy right now, but I'll explain after this nice gentleman leaves."

"Okay, but be careful, or your ass will be grass if you damage the walls or woodwork." I went back into the bedroom and closed the door. Through the walls, I heard a bit more huffing and puffing. Muffled voices came from the hallway, followed by the closing of the front door.

As I walked toward the kitchen, I passed the spare bedroom and glanced at the dresser that now sat in the middle of the floor.

I popped a K-cup into the coffeemaker as he appeared around the corner. "So, what do you think?"

I pursed my lips and didn't look at him. "It's okay." I picked up the streaming hot cup of coffee and headed for the couch.

He caught up with me and placed his arms around my waist. "What's wrong? Are you mad at me for buying it?"

I turned to face him. "No. I'm not mad, just upset you were sneaking around about it. That's not how a relationship works. We're supposed to confide in each other and work together. I wish you'd said something. Actually, I wish I'd thought to suggest we buy you a dresser. Anyway, next time just tell me."

He nodded. "Angel, I didn't want to bother you about it. I needed some place to put my clothes. The piles on the floor were getting old." He put a little distance between us and shrugged. "I'm sorry. Do you want me to return it?"

"No. But we're a team. At least you have good taste. The dresser fits the decor."

"Well, actually, I had Mom pick it out."

I rolled my eyes. "Really?"

He tugged me close. "I'm sorry about not saying anything. You still love me?"

I melted into his embrace, flopping my arms over his shoulders and around his neck. I couldn't stay upset with him. "Of course I do."

By the fifth month, he had moved in and taken over the third bedroom. He had lined one wall with bookshelves from floor to ceiling. A couple of comfortable man-size chairs facing a flat-screen TV also steered their way into the "mini-man cave." I kept the third bedroom as a study and studio. It was an excellent compromise.

~ *Robert* ~

On Saturday, the day before Christmas Eve, I made reservations at an upscale restaurant in the Sugar Land Town Center. The steakhouse had an elegant, quiet atmosphere, the type of place where you didn't feel rushed by the waitstaff. A couple could sit and talk all night, enjoying their meal and each other's company. The perfect place to execute my plan.

I finished dressing and sat in the living room waiting for Belinda. She usually was on time, but today it took her longer. I walked to the closed bedroom door and tried to turn the doorknob. It didn't open. I rapped with one knuckle.

"Angel, are you almost ready?" I couldn't figure out what could take her so long. She had spent the last hour and a half locked in there.

"I'm almost ready. I'll be out in a minute. Go back into the living room."

I let out a sigh and had no choice but to go wait. I sat on the couch and felt like a high school kid sitting next to the hovering father of his date, minus the father, of course. My nerves grated on me. Tonight had to be perfect. I had a lot riding on this evening.

The sound from the bedroom door lock caused me to raise my head to see my Angel. She floated out into the glowing light of the living room Christmas tree. At first, I couldn't move or say a word. I could only stare.

"Robert, say something. Do I look all right?" She twirled around in a light blue chiffon dress.

I stumbled over my words. "You…you look terrific." I stood and walked toward her. "Is that the same dress you wore on New Year's Eve and to the Spring Formal in our dream?"

"Yep. I had Mom shorten it for me." She swished the skirt from side to side. "I remembered how much you liked it in our dream."

Her hair fell softly over her shoulders, but she had it pulled up at the sides. "I wanted to look special for tonight." Her fingers toyed with a single diamond drop at her slender neck.

I held her upper arms and slid my wanton lips up her shoulder to her ear. She quivered as she took in a deep breath. "You know what this dress does to me. I can cancel the reservation and peel it off of you right now." I pulled the phone from my jacket pocket and waved it.

She stiffened as she swung her head around until her luscious mouth came within an inch of mine. "You put that thing away, take my arm, and walk straight out that door." She nodded toward the foyer.

I smiled. "There's my little lawmaker. Do you think you'll need a coat? It is December."

She tightened her lips. "I forgot about that." She spun around and disappeared into the bedroom. Seconds later, she returned with a black velvet cape draped over her arm.

I placed it over her and ran my hands down to her wrists. I rubbed my lips against her ear. Her breathing quickened as she molded herself to me. "I can still cancel the reservation."

To my surprise, she didn't move. She stayed pressed against me as she fastened the cape at her neck. Her breathing shortened and her breasts heaved as she continued to meld against me.

I didn't expect that reaction. She'd been so excited about tonight that I didn't think any amount of sexual teasing would deter her. Now I wasn't sure. Did I just ruin my plans by going too far?

"No way. I've waited all week for tonight." She turned toward me and raised her arms to encircle my neck. She leaned in close and brushed her lips over my ear. "But after we get back…." She smacked her lips. "You can do anything you want with me." She broke away and took a couple of steps, looking back at me. My mouth dropped open. She placed her fingertips under my chin. "Here, let me close that for you."

∞

I walked behind her and a sense of pride swelled within me as the patrons turned to admire my date. Men and women alike took notice.

The hostess led us to a table in a quiet corner of the restaurant. As soon as we were seated, the waitstaff appeared and offered us water, took our drink order, and gave us our menus. As quickly as they appeared, they vanished like a swarm of honeybees buzzing on to their next flowering bush.

The drinks arrived, and the waiter took our order. I lifted my glass to Belinda. "To a beautiful lady who fills my heart and life."

She smiled, and her glass met mine, making a clinking sound.

"And to a wonderful man who completes me." Another clink followed.

She lifted her glass to her lips and then took a sip of wine, zinfandel of course.

~ *Belinda* ~

I glanced over my shoulder at a table behind us. I turned back and pressed my lips to the glass, about to take another sip, when the room began to spin. I put the glass down and stared straight at Robert. His face faded away into a blur. My chest tightened and my breathing shallowed so much I thought I'd pass out from the lack of oxygen. The spinning sped up. I reached for his hands and held on, digging my nails into his flesh. A stabbing pain penetrated my brain from temple to temple. I gritted my teeth, wishing the spinning stopped. And it did, just as it had so many times before. Like a roulette wheel, the surrounding blur slowed and chunks of a memory fell into place.

Robert came back into focus. His expression was one of horror. "Belinda, are you okay?" His voice sounded shaky.

I forced myself to concentrate. A memory episode hadn't happened in months, and this one came on faster than any of the others. I couldn't talk at first and attempted to fill my lungs. I never let go of him, but eased up on the grip.

Finally, I looked up. "This is where it all started."

His brows knitted. "What started?"

"Us. This is where I first saw you." My pitch rose as I talked, as if I wouldn't have enough time to say everything that floated around in my head.

"I was sitting where you are. You were at the table over there." I pointed to the table I had glanced at earlier. "You caught me looking at you, and then you started staring at me. You were the most gorgeous guy I had ever seen, and I couldn't stop watching you. I tried to hide and let my hair cover my face. I thought you wouldn't notice my glances if I hid, but that didn't stop you. You just kept looking at me." My words came fast until I dragged a breath and stopped talking.

"Should we leave?" Concern filled his voice.

Then I remembered he had never witnessed a memory episode. The first one my mother saw almost had me in the car and on my way to the emergency room.

"Oh, Robert. I'm sorry. You must be scared to death." I looked at the indentions my nails had made. "Oh my God! Did I hurt you?"

"No. Look, you didn't even draw blood." He flipped them over and then rubbed at the marks. "I'm just worried about you. Will you be all right?"

"Yes. I'll be fine." I waved, attempting to dismiss how it really felt—confused and elated all at the same time. I smiled to myself. *Very much like sex.*

I ran a finger over a nail indent. "You sure I didn't hurt you?"

"No, I'm fine."

With spread fingers, I gently placed them over his. "Okay. Now let me finish telling you about this memory."

CHAPTER 28

~ Belinda ~

I SHIFTED IN my seat and bounced forward, leaning over the table toward Robert. A tug on his hands signaled him to do the same. I had recovered from the episode and my adrenaline rush lowered.

"I was home for summer break after completing my sophomore year of college and because I made good grades, my parents treated me to a fancy dinner. The hostess seated my family at this table. Your family was seated at that one." I tilted my head toward it.

He looked in the direction I indicated. His head moved in small motions from side to side. His eyebrows knitted closely together. "Belinda, I'm sorry, but I don't remember."

"That's okay. I wouldn't expect you to. This happened years ago, and I wasn't much to look at back then, anyway. The dinner took place before I matured physically, and my mother forced me out of my cocoon."

I rolled my eyes. "But boy, did you make an impression on me." I feigned a swoon covering my heart, patting over it.

"At first, I gave you a few fleeting glances, but the more I watched you, the more you drew me in. The way you moved fascinated me and the few subtle inflections of your voice I could hear. I found myself just flat out staring, but when you caught me watching, you flashed me that smile of yours and I was in love."

I adjusted myself and drew in a breath, focusing back on him. "In that split second…I imagined a life with you. I had us in love, married, raising children, and sitting on a porch in rocking chairs, growing old together."

My eyes moistened. I fanned at the tears. After all, I didn't want mascara running down my cheeks. The memory episode had been enough drama, and he'd been the only one in the restaurant who knew anything had happened.

I leaned forward again, this time planting my hands on the table to emphasize the next point. "Now it gets better." My eyes widened. "I'm over here falling in love with you. Then you get distracted by a petite blonde dressed in a fitted, pink suit, white pumps and matching purse, but that isn't important."

He snorted. "Seems to have been if you remembered all that."

I narrowed my brows and then waved him off. "Let me get back to the story." I took a breath. "It was Sharyn with her father. He called your dad by his full name. All I heard was 'Pen.' I never got the last part."

His mouth opened, and he looked dumbfounded.

"Honey, your mouth is open. Do I need to close it?"

He dropped his chin to his chest for a second, and then stared up at me as a sweeping smile crossed his face. "I remember that. It was a Sunday afternoon. She and her dad had just finished eating and came over to say hello." His smile grew wider. "I remember you now."

His expression became more serious as he recalled the memory. "My parents took me out to eat before my flight back to school for the summer session. I was starting my master's degree. I had just graduated from Brownston University and had been home visiting with them for a few days."

I rested back against the chair and let out a sigh. He remembered.

"And you're right. You weren't much to look at then." He let out a smothered snicker.

"Robert!" I smacked his hand.

"Well, you're the one who said it first."

I squinted my eyes and glared, letting him know I didn't appreciate his last comment. I knew I had lacked in the attractiveness department, but hearing the words come out of his mouth struck me in the heart a bit too hard.

"You don't get it, do you?"

"No…Oh yeah, I think I do. That's how I got plugged into our dream. I remember I took Sharyn's arm to lead her away from the table to talk. I glanced over at you and you were watching us. Your face looked sad, almost like you would cry. It threw me a bit because I realized I'd hurt you."

"My fantasy about you had hit a brick wall. At that moment I knew I wasn't your type, and a girl like me would never in a million years have a chance with someone like you." I heard the sadness reflect in my voice. He must have as well. He reached over and stroked my cheek.

The buzzing around of the waitstaff erupted as our food rolled up on a cart. One waiter cut the meat into slices, and then served it, while another filled the wineglasses. Everything we needed to complete a meal magically appeared before the waiters retreated. In the background, the soft soothing music of a violin filtered through the dining area.

Robert wasted no time picking up the conversation where we left off as soon as we were alone. "Belinda. You affected me as well. Something about the way you looked at me intrigued me. I remember how graceful you were."

I scoffed. "You must've had your glasses off."

"I didn't wear glasses. I saw what lay beneath that long, straight hair. Your big, blue eyes peeked out at me, and they grabbed me." He made a fist and placed it over his heart.

"Now you're just trying to save your rear. Go ahead. You can take your foot out of your mouth. I'm not stupid."

He frowned. "Okay. You believe whatever you want." He tapped his chest with his finger as he leaned in. "I know I'm telling the truth."

I could see his miffed expression, but how could he blame me? Back then, I knew he would've never asked me out, even if I were the last female alive.

The conversation had run its course. I cut a piece of the pork chop and took a bite, thinking before I washed the food down with a sip of wine. "You know, since I only got part of your last name at the restaurant. I bet that's why I had it wrong in our dream. I just used what I remembered, then filled in the blanks."

"What about the magazine article you saw? Our names were in it."

I had just taken another bite of food. So I thought while I chewed, then swallowed.

"I must have scanned the article or didn't remember. Apparently, the pictures and your first names didn't catch my attention." I let out a sigh. "What's important is I remembered an enormous chunk of something I had forgotten."

I sat and reviewed the memories, how bits and pieces had returned over the past year. "You know, I think the only mystery left is how you lived the dream with me."

"Yep. That's a mystery we may never solve." He lifted his glass toward me, and I did the same until the rims of the glasses touched, making a clinking sound. "To our unsolved mystery."

"Our unsolved mystery."

The rest of the meal chat focused on a wide spectrum of topics. We never came back to the memory the episode stirred up. I figured we exhausted the topic. During the invigorating conversation, we lost track of time.

At one point, I scanned the room and realized we were the only customers left. Several of the waitstaff leaned against walls with their arms folded in front of them.

I opened my mouth, about to suggest we leave, when the violinist appeared at our table. The violin's tone played our song, "Forever in My Mind." With every upward and downward motion of the bow, the melody floated on the air in soft notes. I reached over and took hold of Robert's watch. It read five minutes after midnight, Christmas Eve morning. A brief rush of excited butterflies stirred.

I noticed movement from the staff. They walked over and formed a semi-circle around the violinist. Just as they completed their formation, Robert pushed away from the table. I watched him fiddle with something in his pocket. Now, my little butterflies grew into an erupting volcano. He came around to my side of the table, went down on one knee, and pulled a small, black velvet box from his pocket. I stopped breathing as I concentrated on the man I loved kneeling before me.

He opened the box and presented it. "Ms. Belinda Davies, would you do me the honor of becoming my wife?"

I gasped and then held my breath. I reached for the box that held a three-stoned diamond ring.

"It looks like the one in our dream," I said as air passed through my words.

With a light touch of my finger, I rubbed over the stones and then took the ring from the box and held it up.

The halogen lights made the diamonds dance as I rotated it in my fingers.

"Is it your mother's?" I glanced up at him as he nodded. My gaze fell back on the ring as I continued to admire and play with it.

"Your mother got this from her mother, your grandmother?" I glanced back at him. He nodded. I went back to my fixation on the ring. Seconds passed. His throat cleared and made me look at the patient man kneeling in front of me.

"Well?"

"Oh!" I sucked in a breath as I realized I hadn't given him an answer. A smile swept across my face.

"Yes, I'll marry you." A tear rolled down my cheek, followed by another and then another as he took the ring and slipped it onto my finger.

"I love you, Ms. Davies. Forever."

"And I love you, Mr. Pendleton. Forever."

He rose, lifted me to my feet, and twirled me around, squeezing me at the waist as he planted a kiss on my willing lips.

I flung my arms around his neck while the violinist continued playing our song in the background. Over the melody, the restaurant staff burst into a clamor of cheers, while one snapped pictures. I wasn't sure if their jubilation was in congratulations for our new engagement or that now they'd finally get to go home.

∞

On the car ride home, I held my left hand in front of me and watched the ring sparkle in the dim light of the streetlights. I loved to watch the light jump through the perfectly cut gems. The streaks of color mesmerized me.

"How did you know about the ring in our dream?"

"Your mother was wearing it in the picture of the three of you sitting in the family room in the magazine article. I just assumed it was an heirloom."

"Do you remember your promise to me before we left tonight?"

A half-grin slithered across my mouth. "Oh, yes, I do."

"Good. I was just checking."

After we entered the house, I started toward the great room, fully expecting Robert to release my hand as I continued on, but he didn't. I snapped back on the ball of my foot as he tightened his grip. As I turned toward him, his eyes turned lustful and the glacier-blue color magically darkened to a deep ocean hue. His expression gave me everything I needed to know about his plans.

He tugged me to him and released the clasp on my cape. "Don't move. Keep your hands at your side." Memories of the fraternity Spring Formal from the dream flowed, and I did as he asked.

He ran his fingertips under the cape until they found the nape of my neck. I swallowed hard as I watched him concentrate on his actions. His fingers moved softly over my shoulders, causing the black velvet cape to slip off and puddle at our feet, and then he held me by my upper arms. He never looked at my face, but studied me until his soft mouth brushed against my neck. His warm breath prickled my skin. He flicked me with the tip of his tongue mixed with little nibbles, occasionally just brushing his lips against me.

My heart galloped, and I bit my lower lip as my back arched, anticipating his next move.

He moved to my side and locked my arms behind me as he gripped my wrists. With his other, he explored my body, igniting every nerve in me.

I loved it when he touched me. The touch of his fingers sent sizzling impulses through me, making me want more of him. I leaned back into his hand, the one that clasped my wrists. My breathing became shallow as my head fell back and I moaned.

I remembered my promise to him, one that would not be the least bit hard to keep.

CHAPTER 29

~ Belinda ~

IN THE MORNING I picked up the chiffon dress and velvet cape lying in a pile on the foyer floor. I arranged the garments over the back of a dining chair and headed straight for the coffee brewer. There I found a vase and a single rose. No card this time, but when did he do this? I was with him all night. "That's my man."

I cupped the bud and brushed the soft petals with my fingertips, taking a whiff. Robert had thought of everything. Like its predecessors, when dried, this one too would find its way into the box, which held all my dried roses.

I remembered his endearing expression the first time he discovered a drying rose in the laundry room hanging from the cabinet knob. "Wait. Don't tell me. It's for your treasure box. Like I didn't know that already?" He let out a grunt. His reaction reminded me why I fell in love with the man.

Steam rose from the cup of hot coffee. The heat radiated through the cup and warmed my hands, chilled from the cool morning air, as I settled down on the couch.

The Christmas tree had remained lit from the night before. Their glow, the only light in the semi-dark room, made the atmosphere warm and cozy. To add to the ambiance and ward off the chill, I lit a fire in the fireplace and made myself comfortable on the couch nearest the tree. I took a sip of coffee. I loved the early mornings, the way the light slowly filled each room as the sun rose higher in the sky. A quiet morning like this gave me a few stolen moments for myself.

I placed the cup on the end table. A flicker of light from my ring finger caught my attention, and I held it up in front of me. The diamonds came alive in the dim light, showing off the V-shaped, multi-colored facets.

"I'm going to be Mrs. Robert Pendleton," brushed over my lips.

Although the ring resembled the one in the dream, the real version seemed more intense. Everything in my "New Reality" seemed more intensified—Robert's touch, how I responded to him, our lovemaking. Even Abby seemed higher-strung—as if that were possible. A slight smirk slipped across my face.

"Good Morning." Robert disrupted my serenity. He rubbed the back of his neck and yawned before disappearing into the kitchen.

Even in the morning, when his appearance was the most unkempt, I found him sexy as hell. I loved his stubble, his unruly hair, his bare, muscular chest...and backside, and how his flannel pajama bottoms hung low on his hips. A shiver rocked me.

I propped my feet on the coffee table and picked up the cup. A muffled shuffle from the kitchen told me he'd be on his way to join me.

"What are you doing up? I figured after last night you would've wanted to sleep in." He plopped down beside me, careful not to spill his hot coffee.

I studied him. "Well, I could ask you the same thing."

He snorted. "I rolled over and felt around for you, but the bed was cold and empty. So I came to hunt down the future, Mrs. Pendleton." He took a sip of coffee and let out a spurt of air. "Hot. Hot."

"Careful, Baby." I took another sip. "I like the quiet of the mornings, and I don't get to enjoy too many anymore. Before a certain someone moved into my life, I had lots of them." I elbowed him softly in the ribs.

"Oh. Do I interfere?"

"Of course you do, but I wouldn't have it any other way. If I had a choice between all the times I spent without you and having you with me...well, I think you know which one I'd prefer."

He placed his arm around my shoulders, and I snuggled against his chest. We sat sipping coffee in silence, basking in the fireplace's warmth, waiting for the soft sunlight to fill the rooms.

Despite the caffeine in our systems, we ended up back in bed to enjoy sleeping.

We had nothing to do until our expected arrival at his parents' home for dinner that evening. The gathering would include my parents for our Christmas Eve dinner and gift exchange.

~ *Robert* ~

The minute I opened the front door of my parents' home, Mom and Dora hurried into the foyer and hovered around Belinda.

"Let me see it." Mom lifted Belinda's hand and eased it from side to side. She stepped aside so Dora could admire her daughter's recent present.

"Oh Honey, it's beautiful. Have you talked about a date yet?"

She panned between the two most important women in her life. "No, I just got it a few hours ago. I...We haven't had time."

My mother placed an arm around her waist, and Dora did the same. Sandwiched between them, they ushered her toward the family room, tossing ideas of wedding plans back and forth. She looked over her shoulder at me and mouthed, "Help me."

I knew this was a battle not worth fighting and offered my bride-to-be no assistance. I stood there with one hand tucked into my pocket and shrugged. With the other, I feigned a half-wave. "Hi, Mom. Dora."

My greeting to the elder women went unnoticed. I took in Belinda's pitiful expression and wished I could save her. Instead, I gave her a salute and whispered, "Good luck," just before I turned on my heels and disappeared into the dining room.

I ducked through the butler's pantry into the kitchen. Dad and James were standing by the island sipping drinks and watching her captivity unfold.

"Hi, Dad. Mr. Davies." I nodded.

James gave a throaty chuckle. "I think you can call me James or Dad, whichever you prefer, now that you're part of the family."

I took his hand and gave a manly shake. "Thanks, Dad."

"Robert, interested in a drink?" my father asked. "Your usual?"

I nodded and glanced into the great room. "She's their prisoner now."

The three of us let out a mixture of snorts, grunts, and ah ha's.

He handed me my glass of scotch on the rocks.

I rolled the cubes against the side of the glass before taking a stiff swallow. "Do you think I should step in to save her?"

"Son, let them be. She'll be fine. She knows how to handle her mother. Besides, the more they're preoccupied, the less they bother us. A little something you'll need to learn. Always let them think they're getting their way." James nodded toward me. "You'll learn soon enough it makes for a grand marriage."

"He's right. I love your mother to death but sometimes…." Dad looked at me. "You know how she gets when she's on a mission."

I rolled my eyes and nodded.

Dad nudged me. "You'll figure it out."

James spoke up. "Rob, you have a fine young man here. You did a good job raising him. You know, he came over about a week ago and asked my permission to marry my daughter."

One side of my father's mouth shot up. "Well, thank you. I'm proud of how he turned out, and I'm glad you're giving me some of the credit."

The conversation drifted to the latest football victory, losses, and potential playoff scenarios. Eventually, it moved on to recent newsworthy topics. I positioned myself so I had a clear view of the three women sitting on the couch in the great room. Belinda remained sandwiched between her mother and mine. I swore she hadn't said a word or most likely the pair hadn't given her a chance.

It appeared they had planned their attack beforehand. Mom came armed with a binder loaded with paper. While they talked, she made notes. I knew what that meant. I had seen this side of my mother on numerous occasions. She was in party-planning mode.

"Robert. We're going into the den to kick back and enjoy our drinks while we watch the Dallas-Washington game I recorded. Care to join us?"

I focused on my father. "I'll meet up with you later. I think I need to get her out of there for a bit." I nodded in Belinda's direction. "Dad, make sure you use coasters under your drinks. You don't want Mom—"

Rob interrupted with a half-grin and a wave. "Trust me. I know how to stay on your mother's good side. Besides, she's trained me well." He raised his eyebrows up and down.

Another low laugh erupted as the older men retreated through the butler's pantry to avoid the women in the great room. I heard my dad ask my future father-in-law, "Do you play golf?" as they made their way to the den.

I rested against the counter and finished the drink, then walked toward the henpecking session taking place on the couch. My approach went unnoticed and the two older women never skipped a beat as they continued to talk, with Mom taking a myriad of notes. They only stopped when I leaned over Belinda's shoulder and spoke. "Ladies, I'm going to steal my future wife. There's something I need to show her."

She let out a sigh, as if she'd been sitting there holding her breath the entire time. When I touched her shoulder, I felt her tension ease. I whispered in her ear, "Come on. Let's get out of here."

In that second, she shot to her feet, waving frantically through the air. "You ladies continue this and fill me in later." She turned toward the door and ran for it.

Her exit took me off-guard. It took me a few moments to register that she had almost made her way across the room. In full stride, I caught up and reached for the handle to the patio door.

She didn't wait and darted through her escape route. I saw a coat draped across one of the kitchen chairs and grabbed it, then raced after her. She stepped out from under the covered patio as I dove for her shoulder. I pulled her back, and she twirled around before she landed in my arms. "Slow down, Angel." I stroked her hair, and she buried her face in my chest.

She looked up, and I saw the most pitiful puppy-dog expression peering at me. "Can we just elope?"

I gave out a snorty, muffled laugh that forced the air out of my nose. "Let them have this. If they want to plan, let them. We'll set limits when necessary on the important stuff, like the budget, invitations, the dress, our vows." I lifted her chin and placed a quick kiss on her mouth.

"But you haven't heard half of what they're planning. It'll be a three-ring circus." She bit the side of her lower lip.

"Come on. We're stronger than both of them together. You know how to say 'no'. I know you do. You tell me 'no' all the time."

A faint smile swept across her face.

"We'll sit down and lay out some ground rules for them. Then we'll just have to make sure they stick to them and we have the final say on what we want to control. Okay?"

She smiled and nodded.

"Besides, I think I'd like the biggest wedding we can manage."

Her nose scrunched as her head tilted back.

"Ah. I see you need an explanation."

Her head bobbed. "An explanation might be nice."

I gave her nose a soft tap. "You missed out on a big wedding the first time, and since this is the last time I plan on marrying you…I want to remember it. Is that a good enough explanation?"

"Yes." She pushed the center of my chest with a forceful finger. "But if they get out of line, I pull the plug. Agreed?"

"Agreed."

I tilted my head toward the barn. "Come on. I have something to show you."

I helped her slip on the coat and then held her hand as we walked across the lawn.

The barn door creaked from the strain of the rollers as I pushed it aside and ducked in to flip on the lights.

"Come on. What I want to show you is over here." I led her to the back stall, the one the family used for tack.

Just before we entered, I turned toward her to block the view. "Close your eyes. No peeking."

Her eyelids squeezed shut.

I held her by the forearms and maneuvered her inside the stall. The smell of new leather filled my nostrils. Her head tilted up as her cute nose sniffed at the air. Her graceful, subtle movements were one thing I loved about her, and I wished I could freeze this moment in time.

"What did you want to show me?"

I stood behind her and maneuvered her into the best vantage point, then leaned into her back and whispered, "Open your eyes."

Her back straightened as a loud gasp escaped. I imagined her eyes were as wide as silver dollars.

"Robert…" She rushed forward and stroked the leather of the new English saddle with the big red bow. "It's beautiful."

I stepped closer. "Merry Christmas."

She spun around and flung her arms around my neck. She showered me with tiny kisses. I tightened my grip and found her warm, moist lips. Her reaction told me all I needed. Yeah. She likes it. I lifted her off her feet and continued the kiss while I carried her back into the corridor of the barn. Once steady her on her feet, I released her from the kiss. From my pocket, I pulled out my phone and punched a few buttons until the barn filled with a melodious sound. Stepping away, I bowed. "May I have this dance?"

She giggled, fell back into my arms, and we glided around the dirt floor.

~ *Belinda* ~

After dinner, we buried ourselves in the kitchen cleanup to get away from the Christmas gathering turned wedding planning. I handed Robert the last serving dish to place in the upper cabinet. His extra height gave him an advantage. As he closed the door, our parents entered.

"Sweetie, we're going to leave. We'll talk more in a few days." My mother reached over and gave me a kiss on the cheek.

Mom's face lit up. In that second, I realized I hadn't seen her this happy in years. The joy I saw convinced me Robert's idea to let the moms plan their hearts out was the right way to go. I leaned into her and gave her a kiss back. "In a few days."

Rob and Sandra escorted my parents to the front door and then returned to the kitchen.

"Mom, Dad, I guess we'll get going as well." He folded the dishtowel and placed it on the counter.

He slipped his arm around my waist. I noticed Sandra's frown as she entwined her arm around Rob's.

"Is something wrong?" I looked at Sandra and then at him.

Rob rubbed his chin. "Ah." He placed his hand over his wife's. "Can you two hang around? Um…we have something we'd like to talk to you about."

His request made me feel uneasy. Robert tugged at my waist. "Is that okay with you?"

"Yeah. I don't mind."

Rob pointed to the kitchen table. "Let's sit in here. Can I get anyone something to drink before we get started?" Everyone placed their order and then nestled around the table. Rob and Sandra sat on one side with us facing them.

I wrung my hands as my head filled with questions of what could be so serious. I reached for my drink but put it down as Rob started talking.

"Your mother and I have a confession."

I turned toward Robert. Up to this point, he didn't act concerned. Now his brows knitted, and he sat upright in his chair, staring at his father.

"Robert, Belinda. Sandra and I pushed you two together."

Robert snorted as he jerked his head back.

I chuckled under my breath.

I chuckled under my breath. "We know that. You two didn't hide it very well." His parents exchanged glances. "Belinda, honey, we manipulated you. But it was for your own good," Sandra chimed in.

"I don't understand." Manipulated? "How?"

"Sandra hired you when we knew Robert would be gone for a few weeks. Then I talked you into keeping Beau here. We wanted you to feel comfortable being around us before Robert came home."

I bounced my glances from Rob to Sandra. "I don't understand why you'd do that."

Sandra spoke first. "Because you two belonged together." She reached over and clutched my hands. "From the first time I shook your hand the day I came over to your house, I knew you were going to marry Robert. I felt it in my soul the second I touched you. Rob felt it too, when he shook yours at the cocktail party. After that, we knew we had to move you two along."

Robert started to say something, but Sandra cut him off. "We had to do something." She flipped her wrist in his direction. "You were running from her at every opportunity."

He just stared at his mother.

She continued. "Belinda, you've noticed how Rob and I just know what the other wants without saying a word. I know you've seen us pass something to each other when we're in the kitchen or when I pick up the phone before it rings and Rob is on the other end."

I nodded.

"Well, in time, you and Robert will start doing the same thing. You have a deep connection with each other. When you touch each other, is the feeling like nothing you've ever experienced?"

Robert and I exchanged a glance. We both nodded as we turned back to their expecting look.

"It's the same connection we have. The same connection Rob's mother and father had and his grandparents had. That's why we pushed. I hope you can understand why we interfered and can forgive us."

I slowly turned toward Robert. He returned my gaze. We both let out a muffled laugh, then turned back to his now confused parents.

"Mom, Dad. We have a story for you."

An hour later, Robert and I finished the recounting of my "Old Reality" and our "Dream Reality."

"We haven't been able to figure out why and how I could enter her dream. We even talked to her doctor to see if he had any idea, but he couldn't help, and his research into the matter has led nowhere."

"Okay, here's a thought," Sandra added. "Belinda, you said the first time you remembered seeing Robert was at the restaurant."

"Yes, that's right."

"Did you feel connected to him?" she asked.

"I knew he was the most handsome guy I had ever seen, and I couldn't keep my eyes off of him."

"Anything else?"

I searched my memories. "During that meal, I planned a lifetime with him." I reached for his hand. "Until Sharyn and her father showed up."

Sandra scoffed. "Even back then, she was a problem. Anyway, she's gone now and good riddance." She looked at me. "Don't you see? Your first meeting was the foundation for your 'Dream Reality.' That's what you called it, right?"

"Okay, maybe our first encounter and seeing the pictures of your family in the magazine, the ones now hanging in your office, could explain how I put him into my dream. That still doesn't explain how he experienced it?"

Sandra's attention turned toward Robert. "What did you feel when you saw her the first time?"

His fingers rubbed over his mouth. He placed his arm around me and pulled me closer. "I thought she was cute. She fascinated me and I enjoyed flirting with her. Sharyn and her dad changed the mood. After that, Belinda and her parents left. So, if we connected, I can't say."

Sandra appeared disappointed, as if she were hoping he'd had a deeper connection with me at the restaurant. A hushed "Oh," escaped her lips.

Suddenly, my breaths became short. The room started a slow spin. "Robert!" I grabbed for his hand. His fingers crushed in over mine just as the spinning sped up. Everything around blurred as I became unaware of my surroundings.

Feeling a hard surface press against my temple, I batted my eyes open. I realized I had passed out. My head ached. As I sat up, I noticed the concerned on my in-laws' faces. "How long was I out?" I rubbed my head.

"A few seconds. Are you okay?" Robert asked.

"I'll be better once my head stops throbbing." I buried it in my hands. "Did you explain what was happening?"

"I told them."

I lifted my head and peered at Sandra through my hair. Rob had his arm around her. Her expression was sheer shock.

"Are you sure you're okay?" Sandra reached over and patted my arm.

I straightened and sucked air in through my teeth. "Yeah, I'm fine, but better yet, I remembered something." I turned toward Robert. "I was in your car the night of the accident."

"Angel, we know that's impossible."

"No. You had on a light blue Oxford shirt, and your tie was loose around your neck. You were cussing at yourself while you were wiping up a drink you spilled all over the passenger side floor." I paused. "Am I right?"

His head cocked to the side. "Yeah."

"You reached over to pick up the cup, and I thought you would touch my leg, but your hand went right through it. I realized you didn't know I was there. I reached over and just as I was about to touch you, the ambulance drove away and the next thing I knew, I was sitting next to an EMT looking at myself on a stretcher." A tear rolled down my cheek. "I looked out the back window and watched your car fade out of sight."

Sandra jumped in her seat. "You had an out-of-body experience." Her fist smacked the table. "That's it! That's why you connected."

"Mom, what do you mean?"

"I'm suggesting her subconscious reached out to you because she was neither dead nor alive. She was someplace in between. She knew you two were supposed to be together, and she found you in her limbo state."

"Then you reached back when you were asleep, because sleep is the closest thing to a coma for you. Your subconscious knew she was meant for you. Robert, when you were sleeping, you had an out-of-body experience." She shrugged. "The mind is a strange and fascinating thing, and many times in our conscious state, we ignore subtle signs. At the restaurant, you two connected, but because you were both young and into your own stuff, both of you ignored it. Hell, even as adults, you almost let it slip by."

"Mom, you really believe this stuff?"

She tilted her head. "And you don't after what was just described? We have an amazing connection." She motioned between her and Rob. "Your grandparents and great grandparents knew each other's needs and wants, but you two..." She held her hand to her cheek. "You two have taken the Pendleton connection to a whole new level." She sat back against Rob's arm, exasperated.

Robert crossed his arms over his chest and leaned back in his chair. "Okay. Let's say your theory is right. That still doesn't explain why I had no control over the dream. She ran everything."

Rob chuckled. "Son, that's just the way it's supposed to be. The woman controls everything."

Sandra gave Rob a quick jab in the ribs with an elbow. "Rob, that's not true."

"Yes, it is. It was Belinda's dream, so she controlled it. This is your house and I'm your husband, so you control me while I'm here. I may not always agree with it, but you have the control, Sandra," he teased.

Her theory made more sense than anything I'd heard so far, and I couldn't deny it—Robert and I were connected.

"So we're good here?" Rob slapped the table and threw a glance from me to his son.

A snicker came out of Robert. "We're good here, Dad. We're real good."

CHAPTER 30

~ Belinda ~

THE WEDDING MARCH begins to play. My heart starts to race ninety to nothing. I can't believe the day is finally here, that I'm becoming Mrs. Robert Pendleton, IV.

I latch onto Dad's arm, then look down at myself to make sure everything is in place before we start down the aisle. To my horror, my beautiful ivory wedding dress is dingy and rumpled. I run my hands down the sides and front to smooth the material, but that doesn't seem to help. And to make matters worse, I discover a long tear down the side of the skirt.

Oh, God! What will everyone think of me? What will Robert think?

We make our way toward the lattice arch of tulle and satin ribbons…oh no! The red roses are wilting before my eyes. My stomach squeezes.

My eyes shoot over to Robert. A big smile is plastered across his face as I approach him. I reach for his hand, but I'm met with a cold, stiff one. Smooth skin, like a mannequin.

To my relief, he softens and molds his hand around mine.

A chill races down my spine as a deep, strange voice catches my attention. There before us stands a tall, thin man dressed all in black with skin as pale as a full moon. As he speaks, I swear I see fangs. What happened to the minister we hired?

"Belinda, do you take Robert to be your lawful wedded husband, to have and to hold from this day forward, in sickness and in health, 'til death do you part?"

A glint appears in Robert's eyes and my favorite signature smile spreads across his face as he squeezes my hands, easing my tension.

I say, "I do."

"Robert, do you take Belinda to be your lawful wedded wife, to have and to hold from this day forward, in sickness and in health, 'til death do you part?"

The words I had longed to hear are about to pass over his lips.

Robert says, "I—"

"No, you don't."

Robert and I whip around to look down the aisle toward the screeching voice.

"You promised to marry me. That bitch stole you away from me," screams Sharyn, running toward us, pointing at me, with a crazed look in her eyes.

∞

I shot up in bed and gasped for breath, my heart pounding as I glanced around the bedroom. I rubbed my damp hair and the beads of sweat from my face.

"Oh. Thank God. It was only a dream." I took a deep breath and exhaled, flopping back on the bed. How disastrous. A vampire for a minister, torn dress, wilted roses, and Sharyn? I rested my arms under my head. "I need to get a grip."

Why would I put Sharyn in my dream? Guilt? Why?

I didn't think I felt guilty for taking what had been mine. Maybe not in the physical sense, but we met and fell in love even before Sharyn appeared in the picture. Surely, she wouldn't humiliate herself by barging in on the wedding. We hadn't seen or heard a word from her since the breakup.

My head lie on my laced fingers. The nightmare had to be from all my worry that something would go wrong at the wedding. And probably because last night was the first night I'd spent away from Robert. I missed being in his arms.

A more pleasant thought made the corners of my mouth to kick up into a big smile. The day I'd long awaited had finally arrived. The day I'd become Mrs. Robert Pendleton, IV, for real. I couldn't wait to experience a lifetime of married bliss with the Real Robert. The last few months we'd spent together had been wonderful. Now, the wedding would go as our mothers planned. Whatever that is?

As agreed, our moms had taken over the actual planning of the event and excluded me from the decision-making process. I wished I'd insisted on being included in more of the whole affair, but they didn't want me to be stressed with the details. Little did they know being left in the dark was more stressful.

I took the week off before the glorious day and was forbidden to go to my future in-laws' home. Sandra and Mom wanted it to be a surprise when I walked down the aisle on the Pendletons' estate.

I pried Robert for details, but he was sworn to secrecy. I had only gotten an index finger and thumb slid across his pursed lips, as though they were being zipped shut.

To add to the frustration, I didn't know the full details of the honeymoon. The only hints given were "warm and casual." Based on that information, I needed to figure out how to pack. Even he didn't know where we were going. Only our parents and the pilot of the corporate jet knew the details.

∞

My nose picked up the aroma of freshly brewed coffee wafting upstairs. Pushing the nightmare aside, I took in another deep breath.

Mom assured me sleeping over would make my prep time easier. But I figured they wanted to make sure I behaved myself and didn't peek.

Right now, I didn't care. I had coffee on my mind.

I rubbed my eyes and focused on the alarm clock—10:30. I sat up and stretched my arms out wide as a big yawn escaped my mouth. I wanted to stay in bed, but I sucked in a deep breath. The mouthwatering scent of pancakes filled my nose. I tilted my head back and took another whiff. The worries over the wedding drifted away as a growl erupted from my stomach. I slid to the edge of the bed and pushed off, bounding my way to the kitchen.

Mom turned and glanced at me. "Good morning, Sweetie. Pancakes okay with you?" About to pour another measuring cupful of batter, she turned back to the stove, and made several perfect circles on a square griddle.

"Yeah. You know that."

"I do. Did you sleep okay?"

I slipped into a chair at the table. "Not really? I dreamt all kinds of bad things happened at the wedding. Really strange things. My mind was in overdrive."

"Don't worry. Sandra and I have everything under control. Just enjoy your day." She walked to the table carrying a plate of pancakes and placed it in front of me. "Would you like coffee and orange juice?"

"Coffee. I'll get it. How about you?" I got up.

She placed a hand on my shoulder. "No, you stay seated. I'll get it. Your pancakes will get cold." From an upper cabinet, she grabbed the mugs, then poured two cups of coffee. She returned to the table, set them down, and joined me. "Do you want to talk about your dream?"

"More like a nightmare, but no, not really. It was stupid. I'm just a little stressed, not knowing what to expect, and I missed Robert last night."

"Well, I assure you everything will be perfect. So stop worrying." She stood and went to the stove. "Sweetie, I'm going to fix myself some pancakes. Do you want any more?"

"Sure. Two. Thanks."

She returned to the table with the pancake order. We ate and talked for a while about several topics, one of which was how she had met my father.

I had heard the story many times before but enjoyed a repeat. I thought how great it was that they had been high school sweethearts and remained so even though they went to different colleges.

The fork lay on the plate, which held the remnants of my breakfast. I pushed away from the table and helped clean up the kitchen. The breakfast calmed me.

At around 2:30, my mother nudged me. "You need to think about getting cleaned up, and your hair washed and dried. The cosmetologist will arrive at four."

I strolled back upstairs where I took a long relaxing shower, washed my hair, and then put on a robe. After blow-drying the long tresses, I lay on the bed admiring my gorgeous wedding dress hanging on the closet door.

I snickered, remembering how Abby and I had run my mom around town for two days to four bridal shops, trying to find the perfect dress. I must've tried on at least two dozen dresses, but none of them seemed to be "the one."

On the second day, Abby found a pale blue taffeta, off-the-shoulder bridesmaid dress. It looked terrific on her, so she ordered it.

That afternoon, my mom mentioned that she really liked the strapless ball gown at the last shop. So we went back the next day. Abby had an appointment and couldn't come.

"This is something you need to do with just your mom. I can't wait to see it, though," she said before hanging up.

With Mom's help, I tried on the dress again, but it just didn't wow me. The saleslady recommended a few more dresses. Still nothing.

I had almost given up when the saleslady knocked on the dressing room door. A new shipment had just arrived and asked us to wait while she searched through the selection.

She returned with two more dresses. Mom hung them up. We studied each one through the plastic covers. The second dress, an ivory strapless, sweetheart-cut bodice of beaded lace that extended down to a cascading tulle skirt, put a smile on my face. Something about this one spoke to me.

When I ran my fingers down the length of the skirt layers a shiver raced up my spine. Tiny beads shone like stars in the night when I glided my fingers over them. The stiffness of the cascading tulle held the layers out away from the hips. They lay over a softer, more moveable fabric.

I studied myself in the full-length mirror and my breath hitched. My reflection had caused tears to well. "This is the one." The perfect one. It had even put a huge, admiring smile on my mother's face.

I got up from bed and stood in front of the dress, running the pads of my fingers over the nubby texture of the beaded lace. From the dresser, I picked up a rhinestone and beaded grosgrain ribbon belt and held it up against the waist of the dress. The sparkle of the rhinestones added a bit more bling to the dress's elegant design.

The doorbell chimed, then mother's muffled voice greeted a person.

"Belinda, Ms. Walters, the cosmetologist, is here. Are you ready for her?"

The time had arrived for all the beauty pampering Sandra had arranged.

I rushed to the stairway. "Yes, send her up." I waited at the top of the stairs.

As Ms. Walters ascended, she turned and addressed us. "Please, my friends, all call me Wendy."

"Hi, Wendy." I escorted her to my bedroom and then seated myself at the vanity. "I'd like my makeup to look natural, and I think I want my hair in an updo, or maybe pulled back and cascading down."

She gathered my hair back and studied me in the mirror. "Will you wear a veil?"

"No, ma'am." I reached over and picked up a rhinestone headband from the vanity. "This."

"Oh, that's lovely. I know exactly what to do. You'll be easy to work with. I'll have you looking amazing. Your future husband won't be able to take his eyes off you. Before I get started, let me paint your fingernails and toenails with this light pink polish."

She held out the bottle for my approval. I nodded.

"They can dry while I do your makeup and hair."

The final hour arrived. The cosmetologist had fulfilled her promise. My makeup looked just like I had imagined, only better. And my hair. It was beautiful, with wistful tendrils around my face and cascading curls down the back. The headband added the finishing touch.

"Well, I think this does it." Wendy packed up her belongings. "I'll let myself out and congratulations."

My mother peeked in. "May I come in?"

"Sure."

She entered dressed for the evening event in a light blue brocade long dress.

"Oh. You look beautiful. And your hair. Did you do it? It's gorgeous."

"No. I asked Wendy to style it before she left." She reached up and fluffed her hair in the back. "She's amazing and so nice. We have to thank Sandra."

Mom walked over to the wedding dress, still hanging on the door. "You're going to be the most beautiful bride." She turned toward me and smiled. "I can't wait to see Robert when you walk down the aisle."

"Me too."

"Are you ready to put it on? I'll help you."

"Yes." I carefully removed it from the hanger and handed it to her. Slipping the robe from my shoulders, I let it fall to the floor and then kicked it aside.

"Aren't you going to wear a bra?"

"No. I don't need one."

In fact, I'll wear nothing under this dress. I can't wait to see his face when he peels it off me.

I steadied myself with the help of her shoulder and stepped into the wedding gown, pulling it up into place. She ran the zipper up the back. Then she collected the embellished belt from the dresser and tied it around my waist, finishing the effect with a perfect bow. She then placed the glistening silver shoes on the floor in front of me. Lifting the front of the dress to see the shoes, I slipped them on. We walked over to the full-length mirror.

Her fingers splayed across the base of her neck. "Oh, Sweetie. You look so beautiful."

"Thanks, Mom." Just like the first time I tried on the dress, my breath hitched and tears threatened, but I blinked them away to avoid ruining my makeup. I prayed that when Robert saw me, it would have the same effect on him.

She walked to the door. "I'm going downstairs to watch for your ride."

"I'm not riding with you and Dad?"

"No. You drive over by yourself. We'll meet you there." She started out the door, but stopped and turned back. "Oh. I almost forgot something. I'll be right back."

I took advantage of her absence to remove the last undergarment—my panties. Lifting the left side of the dress, I hooked a thumb in the side of the bikini's, pulling them down. Then I shimmied them to the floor and kicked them under the bed out of Mom's view.

I wiggled my hips as I shook the layers straight to adjust the front of the dress. A mild shudder ran through me as the smooth, under layer brushed against my backside. The subtle touch of the fabric reminded me of Robert's gentle hands dancing across my skin. I closed my eyes and took in a deep breath that tightened the bodice, making me very aware of my naked body beneath it.

I let my breath out as Mom opened the door.

"You need something new, something old, something borrowed, and something blue. Your dress is new. Your engagement ring is an heirloom, something old. I'd like for you to wear my diamond drop necklace for something borrowed, and Sandra bought this blue garter for you to wear." She held up the necklace and garter for me to see.

"Thanks, Mom." I hugged her and kissed her cheek, then turned my back to her, lifting my hair. She fastened the necklace around my neck. Then I sat on the bed and lifted the dress just above the knee, careful not to expose myself, as she slipped on the garter. I fluffed the layers of the skirt back into place, enjoying the sensation.

She stepped back and sighed. "I guess that's all." Her finger swiped away an escaping tear.

"Mom." I took a step toward her.

Her hands flew up to stop me. "No. No." She tucked her chin down. "We can't touch because we'll both start crying." Raising her head, she peeked through her lashes at me, smiled, and walked to the door. "I'll see you downstairs."

"Okay." I walked to the dresser and picked up Robert's wedding ring and slid it onto my thumb. It spun with ease, so I clinched my fingers around the thumb to hold the ring in place. I walked to the mirror and stared at myself, fingering the necklace. It's almost time. Time to become Mrs. Robert Pendleton, IV and my dream about to become reality. Butterflies fluttered around in my stomach. Please let my wedding day turn out perfect and not like my nightmare.

"Belinda, your ride is here."

"Okay. I'm coming." I took a deep breath and then dashed out of the room.

CHAPTER 31

~ Belinda ~

STARTLED BY THE flash from a camera, I stopped after taking only a few steps down the stairs.

"Don't stop. Keep coming," the photographer said as he continued to snap pictures.

"Oh, my little girl is so beautiful." Dad walked up a few steps and escorted me down the rest of the way. He kissed my forehead. "Robert's a very lucky man."

"Thanks, Dad." I kissed his cheek. I raised my head and eyelids toward the ceiling and fanned my eyes with my fingers to control the threatening waterfall. Beside me, I could hear him suppressing his chuckles.

"James, don't make her cry," Mom scolded.

"Okay." He took hold of my elbow and escorted me to the front door where she waited.

"Wow!" I couldn't believe what I saw parked in front of the house—a shiny white limousine.

Arm in arm on either side of me, my parents walked me down the path to the waiting vehicle, where a chauffeur stood at attention by an opened door. The photographer hovered around, snapping pictures. He'd halt our movements to ask us to smile and pose. At the car, I hugged them and slipped into a back seat. Then, with my fingers pressed against my lips, I blew them a kiss as they faded from view as the door closed.

The limo pulled into the circular drive at the Pendletons' house and stopped at the front entrance and aligned with the walkway. The chauffeur spoke through the dividing window, "Miss Davies, Mrs. Pendleton, instructed me to let her know when we arrived so she can make sure your fiancé wasn't in the house. I'll be right back."

I saw my parents make their way toward the limo as the chauffeur conversed with Mrs. Pendleton. She nodded. He turned and stepped down the path to open the limo door. He smiled and offered his hand. "The coast is clear. Let me assist you."

"Thank you." I placed one foot on the pavement. The photographer came out of nowhere. He instructed me how to pose as he snapped pictures from all angles.

When I could stand, Mom swooped in and started working with the layers of my gown, fluffing and smoothing everywhere needed. The photographer continued clicking away. I thought of smacking him the same way one would swat an annoying bug.

The spontaneous flurry settled down, and the chauffeur extended his elbow to escort me toward the front door. My parents walked ahead as the pesky photographer continued his irritating shooting spree.

A big smile formed across Sandra's face as I stepped into the foyer. "You look gorgeous."

"Thank you, and so do you." I admired her beautiful long dress of gold brocade.

"Wait here. I'll go get your flowers."

"Oh! My! God!" came from the top of the stairs. Holding a nosegay of red roses, Abby came bouncing down toward me with a huge smile. "You…You…there isn't a word expressive enough. You're right. This dress is 'the one.' It's perfect and worth the wait." She took me by the shoulders and touched each of her cheeks to mine. "I'd hug you, but I'm afraid I'll muss you up." She stepped back. "You're going to knock that hunk of yours flat on his ass when he sees you."

I let out a little giggle and held her by the hands. "You look beautiful too."

A twinge on my thumb from the pressure of her grip reminded me about Robert's ring. I slipped the band off and held it out for her. "Here put this on your thumb." I pressed it into her palm. "Make sure Colin gets it and *don't* lose it."

"Right." In an exaggerated motion she slipped the ring on her thumb and made a fist. "See all safe."

"Abby. Be serious."

"I am."

Sandra returned with a cascading bouquet of red roses, baby's breath, and long, ivory satin ribbons. "I hope you like it."

"It's beautiful." I lifted the roses to my nose and inhaled a deep breath. "They smell wonderful. Did Robert tell what roses mean to us?"

She and Mom nodded simultaneously.

"It's time to start. All the guests are seated and we need to head for the back." Sandra placed her hand under my elbow and led me to the back door, where my dad stood waiting for me. Mom followed.

"Come on, Dora. Let's go take our seats." She guided her out the door to where the ushers waited.

Dad turned toward me. "Well, Sweetie, this is it. Are you ready?"

My heart began racing, and butterflies began bouncing from side to side in my chest. They made my voice quaver as I spoke. "I think so." I examined my ivory gown, checking its condition. Relief washed over me. It hadn't turned dingy and rumpled like in the nightmare, and thank goodness, it wasn't torn. Now, if I could only make it down the aisle without tripping and falling.

Soft music drifted in through the open door. The tempo changed and Abby started her procession.

He extended his elbow, and I latched on. My knees wobbled, and he tightened his grip to steady me. "Come on, Sweetie. You can do this. You've waited a long time for this day. Think only about Robert."

I had waited a long time. In fact, sixteen agonizing months had passed since he proposed. Waiting was the price I paid for a May wedding. But now the day had arrived, and I'd be Mrs. Robert Pendleton, IV within the next fifteen minutes, as long as nothing went wrong. Sharyn. She'd better not show up!

I tucked my chin and let the vision of Robert's charismatic smile chase all my thoughts away. With a deep breath, I straightened and smiled. "I'm ready."

We walked out to the backyard and down the carpeted walkway toward the last aisle between the guests.

My breath caught as I glanced around. The decorations were amazing, and in some aspects, reminded me of the dream wedding reception. Tiny white lights twinkled throughout the trees. Floating candles and white pearl-colored balloons drifted over the pool's surface. The flickering flames between the bobbing balloons gave them an effervescent appearance and mimicked giant champagne bubbles. It had to have been Robert's contribution. He must've remembered those details from the dream.

My gaze drifted to the huge white tent. What little I saw through the plastic windows looked like twinkle lights were strung everywhere, and I thought I saw bits of a chandelier. I stretched my neck, trying to get a glimpse of the furnishings, but with the door flaps closed, it was impossible.

I turned my head as much as I could, without appearing to be a fool, and attempted to take it all in. I cursed myself for agreeing to be kept in the dark. Sandra and Mom did so much, and what I saw so far, I loved.

We stopped before we reached the last row of guests and waited for the wedding march to start. On que, the guests stood and just like in my dream I took my first step toward my love.

My father led me up the aisle. As I past each row, I'd scan for Sharyn. I was relieved she didn't crash my big day, but the ceremony wasn't over yet. A sick feeling erupted in my throat, and I took a spontaneous deep breath, which help.

Thoughts of Sharyn vanished when I saw the beautiful lattice arch of tulle, satin ribbons, and perfect red roses. Under it stood my waiting groom. His eyes glistened, and he had a heart-stopping smile. He rocked back on his heels before shifting his weight from one foot to the other. For the first time in our lives, he looked nervous. I became lost in his expression, and it washed away all my fears.

My heart quickened, but my gaze never faltered from his. He became my rock who drew me into our *Destiny Reborn*.

Totally focused on my fiancé, everything became a blur until he reached for my hands. I fumbled with the bouquet and passed it to Abby, then placed my hands in his. The minister began, "Repeat after me."

As Robert finished saying, "til death do us part," his face lit up.

The haunting memory of the nightmare crept back. Holding my breath, I glanced down the aisle just to reassure myself Sharyn wasn't running toward us. I closed my eyes and let out my breath, relieved the devil herself was nowhere in sight.

I refocused on his glacier-blue eyes. As I repeated my vow, my heart hammered and my breath seized. A tear of joy escaped with my ending words. He gave my hands a few quick squeezes.

As the ring ceremony began, I noticed Colin, the best man, for the first time when he handed Robert the ring. Colin winked.

He slid a white gold band onto my finger. "With this ring, I thee wed."

The band looked just like the one from the dream. I smiled up at him and he whispered, "Forever."

Abby handed me his ring. I slid a matching wider band onto his finger. "With this ring, I thee wed."

He smiled, and I whispered, "Forever."

"I now pronounce you husband and wife. You may kiss your bride."

I wrapped my arms around his neck and he embraced me as our lips crushed together. I floated backward when he dipped me in his muscular arms, allowing the kiss to linger. The minister cleared his throat and snickers erupted from the guests. The kiss...well, Robert had to peel me off him after we were upright. It was a kiss he'd never forget, and even better than the one in our dream wedding.

Another song played as Abby and Colin retreated down the aisle. Robert surprised me and whisked me off my feet. I hugged his neck and kissed his cheek. "I love you, Mr. Robert Pendleton."

"I love you too, Mrs. Robert Pendleton."

"I like how that sounds."

"Me too."

The parents joined us in the reception line and greeted the guests as they headed for the tent. Afterwards, the wedding party returned to the lattice arch, where the photographer took numerous pictures, finishing just before twilight.

Sharyn never materialized.

CHAPTER 32

~ Belinda ~

MY FINGERS FLEW up to my parted lips as I gasped when we entered the air-conditioned tent. The sight was beyond anything I could've imagined.

"Oooh, Robert. It's gorgeous."

He squeezed my hand and grinned. "I'm glad you like it. I told our moms about our dream wedding reception. They did a good job."

Twinkle lights ringed the perimeter at the ceiling and crisscrossed the top of the tent several times, like the spokes of a wagon wheel. At the peak hung a beautiful chandelier. Just enough light glowed to set a mystical mood. To the left of the entrance sat a long, rectangular table draped in a pale blue floor-length tablecloth, piled full of wrapped presents. Round tables flanked the dance floor, forming a horseshoe. A floor-length, pale blue linen tablecloth and a smaller white topper adorned each table. In the center of each sat an arrangement of red roses and baby's breath around a clear glass hurricane shade containing a flickering white candle. Crystal glasses and silverware adorned the place settings.

A crackle from a microphone followed by a high, ear-busting shrill caused the guests to turn toward a man standing in the middle of the dance floor. "Honored guests. Allow me to present to you, our newlyweds, Mr. and Mrs. Robert Pendleton, IV."

Robert led me down the aisle between the tables toward the dance floor. Once in the middle, we turned to face the guests, and he thrust our clenched hands into the air above our heads. The room went wild. People stood and applauded. A few shouted, snide remarks from his coworkers sent a ripple of laughter around the room. He made a "V" with two fingers and pointed them from his eyes to the hecklers standing around their tables.

The crowd returned to their seats while we continued to make our way across the dance floor toward the head table.

I gazed around the room, wanting to take it all in. Between each window stood a tall, thin, white tree with white blossoms and draped with more twinkle lights. Elegant, soft music touched my ears above the chatter of the guests. I turned to the far left side of the tent to see a quartet—a harpist, a violinist, a cellist, and a flutist. I realized they were the ones who played the wedding music. When we reached our table, I noticed the man who announced our entrance standing behind a deejay station with several huge speakers on either side. I figured he'd step up the night's entertainment later.

The waitstaff started serving salad on elegant bone china plates.

I glanced all around the tent to take in more of the surroundings. There was so much. I darted my eyes from one side to the other. Would I be able to experience every aspect of my special day?

The touch of warmth encompassed my hand, followed by a mild tightening sensation. I turned to meet Robert's eyes and the chaos that roared inside me melted away.

As the delicious meal ended, Robert's father stood and made a toast to us, followed by my father, then the matron of honor, Abby, and finally the best man, Colin. Of course, he had to make a joke about Robert stealing me away from him. "I hope I'll meet someone as sweet and lovely as Belinda, someone who makes me as happy as she makes Robert." He looked at us, raised his glass, and smiled. "No hard feelings, man."

A burst of laughter erupted from the guests.

The quartet played a soft, barely audible tune in the background. "Dear guests, please follow the bride and groom to the stables so they can have their first dance." Colin bent down toward us. "Come on. Get up." Arm in arm between us, he led us into the stable and directed us to stand in the middle.

"Ladies and gentleman, you may think it's strange for the first dance to be held on the dirt floor of a stable. And I agree—it is strange…well, so is the couple standing in front of you. But dancing on this ground is something they have shared and I hope will share for years to come. Ladies and gentlemen, I present to you, Mr. and Mrs. Robert Pendleton, IV, in their first dance as husband and wife." Applause from the guests standing at each opening of the stable filled the space as Colin backed away.

In the background, the quartet music filled the dimly lit barn. Just like in the tent, twinkle lights gave the space a romantic ambiance. The horse stalls displayed light blue and white ribbons.

Robert held me around the waist and positioned us to dance. "Are you ready, Angel? Our audience awaits."

I glanced around at the guests watching us. He lifted my chin and his gaze captivated me. "Now follow me." I nodded. He took a step, and I followed his lead. He twirled me around and made me feel like a princess dancing with my prince charming, even though the dance floor was dirt. I wouldn't have had it any other way.

We returned to the tent, and the party went into full swing. The deejay had the room hopping as the drinks flowed.

Earlier, Colin caught the garter to the relentless whooping and hollering of his ex-office mates. He wore it on his bicep like a badge of honor while he danced with every single and some not so single females who would say "yes."

Rob's secretary caught the bouquet. I knew very little about her, but she glowed as she emerged from the huddled mass of ladies scrapping over it. She thrust it above her head, holding it like a torch.

After we made the rounds to talk to all our guests, Robert and I retreated to the front table to relax. Colin had a "one too many" sway to his walk as he gave Robert a slap on the back. "Your moms sure know how to throw a party." His speech came out slurred.

"Colin, you're in the guest house tonight. Give me your keys." He held out his hand, palm up.

"Nope. I'm fine."

Robert gestured with an upward motion of his hand and pointed to it.

I giggled. He tsked, but dug in his pocket and relinquished the keys to his beloved car.

"I'll give these to my mother. There's t-shirts and shorts in the dresser. Everything you'll need to clean up with in the morning is in the bathroom. I'm sure she'll throw in brunch and a swim in the pool for her favorite adopted son."

With a lopsided grin, he centered himself between Robert and me, throwing an arm over each of us. "You know, you two are my favorite people and I love you both."

Robert took a deep breath.

I snickered under mine. "We love you too."

"Hey, I was wondering…did you think about inviting Sharyn? Now *that* would have made things interesting," he slurred out.

I lifted my head. My back went rigid. I knew the alcohol made his judgement fuzzy, but hearing that name sent chills up my spine.

Robert intervened in an instant. "We didn't think that's a good idea. Besides, her father told my dad she's moved to Europe. He told me she took over her father's holdings."

Robert shot me a steady look and nodded. He stood up and put his arm around Colin. "Come on, let's go find you someone to dance with." He mouthed, "I'll be right back," as he led Colin away.

It didn't take too long before he returned and placed a kiss on my cheek. He sat and bounced his chair close, then put his arm around me. "I'm sorry about that."

His head tilted until his forehead touched mine. "Are you okay?"

"Yeah, I'm fine. How come you didn't tell me about Sharyn moving?"

"I didn't think it was important, and I didn't want to upset you. I found out months ago."

"I would've loved knowing she was out of the country. I've been worrying myself sick she would crash our wedding."

With my thumb and index finger about a half inch apart, I said, "That little piece of information might have calmed my nerves a bit."

He stroked my forearm. "Am I forgiven?"

"Of course you are, you goof."

"Good, let's dance!" He picked me up by the waist and led me to the crowded dance floor.

With my head against his shoulder, the sway to the slow dance coaxed me to sleep as the exhaustion from the day caught up with me. He leaned close to my ear. "Come on. Let's get out of here. We can take a nap before we leave for the airport."

I raised my head. "But what about our guests?"

A laugh burst out of him that confused me.

"What's so funny?"

He leaned forward again so I could hear him. "You said the same thing in our dream at the Homecoming frat party, and my answer is the same as it was then. Who cares?" He held out his hand. I hesitated a moment, took it, and followed him out of the loud, music-filled tent.

In the upstairs guest bedroom, Robert closed the door behind him. I toed-off my shoes and walked backward toward the bed, waiting for him to turn around. As he did, I beckoned him with my finger, swaying my hips from side to side.

A half-grin formed on his face. "I thought you were tired?"

I reached out and grabbed the lapels of his tux to pull him along. When the mattress touched the back of my legs, I sat down and motioned for him to kneel in front of me. He raised a brow, but did as I asked. I clasped his hand and guided it up under the hem of my skirt and onto my calf. It didn't take him long to figure out my plan. I let go and rested back on my hands, watching him. His eyes never left mine as he maneuvered closer up my thigh, exploring. My breath became more irregular with every upward movement of his soft touch toward my inner thighs. My back arched, but I refused to break our gaze.

Suddenly, he stopped as he reached his destination. His half-grin grew to a full smile. "You naughty girl! Going commando for our wedding? Tsk. Tsk."

I lunged forward and grabbed his lapels, pulling his lips within an inch of mine. "Nothing but the best for you, Mr. Pendleton."

∞

Robert changed into a simple white t-shirt and jeans. He put on his lightweight flight jacket and then reached for his phone and started texting.

"Who are you texting?" I leaned around him to see.

"Sharyn. We didn't invite her to the wedding, so I thought the least I should do was text." He gave me an impish grin.

I popped him in the arm and then backed away. "That's not funny!"

"Come on. You know I'm joking." He walked over to show me the screen. "Look, I'm just texting Mom. She wanted me to tell her when we were ready to leave."

He held up his finger while he read her response. "Okay. We have to wait a few minutes."

He pivoted and wrapped his arms around me. "Have I told you lately how much I love you?" He kissed my nose.

"Does your moaning before our nap count?"

His head tilted, and an eyebrow raised. "Technically, you did more moaning than I did, but you can consider my contribution to the noise level as a 'yes'." He gave me a soft kiss on the lips. "Am I forgiven?"

I hesitated before answering. "Hmm. I'll think about it."

His phone pinged and he read the text. "Okay, you think about it, but we have to leave now. Let's go." He waited for me to put on my jacket and grab my bag, then escorted me down the stairs.

Sandra waited for us at the front door. As we approached, she opened it to show off the remaining guests lining the walkway to the limo. As Robert and I rushed toward our ride, tiny bubbles filled the path and floated all around us as the guests cheered us on.

Once inside the limo, he pulled me toward him and wrapped his arms around my waist, and then he planted a slow, sultry kiss on my lips. My eyes drifted shut as I reveled in the electrifying sensation buzzing up my spine. As the limo pulled onto the street, I raised my eyelids and looked over his shoulder, out the tinted window. What I saw shocked me. A familiar Mini Cooper sat parked alongside the curb. In the driver seat sat a female with short blonde hair—her narrowed eyes shooting daggers as the limo drove by. *What the hell is she doing here*?! My back straightened, my muscles tensed, and my heart skipped a beat.

He rubbed my back. "What's wrong?"

I only smiled, not wanting to ruin the rest of our night. "Nothing. I'm just enjoying being Mrs. Pendleton." I leaned in and placed my mouth over his, brushing Sharyn out of my mind.

The trip to the Sugar Land Airport took no time at all. We boarded the jet and made ourselves comfortable. Jessica, the flight attendant, saw to our needs and brought us drinks.

Before takeoff, the captain came out of the cockpit and spoke to us. "Congratulations, Mr. and Mrs. Pendleton." He sat down facing us. "I've been sworn to secrecy by my boss, your father, not to tell you where you're going. What I can tell you is, you'll have approximately twelve hours of travel time. We'll be making one stop to refuel before we touch down at the final airport. There will be a limousine waiting to take you to your final destination about two hours away. Once you arrive, you will receive a binder with all the information needed to complete the first half of your trip. At your next destination, you'll receive another binder with the itinerary for the last half. So for now, relax and enjoy the flight. We have made the bedroom up if you choose to use it."

I saw a slight rise of the captain's brow. A smirk brushed across Robert's face as he stared at the captain. I assumed some guy-speak was taking place.

I looked at the captain. "This all sounds so cloak-and-dagger, but I'm hooked."

"Sorry. I can't give you any more information." He got up and closed the door of the cockpit behind him.

A garbled, "Please fasten your seatbelts," came over the intercom. "Jessica, prepare for takeoff."

The cabin lights dimmed, and within minutes, the ground fell away. The lights below blended with the stars in the clear night sky. I lolled my head against the backrest and remembered our first date in a blue Beamer on "Make Out Ridge," from a dream that seemed so long ago. The jet banked to the left and then level out as it flew east.

"It is now safe to move about the cabin," blared over the intercom.

The attendant approached. "Can I get you anything?"

"No. I'm fine."

Robert unbuckled his seat belt before he answered. "No. I'm good as well. We'll be in the bedroom. Please wake us two hours before we land. We'd like a light breakfast. Bagels, coffee and orange juice will be fine."

He waited for the attendant to leave and then leaned over to me. "Unbuckle your seatbelt. We're about to become members of the 'Mile High Club.'"

The jet touched down and rolled onto the tarmac. The sign across the hangar doors told me we had just landed in Paris, France.

As I stepped out, I felt refreshed despite our antics that made me an official member of the "Mile High Club." The sun rose in the east and the air was balmy.

As soon as we deplaned, a uniformed chauffeur escorted us to a black limousine parked a few feet from the jet's ramp.

The drive north to the final destination took two hours. We made a game out of guessing where we were heading, but I figured out we were somewhere in the Champagne region of France.

The limo stopped in front of a magnificent chateau. The chauffeur opened the door and one of the chateau's staff greeted us. "Welcome, Madame and Monsieur. Please follow me."

The three of us hopped onto a waiting golf cart that sped off on the path leading to the back of the main house. It stopped outside a quaint cottage, and he escorted us in.

"I hope this will be to your liking?"

I couldn't believe the expense and time our parents took to make our honeymoon so extraordinary.

Robert walked around the cottage with his fists on his hips, exuding a sense of confidence, as if he did this sort of thing all the time.

The man walked over to the table in the center of the room and picked up a black binder. He then pulled a white envelope from his inside pocket. "They asked me to give both to you on your arrival. Please, Monsieur, open the envelope first."

He took them and the man stepped back toward the door and waited. After opening the envelope, he let out a chuckle. He pulled out what looked like French currency, then walked over and handed the man a bill. "Thank you. Everything is perfect. I'll call the front desk if we need anything."

The man bowed and relinquished two sets of keys. "Monsieur, the first set is for the golf cart. It is for you to use around the grounds. This set is for the cottage. Your luggage will arrive shortly. Information about the chateau's services is on the table." When he finished, he left.

Robert held up the envelope and shook it at me. "They thought of everything."

He walked over and picked up the black binder on the table and plopped down on the couch. With a flip of the cover, he studied the contents, never raising his eyes. He patted the seat beside him. "Aren't you interested in knowing how our parents have planned our lives for the next week?"

CHAPTER 33

~ Belinda ~

A COOL BREEZE lifted the lace curtains as they floated on the current. The song of a nearby jay filled the air. I stretched and took in my surroundings. The morning sunlight flooded the room, casting shadows on the walls. I swung my feet over the edge of the overstuffed bed. We had done very little the last day and a half but eat and sleep. Jet lag had set in.

I walked into the sitting area of the honeymoon cottage to find Robert lounging on the couch, reading a book. He sported a wide grin as I approached. "Sleep well? I ordered us some breakfast. Coffee is on its way."

"Coffee. I need coffee." I curled up next to him and nestled into his chest. Strong arms encircled me. They gave me a sense of security. I liked that feeling.

"Well, what should we do today? We really should get out of the cottage and at least see what this area offers. Who knows when we'll get back to France again?" He tightened his arms around me.

"I'm happy just where I am, but I guess you're right. It'd be a shame not to take advantage and do some sightseeing. How about we take a ride in the golf cart to see what the grounds look like? We could go up to the chateau to see if they have any sightseeing information. Also, let's eat dinner in the main dining room tonight." I patted his chest.

"While you were snoozing, I looked over the information the place supplied in the room. Did you know there is a nine-hole golf course on the grounds? Have you ever played golf?"

"No, but do you really want to spend time on a golf course? It's our honeymoon."

I adjusted to see his face. His pushed out lip and pouty expression gave me the answer I wasn't looking for. "Tsk. I guess I'm going to get some golf lessons."

His expression changed and perked up. He tightened his arms around me. "You'll like it. The course can be very peaceful and it's relaxing."

A knock at the door alerted us that breakfast had arrived. He climbed over me, nearly tossing me onto the floor. His quick maneuvering placed me on the couch before he headed for the door.

The aroma of freshly brewed coffee hit me. After a few cups, I'd be ready to take on whatever France offered, including golf lessons.

By the end of mid-morning, not much had change. We had moved to the side patio, still clad in pajamas, to have breakfast.

I propped my feet up and sipped at my third cup of coffee while he went inside to set up a tee time for my first golf game ever.

I closed my eyes to enjoy the quiet and the fresh air. A gentle breeze rustled the leaves as the chirp of birds drifted through the air. From the other room, I heard him speaking French into the phone. French? Robert can speak French? I listened closer. From what I could tell, he was fluent in the language.

"Well, we have a three o'clock time set up."

I stared at him.

"What? Is something wrong? I figured we'll play nine holes and still have plenty of time to come back and get duded up for a nice dinner."

"The time is fine. How come you didn't tell me you speak French?"

Robert furrowed his brow. "It never came up." His shoulders lifted. "I took it in high school and then in college. After I started working with my dad, I found it came in handy with some of our French-speaking Canadian clients." He dropped next to me. "Maybe that's why we're in France?"

"I enjoy hearing you speak French. It sounds sexy. What other little secrets will I learn about you?"

He leaned back and crossed his arms. "Je suis sur autant que je vais decouvrir de toi."

"Ooh." A shiver ran along my spine. "What did you say?"

"I'm sure as much as I'll discover about you."

Golf, was interesting. Although I had little power in my swing, I hit the ball straight and kept it on the fairway, unlike Robert, who walloped the ball several hundred yards.

He lost four balls. With each loss, he spent at least fifteen minutes raking his club through the brush, attempting to find the lost sphere. The entire time he mumbled obscenities under his breath.

"Baby, I thought golf was supposed to be relaxing. You seem so stressed looking for those balls."

He gripped the steering wheel of the cart and winked. "It's just part of the game." The cart jolted forward as he made a sharp turn toward the clubhouse. I shifted and would've fallen out if my instincts hadn't caused me to grab onto the cart's roof. I scowled at him.

"It's all part of the game." He snickered.

~ *Robert* ~

I scanned Belinda from head to toe as she pivoted around. She looked sexy as hell in her black dress. It had long sleeves with the top half covered in lace. The tone of her smooth skin peeked through over her shoulders and arms while the back plunged in a "V" to her waist. The skirt came mid-thigh and bounced as she moved. Her heels gave her legs a long, slender appearance. She wore her hair up, twisted in curls on top of her head, exposing her neck.

I could tell she had very little on underneath, and the sheer sight of that little black number draped over her delicate frame made me want to explore. From what I could tell, one shiny button at her waist was all that kept the dress in place.

At dinner, I watched her lift her fork and take dainty bites. If she keeps eating like that, I'll never get that dress off of her. A ray of light bounced off that button and teased me. Excitement stirred within me. But I just smiled, raised my glass to her and took a sip of champagne, biding my time.

The dress intrigued me. She obviously wasn't wearing a bra or stockings. I caught a glint from her side. What would happen if I unfastened that button?

On the way back to the cottage, we walked down a path lit by ornate dim lamps. I rubbed my fingers over her bare back. She snuggled in closer. A slight quiver rushed over her skin as I floated my fingers under the "V" of the dress. I reached in under her arm and brushed the underside of her breast. She giggled. I pulled her closer.

As soon as I closed the cottage door, I took her in my arms. She rolled her head back and let out a gasp while I kissed the crevices of her neck. I toyed with the button. Next to her ear, I whispered, "I've been wondering about this button all night." I nibbled at her earlobe. "And what would happen if I unbuttoned it?" With a slight flick of a finger, the button released and the dress back fell open.

I glided my hands down her bare ass. "Commando again?" I squeezed each cheek and her gasp filled me with desire. I turned her so her back was against my chest and teased her soft flesh as I peeled off the dress.

She melted against me, swaying her head from side to side, and moaned, "Robert, please. I want you." Her breaths came fast and her chest heaved.

I placed my hands on her shoulders to steady her. "Stand here and don't turn around."

As I slid my hand over her backside, she went to turn toward me. I nibbled at her ear and repeated, "Don't turn around."

She tucked her chin and looked forward.

I ducked into the bedroom.

A few seconds later, I pulled the pins that held her hair in place and let it cascade down. I buried my nose and inhaled, taking in her scent. Next, I continued my exploration of her body, this time pressing my naked flesh against hers.

She molded to me and cooed. I turned her toward me. Her eyes widened as I stroked my fingers over the side of her face. Placing a hand on either side of her chin, I kissed her hard and backed her up to the edge of the couch. We fell backwards and spent the night in the living room.

~ *Belinda* ~

Early Monday morning, the limo arrived and whisked us back to Paris. We still had one week left but did not know what lay in store for us.

The sleek, black limousine came to a stop in front of the Ritz, on the north side of the Seine River. A bellman took charge of our luggage. A concierge greeted and escorted us to a private elevator, which took us to the penthouse suite.

I gasped when the double doors opened to reveal the two thousand square foot suite of pure luxury. As before, a black binder and an envelope stuffed full of French currency lay on the table in the foyer.

I wanted to run around and touch everything but controlled the urge by tucking my arms close. I took small steps and strolled around the room, trying not to be too obvious in front of the concierge.

Once we were alone, the story changed.

"Oh my God! Can you believe this place? What the hell were our parents' thinking?" I ran to the French doors leading to the terrace and flung them open. "I'm dreaming….I thought the chateau was magnificent, but this is insane."

I stepped onto the terrace to a full view of the Seine River and the Eiffel Tower just beyond. His arms wrapped around me from behind, and we stood admiring the view. "This is…I can't describe what this is."

With a quick jerk, I turned. "The bathroom. I have to check it out."

"We have Paris at our fingertips and you want to check out the bathroom?"

I made it halfway into the living room with him following. I checked out the door placement and chose the one I deduced would lead to the primary bedroom. My exaggerated hip movements and beckoning finger enticed him to continue to follow a few paces behind.

Grabbing the handles, I put a bit of drama into opening the doors, making wide arm gestures. "Voila! Success!" After I stepped inside, I focused on the open door leading to the bathroom.

He caught up to me, standing, hands on hips, in a bathroom the size of Paris. In the middle stood what looked like a small swimming pool. "Is that the tub?"

"Yep." I reached for the first button on my blouse. "And I'm getting in it." The blouse fell to the floor. "Care to join me?"

A hint of a smile graced his face. "Fill it up. I'll go get the champagne and chocolate-covered strawberries from the dining room table."

"Robert, baby." I stood in my bra and panties, pouring bubble bath near the jetting water. "Don't forget the 'Do Not Disturb sign.'"

∞

According to the itinerary in the binder, the first day belonged to us. After the bath and nap, we ventured out onto the streets of Paris. We strolled alongside the Seine, stopped for a late lunch in a quaint street-side café, and ducked in and out of many shops. The day was the perfect description of romance. After all, we were in the "City of Love."

I flipped through a rack full of dresses in a very chic boutique and glanced at Robert. He walked around acting as if he was interested in his wife's shopping, but he was bored stiff. How could I not love this man? With several fast sweeping motions, I completed one rack and moved on to the next, attempting to speed up the process.

A glimpse of a petite blonde walking out of sight of the shop window caused me to freeze. Was my mind playing tricks on me?

I turned toward him at the next rack. I continued to browse through the clothes.

"Robert, what country did Sharyn move to?"

He stopped his meandering, and his brows knitted. "I don't know. What made you think of that?"

"I was just thinking about it and wondered if you knew."

"No clue."

"Come on, let's get out of here. I see nothing I can't live without."

I tucked my arm around his, and we walked out to the street. I looked in the direction I'd seen the blonde, but couldn't find any remnants of her existence. Was my mind playing tricks on me? I blocked the possibility and focused on the man of my dreams. "What's next?"

The rest of the week was jam-packed with visits to the Louvre, the Eiffel Tower, and multiple museums. In mid-week, we had a private tour of Bes de Boulogne, which included a picnic alongside a lake in an English garden setting. Our evenings also followed a plan, which included dinner while cruising on the Seine and a night at the Moulin Rouge.

Robert and I laughed that we'd need another week off to recover from the honeymoon. Yet, neither of us would've given up the experience, no matter how exhausting.

On Saturday morning, we met the limousine at the front door. They chauffeured us to the private terminal, where we boarded the corporate jet bound for Texas. As before, the bedroom had been prepared for us. This time, the "Mile High Club" folly didn't even enter our minds. He wrapped his arms around me and we slept.

"Jessica, prepare for landing." The pilot's voice crackled over the intercom.

A tall woman stood in the aisle next to Robert. "Please fasten your seat belts." She reached for the empty glasses and then vanished to the rear of the jet.

I rolled my head toward the window. The clear night sky filled with small pinpoints of light blended with the lights below. The jar of the wheels hitting the pavement brought a hint of a smile across my face. I settled my hand over his. He curled his fingers around mine. I rolled my head to face him. We sat locked in each other's gaze as I imagined the rest of our life. ♡

ABOUT THE AUTHORS

Linda Fagala was born and raised in Texas, and currently resides there with her husband. She graduated from Stephen F. Austin State University as an art teacher. She retired from writing several years ago, but assisted in the second edition publishing.

Karen Pugh was born in Chicago, Illinois and graduated from Amundsen-Mayfair City College with an ADN in Nursing. She has had a long interest in writing. She helped create the League of Romance writers based in Houston, Texas where she lives with her husband.

**Shattered Fate** The Belinda and Robert saga came to Linda after reminiscing about her experiences during her college years and is loosely based on those events. She approached Karen with the idea of a romance novel. Karen's experiences in nursing, contributed to the theme of the plot. Combining their talents and ideas, they embarked on their first novel.

**Destiny Reborn** is the sequel of Belinda and Robert's life, as the two discover the reasons for their attraction.

**Paper Snowflakes for Christmas** continues the adventures of Colin Brockman, after his breakup with Belinda and his move to Canada in _Destiny Reborn_. This short Christmas novel is promised to delight the reader and spark romance.

**Fulling Destiny** is the final chapter in the lives of Belinda and Robert as they navigate learning about each other, life, and family as the pair prove A Happy Ever After can be forever.